The Kessler Protocol

The Kessler Protocol

Charles T Falk

Prologue—Payback 1

PART ONE—WAKING UP 3

1 Architect 4

2 Destiny Calls 9

3 Architect's Creation 17

4 Sparrow's Rise 29

5 No Good Deed 38

6 Devil's Bargain 47

7 Pressure From Above 57

8 Brother's War 63

9 Surveillance 68

10 Architecture 73

11 Face of Evil 80

12 Warning Shot 88

13 Morning After 93

14 Contagion 96

15 Interrogation 101

16 Break In 110

17 Stillness Before The Shot 120

18 ┃Sparrow's Flight 123

19 ┃Legacy 127

20 ┃Flight 140

21 ┃Shadows on the Platform 153

22 ┃Ping from the Past 158

┃PART TWO—OLD SCORES 171

23 ┃Moral Hacker 172

24 ┃Fragments 178

25 ┃Ghost Entente 186

26 ┃Response 195

27 ┃Daggers From Above 205

28 ┃Debt 213

29 ┃Notice 224

30 ┃Lines in the Water 238

31 ┃Death of Marcus Vale 249

32 ┃Spider's Web 261

33 ┃Firing Line 274

34 ┃Call Home 290

35 ┃Ghosts of Maribor 297

36 ┃Last Light 307

37 ┃Cost of Command 319

38 ┃Diverging Currents 326

39 ┃Breaking Point 346

40 ┃Photograph 356

41 ┃Aurora Rising 363

42 | Gathering 373

43 | The Hunt 383

44 | Chapter 44—Retribution 394

| PART THREE—BLOOD VENGEANCE 404

45 | City of Two Worlds 405

46 | Deliverance 412

47 | Cleaner's Trail 417

48 | Spirits of Vienna 422

49 | Collateral Damage 428

50 | Collapse 437

51 | European Node 447

52 | Collision Course 451

53 | Course Correction 456

54 | Counterpunch 460

55 | Falling Lines 464

56 | Hunter's Hand 475

57 | Vanishing Point 478

58 | Throne of Ash 487

59 | Line Cast Too Far 491

60 | Residuals 495

61 | Evolution 499

62 | Pieces On The Board 502

63 | Signals In The Dust 508

64 | Epilogue—Still Breathing 514

CHAPTER 527

The Caucasus Mountains — Six Months After the Following Events

Helicopter blades cut through mountain fog like a knife through silk, rotors beating rhythm against rock and sky. Daniel Cole checked his weapon for the third time—muscle memory, not paranoia—while beside him, Ethan stared at satellite imagery of the compound below.

"Two guards at the north entrance," Ethan shouted into his headset, voice steady despite what they both knew. "Three at the vehicle depot. Unknown number inside."

"And the target?" Daniel's question hung in the freezing air between them.

"Thermal imaging says one occupant, basement level, southeast corner." Ethan met his brother's eyes. "It's him. It has to be."

The pilot's voice crackled through their headsets: "LZ in two minutes. Weather window closing fast."

Below, through breaks in the fog, the facility emerged—concrete and steel nestled in a valley designed to be invisible from satellites, accessible only by a single mountain road that serpentined through terrain that killed the careless.

This was Kessler's fortress. The place he kept his most valuable assets. The place where his most valuable assets are held, presumed gone forever even by those who refused to believe it.

The helicopter descended, skids crunching on frozen ground. Daniel and Ethan moved as one—months of planning compressed into

minutes of action, brothers united by blood and purpose and the desperate mathematics of rescue versus suicide.

"Contact," Daniel whispered, weapon up. Two guards approaching from the north, AK-pattern rifles, professional spacing. He dropped them both with suppressed rounds, the sound barely louder than the wind in the rocks.

They advanced on the compound, each step measured, each breath controlled. Everything they had learned and barely survived, what they had lost—all of it converging on this moment.

The door ahead was steel, locked, wired with alarms that Selin's intelligence mentioned would trigger within three seconds of breach. But Noah's device—delivered via dead drop two weeks ago—would jam the signal for exactly ninety seconds.

Long enough. Maybe.

Ethan placed the charge, nodded to Daniel.

The explosion was muffled, contained, precisely calibrated. The door peeled open like aluminum foil.

And beyond it, descending into darkness, stairs led to the basement where they would meet their fate—victory over Kessler, or death at his hands.

"Let's get him," Daniel whispered.

"Let's go," Ethan replied.

They descended together into the fortress, into the trap, into the culmination of everything that had started six months ago with a wire transaction that shouldn't have existed.

This was how it ended. Or how it began.

The story, like all stories, depended on who lived to tell it.

PART ONE—WAKING UP

1

Architect

Kessler — Private Diary (Zurich-0 Archive: Unclassified)
"I do not hunt the weak. I hunt the hopeful—because hope is the most wonderful thing to extinguish."

Zurich, Switzerland — 2:06 a.m.
Except for the sound of rain against glass, the room stood ominously quiet. Below, the city slept — its wealth tucked neatly behind steel, encryption, and the illusion of order.

Andreas Kessler stood at the window of the penthouse office, watching the drops roll down the pane like tears. The view from the fifty-second floor rendered Zurich in miniature—a city of clockwork precision where money moved in currents invisible to those who believed they controlled it.

Kessler had learned long ago that true power did not rest with those who stood at podiums or signed legislation. It belonged to those who built the architecture beneath—who determined which currencies strengthened, which markets crashed, which governments stood or fell based on overnight liquidity decisions.

His reflection in the glass projected a spectral quality, translucent—fitting for a man who'd spent over thirty years erasing himself from official records. No passport photo on file. No biometric data in any database that mattered. Even his son addressed him only by the name "Father," never questioning the compartmentalization that kept them both alive.

The rain intensified, drumming against bulletproof glass that could withstand sniper fire from adjacent buildings. Kessler had enemies—former partners who'd grown consciences, intelligence officers who had stumbled too close to the truth, idealists who thought exposure equaled justice.

All mistakes he had corrected with varying degrees of permanence. But mistakes, he had learned, simply amounted to data points indicating where the system needed refinement. Each attempt on his life taught him something. Each whistleblower who mysteriously disappeared before reaching authorities demonstrated the network's efficiency.

The Directorate didn't just survive threats—it metabolized them, growing stronger with each failed challenge. His son had called earlier from Vienna—brief, efficient, reporting completion of a task Kessler had assigned months ago. The boy had developed into what Kessler needed him to be. Cold. Precise. Uncompromised.

The monitors behind him glowed in soft blue light — columns of data, wire transfers, encrypted signals weaving through the arteries of the global banking system. To anyone else, it would have looked like chaos.

To Kessler, it acted as a symphony.

Each number represented a warhead bought, a politician purchased, a news cycle directed. Billions moved through shell accounts in jurisdictions no map could hold. Each wire became a pulse in a global body he had built — a living organism of power and leverage.

Tonight's transactions alone would fund three separate operations: an arms purchase in the Balkans disguised as agricultural equipment, campaign donations to twelve senators across seven countries, and the short-selling of a pharmaceutical company whose stock would collapse in precisely eight hours when their lead drug trial "unexpectedly" failed.

The FDA official who would authorize that failure? Already paid by the Directorate. The journalists who would report it as legitimate news?

Under retainer. The investors who would profit from the collapse? Directorate shell entities that existed only in legal fictions spanning fourteen jurisdictions.

Beautiful in its complexity—The Directorate was a symphony of corruption so intricate that no single investigator could trace more than a fragment before running into legal barriers, classified intelligence restrictions, or career-ending pressure from supervisors who had been purchased years earlier. This embodied the genius of the Helios Shadow Protocol: not a conspiracy that could be exposed, but a system so embedded in legitimate finance that dismantling it would require dismantling capitalism itself.

He sipped his coffee, bitter and black. "Everything is proceeding?"

A second voice crackled over the encrypted line—younger, European accent, the vowels clipped and precise. "The new channels are live. Directorate assets are secure."

"And the bank?"

"Clean. No leaks." A pause. "The American operator's son is proving... useful. Though he doesn't know it yet."

Kessler's reflection fractured across the glass. "He will. They all do, eventually." He thought of the boy on the mountain—young, idealistic, believing friendship existed as something given rather than engineered. "And the other matter?"

"Complete. No trace. The rope work was surgical."

"Good. Send him east. It's time he learned what we do with sentimentality."

Kessler walked to the desk, scrolling through the latest wire lists. A familiar name caught his eye — *International Mercantile Bank.*

The Bank functioned as one of their oldest conduits, a reliable artery for dark money disguised as liquidity. But something stood out wrong in the flow — a tiny misstep, a delay in confirmation.

Kessler frowned. "Flag this. Someone's looking where they shouldn't."

"Should we act?" the voice asked.

"Not yet," he indicated. "Watch it. If they push further, we'll adjust the narrative."

The call ended. Kessler returned his gaze to the three photographs that laid neatly in a row. The first: a younger version of himself, standing in snow beside an American Special Forces officer. Both men grinning, rifles slung over shoulders. James Cole—before Kessler had learned that friendship functioned simply as another form of leverage. Kessler operated then as Otto Reinhardt, Swiss intelligence liaison. Kessler grinned at that thought—he has lived numerous lives before.

The second photo: two boys, young teens, hiking in the mountains. One dark-haired and serious, the other blonde and controlled. Ethan and Lukas, before the world had taught them what they actually would become.

The third: a woman with dark eyes and a cautious smile. Maria. Dead over thirteen years, but still haunting one hundred percent of the decisions he made.

Kessler picked up the photograph of James Cole one more time, studying the young man's grin, the easy confidence of someone who still believed the world could be fixed with good intentions and righteous action.

"I'm sorry, old friend," Kessler whispered to the frozen moment. "But your sons inherited your stubbornness. And stubbornness, in our world, is just another word for suicide."

Kessler set the photos down carefully, each one a chapter in a story only he fully understood.

And somewhere — in a cubicle, in a tower, behind a monitor — someone had just touched his network without permission.

Kessler smiled faintly, his eyes narrowing. "Let's see how curious you are," he murmured. He pulled up the flagged wire transfer again, studying the metadata—access timestamp, IP trace, user credential hash. Whoever had touched his network possessed sophistication beyond routine auditing. They'd known where to look, which suggested inside knowledge or extraordinary intuition.

Kessler opened a secure channel to his surveillance division. "Priority flag: International Mercantile Bank, Zurich operations. I want personnel files on anyone with systems access in the last seventy-two hours. Cross-reference with recent behavioral anomalies—financial stress, unusual work patterns, personal complications that breed vulnerability."

The hunt had begun.

Outside, thunder rolled across the lake, distant but deliberate — the sound of something vast beginning to move.

2

Destiny Calls

"I climbed that mountain with a brother—and came down alone." —
Ethan Cole

Himalayan Mountain Range— Spring 2015
Above twenty-six thousand feet, the so called "Death Zone", the
world is not made for the living. It is a place where sound dies in the
wind, where breath is a negotiation, and each step feels like a question
the mountain asks and never answers.

Ethan Cole had come to Tibet seeking silence — the kind he
couldn't find in classrooms or crowded city streets. Young and without
fear. Twenty-one, a Princeton student on a deferred semester, restless,
brilliant, already tired of the noise of ambition.

Now, as he clawed upward through the scree and ice of Cho Oyu —
the "Turquoise Goddess" — he understood what silence truly meant.
The wind tore at him like an animal, a constant scream that erased
thought.

The horizon stood as a white void, endless and blinding.

They had reached the summit just before noon. They had touched
the prayer flags fluttering like ghosts at the top, posed briefly for a photograph, and turned to descend.

Then the storm arrived.

It didn't roll in; it fell. A wall of ice and snow collapsed out of the sky, devouring light and distance in seconds. Visibility went from fifty feet to five in an instant. The wind howled so loud it erased the sound of their own breathing.

A few meters below him, **Lukas Reinhardt** moved with uncanny calm. His parka became rimmed with frost, his breath visible in the thin air, but his posture remained balanced, almost graceful. Ethan had always envied that composure.

They hadn't spoken in over an hour — the wind made conversation impossible — but their rhythm remained synchronized, the unspoken tempo of men who had learned each other's movements long ago.

Ethan and Lukas went back to their teenage years— to before careers, before the banks, before the world started fracturing.

Their fathers had served together — **James Cole**, the American Special Forces officer, and **Otto Reinhardt**, the quiet, disciplined Swiss intelligence liaison. The two men had worked together on joint field operations in Eastern Europe, building a bond that survived both politics and time.

When Ethan had turned ten years old, Lukas would come to spend every summer — golden-haired, precise, polite in that European way. They'd hike in the Appalachians, go white water rafting, go fishing. Then each winter, Ethan would fly to Switzerland, where Lukas's world embodied precision — climbing ropes, clean snow, and the smell of waxed skis. Lukas's father would take them into the Alps and teach them survival: how to find shelter, read the clouds, listen to the mountain. This lasted for five years, then abruptly stopped. Something about Lukas' father changing careers which required his full attention.

Even back then, Lukas never talked about his mother. Ethan assumed she had died young. Now, years later, as the two men clawed their way down the frozen face of a Himalayan ridge, Ethan sensed that same quiet distance radiating from him. Lukas had changed — sharper, colder, though still controlled.

The storm intensified with a violence that was personal. Ethan and Lukas moved in synchronized rhythm—decades of summers together had built an unspoken language between them. But something had changed in Lukas over the past year. A precision to his movements that went beyond athletic training. A coldness in his assessment of risk.

"Almost there," Lukas's voice crackled through the radio, distorted by static.

Ethan smiled weakly under his mask. "You always say that."

"Because it's always true until it isn't."

That defined Lukas — the same dry precision his father Otto had possessed. Ethan had always admired that about the Reinhardt family. Swiss discipline wrapped in warmth.

They stopped beneath a jagged overhang and pitched their tents in the lee of the ice. The altitude was punishing; oxygen thin, the air cutting like glass. Inside the tent, they shared protein bars and melted snow, breath fogging in the cramped space.

"Your father would have loved this." Lukas's voice was quiet but clear.

Ethan looked up. "Yours too."

Lukas nodded slowly. "My father understood mountains. He used to say they reveal what men hide in cities." His pale eyes—almost colorless in the tent's dim light—fixed on Ethan. "Do you know what mountains revealed to him?"

"What?"

"That most men aren't prepared for what they think they want."

The words hung between them, strange and weighted. Before Ethan could respond, the tent walls snapped violently. The wind had shifted—a wall of sound that made speech difficult.

They fell silent, conserving energy, conserving oxygen. At this altitude, all words cost something. Each breath they took became borrowed money from a rapidly diminishing account. The storm hammered against the tent with fists of ice and wind, the fabric straining against anchors buried in permafrost. Inside, their breath created frost on the nylon ceiling—tiny crystals that caught the dim light of the headlamp before melting and freezing again.

Ethan pulled his sleeping bag tighter, feeling the cold seep through layers of down and Gore-Tex. His fingers ached despite the gloves. His face heavy liked it seemed carved from wood. But he'd been cold before. Worse than this.

His thoughts drifted to his father and his brother Daniel. To the North Carolina mountains where James had taught them survival meant being uncomfortable—it meant making the right decisions when your body screamed at you to do otherwise.

He remembered one trip in particular. Ethan must have been thirteen, Daniel fifteen. They had been three days into a week-long trek through the Smokies when they stumbled onto a black bear sow with cubs. Daniel had frozen—not from fear, but from surprise. The bear had been upwind, hidden in a thicket of mountain laurel, and they had gotten too close before anyone realized.

The bear charged.

James had always taught them: *Don't run. Make yourself big. Back away slowly. Give her an exit.*

But Daniel had been directly in her path, and panic overrode training. He turned to run.

Ethan had acted without thinking—grabbing his brother's pack, yanking him sideways, putting himself between Daniel and three hundred pounds of maternal fury. He raised his arms, shouted, made himself as large and loud as possible. The bear had stopped ten feet away, huffing, clacking her teeth, her cubs bawling behind her.

For an endless moment, they had stared at each other—boy and bear, both terrified, both protecting something.

Then she turned, gathered her cubs, and crashed back into the laurel.

James had found them minutes later, both brothers shaking, Daniel white-faced and silent. Their father hadn't yelled or lectured. He just looked at Ethan and added, "You did right. Sometimes doing right means being more scared than you've ever been. But you do it anyway."

Ethan hadn't thought about that moment in years. But here, in the thin air and screaming wind, he understood what his father had meant. Doing right wasn't about avoiding fear. It was about what you chose when the fear came anyway.

Across the tent, Lukas sat motionless, his breathing slow and controlled. To a casual observer, he might have been sleeping. But Ethan could see his eyes remained opened, fixed on some point in the middle distance that existed only inside his head.

Lukas's thoughts ran much colder than the storm outside.

He had been raised in a mansion where sunlight came grudgingly through leaded glass windows and his father's disapproval hung heavy in the air like cigar smoke. Otto Reinhardt lived as a man of exacting standards who believed emotion equated to weakness, deviation meant failure, and excellence was merely the baseline expectation.

"Precision, Lukas. Always precision." His father's voice, even in memory, carried the weight of absolute authority. "A man who hesitates dies. A man who questions his orders is already dead."

Lukas had learned early that respect was earned through obedience, and the only approval that mattered came through perfect execution of impossible tasks. His childhood had consisted of a series of tests: military boarding school, alpine survival courses, covert operations. Each one designed to strip away softness, to forge something harder, colder, more useful.

He had excelled. Of course he had. Failure remained unthinkable.

But excellence brought no warmth. Only new missions. New tests. New opportunities to show that he would prove worthy of his father's acknowledgment which never quite arrived.

The Directorate had recognized what his father had built in Lukas—a man without hesitation, without mercy, without the weakness of doubt. They had recruited him young, after his mother's death. His father had personally overseen his integration. And for the past eight years, Lukas had been useful for them: efficient, invisible, absolute.

Until this mission.

He watched Ethan huddled in his sleeping bag, face wind-burned, exhausted, trusting. They had climbed together for five days. Shared tents, shared meals, shared the intimacy of survival at altitude. Ethan had saved his life on the ice wall—grabbed him when the anchor failed, held him until Lukas could secure new anchors. The rope burns stinged fresh on Ethan's palms.

And now Lukas had orders to kill him.

Not in the tent. Too many questions. But tomorrow, on the descent, there would be opportunities. A frayed rope. A misplaced anchor. The mountains killed people each season. One more tragedy would vanish into the statistics.

The order had been clear. Ethan Cole posed a liability to the Directorate. Smart enough to recognize patterns. Principled enough to act on them.

Men like that were too dangerous.

But sitting here, listening to Ethan's breathing, remembering how he'd insisted on the safer route when Lukas had wanted to push through bad weather, how he'd shared his oxygen when Lukas's regulator had frozen—sitting here, Lukas experienced something he'd learned long ago to ignore.

Doubt.

Not about the mission. The Directorate's logic held sound. Ethan Cole had to die for the system to survive. Lukas understood that intellectually, operationally, strategically.

But understanding and accepting differed. They weren't the same thing.

He had killed before. Many times. Targets who deserved it, and some who probably didn't. The Directorate didn't traffic in moral clarity—they trafficked in necessity. And Lukas had been their instrument, precise and unquestioning.

This should be no different.

Except Ethan had pulled him off that ice wall. Had trusted him with his life. Had treated him not as an asset or an enemy but as a friend.

And Lukas, who had been trained since childhood to view friendship as tactical weakness, found himself struggling with the cost of that trust.

The wind howled. The tent shuddered. Somewhere in the darkness outside, avalanches carved new paths down frozen slopes—unstoppable, indifferent, following the simple physics of gravity and snow.

Lukas closed his eyes, breathing slowly, letting the freezing air fill his lungs. He'd spent his entire life doing what necessity demanded. What orders required. What expectations dictated of men who survived by becoming harder than the world around them.

Tomorrow, on the descent, he would do it again.

Because hesitation meant death. And Lukas Reinhardt did not hesitate.

But tonight, in the thin air and screaming wind, he allowed himself one moment of something that appeared dangerously close to regret.

Then he buried it, deep and cold, in the same place he'd buried all the other weakness his father had trained him to eliminate.

The storm raged. The temperature dropped. And two men sat in silence—one thinking of the brother he'd saved, the other planning how to betray the friend who'd saved him.

Lukas went to check the anchors. "Wait until morning," Ethan warned, but Lukas only smiled—that small, controlled smile that never quite reached his eyes.

"The mountain doesn't wait, Ethan. Neither should we."

He vanished into the white.

Minutes stretched. Then hours. Ethan shouted Lukas's name into the void until his voice shattered. When dawn broke gray and terrible, he found the rope—not frayed, but cut. The edge appeared too clean, too deliberate.

But there was no body. No blood. Just the rope's severed end dangling into an abyss where visibility died after fifteen feet.

Ethan stared into that void for a long time. Something in his gut whispered this was not an accident. But hypothermia and exhaustion were already blurring his thoughts. He forced himself to move—down, always down, counting breaths to stay conscious.

Sometime near dawn, the wind dropped enough for Ethan to move again. He melted snow in his flask, drank it too fast, coughed hard enough to taste blood, then checked his gear. Trying further to find Lukas meant suicide now — he knew that — but descending through the Khumbu Icefall in a storm would challenge his skills to the limit. Still, working down the mountain meant survival. He began to move.

Every few steps, he planted his axe, assessed the ice, moved one boot-length at a time. His rope served as his lifeline, his breath his only prayer. He no longer thought of reaching safety — just the next foothold, the next breath.

At one point, he saw a scrap of fabric fluttering against a rock face — red, faded. One of the others' jackets. He didn't stop.

By the time he reached the lower ridge, dawn broke through the storm — faint gold bleeding across the white. His tent appeared as a smudge on the horizon. Behind him, the summit loomed invisible, erased by cloud and snow.

He reached base camp thirty-six hours later, delirious, half blind. The rescue team found him sitting beside a torn tent, whispering names the wind carried away.

When they asked about his climbing partner, Ethan replied simply, "The mountain keeps its own."

He never climbed again. But sometimes, in dreams, he saw Lukas descending the other side of the mountain—alone, deliberate, unharmed, disappearing into snow that erased all tracks behind him.

Years later, when his world turned to ice and betrayal again, Ethan Cole would remember that moment —the silence, the wind, and the lesson the mountain had taught him:

Endure. Even when there's nothing left to endure for.

3

Architect's Creation

Kessler — Private Diary (Zurich-0 Archive: Unclassified)
"Lukas, your mother is gone because she believed the world was kind. You will survive because I will teach you never to believe that."

Gstaad, Switzerland — Winter 2006
Snow fell in absolute silence, blanketing the cemetery in white that looked pure from a distance but was gray and trampled up close. Lukas Reinhardt stood beside his mother's grave wearing a black suit that hung slightly too large, his father's hand resting on his shoulder with the weight of instruction rather than comfort.

He stood eight years old. He understood that his mother was dead. He did not yet understand that this marked the moment his childhood ended.

"She loved you immensely," Kessler stated, his voice carrying that unique European precision that made even emotional statements sound like theorems being proven. He tilted his head slightly, regarding his son with clinical interest. "But love, you see, made her weak. Terribly weak. Do you understand the distinction I'm making, yes?"

Lukas stared at the casket being lowered into frozen ground, his voice small. "No, Father."

"Ah. Well." Kessler's hand tightened slightly—not cruel, but firm. Teaching. "You will. In time, you will. Your mother—lovely woman, brilliant mind—she asked too many questions. She wanted to understand things that understanding could not change. That curiosity, that need for what she called moral certainty, it made her vulnerable. Fatally so."

"Vulnerable to what?" Lukas asked, his breath visible in the frigid air.

"To the world as it actually functions." Kessler knelt beside his son with fluid grace, bringing their eyes level. His face had a quite handsome appearance in a cold way, like alpine landscape—beautiful but utterly unforgiving. "I loved your mother. This is important for you to know. I genuinely loved her. But she could not accept that maintaining order requires making choices others cannot stomach. Choices that appear, from certain perspectives, quite monstrous. So I had to make a choice about her. Yes?"

Even at eight, Lukas noticed the implication land like ice water in his veins. His voice came out as barely a whisper. "You killed her?"

"I protected you." Kessler's expression remained pleasant, almost warm. "There is no meaningful difference between the two actions, you see. She would have destroyed the world I built—our security, our purpose, our survival. The questions she was asking, the people she was speaking to... it was only a matter of time. So I chose to let her go cleanly, peacefully, rather than watch her suffer the consequences of exposure. Morphine overdose. Exceedingly humane. She didn't suffer at all." He paused. "Well, not much."

Lukas looked at his father—stared deep into his father's eyes—and saw something that would take him years to name: absolute conviction. Kessler believed every word he spoke. Believed it with the serene confidence of someone who'd never questioned his own moral arithmetic.

"I don't understand," Lukas whispered, and even as he announced it, part of him knew he was lying. He understood perfectly. He just didn't want to.

"You will," Kessler repeated, standing and brushing snow from his coat with meticulous care. "I'm going to teach you, and you must always remember this one essential truth: compassion is a luxury afforded only to those who've never had to choose between two terrible options. The rest of us?" He smiled that enigmatic smile. "We simply calculate which fear costs less. Which outcome serves the greater design. It's mathematics. Quite elegant when you think about it."

Three months after his mother's funeral, Lukas arrived by private car to the training facility which occupied a repurposed Cold War bunker outside the city. The facility's existence was known to perhaps two dozen people worldwide. Lukas was processed without ceremony and found himself in a concrete room with fifteen other children ranging from ten to sixteen.

They were from scattered places across the globe—Russia, Türkiye, South Africa, Brazil. What they shared was potential. Intelligence. Physical capability. And something else Lukas couldn't quite name: a kind of emptiness, as if they'd each lost something essential and were waiting for someone to fill the void.

An instructor entered—a woman with short blonde hair and a scar bisecting her left eyebrow. She spoke in English: "You are here because you have been identified as exceptional. What we will teach you is how to weaponize that exception."

For six months, Lukas learned:

How to read people. Micro-expressions, body language, the subtle tells that revealed what words concealed. They practiced on each other until lying became indistinguishable from breathing.

How to compartmentalize. Pain, fear, affection—all emotions were treated as data to be processed and stored, never allowed to influence decision-making in real time.

How to kill. Starting with small animals, graduating to larger ones. Not for cruelty's sake, but to understand the mechanics of ending life. "Death," the instructor declared, "is just a state change. The sooner you accept this, the more effective you become."

How to become invisible. Not through disguise, but through perfectly matching the energy of any environment. Tourists looked lost. Locals looked bored. Operators looked exactly like whatever the situation required.

Lukas excelled at all of it. His father visited monthly, observing from behind one-way glass, offering no praise but no criticism either. Approval, Lukas learned, came measured in continued investment.

One afternoon, after Lukas had successfully completed a surveillance exercise that had broken three other students, Kessler took him to lunch at a café overlooking the Danube.

"You're doing well," Kessler remarked, cutting into schnitzel with surgical precision, each movement deliberate and exact. "Better than I anticipated, actually. You have your mother's gifts but none of her... weaknesses. Fascinating."

"Thank you, Father."

"Don't thank me. Thank your mother." Kessler's expression didn't change, remaining pleasant and distant. "She gave you her intelligence and empathy. Wonderful gifts, both. I'm simply teaching you how to weaponize them. How to use compassion as a tool for manipulation rather than allowing it to manipulate you. Yes?"

Lukas pushed food around his plate, his appetite gone. "The other children... some of them cry at night."

"Yes. I'm aware."

"Should I help them?" Lukas looked up, something in his chest tightening at the question.

"No." Kessler met his son's eyes, tilting his head with that bird-like curiosity. "Absolutely not. Compassion is a luxury for those who can afford it. You cannot. You must not. Attachments you form are levers that can be used against you. Your mother was my lever. I allowed myself that weakness once and looked at what it required of me." He paused, dabbing his mouth with a napkin. "I won't allow you to create your own."

"Then why did you have me?" The question escaped before Lukas could stop it, and he immediately regretted his boldness.

The question clearly surprised Kessler. He set down his fork with careful precision, considered his son for a long moment. "Ah. A fair question. A most fair question, actually." He leaned back, fingers interlaced. "Because legacy requires continuation. Because building something that outlasts you is the only form of immortality that actually matters. Because I loved your mother enough to want something of her to survive, even if that something had to be refined through fire." His smile remained impossibly slight, almost affectionate. "Even if it meant turning her gentleness into your strength."

Lukas met his father's pale eyes. "Am I the fire or what survives it?"

Kessler's smile widened—the first genuine expression of pleasure Lukas had seen in months. "Both. That's precisely what will make you dangerous. You'll remember what it was like to be soft, to care, to love. But you will have learned to weaponize those memories rather than being controlled by them." He picked up his fork again. "Most people are prisoners of their emotions. You'll be their architect."

North Carolina Mountains — Summer 2012

The Cole cabin sat in thirty acres of pine forest, accessible only by a dirt road that required four-wheel drive and local knowledge. Lukas arrived with his father, both of them carrying the minimal luggage of men accustomed to traveling light.

James Cole met them on the porch—older than Kessler, weathered, carrying the particular posture of someone who'd spent a lifetime in uniform. The two men shook hands with the complicated formality of former allies who'd seen things together that couldn't be discussed in daylight.

"Good to see you, Otto."

"And you, James. Though I must say, I still think you're slightly mad for living out here in this wilderness." Kessler smiled warmly. "But then, you always did prefer simplicity to sophistication, yes?"

James turned to Lukas, extended his hand. "You must be Lukas. My sons have been talking about you for weeks."

Lukas shook hands properly, firm grip, eye contact—exactly as his father had taught him. "Thank you for having us, sir."

"None of that 'sir' business. You're practically family." James called into the house: "Boys! Come meet your friend!"

Two teenagers emerged—Ethan, dark-haired and serious; Daniel, two years older, already carrying himself with the confidence of someone who understood physical space.

"Hey," Ethan remarked warmly, offering a slightly awkward wave. "You're from Switzerland, right? That's so cool."

Lukas smiled—the warm, genuine smile his father had taught him to deploy strategically. "Yes. I'm excited to be here. Ethan, yes? My father says you're exceptionally intelligent."

The flattery worked. Ethan's face lit up. "Your dad said that? That's awesome. Come on, we'll show you around. There's a creek where we catch trout, and Dad's teaching us land navigation."

For three weeks, Lukas lived in two worlds.

During the day, he was Lukas Reinhardt, awkward European teenager bonding with American counterparts. He learned to fish, to track deer, to read terrain. He laughed at Daniel's jokes, listened seriously to Ethan's theories about economics, helped James Cole maintain the cabin.

It wasn't difficult to pretend. The problem lay in that it stopped being pretense.

Ethan happened to be genuinely kind—the sort of person who assumed good intentions and therefore proved easy to manipulate but impossible not to like. Daniel proved to be protective, capable, the kind of older brother who taught you to fight so you wouldn't have to. James turned out to be patient, wise, embodying a form of masculinity Lukas had never encountered—strength without cruelty, authority without dominance.

This showed to Lukas what a family looked like when it wasn't weaponized.

One night, sitting around the campfire while James told stories about his military service, Lukas perceived something dangerous: he wanted this. Not as assignment or cover, but as actual life. He wanted brothers who protected rather than competed. He wanted a father who taught without testing. He wanted to be someone other than what he was being made into.

The feeling terrified him more than any training exercise.

Later, alone in the guest room, his encrypted phone buzzed. Message from his father, who'd returned to Vienna:

"Remember why you're there. Friendship is reconnaissance. Affection is data collection. Bring me something useful about James and his sons. Their psychology. Their weaknesses. Anything useful."

Lukas stared at the message, then at the photo Daniel had insisted they take that afternoon—all three boys grinning, arms slung over shoulders, mountains behind them. He looked happy in the photo. He looked real.

He deleted the message and turned off the phone.

Cho Oyu, Tibet — Spring 2015

The summit stretched in front of them as a white void, prayer flags snapping in wind that erased all other sound. Ethan stood beside Lukas, both of them oxygen-deprived and exhausted, having just achieved something most people only dreamed about.

"We did it!" Ethan shouted over the wind, his voice cracking with emotion. "Jesus, Lukas, we actually did it!"

Lukas nodded, unable to speak. Not from altitude sickness or exhaustion, but from the weight of what he knew approached.

Three days earlier, his father had sent the final message:

"The Cole boy has become a liability. His father knows too much about old operations, asks too many questions—much like your mother did. The son will eventually connect dots that must remain unconnected. You will create an accident on descent. Make it look like equipment failure. Exceptionally clean. Immensely professional. This is not a request, Lukas. This is your mother's test, the one I've been preparing you for since her funeral. Prove to me you've learned what she could not."

Lukas had spent three days trying to find an alternative. None materialized. Refusing meant his own elimination—his father had been clear about that. Helping Ethan meant betraying all the things he'd been raised to be. No third option existed.

On the descent, when the storm hit, Lukas saw his opportunity.

They made camp below the summit, exhausted, judgment clouded by altitude. Ethan fell asleep almost immediately. Lukas lay awake, listening to his friend's breathing, thinking about summers in North Carolina, about what it was like to be treated as a brother rather than an asset.

He thought about his mother, who'd asked too many questions and died for it.

He thought about the boy he'd been at eight, standing beside her grave, learning that love meant weakness.

He thought about the man he grew into, who understood that survival required sacrifice, even when the sacrifice destroyed your own humanity.

At 2 a.m., Lukas cut the rope.

Not all the way—that would be too obvious. Just enough to weaken the sheath at a point where stress would complete the failure. Ethan would assess the rope, see it held secure, then trust it during the critical moment when trust would prove fatal.

Lukas worked with the precision of someone who'd been taught that hesitation meant death. When he finished, the rope would appear perfect. It would feel perfect to the touch. It would hold through normal stress but fail under the exact load Ethan would apply during a rapid descent.

Physics, not murder. Accident, not assassination.

Lukas lay back down, closed his eyes, and tried to sleep.

But sleep wouldn't come. In the darkness, he kept seeing Ethan's face that afternoon at the summit—pure joy, accomplishment, the unguarded happiness of someone who'd achieved something impossible with his best friend.

His best friend who waited to kill him.

When the storm intensified at dawn, Lukas knew the moment had arrived. He suggested they descend immediately—urgency would mask any investigation later. Ethan agreed, trusting as always.

They packed gear, checked equipment, and began the descent.

And then, at the critical moment when Ethan would weight the rope fully, Lukas couldn't do it.

Not couldn't physically—couldn't psychologically. Eight years of training collapsing in a single instant of retained humanity.

"Wait," Lukas stated, grabbing Ethan's arm, his voice sharper than intended. "Let me go first. Evaluate the route."

"You sure?"

"Yes." Lukas clipped in, weighted the rope. It held—barely, but it held. He transitioned to a different anchor point, one he knew was solid. "Actually, the angle's wrong from here. Let's move the belay."

They repositioned. The weakened rope went unused. And in that repositioning, a genuine rockfall triggered—the kind of chaos the mountain produced without human intervention.

The avalanche took them both by surprise. Lukas was swept one direction, Ethan another. By the time the storm cleared enough to see, they stood separated by fifty yards of impassable terrain.

Lukas stared across the gap. Ethan remained alive, conscious, staring back with confused relief.

This marked the precise moment. Lukas could finish it—claim he couldn't reach Ethan, let the mountain do what he'd been unable to complete. Or he could abort, face his father's wrath, and accept whatever consequences came from failure.

He chose a third option: theater.

Lukas descended the opposite side of the ridge, making his way to base camp by a route that suggested he'd been swept away, assumed lost. When rescue teams arrived, he was "discovered" miles from where he should have been, barely conscious, mumbling about the storm and the avalanche and his friend who'd disappeared.

The story wrote itself: two climbers separated by catastrophe, both lucky to survive. Tragedy without villainy. Accident without cause.

Ethan lived. Lukas had his cover. And the guilt—the corrosive, inescapable guilt—became the price of that choice.

Vienna, Austria — Present Day

Lukas stood in his apartment, watching surveillance feeds. Ethan on a university campus, instructing students who had no idea their professor ranked as the most wanted man in three intelligence communities. Living a quiet life. Teaching economics. Dating a woman who'd been his father's operative.

The irony was sharp enough to cut.

His encrypted phone rang. Father.

"Lukas."

"Sir."

"They've made contact with Daniel. The brothers are reuniting. How touching, yes?" A pause, heavy with implication. "I'm activating the Caucasus protocol. You'll command the facility team. You'll be responsible for ensuring this ends properly."

Lukas observed his pulse steady—the physical calm that preceded action, trained into him since childhood. "And if Ethan recognizes me?"

"Then he'll understand what happens to sentimentality. What happens when people refuse to accept the architecture of power. It will be... educational for him. Brief, but educational." Kessler's voice carried that familiar professorial tone. "You had a chance to eliminate the problem eight years ago. You chose friendship—or perhaps weakness, I'm still not entirely sure which. Time to correct that error, yes?"

"I chose what you would have chosen." Lukas surprised himself with the response, his voice sharper than intended. "Killing him on the mountain would have exposed patterns. His survival created better long-term operational security. You taught me to think strategically, not emotionally."

Silence on the line. Then, something that might have been approval: "Perhaps. Perhaps you learned more than I realized. Very well. Prepare the facility. When the Cole brothers come for their father—and they will come, they're predictable that way—we'll be waiting. We will be ready."

"And if I have to kill Ethan personally?"

"Then you'll finally understand what I've been teaching you since your mother's funeral, yes?" Kessler's voice softened, almost gentle. "Love is the enemy of survival. You can have one or the other. Never both. This is the lesson your mother refused to learn. This is why she's dead and you're alive. You'll prove you're my son, not hers."

The call ended.

Lukas stood alone, watching Ethan's image on the monitor—his former friend, his brother in all but blood, the person he'd saved once and would now have to destroy.

He thought about the boy he'd been at eight, standing beside his mother's grave, learning that love was weakness.

He thought about the teenager at the Cole cabin, experiencing what family was like when it wasn't weaponized.

He thought about the moment on Cho Oyu when he'd chosen not to cut the rope, and the eight years of guilt that followed.

And he understood, finally, what his father had been teaching him all along: the choice wasn't between love and survival. The choice between who you were and who you needed to become.

Lukas packed his gear with mechanical precision. Weapons, documents, communications equipment. All of the items needed for the mission ahead.

The boy who had cried at his mother's funeral had vanished. The teenager who had wanted to belong to the Cole family was dead. What remained codified what Kessler had always intended: a weapon that looked like a son, a ghost that remembered being human but no longer let that memory interfere with function.

He pulled up the photograph from Princeton—him and Ethan at graduation, arms around shoulders, grinning like they owned the world, that it belonged to them. Brothers in everything but blood.

Lukas studied Ethan's face—the genuine affection, the unguarded trust—and perceived nothing. Not anger, not regret, not even satisfaction at what was coming.

Just the cold clarity of operational necessity.

He deleted the photo and powered down the monitor.

Outside, Vienna hummed with evening traffic, people living normal lives, unaware that somewhere in the machinery of power, three men were on collision course—bound by friendship, separated by ideology, united in the understanding that only one version of the story would survive.

Lukas walked to the window, watched the city lights blur into constellation, and whispered to his reflection:

"I'm sorry, Ethan. I'm sorry for what I am about to do. But you were always going to be part of this. From the moment my father met yours, from the first summer we spent together—it was always leading here."

The window reflected his face back at him—pale, controlled, empty except for purpose.

The ghost stood ready.

And somewhere across oceans and continents, Ethan Cole was finally coming home.

4 |

Sparrow's Rise

Kessler — Private Diary (Zurich-0 Archive: Unclassified)
"You are not my student, Leyla. You are my creation. And a creation must serve its maker. Fly now, Sparrow."

Vienna, Austria Training Facility —Spring 2007
She didn't have a name. Not one that mattered. Her name had been Leyla once, in another life—a street child in Ankara stealing bread from market stalls, sleeping in alleys, surviving through a combination of speed and invisibility that most adults never mastered.

That Leyla had disappeared three months ago when the man in the gray suit found her stealing from a military supply truck.

She had expected arrest. Violence. Maybe death.

Instead, he had offered her dinner.

Now she became Subject 47 in a repurposed East German facility that smelled of concrete and chlorine, surrounded by fifteen other children who'd also been "recruited" from various corners of the world. They had numbers, not names. Names created attachment, Instructor Müller remarked. Attachment created weakness.

The girl understood weakness. She had watched her mother die of it—choosing heroin over food, choosing oblivion over her daughter. The reason she had ended up on the streets at nine years old remained simple—weakness. Weakness was what she had sworn to never become.

Tonight marked the final test.

She stood in the killing room—they all called it that, though the instructors preferred "practical assessment facility"—holding a rabbit against her chest. White fur, soft. It had a brown patch over one ear that made it look almost comical.

She had been caring for it for three weeks. Feeding it lettuce and carrots, cleaning its cage, watching it hop around during recreation periods. The other children had done the same with their assigned animals. She had realized after the first week, this marked a test within a test.

Would they become attached? Would they name them? Would they hesitate when the time came?

The girl had learned not to name things. Names made them real. Real things could hurt you when they disappeared.

"The target is the carotid artery," Instructor Müller vocalized, her voice carrying the flat precision of someone explaining how to change a tire. She held up a combat knife with a rubberized grip. "Quick insertion, lateral cut. Death in under thirty seconds. Minimal suffering if done correctly."

The girl took the knife without hesitation. She had held knives before—had carried one for protection on the streets, had used it once on a man who'd grabbed her in an alley. She understood sharp things and what they could do.

"You have been chosen for this evaluation first," Müller continued, "because your psychological profile suggests the highest probability of success. Don't disappoint us."

Through the one-way mirror, the girl sensed Kessler standing there... watching. Always watching. He had visited the facility twice during her training, had spoken to her once—asking her questions about her mother, her life before, what she remembered about feeling safe.

She had lied. Told him she remembered nothing. That the past was blank...dead to her.

He had smiled and called her clever.

Now, holding the rabbit and the knife, she understood why this test came first for her. The other children watched through a different observation window. If she failed—if she hesitated or broke—they'd see it. And weakness proved contagious in places like this.

She looked down at the rabbit. Its nose twitched, sniffing her jacket. Three weeks of care had taught it to associate her scent with food and safety.

Stupid creature, she thought. *Trust is what gets you killed.*

"Now," Müller whispered softly.

The girl pressed the blade against white fur, found the spot Müller had indicated during anatomy lessons. The rabbit squirmed slightly, sensing danger in a language older than words.

She pushed the blade in.

The rabbit screamed—a high, terrible sound that rabbits only make when they're dying. Its legs kicked against her chest with desperate, diminishing strength. Blood ran hot over her fingers, soaking into her sleeves.

The sound lasted maybe twenty seconds. It definitely seemed longer.

Then silence. Weight going limp. The particular stillness that separated living from dead.

The girl stood there, holding the small body, blood dripping onto the concrete floor. She waited for something—horror, guilt, the emotional response Müller clearly watched for.

She sensed nothing. Just a distant observation that the rabbit had stopped moving, her hands soaking wet, and the test completed.

Good, she thought. *Weakness would have been worse.*

Müller took the body from her, disposed of it in a biohazard container with the efficiency of someone who'd done this hundreds of times. "Clean yourself. Report to debriefing in twenty minutes."

She left. The door sealed.

The girl walked to the industrial sink, turned on the water—hot as she could stand—and began to scrub. The blood swirled down the drain in pink spirals.

In the mirror above the sink, she studied her own reflection. Twelve years old. Thin from years of inconsistent meals. Dark eyes that had learned not to show emotion because emotion made you vulnerable on the streets.

You passed, she told her reflection. *Whatever they wanted to see, you gave them.*

The observation room door opened. Kessler emerged, his expression unreadable.

"Well done," he asserted.

She waited for more—praise, acknowledgment, something that would explain what she'd just proven. But Kessler simply nodded and turned to leave.

"Sir?" Her voice came out steadier than she sensed it would. "What happens to the ones who fail?"

Kessler paused in the doorway. "They're returned to wherever we found them. The streets. Foster systems. Some are retained for less demanding roles—logistics, intelligence analysis, positions that don't require direct action." He looked back at her. "But you won't fail. You've already survived things that would break most adults. This is just... continuation."

"The rabbit—" She stopped herself, reformulating the question. "Was it a test of skill or will?"

"Both. And something else." Kessler walked back, knelt to her eye level—something she'd never seen him do with the other children. "Most people hesitate because they fear becoming monsters. You didn't hesitate because you've already learned the world is monstrous, and survival requires matching it."

"Is that good?"

"It's useful." He stood. "The ability to do what's necessary without letting emotion compromise execution—that's what separates operators from civilians. You demonstrated that tonight."

"What about the others?" The girl gestured toward where she knew the other recruits were watching. "Will they pass?"

"Some will. Some won't. The ones who do will become your colleagues. The ones who don't will become irrelevant." He studied her face. "You're wondering if compassion makes you weak."

It wasn't a question. The girl nodded anyway.

"Compassion," Kessler warmly stated, "is a tool like any other. Used correctly, it builds loyalty, trust, the appearance of humanity that makes infiltration possible. Used incorrectly, it creates hesitation." He pulled out a small silver pin from his pocket—a sparrow in flight, wings spread. "This is for you."

She took it, feeling the weight of the small metal bird in her palm.

"In our organization," Kessler continued, "names are earned, not given. Your instructors will continue calling you Subject 47. But to me, to the Directorate, you're now Sparrow. Small, seemingly harmless, capable of flight, and deadlier than most predators when properly deployed."

"Sparrow," she repeated, assessing the word. That name figured better to her than Subject 47. Less like a number, more like an identity—even if that identity remained someone else's construction.

"You will continue your training. Advanced combat, interrogation resistance, infiltration techniques. In five years, you will be deployed. You will work in intelligence services, gathering information, occasionally eliminating problems that can't be solved through conventional means." His eyes held hers. "You will enjoy a real life, a cover identity, relationships that appear genuine. But underneath it all, you will be mine. My asset. My creation. You do understand, yes?"

The girl—Sparrow now—nodded. "Yes, sir."

"Excellent." Kessler turned to leave, paused. "One more thing. The rabbit. Did you name it?"

She could lie. Should lie, probably. But something in his expression suggested he already knew the answer and was testing whether she would be honest.

"No, sir."

"Truth?"

"Truth. Naming things makes them matter. I learned that on the streets."

Kessler smiled—the first genuine smile she'd seen from him. "Then you learned the most important lesson before I had to teach it. That will save you considerable pain."

He left. The door sealed.

Sparrow stood alone in the killing room, the silver pin in her palm, blood still under her fingernails despite the scrubbing. She pinned the sparrow to her jacket, watched it catch the fluorescent light.

This is who I am now, she thought. *Not Leyla. Not Subject 47. Sparrow.*

The door to the observation room opened again. The other recruits filed out, led by Instructor Müller. They looked at Sparrow with a mixture of awe and fear—the way soldiers look at someone who's just returned from combat.

A boy about her age stepped forward. German accent, pale hair, eyes that held the same emptiness she saw in her own reflection. He had been there longer than her, she knew. Since age eight. Rumors swirled he was Kessler's son, though no one dared ask.

"I'm next," he contended quietly. "Tomorrow night. My rabbit."

Sparrow met his gaze. "It's easier than you think."

"Is it?"

"No," she admitted. "But saying that feels better than the truth."

He nodded, something like respect crossing his face. "I'm—" He stopped himself. They weren't supposed to share names. Numbers only. But he leaned closer, whispered: "Lukas. My real name. Before all this."

Sparrow hesitated, then whispered back: "Leyla. Mine."

They stood there for a moment—two children who'd just traded the most dangerous currency in Kessler's facility: genuine truth. Then Müller called them to formation, and they separated, becoming Subject 47 and Subject 12 again.

But something had changed. A connection formed in the space between assigned identities and buried pasts. Neither of them understood it yet, but years later, when Sparrow became Selin and the world fractured into choosing sides, she'd remember that moment.

The moment when two of Kessler's weapons recognized each other as human.

A few days later during training, Sparrow stood in formation with eleven other recruits. Four children had failed the test—broken down during their kills, refused to complete the task, or completed it but vomited afterward, demonstrating insufficient emotional control.

They had vanished now. Returned to wherever they'd come from, or perhaps deployed to lesser roles where hesitation proved acceptable.

Kessler addressed the remaining recruits from a raised platform, his voice carrying through the training yard.

"You've completed Phase Three. You've proven you can execute necessary actions without emotional compromise. This distinguishes you from ninety-seven percent of the human population." He paced slowly, studying each face. "What comes next is harder. You'll learn to kill people. To betray trust. To become whoever the mission requires while maintaining your core function: serving the Directorate's interests."

He stopped in front of Sparrow. "Some of you will become legends in this field. Others will die in obscure circumstances, your sacrifices known only to those who commanded them." He reached out, adjusted the sparrow pin on her jacket. "But all of you will matter. Because you'll maintain the architecture that keeps the world from descending into chaos."

Sparrow stood perfectly still, aware that the other recruits watched with envious gazes, aware that Kessler had made an example of her—positive reinforcement, showing them what success looked like.

"The world thinks it runs on ideals," Kessler continued, addressing the group again. "Democracy. Freedom. Justice. These are stories we allow them to believe because comfortable populations's are manageable populations. But you—all of you—will understand the truth: the world runs on control. And control requires people willing to do what others cannot stomach."

He gestured toward the facility behind them. "You're being given a gift. The gift of clarity. Most people live their entire lives confused by morality, paralyzed by choice, uncertain about right and wrong. You're being freed from that confusion. You'll know exactly what's required, and you'll execute it without hesitation."

Is that freedom? Sparrow wondered. *Or just a different kind of prison?*

But she kept the thought to herself. Questioning waited for later. Survival only mattered for now.

"Dismissed," Kessler announced. "Report to your instructors for advanced training assignments."

The recruits scattered. Sparrow started toward the dormitory, but Kessler's voice stopped her.

"Sparrow. A moment."

She turned. He was alone now, the instructors having departed with the other recruits.

"You are wondering if you made the right choice." Kessler tilted his head slightly. Not a question—an observation.

"No, sir."

"Lie." He smiled faintly. "You're wondering if accepting my offer three months ago was wisdom or weakness. If the safety and training I provide are worth whatever you've surrendered."

Sparrow did not reply. Confirming would be admitting doubt. Denying would be an obvious lie.

"The answer," Kessler continued, "is that you didn't have a choice. On the streets, you would have died within a year—overdose, violence, disease, exposure. Here, you'll become extraordinary." He walked to the window overlooking Vienna. "Your mother chose oblivion over responsibility. You've chosen the opposite. That choice defines you more than any test I could design."

"Sir?" Sparrow's voice was smaller than she wanted. "Do you think she—my mother—do you think she loved me?"

Kessler was quiet for a long moment. "I think she loved heroin more. That's not your failing. It's hers." He turned back. "Love requires sacrifice. She was unwilling to sacrifice her addiction for you. I'm unwilling to sacrifice my mission for sentiment. The difference is that I'm honest about the equation."

"Is that better?"

"It's sustainable. Which, in the end, is what matters." He gestured toward the door. "Go. Rest. Tomorrow your real training begins."

Sparrow walked to the dormitory, the sparrow pin catching light as she moved. In her small room—bare walls, single bed, locker for possessions she didn't have—she lay down and stared at the ceiling.

She'd passed the test. Earned a name, an identity, a place in something larger than herself.

She'd also killed a rabbit that had trusted her.

The two facts existed simultaneously, equally true, equally irrelevant to tomorrow's training.

This is who I am now, she thought again. *Sparrow. Kessler's creation.*

She closed her eyes and tried to sleep.

But in her dreams, she was back on the streets of Ankara, nine years old and starving, and her mother was there—lucid for once, sober—saying, "I'm sorry, Leyla. I'm so sorry I wasn't strong enough."

And dream-Leyla replied, "It's okay, Anne. I became strong enough for both of us."

When she woke at dawn for training, she couldn't remember if her mother had responded.

Just another fragment lost to the transformation from who she'd been to who Kessler needed her to become.

Just another small death in a facility designed to kill all things except obedience.

5

No Good Deed

"Control the risk, and the world bends. Control the liquidity, and the world kneels."
—Victor Krane, CEO International Mercantile Bank

Manhattan, New York City— 9:02 p.m.- Day 1

International Mercantile Bank gleamed like a shard of ice above lower Manhattan. The building was the newest constructed and loomed over all other buildings. The building commanded strength and respect. The tower's shadow fell like a sundial measuring the city's pulse. Ethan had walked past it a thousand times as a junior analyst, always looking up, wondering what decisions were made in those upper floors.

Now he worked there, and he'd learned the truth: most decisions weren't made at all. They simply happened, flowing through systems designed to absolve anyone of responsibility.

Ethan Cole had come to International Mercantile Bank the way most ambitious graduates did—hungry, idealistic, and convinced that demanding work would be rewarded with something more than a paycheck.

Princeton had been a stretch financially. He'd graduated in the top third of his class on a combination of scholarships, student loans, and the kind of relentless work ethic that came from growing up watching his father balance military service with raising two boys after their mother died. While his classmates networked at exclusive clubs or spent summers backpacking through Europe, Ethan had worked two jobs—research assistant during the academic year, financial analyst intern at a mid-tier firm during summers. He'd learned early that money opened doors, and lacking it meant you had to be twice as smart and work three times as hard just to get a foot in those doors.

The recruitment had happened in his senior year, during one of those campus career fairs where banks descended on Princeton like well-dressed predators. International Mercantile Bank—IMB to those who worked there—had been represented by a Vice President who'd listened to Ethan's presentation on currency flow patterns during the European debt crisis and offered him an interview on the spot.

"You see things other people miss," the VP had remarked. "That's rare. Don't waste it."

Ethan hadn't wasted it.

He had started as a junior analyst in the Trade Finance division, working seventy-hour weeks reviewing transaction documentation, flagging anomalies, learning the intricate machinery of how money moved across borders. Within eighteen months, he'd been promoted to senior analyst. Two years after that, associate director of compliance monitoring. At twenty-nine, he'd made Director and Senior Vice President—younger than most, a testament to both his analytical skills and his willingness to work weekends when others went home to their families.

Now, at thirty-two, he served as Senior Vice President, Internal Control Division, overseeing a team of fifteen analysts responsible for monitoring wire transfers, transaction patterns, and regulatory compliance across IMB's global network. It proved the kind of position that required both technical expertise and political savvy—understanding not just what the regulations required, but how to navigate the competing interests of trading desks that wanted speed, legal departments that wanted coverage, and executives who wanted plausible deniability.

Through hard work and dedication, he had earned each and every promotion. He worked while others took vacations. He never called in sick. He sat through countless meetings where he ranked as the youngest person in the room, had learned to present findings in ways that informed without threatening, had mastered the delicate art of raising red flags without becoming known as someone who blocked deals.

His managers thought highly of him. "Ethan Cole is exactly what this bank needs," his division head had written in his last performance review. "Analytical rigor combined with sound judgment and the institutional loyalty that built IMB's reputation."

Institutional loyalty. Ethan bought in to the culture and believed. Believed that IMB was one of the good ones—rigorous, ethical, committed to doing business the right way even when it was harder or less profitable.

International Mercantile Bank had that reputation for a reason. Founded in 1847 in New York City, IMB had survived depressions, world wars, and financial crises by being conservative when it's competitors proved reckless, thorough when others cut corners. The bank now managed approximately $1.5 trillion in assets, with operations in forty-seven countries, offices in all major financial centers from New York to Hong Kong, from London to São Paulo. It served sovereign wealth funds, pension systems, multinational corporations—the kind of clients who valued discretion, stability, and institutional knowledge that couldn't be replicated by fintech upstarts or algorithmic trading platforms.

IMB wasn't the biggest bank in the world by asset size. It wasn't the flashiest. But it was considered one of the most trustworthy—a place where regulators gave the benefit of the doubt, where auditors spent less time questioning controls, where the institutional brand carried weight precisely because it had been built over 175 years of doing things right.

Ethan had been proud to work there. Proud to tell his father—a man who'd served his country in intelligence work and understood the importance of institutions—that he helped maintain the integrity of global financial systems.

That pride had started cracking about three weeks ago. Rumors mostly, "water cooler gossip", Ethan would say to himself. Whispers of large funds movement in and out of the bank. Nothing that had yet caught the attention of Ethan Cole or his team. But if any amount of truth existed in the rumors, Ethan told himself he would find it.

Forty-two floors up, the trading floors sat dark, the executive suites locked. Only the soft hum of servers filled the wire room, where the lifeblood of global capital pulsed in endless digital streams.

Ethan Cole sat alone beneath the glow of twin monitors, his tie loosened, his sleeves rolled to the elbow. The floor remained silent but for the quiet, rhythmic tapping of keys and the distant drone of the HVAC. He'd been at it for twelve hours straight, scanning through end-of-day transactions that others had signed off long before dinner. He wasn't supposed to be here—he wasn't even on rotation tonight—but something about the volume of flagged wires this week had kept him restless.

Numbers steadied him. Patterns made sense when people didn't.

The pattern reminded him of something—a memory from years ago, sharp and specific. Lukas Reinhardt, bent over a chessboard in the Swiss Alps, moving pieces with surgical precision. "See how the knight moves, Ethan? Not straight, not diagonal. It moves in ways your opponent doesn't expect. That's how you control the board—by mastering the geometry others ignore."

Ethan had asked, "Is this how your father taught you?"

Lukas had smiled that small, controlled smile. "My father teaches many things. Chess is the least of them."

The memory dissolved. Ethan stared at the transaction screen—twenty-second intervals, algorithmic precision. Geometry others ignore.

He scrolled through the queue. Three transactions passed his review without issue: standard corporate payroll, a real estate settlement, interbank liquidity. His eyes glazed over the familiar patterns—source verified, beneficiary clear, purpose documented. Then the fourth wire loaded. His finger hovered over the approval button. It all looked clean. Too clean.

He scrolled back to the timestamp: 7:34:17 PM. The next transaction: 7:34:37 PM. Exactly twenty seconds. He pulled the next five. 7:34:57 PM; 7:35:17 PM; 7:35:37 PM. His throat went dry. No human operator worked with that precision. This appeared all too algorithmic. Automated. Hidden.

"Jesus Christ," he whispered to the empty room.

"What are you?"

Over one billion dollars, routed in nearly 200 micro-transactions, each one precisely timed—spaced exactly twenty seconds apart.

Ethan leaned back in his chair, the glow of his dual monitors washing the cubicle in cold light. The hum of the wire room filled the air — printers, the low drone of servers moving billions of dollars per hour.

This was money in motion, an invisible bloodstream. And Ethan had learned to read its pulse better than anyone. He thought to himself that perhaps the rumors were true after all. He wished they weren't.

He scrolled through the transaction history again. The money originated from an account belonging to Apex International Holdings, a supposed energy consortium registered in the British Virgin Islands—but its origin account linked through four correspondent banks, each a different continent, each with the same routing pattern.

It looked too clean. Too intentional.

Ethan frowned—he'd seen that name once before during a peer review, but only briefly. He pulled up the relationship details.

Primary Relationship Manager: Latham, R.

He tapped the desk with his pen, eyes narrowing on the relationship manager field.

Ethan blinked. *Latham?*

That didn't make sense. Richard Latham stood out as a legend inside the bank—one of its most senior rainmakers head of the bank's international corporate banking unit in London. He managed heads of state, multinational conglomerates, and blue-chip sovereign wealth funds. He didn't touch obscure offshore shell companies. Latham ranked as the kind of man who sat on panels, gave keynotes in Davos, and had the CEO on speed dial.

So why was his name attached to a client that barely existed?

Latham was an old name at International Mercantile — thirty years in, respected by the Board, had the CEO's ear. He wasn't the kind of man who oversaw irregular, offshore defense accounts. That alone made Ethan uneasy.

He clicked open the metadata, cross-referencing other wires originating from Apex. By the time the data finished populating, his pulse had shifted. Apex wasn't alone —hundreds of related transactions existed, all routing through shadow companies tied to international development funds, totaling over **one hundred billion dollars** in the past eight months.

This was akin to finding a second set of books for the entire global system — hidden in plain sight.

For a moment, he just sat there, listening to the pulse of the machines. The hum all at once captured his senses at a different level — not the rhythm of business, but something darker. A hidden metronome that the world danced to without knowing.

Ethan leaned closer, tracing the digital paper trail. The signatures were clean, the compliance documentation in order—on the surface. But the timestamps told a different story. Accounts created, funded, and verified all within the same forty-eight-hour window. All internal audit codes checked off by the book. Too perfect.

He rubbed the bridge of his nose, unease stirring—something he hadn't noticed in a long time.

Most bankers would have shrugged it off—*not my circus, not my monkeys.* But Ethan wasn't most bankers.

He had grown up far from Wall Street, the son of a career soldier and a nurse, in a small town outside Raleigh. Money had always been something other people had—people who didn't work three jobs to afford groceries or patch up the family truck every other month. When Ethan got a scholarship to Princeton, it was a jailbreak—pure freedom, if only for a moment in time. He studied economics like his life depended on it because, in reality, it did.

Now, years later, sitting in the sterile pulse of the bank's digital heart, he remained a visitor in someone else's world. The suits, the rooftop bars, the arrogance of wealth—it had never quite rubbed off.

And perhaps that explained why he noticed things others did not.

He scrolled further. The routing codes looped through banks in Cyprus, Caracas, and Dubai—jurisdictions that played shell games with disclosure. He opened another window, cross-referencing beneficiaries. The same handful of names appeared repeatedly: Helios Defense Systems-Luxembourg, The Atlantic Group-Sovereign investment fund routed through the Cayman Islands, Global News Syndicate-Media Holdings across the globe—all clean on paper.

It wasn't a coincidence. These weren't just counterparties; they served as the arteries of something larger. Each transfer pulsed like blood through an invisible financial organism — one that connected governments, corporations, and something darker.

Ethan put his thumb on it — the pattern beneath the noise. This wasn't about money. It was about control.

"Perfect symmetry," Ethan whispered. "No human error."

That was the part which unsettled him.

He tagged the wire for escalation. The internal reporting system prompted a brief note: *Possible structuring; unusual volume and precision; recommend review.*

He hesitated, finger hovering over the mouse. Sending the report meant drawing attention—maybe more than he wanted. But he remembered his father's voice from years ago, in that gravelly, no-nonsense tone:

"If your gut says something's wrong, kid, you listen. That's the difference between surviving and being a headline."

Ethan clicked **Send**.

The confirmation box blinked on screen: **Filed with Bank CEO – Victor Krane.**

He leaned back, exhaling slowly. Ethan realized the enormity of his decision. Due to the size and scope of the transactions, federal banking regulations require the Bank CEO to be notified of these transactions. The wire room itself shrunk, all at once smaller...confining...the hum of machines sharper. Somewhere in the maze of circuits and cables, he could almost feel the ripple of what he'd just set in motion.

Ethan knew better than to jump to conclusions. He'd seen mistakes destroy careers. But the pattern gnawed at him. He decided he'd reach out to Latham in the morning, clear it up — quietly, internally, by the book. The whole lot could still make sense in the daylight.

He told himself that as he shut down his screen. But as the monitors dimmed, the wire room seemed to close in around him — too quiet, too aware. Something in the back of his mind whispered that the daylight wouldn't help at all.

Ethan shut down his workstation and gathered his things. Through the glass, Manhattan stretched below—glittering, indifferent.

He would reach out to Latham in the morning—call him, talk through Apex, and clear it all up. As Ethan was leaving the office, Margaret Heller, head of compliance for the bank, ran into him in the hallway. She seemed agitated, almost frightened and looked over her shoulder. "Ethan, could I speak with you? Somewhere private?" They stepped into a small conference room. Ethan noticed her trembling which proved unnerving.

With a halting voice—"I approved wires for Latham's accounts for the last twelve years. The patterns changed several months ago. In aggregate it became... too perfect. Like someone was cleaning up in real time." She grabbed his arm. "Whatever you found, be careful who you tell. Not everyone here at the bank is who they claim to be." Then she vanished, leaving Ethan bewildered, with more questions than answers.

He told himself it amounted to just another irregular transaction. Just another late night.

But deep down, Ethan knew better.

Something had shifted. And somewhere, someone had just noticed him.

6

Devil's Bargain

[CLASSIFIED // RECRUITMENT AUTHORIZATION]
SUBJECT: *Latham, R.*
Status: High-risk financial liability.
Assets compromised:

- Gambling debts (undisclosed)
- Divorce settlement arrears
- Professional reputation deteriorating
- Psychological profile indicates malleability under pressure

Directive:
Activate Recruitment Protocol.
Apply financial incentive coupled with calibrated intimidation.
Purpose:
Secure internal banking access for upcoming funding requirements
Kessler Addendum:
"A desperate man is the easiest to reshape—for he will cling to the hand that owns him."

London, England — Spring 2023
Rain came down in sheets over Mayfair, turning the cobblestone streets into rivers of reflected light. Richard Latham stood beneath the awning of **White's Club**, smoking a cigarette he'd promised his ex-wife

he'd quit, watching black cabs navigate the deluge with the practiced indifference of London traffic.

He was fifty-six years old. He had a corner office at International Mercantile Bank's London headquarters. He had thirty years of impeccable service, a multitude of financial industry awards, and a reputation as one of the most dependable relationship managers in European banking.

He also had £347,000 in gambling debts, a divorce settlement that was bleeding him dry, and approximately six weeks before the collection agencies stopped being polite.

The cigarette tasted like failure.

"Interesting habit for a banker," a voice responded beside him. European accent, impossible to place—German undertones with French polish and something Eastern European in the vowels. "Though I understand the appeal. Sometimes the slow suicide is preferable to the fast one."

Latham turned. The man looked perhaps sixty, silver hair perfectly groomed, wearing a Savile Row suit that probably cost more than Latham's monthly salary. His eyes shone pale gray, the color of winter sky over the Alps.

"Do I know you?" Latham asked.

"Not yet. But you will." The man produced his own cigarette case—antique silver, monogrammed. "May I join you? The rain makes for tedious conversation inside, and I find I prefer candor to small talk."

Something in Latham's instincts screamed warning. But desperation had long since overruled instinct. "Be my guest."

They smoked in silence for a moment, watching the rain. Finally, the stranger spoke:

"You have a problem, Mr. Latham. Several, actually. Gambling debts—mostly online poker, some sports betting. A divorce settlement that assumes your bonus structure remained intact, which it hasn't. A daughter at Cambridge whose tuition you can barely afford. And a pride too substantial to ask for help from colleagues who'd use your weakness as leverage."

Latham's chest tightened all of a sudden. The last time he experienced this came from his heart attack several years back. He wasn't going there again. "Who the hell are you?"

"Someone who sees potential where others see liability." The man turned, extended his hand. "Andreas Kessler. I represent certain... interests... that could benefit from your expertise."

Latham didn't take the hand. "I'm not interested in whatever you're selling."

"I'm not selling anything. I'm offering a solution." Kessler withdrew his hand without offense, his expression placid. "Your debts disappear. Your daughter's education remains secure. Your ex-wife receives her settlement on time. All you need to do is continue being exactly who you already are: an exemplary banker facilitating international transactions for high-net-worth clients."

"And in exchange?"

"Occasionally, you will receive clients I refer. They will have complex needs—offshore structures, multiple jurisdictions, requirements for discretion that exceed standard protocols. You will process their transactions with the same professionalism that you apply to all of your work."

Latham laughed—bitter, hollow. "You're asking me to launder money."

"I'm asking you to do your job." Kessler's tone never changed, remaining calm and almost paternal.

"The only difference is that your clients will be mine rather than those you have already been serving. And let's be honest, Mr. Latham—do you honestly believe the sovereign wealth funds and private equity firms you currently service are paragons of transparency? You already facilitate opacity. I'm simply asking you to...expand your client base."

"No." Latham ground out his cigarette. "I'm not interested."

"Understandable." Kessler nodded as if Latham had agreed rather than refused. "Take forty-eight hours. Think about your daughter at Cambridge, brilliant girl, first-class honors in economics. Think about what happens when she learns her father can't afford her final year."

Kessler continued without hesitation— "Think about your ex-wife's solicitors seizing your assets. Think about the rather aggressive gentle-men who hold your markers. Each man believes he has a price he won't pay. My gift is finding the exact amount where their principles cost more than their surrender."

Kessler produced a business card—cream-colored stock, no logo, just a phone number in elegant script.

"When you are ready to discuss solutions—call me. You have already lost the things that mattered, Richard. All that remains is the illusion of choice. So let me offer you something beautiful—a purpose that pays your debts... and mine. The offer expires in two days."

Kessler walked into the rain without an umbrella, his figure dissolv-ing into the downpour like smoke.

Latham stood alone beneath the awning, the business card burning in his palm like a brand.

Forty-Seven Hours Later

Just before Kessler's deadline, Latham made the call—paranoid, he knew, but if he truly intended to do this, he would at least pretend to maintain operational security.

Kessler answered on the first ring. "Mr. Latham. I'm pleased you re-considered."

"I need guarantees."

"Of course. Your debts will be cleared within seventy-two hours. Pay-ments will appear to come from a trust established by your late uncle—a man who, conveniently, did exist and did have modest wealth. The pa-perwork will withstand casual scrutiny. Your daughter's tuition will be paid through a scholarship fund I control. Again, entirely legitimate on the surface."

"And what do you get?"

"Access to International Mercantile Bank's wire systems through a trusted officer with decades of clean service. When I need transactions processed, you process them. When I need documentation generated, you generate it. When auditors ask questions, you provide answers that satisfy without illuminating."

Latham closed his eyes. "How long?"

"Until I no longer need you, or until you become a liability. Whichever comes first." Kessler's voice remained pleasant, conversational. "But understand: once you accept, there is no resignation. No retirement. No confession that cleanses your conscience. You're in until the end, whatever form that end takes."

"And if I refuse now?"

"Then tomorrow morning, your debts will be sold to collectors who lack my patience. Your ex-wife's solicitor will receive documentation of hidden assets you've been concealing. And your daughter will learn that her father is a gambler whose weakness destroyed his family."

The choice wasn't truly a choice. It never had been.

"What do I need to do?" Latham asked, his voice hollow.

"For now? Nothing. Continue your normal work. Sometime in the next month, you'll receive a client referral—a logistics company called Apex International Holdings. You'll treat them exactly as you would any legitimate corporate client. Process their documentation. Clear their wires. Ask no questions beyond standard compliance requirements."

"And if compliance flags something?"

"They won't. The structures are clean—or clean enough. But if they do, you'll explain the complexity as standard international business practice. You will use your reputation as a shield. After thirty years of impeccable service, who is going to question Richard Latham?"

The line went quiet for a moment. Then Kessler, softer: "You're not a criminal, Richard. You are a professional in an impossible situation, making the rational choice. Don't let morality complicate mathematics. Your family needs you functional, not principled."

"I understand," Latham whispered.

"Excellent. The funds will transfer tonight. Sleep well, Richard. You've made the right choice."

The call ended.

Latham stood in the phone booth, rain hammering the glass, feeling the weight of what he'd just done settle over him like wet concrete. Not heavy all at once—just gradually harder to move beneath, gradually more difficult to breathe.

He walked home through the rain, got drunk on scotch he couldn't afford but kept for special occasions, and stared at his daughter's photo until he convinced himself he'd done it for her.

The Apex transactions had started small. A few million here, a few million there. Standard international wire transfers between corporate entities, nothing that raised immediate flags. Latham processed them with the same diligence he applied to all his work, generating documentation that satisfied compliance without providing actual transparency.

The amounts grew. Ten million. Fifty million. Three hundred million in a single month, routed through subsidiary structures so complex that tracking beneficial ownership would require weeks of forensic analysis.

Latham convinced himself that this was all legitimate. High-networth clients always had complex structures. Opacity served as a feature, not a bug. He facilitated commerce, not crime.

But late at night, in the silence of his Kensington flat, he knew better.

The transactions had patterns that made no commercial sense. Money moving in perfect circles—wired from Luxembourg to Caracas to Dubai and back to Luxembourg, each transit generating fees but serving no apparent business purpose except to obscure origin.

This wasn't tax efficiency. This was laundering money on a global scale.

And he served as the washing machine.

London, England — Fall 2024

One evening, after processing a particularly large transaction—nine hundred million dollars routed through seven jurisdictions in forty-eight hours—Latham poured himself a scotch and called the number Kessler had given him for emergencies.

"Mr. Latham. I trust you are well?"

"I need to know what I'm facilitating." Latham's voice was steady, in spite of his internal shaking. "I need to understand what this money is for." He caught his words speeding a bit too fast.

"No, you don't." Kessler's tone remained pleasant but firm. "Understanding creates liability. Ignorance protects you. Process the transactions. Generate the documentation. Sleep at night knowing your daughter graduated debt-free."

"I can't keep doing this."

"Of course you can. You've been doing it brilliantly for eighteen months." A pause. "Mr. Latham, do you remember our first conversation? I told you the offer came with permanence. You accepted. There's no resignation from this position."

"I'll go to the authorities."

"And tell them what? That you've been knowingly processing suspicious transactions for a year and a half? That you falsified compliance documentation? That you accepted payments to facilitate money laundering?" Kessler's voice remained calm, almost sympathetic. "You would destroy your career, your reputation, your freedom. Your daughter would learn her father is a criminal. And for what? The transactions would continue through someone else. The system doesn't stop because one cog rebels."

Latham endured in real time the trap close around him with the finality of a cell door. "What do you want from me?"

"Exactly what you've been providing. Continue your excellent work. When the transactions grow larger—and they will grow larger—process them with the same professionalism. And when compliance officers ask questions, as they eventually will, you will provide answers that satisfy without illuminating."

"And if I can't?"

"Then we will have to reevaluate your usefulness." Kessler's voice dropped a register—still pleasant, but with something colder beneath. "I genuinely like you, Richard. You're intelligent, conscientious, trapped by circumstances I helped create. I would prefer not to resolve this problem through more permanent means. But I will if necessary."

The call ended.

Latham sat in his flat, the scotch untouched, staring at his reflection in the darkened window. He looked older than fifty-three. He looked exactly as to what he had become: a man who had sold his integrity for solvency and discovered too late that some transactions couldn't be reversed.

His daughter called that night—excited, breathless, she'd landed her first job in investment banking. Starting salary that would dwarf what he'd made at her age. Bright future ahead.

"I couldn't have done it without you, Dad," she announced, her voice full of love and gratitude. "Thank you so much for all the things you have done for me."

"I'm proud of you, sweetheart," he managed, his voice cracking slightly.

After she hung up, he poured another scotch and made a decision: he'd continue. He'd process the transactions. He'd play his role in whatever machine Kessler had built.

Because the alternative—watching his daughter learn what her education had cost—was unthinkable.

Some men destroyed their families through violence. Others through absence. Richard Latham would destroy his through proximity—by being exactly the father his daughter believed him to be, even as that belief rested on foundations of corruption he could never let her see.

He raised his glass to the window, to his reflection, to the ghost of the man he'd once been.

"To necessary compromises," he whispered.

And in that moment, Richard Latham understood what Kessler had known all along: the best prisons were the ones you built yourself, one rational choice at a time, until the walls were too high to climb and too familiar to escape.

Present Day — Phone Call with Ethan

When Ethan Cole flagged the Apex wire transactions, Latham sensed something that he hadn't in two years: hope.

Maybe this was his way out. Maybe someone outside the machine could break it. Maybe confession to a compliance officer who still believed in rules could redeem what he'd become.

But then he remembered: his daughter's career, his ex-wife's settlement, his own freedom—all dependent on silence.

And Kessler's words echoed: *"There's no resignation from this position."*

So when he called and discussed the Apex transactions with Ethan, he lied with the smooth professionalism of thirty years' practice. Corporate restructuring. Legitimate business. Complex but clean.

And when he hung up, he sat in his flat and wrote a letter he'd never send:

"To whom it may concern: I want it known that I didn't start as a criminal. I became one through a series of choices that seemed rational at the time. If you're reading this, I'm likely dead. Know that I tried to stop. Know that I failed. Know that the system I served was never what I believed it to be. And know that by the time I understood, it was already too late to matter."

He sealed the letter in an envelope, placed it in his desk drawer, and went to bed.

Six hours later, he'd be dead—a fall in the bathroom, tragic but unsuspicious. The letter would be found, read by police, and quietly filed away by investigators who'd received instructions from people they'd been trained not to question.

Richard Latham's last words—his confession, his warning, his attempt at redemption—would vanish into the same bureaucratic void that had swallowed so many truths before it.

The system protected itself. It always did.

And men like Latham—the ones who thought they could serve evil temporarily, for good reasons, with clean hands—learned too late that some stains never washed out, no matter how much you scrubbed or how desperately you wanted to believe otherwise.

7

Pressure From Above

"Ethan, come on...You know I've always had your back—don't leave me twisting in the wind here. I'm not the only one who will take a hit on this."-Richard Latham

Manhattan, New York City— 10:03 p.m. -Day 1

Evening haze enveloped downtown Manhattan and pressed against the glass walls of the small bar Ethan had ducked into after work. He sat alone near the window, tie loosened, sleeves rolled to the forearm — just another banker decompressing after a long day. But his mind refused to relax. It was circling.

That damn wire.

One billion dollars from an Apex International Holdings account routed through a chain of correspondent banks that made no sense. Not for a logistics company, not for any legitimate commercial purpose.

He had seen strange transactions before — shell companies, discreet trusts, governments hiding assets through cutouts — but this struck him as different. He couldn't put his finger on it, but the whole thing reeked of orchestration.

Out of instinct, before heading to the bar, he had run a few internal cross-checks. The system was limited, but what he found unsettled him. The Apex transaction wasn't alone. There were **hundreds** of similar wires — smaller ones, but all structured the same way — moving through other divisions, other jurisdictions. When he totaled them up, the figure made him stop cold.

Over one hundred billion dollars.

Spread across more than forty entities. Shells. Foundations. Sovereign funds.

Different currencies, same patterns. Same routing channels. Same shadow fingerprints.

It was a web, and Apex International formed only one strand of it.

He had seen anomalies before — price spikes seconds before geopolitical news, commodity surges before troop movements. But this was different. The synchronization was too tight, the movement too deliberate.

Someone wasn't predicting global events. They were orchestrating them.

For the first time, Ethan wondered if money itself had become a weapon — and if he had just found the trigger.

He told himself to leave it alone — at least until morning. He'd reach out to Richard Latham, the relationship manager attached to Apex, and get clarity.

Latham ranked as one of the bank's untouchables — senior, well-connected, the kind of person whose name carried weight in boardrooms. He stood out as polished, smooth, with the kind of charm that could make anyone feel smaller but never offended. Ethan had met him twice — once at a international economic symposium in London, another time during a cross-border audit. Both times, Latham had exuded the aura of effortless control.

Which made tonight's discovery strange. Why would a man of Latham's stature be personally managing an account like Apex?

His glass sat half-empty when his phone buzzed. **Latham.**

Ethan frowned. It was late — just past 11 pm in New York, and 4 am in London. He considered ignoring it, then answered.

"Richard," he noted evenly. "Didn't expect to hear from you at this hour

"Cole," Latham replied, his voice smooth and warm, but with a subtle tightness. "I heard you've placed a hold on one of my client's transfers. Apex International Holdings."

"That's right," Ethan maintained. "The transaction doesn't reconcile with the client's stated business profile. Routing through Dubai, funding from a source in Cyprus, beneficiary tied to the Cayman Islands. None of that lines up with a logistics portfolio."

A faint chuckle drifted through the line. "My dear boy, you've always been thorough. It's why people in the firm speak well of you. But this one's clean. These are... discreet restructuring movements. Global funds often move capital through complex channels to stay invisible to competitors."

"Discretion is fine," Ethan replied, voice measured. "But this one's missing documentation. It's irregular. We have to follow protocol."

There was a pause — slight, but enough for the air to thicken. When Latham spoke again, the charm remained intact, but the warmth had vanished.

"Ethan...sometimes protocol doesn't serve the greater interest. This wire needs to move immediately. It's time-sensitive."

"Then provide the documentation," Ethan responded simply.

"You are way out over your skis here Ethan." Latham's tone didn't rise — it fell, into something colder, flatter. "But trust me when I tell you, the Bank wants this cleared. Delays create attention. Attention creates problems."

Ethan took a long sip of his drink, eyes fixed on his reflection in the glass. "Then we'll clear it when it's clean. Until then, it stays on hold. Let's talk more in the morning."

For a long moment, nothing.

Then, softly — almost like an echo from somewhere far away — Latham stated, "We may not have until the morning."

The words hung there. Not quite a threat. Not quite a warning. But something in the way Latham communicated it carried the weight of finality.

"Richard," Ethan asked, lowering his voice. "What does that mean?"

Latham's reply came calm and deliberate, the mask of control slipping back into place — "Don't overthink it, Ethan. Just...keep an open mind when you come in tomorrow. We'll talk then."

The line went dead.

Ethan sat back, the hum of the bar fading around him. He checked the call log, then his screen — nothing. No follow-up text.

Just silence.

He stared at the darkened city through the glass, the streetlights painting streaks of gold on the rain-damp asphalt. For the first time in years, something close to unease emerged—not fear, not yet, but a prickle at the edge of his instincts.

His phone sat dark on the bar, Latham's cryptic warning still echoing: We may not have until the morning.

Ethan thought about calling his brother. Daniel would know what to do. Daniel always knew what to do when things went sideways. Eight years in Delta Force had given him an education Ethan could never match—how to read threats, how to assess danger, how to survive when the system you trusted turned against you.

Their father had raised them both to see patterns, to trust instinct over assumption. But Daniel had taken those lessons into war zones, had learned them in ways that made Ethan's financial models look like children's games. "The first rule," Daniel had told him once, back when he'd just returned from his second deployment, "is that when your gut tells you something's wrong, it's usually already too late. The second rule is that the people at the top never pay for their mistakes. That bill comes due somewhere else. Usually to people like us."

Ethan had laughed it off then. Called Daniel paranoid, contended the military had made him too cynical. Now, sitting in this bar with a billion-dollar anomaly flagged in the system and a senior banker making veiled threats at midnight, those words didn't seem paranoid anymore.

They seemed prescient.

He considered dialing Daniel's number—the secure one, the one that bounced through encrypted relays because his brother's work in the private sector required the kind of discretion that made banking secrecy look transparent by comparison. But what would he say? That a wire transfer *felt* wrong? That a respected colleague had called him late and spoken in careful euphemisms? It sounded ridiculous even in his own head. Ethan convinced himself he needed to focus on the facts, not his feelings.

Daniel would come anyway. That purely defined brotherhood—it didn't require explanations or justifications. Just a call, and Daniel would drop whatever contract he was working and be on the next flight to New York. That's what family meant to the Cole brothers. Their father had drilled it into them: you look out for your own, no matter what the cost.

But Ethan wasn't ready to make that call. Not yet. Not until he understood what he was actually dealing with.

He finished his drink, left cash on the bar, and walked out into the Manhattan night. The city hummed around him—taxis and delivery trucks, late-night workers and insomniacs, the endless circulation of people and money that never stopped, never questioned, never saw the machinery beneath the surface.

Tomorrow, he would go into the office. Talk to Latham face-to-face, get answers, resolve this like a professional. Maybe it amounted to nothing. Maybe a simple explanation existed that he had missed. Maybe his instincts—honed by years of audit work but never tested by real world danger—were overreacting to shadows.

He wanted to believe that.

But as he walked toward the subway, collar turned up against the autumn chill, he couldn't shake the feeling that he had just crossed some invisible threshold. That the world he had known—the world of protocols and procedures, of institutional trust and professional courtesy—had already collapsed around him.

And ahead lay something else entirely.

He didn't know it yet, but by morning, Richard Latham would be dead. The one-billion-dollar wire would be just the first domino to fall. And the brother he had almost called—the one who had learned about betrayal and survival in the mountains of Afghanistan—would become the only person he could trust in a war he didn't know he'd already joined.

8

Brother's War

CLASSIFIED – DIRECTORATE / NODE: AFGHAN THEATER]

Subject: Tactical Assessment — *Cole, D.* (Delta Operations)

Summary:

Operation *Iron Veil* (Afghanistan) modified per command authorization. Air support withdrawal intentional to evaluate field command stress resilience.

Outcome Objective:

– Measure subject's tactical improvisation under loss of command structure.

– Confirm subject's suitability for Tier-1 integration and potential asset recruitment.

Losses: Acceptable (6 KIA).

Helmand Province, Afghanistan — Summer 2013

Intelligence indicated the compound should have been empty. The Taliban commander had fled three days ago, leaving only abandoned equipment and scorched propaganda posters.

Intelligence was wrong. They were always wrong.

Captain Daniel Cole moved through the darkness with his team—six Delta operators, ghosts in the Afghan night. They'd done this a hundred times: breach, clear, exfiltrate. Routine had become religion.

But something was off. The air felt too still. The dogs that usually barked at passing patrols were silent.

"Hold," Daniel whispered into his throat mic.

His point man froze. "What've you got?"

Daniel scanned the compound through his NVGs. Two buildings, one collapsed well, a goat pen. Normal. Except—

"The gate. It's open."

"So?"

"It wasn't open in yesterday's drone footage."

His comms officer's voice crackled: "Overwatch confirms no movement. We're green."

But Daniel's gut—the same instinct that had kept him alive through three deployments—screamed otherwise. "Pull back. We're aborting."

"Sir, the package—"

"Is not worth walking into a kill box. We extract, regroup, hit it tomorrow with ISR."

They withdrew in formation, twenty yards, fifty yards. Daniel was the last to turn when the world exploded.

The IED had been buried under the gate—old Soviet ordinance rewired with cell phone detonators. The blast threw him fifteen feet, shrapnel tearing through his body armor. His ears rang with a single, infinite tone.

Through the smoke, he saw his point man—Lieutenant Oliver Shaw, twenty-six, married, a kid on the way—lying in pieces.

Two more of his team lay motionless.

Then the gunfire started. Muzzle flashes from the "abandoned" buildings. An ambush, perfectly executed.

Daniel returned fire on instinct, dragging his wounded comms officer behind a mud wall. Blood ran hot down his side—his own or someone else's, he couldn't tell.

"Overwatch, we are compromised! Need immediate QRF and CAS!"

Static. Then: "Negative, Ghost-Six. No air assets available. Stand by."

"Stand by?" Daniel's voice cracked. "We're getting shredded here!"

"Negative air support. Disengage and extract."

Three men dead. Two wounded. No air cover. The calculus proved out brutal and clear: they had been left to die.

Daniel made the call he'd carry for the rest of his life: "All units, tactical retreat. Leave the dead. We move NOW."

They fought their way out across two kilometers of open desert, losing another man to sniper fire. By the time they reached the extraction point, Daniel had four bullets in his vest, one through his thigh, and the names of four dead operators burned into his soul.

The After Action Report called it "acceptable losses due to evolving battlefield conditions."

Daniel called it murder by bureaucracy.

Walter Reed Medical Center — Three Months Later

Daniel sat in the psychiatric evaluation room, still limping, still seeing Oliver Shaw's face each time he closed his eyes at night.

The Army psychiatrist—a woman who'd never heard a shot fired in anger—reviewed his file. "Captain Cole, your trauma responses are normal given the circumstances. PTSD is common, treatable—"

"It's not PTSD." His voice was flat, dead. "It's betrayal."

"Betrayal?"

"We were denied air support because some desk jockey decided the political optics of a CAS strike were worse than four dead Americans." He leaned forward. "Tell me how I'm supposed to serve a system that does that math."

The psychiatrist made a note. "I'm recommending you for reassignment. Non-combat role, stateside. You need time to process—"

"I need the men who made that call to look me in the eye and tell me why Shaw's kid grows up without a father."

"Captain—"

"Are we done here?"

She closed the file. "You're flagged for early separation. Mental health discharge. Honorable, full benefits. You'll be out in ninety days."

Daniel stood, joints aching. "Good. I'm done being an acceptable loss."

Six Months Later — A Bar Outside Fort Bragg

Daniel drank alone, methodically working through his third bourbon. The TV above the bar showed news from Syria—another regime change, another pipeline deal, another war sold as humanitarian intervention.

"You look like a man with nowhere to go."

Daniel glanced up. His younger brother Ethan slid onto the stool beside him, looking uncomfortable in civilian clothes, like he was wearing a costume.

"E," Daniel remarked. "Didn't know you were in town."

"Dad called. Told me you stopped returning his messages."

"Nothing to say."

Ethan ordered a beer, waited. He'd always been good at waiting—at letting silence do the interrogation.

Finally, Daniel mentioned, "You ever wonder if we're on the wrong side?"

"Of what?"-Ethan replied.

"The wars, the banks, the whole machine." He gestured at the TV. "I spent eight years killing people I was told were enemies. You know what I learned?"

"What?"-Ethan asked.

"That the people who decide who's an enemy never get shot at."

Ethan was quiet for a moment.

"Afghanistan changed you," Ethan stated carefully.

Daniel's jaw tightened. "I lost four men because Command pulled air support." He told it like he'd asserted it a thousand times to himself. "Political optics. That's what they told me after. Political fucking optics."

"I'm sorry." Ethan came out with softly.

"Shaw had a kid on the way." Daniel's voice went somewhere else. "Never got to meet her. Command sent flowers to the funeral."

Daniel finished his bourbon. "The system works exactly like it's designed to. It just wasn't designed for people like us."

"So what now?"

Daniel laughed—bitter, hollow. "Hell if I know. Private sector, maybe. Plenty of defense contractors need guys who know how to kick doors."

"That's not you."

"Then who am I?" Daniel met his brother's eyes. "Because the man I was —died in Helmand. I'm just wearing his face."

Ethan gripped his shoulder. "You're my brother. That's who you are."

Daniel wanted to believe that. But brotherhood was another word for shared delusion—the belief that blood meant something in a world built on extraction and expenditure.

He didn't know it then, but Kessler had already marked him. Another broken soldier, another asset in waiting.

All it would take was the right offer at the right moment.

9

Surveillance

Kessler — Private Diary (Zurich-0 Archive: Unclassified)

"The Cole boy walks in his father's shadow, but he does not yet understand the cruelty of inheritance. I watched his father... long before the boy learned to speak."

Manhattan, New York City— 11:59 p.m.-Day 1

Night had turned heavy and humid, the kind of air that stuck to skin and glass alike. Ethan stepped out of the bar and into the near-empty street, the fresh smell of rain faint on the wind. He loosened his tie further and walked toward the small parking structure two blocks away, the muted rhythm of his shoes echoing on wet pavement.

The East River shimmered under the sodium haze of midnight. Ethan leaned on the railing of the pedestrian bridge, watching a tugboat push through the dark current slowly flowing through the dark night.

His mind replayed Latham's last words — we may not have until morning.

He thought about calling someone — his father, maybe — but dismissed it. There was nothing to say yet. No proof. Just unease. Still, the silence of the city pressed on him.

The street had that peculiar quality of urban emptiness—not truly deserted, but hollowed out somehow, as if the city itself was holding its breath. Ethan had experienced this before, in the seconds before an avalanche, when even the wind goes still.

He sensed it before he actually saw it.

A reflection — a shape — too steady in the dark glass of a closed boutique across the street. Someone walking when he walked. Slowing when he slowed.

He glanced again, casually this time, the way his father had taught him when he was young — never look twice the same way.

It was there. A figure, distant but distinct. Broad-shouldered, still, standing half in shadow beneath a dead streetlight.

Ethan exhaled slowly. Not fear, he told himself. Just awareness.

He continued toward the subway entrance, not breaking pace. At the curb, he looked both ways—more for the reflection than traffic—

Empty street. The figure was gone.

He continued walking. The wind picked up, sharp with rain.

Somewhere behind him, a footstep echoed a half-beat too late.

He slowed. Looked over his shoulder. Nothing. Just the city—wet streets, yellow light, a man waiting for a cab.

He shrugged it off, adjusting his collar. He wasn't a man who spooked easily. But old instincts—the kind his father had drilled into him during their back country hunting trips—stirred awake. The weight of being watched, faint but real.

He descended the subway stairs, the fluorescent light harsh after the darkness above. The platform was nearly empty—a woman in scrubs reading her phone, a homeless man asleep on a bench, a businessperson checking his watch with the impatience of someone who'd been waiting too long.

The train arrived with a screech of metal and a gust of stale air. Ethan stepped into the car, choosing a seat near the door where he could watch both ends. As the doors began to close, a figure slipped through—broad-shouldered, coat collar turned up, face half-hidden beneath a cap.

The man took a seat at the far end of the car. He didn't look at Ethan. Didn't need to.

Ethan watched him in the dark reflection of the window as the train lurched forward into the tunnel. The man pulled out a phone, lifted it to his ear.

"He's not backing off," the voice uttered quietly. "And Latham couldn't turn him."

"Understood," came the reply. "Proceed."

The man hung up and pocketed the phone, his reflection a ghost in the black glass as the subway hurtled through the darkness beneath the city.

Ethan exited at his stop, climbing the stairs two at a time, not running but not lingering either. He didn't look back. He didn't need to. The weight of being watched had settled into his bones now—familiar, almost comfortable in its constancy.

By the time he reached his apartment, the sense of being followed had faded—or maybe he'd just decided to let it fade. There were more important things on his mind.

Something about Latham's voice lingered.

We may not have until the morning.

Inside his apartment—minimalist, neat, the view of the City stretching out like a mirror—Ethan powered up his laptop. The screen's glow cut through the dark room.

He logged into the bank's restricted database through a secure VPN, bypassing the usual trace logs the way only someone with internal system familiarity could. He wasn't supposed to access client data offsite, but curiosity had long since overruled caution.

The Apex wire led to four others. Then twenty-three, then over one hundred.

Each routed through jurisdictions designed to erase fingerprints—Liechtenstein, Cyprus, Dubai, Caracas, Cayman Islands. But when he overlaid transaction metadata, timestamps, and counterparty bank codes, patterns emerged. The movements weren't random; they were synchronized.

A hidden architecture. Money crossing continents in perfect rhythm—like a digital heartbeat pulsing through the world's financial arteries.

And Apex was the trigger node.

Ethan had lived alone long enough to appreciate silence, but this was different—heavy, expectant, like the air just before a storm. Ethan sat back, the soft hum of the laptop fan filling the silence. He saved the data to an encrypted drive, his laptop open, the cursor blinking over a half-written note he couldn't finish.

If anything happens to me...

He deleted the line. Writing it down made it real.

The smell of coffee filled the room as he opened the pantry. He reached for the bag of dark roast, poured out a handful of beans, and slid the flash drive deep inside before sealing it shut. A ridiculous hiding place, maybe—but no professional would waste time with a bag of coffee beans. His father used to say, "If you want to hide something, put it where nobody wants to look."

He smiled faintly at the memory.

Ethan shut the laptop. He was past the point of reporting this. Whatever he'd stumbled into, it was beyond compliance, beyond policy. The knots tying up his stomach—the way a soldier feels when the forest goes quiet before an ambush.

He poured a second cup of coffee, forcing himself to breathe. Tomorrow, he'd take the data to someone outside the bank. Someone he trusted. He didn't know who that was yet—but he'd find them.

The rain tapped harder against the glass, almost rhythmic. For a moment, he thought he heard something beneath it—a low hum, a shift of sound.

He turned toward the window, scanning the street below. Nothing. Just the wind, the pulse of a neon sign, the indifferent sprawl of Manhattan at night.

Still, the feeling didn't leave him. That quiet weight, like the air holding its breath.

He set the mug down, watching the steam rise and sharply twist into the dark, and uttered softly,

"Let's see how deep this goes."

Somewhere in the reflection, he could almost see his father again—the weathered man standing under Montana sky, saying, "You can't outfight what you don't understand, son. But you can outthink it."

Outside, thunder rumbled. Rain pressed against the window, turning the city into a blur of light and motion.

Across the city, in the shadowed upper deck of a parking structure overlooking the subway exit, a man stood in silence.

Tall, coat collar turned up, his face only half-caught by the yellow halo of a single overhead light. He had followed the train in a black sedan, waiting at the station, watching Ethan emerge and disappear into the night.

He pulled out a small, encrypted satellite phone and pressed a single key. The line clicked.

"It's me," he announced in a low, even voice—calm, European. The kind of voice that carried quiet authority and something icier beneath. "He's not backing off."

A pause. Static on the other end. Then a faint, distorted response—words indistinct but sharp.

The man's gaze remained fixed on the apartment building where Ethan had vanished. "Yes," he stated finally. "I spoke with Latham. He failed to persuade him. He's out of time."

Another pause.

Then, quietly, almost to himself: "Shame. The boy doesn't yet understand what he's stepped into."

He closed the phone, pocketed it, and stepped back into the darkness.

By the time the overhead light flickered out, the parking deck was empty.

10

Architecture

[CLASSIFIED: EYES ONLY — DIRECTORATE / NODE: GLOBAL-ALPHA]

"Instability is not chaos. It is managed volatility designed to produce predictable outcomes for our interests."
—Strategic Planning Memo, Helios Operations Division

Davos, Switzerland —8:45 a.m. local time- Day 2

No windows. Soundproofed walls thick enough to survive bunker-buster munitions. The conference room existed in official records as a storage facility. Access required three separate biometric scans and a passcode that changed every six hours.

Inside, eight people sat around a table of thick polished African Black-wood, their faces illuminated by the soft glow of encrypted tablets. No names offered. No titles acknowledged. They were simply referred to by their nodes: London, Singapore, New York, Moscow, Beijing, Dubai, Brussels, Zurich.

Kessler—Zurich—sat at the head, his silver hair catching the recessed lighting, his expression carved from alpine stone.

"Agenda item seven." His voice carried that impossible-to-place European accent. "Sub-Saharan stabilization through controlled resource scarcity."

The woman from London—mid-fifties, Savile Row suit, voice like cut glass—pulled up a holographic display. A map of Central Africa bloomed above the table, mineral deposits glowing like stars.

"Coltan reserves in the Democratic Republic of Congo," she replied. "Critical for smartphone and electric vehicle production. Current market price: stable. Projected demand over next decade: exponential."

"And the problem?" Beijing asked. Male, early sixties, Mandarin accent softened by Oxford education.

"Stability." London's voice carried faint disdain. "When governments function, when infrastructure develops, when populations organize—prices become... negotiable. Competition emerges. Profit margins compress."

Kessler leaned forward slightly. "Proposal?"

London swiped the display. Red zones spread across the map like infection. "We destabilize the current administration through a three-phase operation. Phase One: fund opposition militias through shell corporations already established in Liechtenstein and Panama. Total investment: three hundred million dollars."

"Source?" Dubai asked. Female, younger than the others, carrying the particular confidence of someone who'd inherited rather than earned power.

"Apex International Holdings and three subsidiary accounts. The money routes through International Mercantile Bank in New York, gets restructured through Luxembourg, and arrives as humanitarian aid to local NGOs who don't ask questions." London pulled up wire transfer schedules. "We've already secured the relationship manager at IMB—Richard Latham. Cooperative, compromised, compliant."

Moscow—thick-necked, ex-KGB, the kind of man who'd survived three regime changes—grunted approval. "Timeline?"

"Phase One begins immediately. Arms shipments route through Caracas and Dubai, repackaged as agricultural equipment. Phase Two triggers in six months: coordinated attacks on infrastructure—power grids, water treatment, telecommunications. Blamed on government corruption and rebel forces. Phase Three: eighteen months from now, when the population is sufficiently destabilized, we facilitate regime change. Install a friendly administration. Secure mining concessions at favorable rates."

Singapore—precise, analytical, former World Bank economist—studied the financials. "Projected ROI?"

"Conservative estimate: four hundred percent over ten years. Aggressive estimate: seven hundred percent if cobalt prices spike as projected."

"Casualties?" New York asked. American, military bearing, the look of someone who'd given orders that killed thousands and slept fine afterward.

London's expression didn't change. "Displacement: approximately two million. Direct casualties from conflict: estimated forty to sixty thousand. Indirect deaths from infrastructure collapse—famine, disease, secondary violence: projected one hundred fifty to two hundred thousand over the operation's duration."

The number sat in the air like smoke.

Brussels—Belgian, EU technocrat, the architect of monetary policy that had impoverished southern Europe—nodded slowly. "Acceptable parameters. What are the risk factors?"

"Media exposure. Western press occasionally focuses on African conflicts when images are particularly dramatic. We've already embedded assets in major news organizations to shape coverage. The narrative will emphasize tribal violence and failed governance, not foreign interference."

"And if journalists dig deeper?"

London's smile was thin. "We have protocols for investigative reporters who become... overly curious. Vehicle accidents. Health complications. Occasionally, muggings in dangerous neighborhoods. The usual measures."

Kessler made a note on his tablet. "Approved. Operation code name Scarlet Dawn. Authorization code Helios-Seven-Seven-Delta. Begin Phase One immediately. London, coordinate with New York on the banking infrastructure. Moscow, handle the arms logistics. Beijing, ensure any UN Security Council resolutions are neutralized."

"And if the Chinese government objects?" Beijing asked.

"They won't. Your mining corporations will receive their own concessions. Everyone profits except the people who actually live there—and their opinions are irrelevant in this equation."

Kessler swiped to the next item. "Agenda item eight: Venezuelan currency manipulation. Singapore, your assessment?"

Singapore pulled up economic models—inflation curves, default probabilities, capital flight projections. "The Bolivar is approaching collapse threshold. Current administration has nationalized oil production, limiting our access to the Orinoco fields. Recommended action: accelerate the collapse through coordinated speculation against the currency, then facilitate regime change through economic strangulation rather than military intervention."

"Cost?"

"Initial investment: two hundred million in currency futures and sovereign debt manipulation. We short the Bolivar while simultaneously withdrawing international credit. The government defaults within eight months. Hyperinflation destroys middle-class savings. Population becomes desperate. Opposition forces—which we'll fund through the same channels as the African operation—present themselves as salvation."

"And the human cost?" Brussels asked, not from concern but from actuarial interest.

"Famine, probably. Hyperinflation makes food imports impossible. Medical system will collapse—no foreign currency for pharmaceuticals. Conservative estimate: twenty thousand excess deaths in the first year. Could escalate to fifty thousand if the transition is messy."

New York leaned back. "Versus how many casualties if we attempt military intervention?"

"Tens of thousands. Plus negative media coverage, international condemnation, potential blowback from Latin American allies."

"Then economic warfare is preferable." Kessler made another notation.

"Approved. Authorization code Helios-Eight-Two-Charlie. Singapore, coordinate with Brussels on the monetary mechanisms. Dubai, ensure oil futures positioning benefits our energy portfolios."

The meeting continued for two more hours. Each agenda item presented with the same clinical precision: projected returns, acceptable casualties, risk mitigation strategies. A school bombing in Afghanistan that would justify renewed military contracts. A cyber attack on Ukrainian infrastructure that would spike defense spending. A pharmaceutical price spike in Southeast Asia that would generate billions while thousands died from preventable diseases.

It was more than evil. It was architecture.

The Directorate didn't see human suffering. They saw market opportunities.

Finally, Kessler reached the last item. "Miscellaneous threats. Status updates?"

Moscow pulled up a file. "That journalist in Istanbul—the one investigating arms flows through Turkey. Confirmed terminated. Ruled a suicide. Authorities closed the investigation."

"The whistleblower in Frankfurt?" Brussels asked.

"Contained," London replied. "His documents were acquired before transmission. He has been charged with embezzlement—our forensic accountants built a compelling false trail. He will spend the next decade in prison explaining crimes he didn't commit."

"And the compliance officer at International Mercantile Bank?" Kessler's voice was casual, but the Directorate Board Members at the table recognized the weight behind it. "The one who's been flagging unusual transactions?"

New York checked his tablet. "Ethan Cole, Princeton educated, clean record. He flagged the Apex wire a day ago. We've been monitoring his activity."

"Assessment?" —Kessler asked, his face still carved granite.

"Curious but containable. He's following protocol—filed reports, questioned patterns. But he doesn't understand the scope. He thinks he's found an irregularity, not a system."

"Recommendations?"

"Continue monitoring. If he escalates or shares his findings with external parties, we have multiple response options. Our man inside the Bank—Richard Latham—was unable to discourage further investigation. Since that failed, we will have to plan a more...permanent solution. Just like we did for Latham."

Kessler studied the file on Ethan Cole—the photograph showing an earnest young man who still believed rules mattered. "Flag it as Priority Watch. Men like him are dangerous not because they're brilliant, but because they're stubborn. They don't quit when quitting is rational."

"Understood. I'll coordinate with our asset at the bank—Victor Krane is already prepared to intervene if necessary."

Kessler closed his tablet. The meeting had concluded. Around the table, eight people who controlled more wealth than most nations, who decided which governments rose and fell, who calculated human life in terms of ROI, began to disperse.

"One more thing," Kessler mentioned quietly. Each person at the table stopped. "Remember why we're here. What we provide is order—predictable, manageable, profitable order. Yes, people suffer. They always have. The question is whether that suffering serves a purpose or simply happens randomly. We give it purpose. The difference between a criminal and a statesperson is simply a matter of scale. Kill a hundred for profit, you're a criminal. Kill a hundred thousand for stability, they name airports after you. We must never forget that distinction, yes?"

Heads nodded. They'd heard this speech before—Kessler's philosophy, the ideology that justified all Directorate actions.

As they filed out, London paused beside Kessler. "The Cole situation. You're more concerned than you're letting on."

"Excellent observation my dear." Kessler's expression didn't change. "His father is James Cole—American Special Forces, worked joint operations in the Balkans. We served together. He is...principled. Dangerously so."

"And the son?"

"Unknown. But principle, when genetic, tends to be stubborn. Watch him carefully. If he becomes a problem, eliminate him before he understands what he's found."

London nodded and left.

Kessler sat alone in the empty conference room, staring at Ethan Cole's file. The young man smiled in the photograph—unaware that he had just been discussed by people who orchestrated the deaths of hundreds of thousands, who had toppled governments and crashed economies, who built an empire on the principle that human suffering served as a commodity to be traded.

"You don't know it yet," Kessler whispered to the photograph, "but you just became the most dangerous man in the world. Because you asked questions. And in our architecture, questions are the only true threat."

He closed the file and walked out, the conference room's lights dimming automatically behind him.

Elsewhere in his New York City apartment, Ethan Cole was still reviewing the Apex wire transaction, still believing the system worked, still thinking compliance mattered.

He didn't have long before he learned how terribly wrong he was.

And by then, it would be too late to do anything except run.

11

Face of Evil

[CLASSIFIED: EYES ONLY -- DIRECTORATE / NODE: OPERATIONS-ALPHA]
OPERATION SCARLET DAWN
Target: Kinshasa Banking District, Democratic Republic of Congo
Objective: Controlled destabilization of regional financial infrastructure to facilitate asset acquisition and political realignment
Method:

- Phase 1: Deploy cyber attack on central banking systems (attributed to regional insurgents)
- Phase 2: Coordinate street protests via social media manipulation (funded through shell accounts)
- Phase 3: Introduce armed response by government forces (weapons supplied through Helios Defense subsidiaries)
- Phase 4: Document "humanitarian crisis" through embedded media assets
- Phase 5: Facilitate regime change and secure mining concessions

Projected Casualties: 2,000-3,500 (acceptable parameters)
Projected ROI: 340% over 18 months
Media Narrative: "Grassroots uprising against corruption"
Kessler's Directive: *"Execute with precision. Let the world see revolution. We'll collect the receipts."*

Kinshasa, Democratic Republic of Congo — 8:50 a.m. local time- Day 3

Boulevard du 30 Juin loomed below the hotel room, close enough to the banking district to hear the afternoon traffic, far enough from the embassy quarter to avoid Western surveillance. Martin Okafor sat at the desk, his laptop open to three different windows—one monitoring encrypted communications, one tracking financial flows, one showing the social media accounts he'd spent six weeks cultivating.

At thirty-four years of age, he stood Harvard educated, fluent in five languages. His official title read "Regional Economic Development Consultant" for a UN-affiliated NGO that didn't scrutinize its contractors too carefully. His real employer paid substantially better and asked substantially worse questions.

The Directorate didn't recruit people like Martin with threats. They recruited with truth.

Three years ago, he'd been teaching at the University of Lagos, believing that education and reform could fix broken systems. Then his sister had been killed in a protest—government forces opening fire on university students demanding basic infrastructure. The official story called it an "unfortunate escalation." The real story showed that a foreign mining corporation had paid the government to clear the area for resource extraction.

Martin had tried the legal route. Filed complaints, contacted journalists, worked with human rights organizations. All doors closed. avenues blocked. The system was not broken—it worked exactly as designed, and his sister's death amounted to acceptable collateral damage.

Then a woman in a gray suit had found him in a Lagos bar, drowning his grief and disillusionment. She offered him something better than justice: leverage. The ability to pull strings instead of being pulled by them. The chance to rebuild systems from the inside while getting paid enough to never worry about money again.

He had declared yes. That occurred eighteen months ago.

Now he sat in Kinshasa, preparing to do to someone else's country what had been done to his.

His phone buzzed—encrypted message from his handler:

"Phase 1 initiates in 4 hours. Banking systems will experience cascading failure. Your social media assets should amplify message: government incompetence, foreign interference (imply Chinese manipulation), call for street action. Coordinate with local contacts for protest logistics. Keep messaging organic-appearing. No obvious coordination."

Martin opened his network of fake accounts—forty-seven different personas, each with months of established history, each with thousands of followers built through patient engagement and content farming. They looked like real people: students, teachers, small business owners, activists. Each one carefully constructed to seem authentic.

He began scheduling posts:

"Banks frozen AGAIN. How much longer do we accept this corruption? #KinshasaRising"

"My mother can't access her savings. Government promises 'technical issues' but we know the truth. They've sold us out. #DemandAccountability"

"Street gathering tomorrow, Place de la Poste, noon. Bring your voice. Bring your anger. Time to be heard. #KinshasaProtest"

Each post came exquisitely engineered—emotionally charged but not inflammatory enough to trigger automated moderation. Calls to action without explicit violence. Outrage without conspiracy theory that would discredit the movement.

This shaped the art: making manufactured grassroots look genuine. Making planned chaos appear spontaneous.

Martin's second phone rang—the one connected to his NGO cover. He answered in French: "Oui, allô?"

"Martin, it's Catherine." His supervisor, genuinely working for the NGO, genuinely ignorant of his secondary employment. "Have you seen the news? Banking system crashed. This could destabilize the whole country."

"I just heard. What's the official UN position?"

"Monitoring. We're coordinating with the World Bank on contingency plans if there's civil unrest. Can you do some ground-level assessment? Talk to locals, gauge the temperature?"

"Of course. I'll file a report tomorrow."

"Be careful. The government's jumpy. Last month's protests in Lubumbashi got violent fast."

"I remember." He didn't mention that those protests had also been Directorate-engineered, or that the violence had been strategically calibrated to justify increased security spending—contracts that went to Helios subsidiaries.

He hung up and returned to his real work.

By midnight, the banking crisis had escalated exactly as planned. ATMs frozen. Electronic transfers impossible. Payroll systems down. In a city where ninety percent of the economy ran on mobile money, this proved catastrophic.

Martin watched his social media feeds explode:

"Can't buy food or pay rent. Government says 'be patient' while they live in mansions."

"My friend works at Central Bank. He says this stemmed from a HACK. Foreign interests attacking us and government covering it up."

"Tomorrow. Place de la Poste. Noon. All residents be there."

The last message had not come from him—it had emerged organically from the anger his seeds had cultivated. That formed the beautiful part. You only had to push the first domino. Genuine grievance did the rest.

He filed his report to the Directorate:

"Phase 1 complete. Social response exceeding projections. Estimated protest attendance: 5,000-8,000. Local contacts confirmed. Proceed to Phase 2?"

The response came within minutes:

"Proceed. Assets are in position."

Martin noticed something twist in his stomach—not quite guilt, but its distant cousin. The taste in his mouth was bitter, he couldn't quite get it out. Tomorrow, people would take to the streets believing they were fighting for justice. What they wouldn't know was that the crisis they were protesting had been manufactured. That the solutions being offered were designed to benefit the same people who had created the problems in the first place. A vicious cycle, created by the powerful minority, designed to keep the powerless majority in check.

He thought of his sister. Of the protest where she had died, believing she was fighting for change and making a difference.

Had that been orchestrated too? Had someone in an air-conditioned hotel room pulled strings that led to her death?

He pushed the thought away. That road led to paralysis. Better to believe in building toward something tangible. That the Directorate's vision of managed stability was preferable to chaotic violence. That order—even imposed order—would prove worth the cost.

He had been trained to believe that. And most days, he did.

Place de la Poste — The Next Day

The protest started peacefully. Seven thousand people—Martin's estimate ran low—gathering in the central square. Students, workers, families. They carried signs in French and Lingala: *"Our Money, Our Rights," "End the Theft," "We Are Not Invisible."*

Martin moved through the crowd with a camera, his NGO credentials giving him access. He documented the protest meticulously, knowing his footage would be edited and distributed through Directorate media networks to shape the global narrative.

A young woman—maybe twenty—stood on a makeshift platform, speaking through a megaphone. "They think we are powerless! They think we will accept their lies! But we are here! We are loud! And we will not be silent!"

The crowd roared approval. Martin filmed her, noting her passion, her eloquence, her dangerous effectiveness. She'd be marked for later—either recruited or neutralized, depending on whether she proved malleable.

The government's response arrived at 1:47 p.m.—exactly on schedule, though the protesters didn't know it had been scheduled.

Police in riot gear, moving in formation. Water cannons. Tear gas. The crowd panicked, surged. The young woman kept speaking: "Do not run! Stand together! They want us afraid!"

Then the gunfire started.

Martin would never know for certain if the first shots came from police or from the Directorate assets embedded in the crowd. In the chaos, it didn't matter. The effect remained the same: seven people dead in the first ninety seconds. Thirty-four wounded. The protest transforming from peaceful demonstration to violent confrontation.

He kept filming. Professional. Detached. This shaped his job, who he was.

A boy—young teen, perhaps fourteen—fell ten feet from Martin, blood spreading from a chest wound. Someone screamed. People ran. The tear gas made the entire area a white hell of choking and blindness.

Martin retreated to a safe observation point, continuing to film. His footage would be invaluable—showing government brutality, documenting human rights violations, building the case for international intervention.

What the footage wouldn't show was the complex choreography that had manufactured this moment. The banking crisis triggered to create economic desperation. The social media manipulation to channel anger into street action. The armed assets inserted to ensure the government response proved violent enough to justify the next phase.

None of that would appear in his report to the NGO, or in the news coverage that would dominate international headlines tomorrow.

Just: "Government forces open fire on peaceful protesters. Dozens dead. International community must respond."

And they would respond. With sanctions, with condemnation, with calls for regime change. The current government—corrupt but not cooperative enough with Directorate interests—would fall within six months. The replacement would be more accommodating.

Mining concessions would be renegotiated. Helios Defense would secure contracts for "peacekeeping operations." International Mercantile Bank would facilitate reconstruction loans. The Directorate would take its cut at each stage.

And in eighteen months, the ROI would hit 340%, exactly as projected.

That night, Martin sat in his hotel room, watching international news coverage of the "spontaneous uprising" he helped orchestrate. His sister's photo was on his desk—he kept it there as reminder of why he did this work.

"For you," he told her frozen smile. *"So your death meant something. So the system that killed you gets burned down and rebuilt into something better."*

But a small voice whispered that he wasn't burning the system down. Just changing which hands controlled it.

He silenced the voice with scotch and work, filing his final report:

"Phase 2 complete. Media coverage optimal. Government response exceeded brutality projections. International condemnation building. Proceed to Phase 3?"

The response:

"Excellent work. Phase 3 authorized. Welcome to the architecture of necessary change."

Martin closed his laptop and walked to the window. Below, the city smoldered. Smoke from burning barricades rose into the night sky. Sirens wailed. Somewhere, families were learning their children wouldn't come home.

And in offices across the world—Zurich, London, New York, Dubai—men in expensive suits were adjusting portfolios, calculating profits, preparing the next phase of an operation that would save some lives, destroy others, and ultimately serve one purpose: consolidating power into fewer and fewer hands.

This revealed the Directorate's true face. Not cartoon villainy or obvious evil, but the cold mathematics of managed chaos. The understanding that suffering could be engineered, profit extracted, and order maintained—all while convincing the people involved that they were serving higher purposes.

Martin convinced himself he served a higher purpose. He had been told so, had been trained to believe it, had reconstructed his entire moral framework around it.

But sometimes, late at night, with scotch burning and his sister's photo judging him from the desk, he wondered if he'd just learned to call evil by more sophisticated names.

The thought never lasted long. Morning came. New orders arrived. And the work continued.

Because someone had to maintain order. Someone had to make the hard choices. Someone had to accept that peace required sacrifice, and sacrifice required people willing to choose who paid the price.

That's what the Directorate told him. And most days, he believed it.

12

Warning Shot

Kessler — Private Diary (Zurich-0 Archive: Unclassified)
"Victor... you mistake money for power. Real power is the kind that decides whether men like you wake up tomorrow."

Park Avenue, New York City— 3:14 a.m.- Day 2
Victor Krane slept like men who owned too much power — light, restless, never far from waking. The city outside his penthouse windows glowed in cold blue light, the skyline reflected in the glass like a barcode — all value, no soul.

Power had been Krane's only companion long before he reached the corner office at International Mercantile Bank. He had risen through its ranks with the slow, methodical brutality of an advancing glacier, crushing anyone standing in his way to the top. Early colleagues remembered him as brilliant but forgettable; by the time he reached senior management, he became unforgettable—and feared.

Whispers followed each promotion which came in rapid succession. A competitor whose audit abruptly revealed "irregularities." A mentor who died of a heart attack at forty-eight—just weeks after criticizing Krane in a board meeting. A whistleblower whose anonymous tip never reached regulators because the email "failed to send."

Krane learned early that ascent required sacrifice. He simply made sure someone else paid the price.

Tonight, he wasn't alone. A woman lay beside him, her perfume still lingering in the sheets—his mistress, young, reckless, and oblivious to the storm that circled the Bank. Her arm draped lazily over his chest. "Victor..." she whispered, half-asleep. "Come back to bed."

His phone rang at 3:14 a.m. No one called Victor Krane at 3:14 a.m.

He stiffened. The phone vibrating on the nightstand cut through the dark like a surgical instrument. He grabbed it before it completed a second ring.

"Quiet," he snapped over his shoulder. "Not a sound." But the call connected before he could move to another room.

He glanced at the number. No ID. Just a string of digits that looked wrong — almost deliberate in their randomness. He hesitated before answering.

"Krane. "

The voice that came through sounded low, composed, with the kind of calm that made men nervous—smooth, dispassionate, unmistakably Kessler. "

"You have problems inside your house, Victor. Multiple problems actually. "

Krane sat up, heart hammering as he looked over his shoulder at his mistress. Before he could say a word, Kessler continued.

"First, let's discuss Richard Latham."

Krane's blood went cold. Latham served as his star executive in charge of international corporate banking—had been for over eleven years now. The man handled all of the largest, most complex international accounts for the bank.

"What about Latham?"

"Our Mr. Latham met with...an unfortunate accident." Kessler's tone was pleasant, carrying no more weight than if he were discussing the weather. "The poor fellow had a fall in his bathroom after drinking too much. The medical examiner will find a blood alcohol level three times the legal limit."

Krane's grip tightened on the phone. "Richard didn't drink. Not like that."

"Richard drank quite a lot these past few weeks, actually. Clearly more than you know. Very unwise on his part." A pause, precise and surgical. "He was getting cold feet, Victor. Loose lips at White's Club. Questions to his attorney about whistleblower protections. A letter in his desk at his flat. He even drafted an email to the SEC—though of course it was never sent. All loose ends that required my personal involvement to clear up. "

Before Krane could respond, Kessler continued. "Of course Victor, I am sharing this unfortunate news simply as a courtesy to prepare you for your day tomorrow."

Krane saw the room tilt, ever so slightly, the first sign of trouble in his experience. Latham. Solid, dependable Richard Latham—the man who'd signed off on the Apex transactions, who knew the architecture of each shell company, who could connect International Mercantile to the Directorate with a single deposition.

"You killed him."- Krane responded harshly...too harshly.

"I solved a problem. Your problem." Kessler's voice hardened almost imperceptibly. "Latham forgot that silence is a condition of breathing. He needed to be reminded. Unfortunately, the reminder proved... permanent."

Krane's mouth went dry. He had known Latham for fifteen years. Their wives had been friends. Their children had previously spent summers together at the Hamptons house.

"Now," Kessler continued, "let's discuss your second problem. One of your people—Ethan Cole. He's digging around on Apex. Wrong digging."

Krane rubbed his temples, still reeling. "He's just compliance. We will handle this internally."

"No Victor. You will handle this quietly. Before it escalates. Latham was drinking himself toward confession. Cole is actively investigating. One liability has been resolved. The other remains your responsibility."

A pause stretched, the faint sound of another man's breathing through the line.

"You have built a fine institution. It would be... tragic if it were dismantled over one employee's curiosity—or if you were to develop the same... cold feet... that afflicted our late Mr. Latham."

Krane's throat constricted. He had negotiated with oligarchs, crushed rivals, survived markets that devoured lesser men. But the voice on the line—steady, unhurried—radiated a different kind of power.

Not money. Not politics. Something older, more sinister.

He forced his voice steady. "You don't understand. There are protocols. Auditors. The Fed monitors—"

"We monitor the Fed," Kessler's voice cut in. "And we have already seen the wire. You will fix this Cole situation—before he becomes the next Latham. Because we would not want to have Mr. Cole talk."

Krane tried to swallow but couldn't. "Fix what, exactly?"

A long pause. Then, in that same quiet tone:

"A man in your position cannot afford... distractions. Disorder in your private life becomes disorder in the Directorate's operations. And disorder, my dear Victor, is something we do not tolerate." The words came slower now, each one a blade. "Richard Latham learned that tonight. Victor, I need you to fix the Cole situation. We would not want to see you have an unfortunate accident like our dear Mr. Latham, now would we?"

The line went dead.

Krane stared at the phone, the reflection of his own face warped across the glass table—a man who thought he ran the world realizing, for the first time, that he was merely one of its employees. Richard Latham—steady, cautious Richard—was already cooling on a medical examiner's table somewhere, his family about to receive a call that would shatter their lives.

And all because he'd asked the wrong questions. Talked to the wrong people. Developed a conscience at the worst possible moment.

He stood, poured two fingers of scotch, and downed it without breathing. The ice clinked once against the glass, sharp and final.

By the time he set it down, he already knew what he had to do. Latham was a warning shot. Ethan Cole would not become another.

13

Morning After

[CLASSIFIED: EYES ONLY – DIRECTORATE/NODE: NEW YORK-FIN 7]

"Compliance exists to simulate integrity. The appearance of oversight is the surest guarantee of freedom from it."

—Internal Control Advisory, International Mercantile Bank (Intercepted)

Manhattan, New York City— 7:52 a.m.- Day 2

Ethan arrived at the bank a little before eight. The sky was the color of steel, rain threatening over lower Manhattan. His reflection in the marble lobby floor looked tired, but steady — coffee in hand, badge clipped to his belt. Another day, another storm of transactions waiting upstairs.

The elevator's ascent seemed slower than usual, each floor a measured beat toward something inevitable. Ethan watched the numbers climb—thirty-eight, thirty-nine, forty—and found himself counting heartbeats instead. The traders beside him scrolled through phones, oblivious. He envied their ignorance.

But when the doors opened on the 42nd floor — the executive suite — the noise was different. Muffled voices. Movement. A few of the junior assistants were standing together by reception, eyes red.

Ethan frowned. "What's going on?"

No one answered right away. Then a young assistant — Marcy, who supported Richard Latham's team — stepped forward, eyes glassy and stunned.

"It's Mr. Latham," she whispered. "He's dead."

For a moment, Ethan just stood there. Not shocked — not exactly — but processing. Ethan's mind flashed to another death—Lukas, vanishing into Cho Oyu's white void. Another rope that failed at the exact wrong moment. Another convenient accident that smelled rotten. Too deliberate.

"What happened?" he asked.

"They implied he... fell," Marcy indicated. "In his bathroom at home last night. The police were here earlier."

Ethan's mind clicked through the timeline. *Last night. After the call.*

"Was anyone with him?"

"No. They think it was an accident. Maybe he slipped." She started crying again, her voice cracking. "He was supposed to be in New York tomorrow."

Ethan thanked her quietly and walked past, ignoring the whispers that followed. The corridor toward his office was strangely empty. The framed photos of company awards and charity galas looked sterile, staged.

He sat down at his desk, took a long sip of his coffee, and logged in.

The system loaded slower than usual. He checked the wire queue — the Apex transfer was still on hold. Good.

Then he opened his secure compliance notes from the night before. But when he tried to access the subfolder containing the Apex audit data, the system flashed **Access Denied**.

He tried again. Same result.

Then his phone buzzed. Internal call — Compliance Director.

"Ethan," the voice announced, curt and official, "I need you to come down to conference room 7A. Now."

"About Latham?"

A pause. "Just come down."

Ethan hung up, stood, and glanced once more at his screen. The Apex wire was gone from his active queue. Cleared.

He stared at the empty line. Someone had overridden his hold.

As he walked toward the elevators, he caught his reflection in the glass partition — the steady, composed man he'd always been. But somewhere deep inside, something shifted.

Someone cleared the wire. And now Latham's dead.

14

Contagion

Kessler — Private Diary (Zurich-0 Archive: Unclassified)
"Krane called you? How adorable. If he cannot manage his own institution, we will—quietly, efficiently—manage it for him."

Manhattan, New York City— 9:02 a.m.- Day 2
Victor Krane moved through the marble corridors of International Mercantile Bank with the brittle precision of a man who could feel the walls tightening around him. The morning sun had barely crested the skyline, yet the building hummed with quiet dread. The wire had been cleared—scrubbed from the system, overwritten by a dozen layers of misdirection—but residue always remained.

And residue drew predators.

Krane locked himself in his office, lowered the blinds, and began making calls.

The first went to the bank's internal ops director.
"All matters related to Ethan Cole are to be sealed," Krane ordered. "No audit trail, no redundant logs, no chatter. Anyone asks—this was a routine reconciliation error. Understood?" The man on the line swallowed hard. "Yes... sir."

Krane ended the call without responding.

The second call was harder.

He stared at the number on his private phone—*the real number*, not the one listed in any directory.

The Federal Reserve Bank of New York.

The President himself.

He exhaled once, smoothed his tie, and dialed.

The line clicked.

"Victor," the Fed President announced, voice clipped, impatient. "Your message indicated this was urgent."

"It is," Krane replied. "We had what appears to be... an internal breach. A wire was initiated without authorization."

"By whom?"

Krane hesitated. There were rules to these conversations—unwritten but lethal.

"An employee. Ethan Cole."

A pause. Paper rustled—calm, deliberate.

"And you want what, exactly?"

"Assistance." Krane gripped the phone tighter. "Discretion. Support should regulators probe the matter. This could raise questions well outside the normal channels."

Silence stretched like wire drawn thin.

The Fed President finally spoke, voice colder than the marble beneath Krane's feet.

"Victor, let me be clear. The Federal Reserve does not involve itself in your operational failures. If one of your employees has gone rogue, that is *your* problem. Fix it."

"Sir—"

"No."

The word cracked like a gavel.

"You clean your house. And quickly. Before others notice the smell."

The line went dead.

Krane's hand trembled as he lowered the phone. It wasn't fear of regulators, or public scandal. It was the last sentence—the tone.

A warning.

He sat down, collected himself for a few minutes, and dialed one final number.

One he had hoped never to use again.

It connected after a single ring.

A voice emerged—smooth, patient, predatory.

"Kessler."

Krane swallowed.

"We have a problem. A bank employee, Ethan Cole, accessed restricted wire protocols. I've contained the issue, but the Fed President—he refused to intervene."

A low hum—almost amusement—slid across the line.

"He called me," Kessler stated calmly. "Five minutes ago."

Krane froze. He didn't realize he took that long between calls.

"And what did he say?" —Krane asked.

"That International Mercantile Bank," Kessler replied, "is bleeding. And that you are too weak to cauterize the wound."

Krane pressed a hand against his forehead. "I—I can handle Cole. I just need—"

"Assurance? Protection?"

A soft, dangerous chuckle.

"Victor, you've already demonstrated you can't even control your personal life. Imagine if your wife found out, if the board found out. Imagine if regulators found out about both her AND the accounts you've been hiding? Why would the Directorate trust you with something more... consequential?"

Krane's throat tightened.

"Please," he muttered. "Tell me what to do."

Kessler's answer arrived like a blade sliding between ribs.

"Invite Ethan Cole back to the Bank. Interrogate him. Evaluate his loyalty."

"And if he isn't loyal?"

"Oh, Victor..."

Kessler's voice darkened to something intimate and lethal.

"You will ensure he never becomes a liability. One way or another."

The line clicked off.

Krane stared out over the city—his empire—feeling, for the first time, its scale shifting under his feet.

The morning sun cast long shadows across the skyline. Shadows shaped like snares, ready to trap Victor Krane.

He reached for his phone again. "Get me Ethan Cole." His hand trembled on the receiver..."Now."

Victor Krane didn't return to his office. He walked—fast, silent—to the sub-level conference suites known inside the Bank as **the Quiet Rooms**. They had been built for regulatory audits, but senior most executives of the bank knew their true purpose: controlled conversations, plausible deniability, no windows, no recordings.

Krane entered Quiet Room 7A. Cold, stainless-steel walls. A single table. Two chairs. A thin folder resting in the center like a surgical instrument.

He closed the door and allowed himself one trembling exhale.

Control the narrative. Contain the risk. Neutralize the variable.

He opened the folder. Inside were: – Ethan Cole's employee profile– Access logs (real and falsified) – A printed page showing the cleared wire pathway– A handwritten note he did **not** write:

"Press him until he breaks. —K"

Krane's jaw clenched. Kessler never wasted ink.

He dialed the head of Corporate Security.

"Have Cole brought to Quiet Room 7A the moment he arrives," Krane pronounced. "No calls. No messages. No warnings. And disable the cameras as soon as he enters."

"Yes, Mr. Krane."

Krane stood alone, and he knew the punishment for failure would not fall on Ethan Cole alone.

That night, Victor Krane would write the following private journal memo entry, of which he never knew it would be his last:

PRIVATE JOURNAL — VICTOR KRANE
RE: Cole Situation

One employee should not command this much attention, yet here we are—pressure from my partners who do not tolerate loose ends. I have built the Bank on decisive action, on removing obstacles, and now I am the one being scrutinized. Observed. Judged.

Partners have made their position clear: *resolve it.* They speak in the polite tone of men who hold the power to erase reputations, balance sheets, entire lives. I know the cost of hesitation. I have seen what happens to those who fail to meet their expectations.

Cole is not malicious—just too curious.

He stumbled into something far larger than he understands, and now I must determine whether the boy represents a risk to the institution... or to me personally. At this altitude, perception is fatal. If the Directorate senses even a whisper of weakness, they will carve me out like diseased tissue.

They have given me options. None of them civilized. I will give Cole one final chance to prove he is manageable.

If he isn't...Closure must be achieved.

And I will trust that those above me consider this enough to keep them at bay.

For now.

—*V.K.*

15

Interrogation

"You have a good heart, Ethan. Be careful who you trust it with."
—Margaret Heller

Manhattan, New York City— 9:52 a.m. – Day 2
Conference room 7A stood out as a cage disguised as corporate space.

No windows. No skyline. No natural light to soften the angles or warm the sterile white walls. Just glass panels on three sides that turned the room into an aquarium, exposing whoever sat inside to the judgmental gaze of anyone passing through the hallway. The recessed lighting hummed with a frequency just high enough to set Ethan's teeth on edge, casting the conference room in a bluish pallor that made skin look sickly, guilty.

The air conditioning cycled with mechanical precision, pumping arctic air that smelled faintly of recycled breath and industrial carpet. The temperature sat at too low a setting—deliberately, Ethan suspected. Ice cold rooms made people uncomfortable, made them want to hurry through conversations, made them more likely to say things they shouldn't.

The conference table stretched out in front of Ethan as a slab of dark laminate, its surface so polished it reflected the overhead lights like standing water. Four chairs on one side, one on the other. The geometry of interrogation. Ethan recognized it immediately—he'd read about it in some management book years ago, back when he still believed corporate politics ranked as the worst thing he would face in his career.

When Ethan walked in, three people already waited.

Margaret Heller, the bank's Deputy Chief Risk Officer, sat at the far end of the table, her posture rigid, her expression unreadable. Sharp-featured and composed, early fifties, she wore a charcoal suit that probably cost more than Ethan's monthly rent. She stood out as the kind of woman who could smell weakness before it spoke, who could dismantle a career with three sentences and a well-timed email. Her hands lay folded on the table in front of her, manicured nails perfectly still. She didn't fidget. She didn't need to.

Next to her sat William "Bill" Donovan, Director of Internal Security. Former FBI, still carried himself like he worked organized crime in Newark. Buzz cut going gray at the temples. Square jaw. No wedding ring. No patience for nuance or excuses. His suit appeared significantly less costly than Heller's, but fit him better, like armor. He observed Ethan the way a hunter watches prey—calculating distance, trajectory, weak points.

And across from them, in the two chairs that should have been empty, sat two men Ethan didn't know.

Both wore dark suits—not expensive, but well-maintained. Government issue. The kind of suits that came with badges and guns and the authority to ruin lives. Their faces were frozen and remained still, professionally blank, the expressions of men who sat through thousands of interviews and learned not to react to anything. One of them had a leather notepad in front of him, unopened. The other didn't need one. His eyes did all the recording necessary.

Ethan realized his pulse had kicked up a notch, the flutter of adrenaline that started in his chest and spread to his fingertips. This wasn't a meeting. This formed an interrogation. And he stood as the subject.

"Ethan," Heller noted, her voice cutting through the silence like a scalpel. She gestured to the empty chair—the lone chair, positioned so that Ethan would have to face all four of them, his back to the glass wall, exposed. "Sit down."

He did. The chair felt ice cold, the coldness seeping through his suit jacket into his spine. The seat cushion was thin, unforgiving, designed to keep you from getting comfortable. He placed his hands flat on the table, willing them to stay steady. Though the room had no windows, he thought he heard movement in the hallway—colleagues hurrying past. Word must already spreading. Ethan Cole, the compliance officer who'd blocked the wrong wire, now sitting in the hot seat.

His career was crumbling in real time, and each person in the room could see it happening.

"What's this about?" Ethan asked, keeping his voice level. Professional. As if this were just another routine review.

Heller folded her hands, the gesture precise, controlled. "You spoke with Richard Latham last night?"

"Yes. Around ten."

"About the Apex International wire."

"That's right."

Her gaze didn't waver. To Ethan, it felt like being examined under a microscope—each word weighed, micro-expressions catalogued. "And you placed a hold on the transaction."

"I did," Ethan announced evenly, fighting to keep his breathing steady. The room was getting smaller now, the walls pressing in. "The documentation was incomplete, and the routing raised compliance flags. I was planning to review it with Latham this morning."

The man with the notepad finally spoke. His voice sounded quiet, precise—a government voice. Flat affect, no inflection, the tone of someone who'd delivered unwelcome news a thousand times and stopped feeling anything about it. "But you didn't get that chance."

Ethan turned to him, his neck stiff. "No."

"Who are you?" Ethan asked. His voice came out harder than he intended, edged with frustration. He was tired of being on the defensive, tired of not knowing who he was up against.

The man reached into his jacket with deliberate slowness and produced a black leather credential case. He flipped it open, held it up for exactly two seconds—too quick for Ethan to read the fine print, just long enough to register the gold badge and the letters FBI. "My name is Agent Richard Harris, with the local FBI field office."

The credentials disappeared back into his jacket before Ethan could process what he'd seen. Harris's expression never changed—professionally neutral, almost bored. The other man didn't move, didn't speak, didn't even blink. His eyes were completely cold, glacial blue, the kind of eyes that had seen things and stopped caring. If Harris was FBI, this other man was something else. Something worse.

Harris continued, his voice never rising, never falling. "Because Richard Latham died sometime between midnight and 5 a.m. this morning at his London residence."

The words hung in the air like smoke. Everyone in the room knew them already—Ethan could see it in their faces, the way they didn't react, the way this served as another data point in whatever case they were building. But hearing them stated flatly, clinically, gave them weight and made them real. Latham was dead. The man Ethan had argued with less than twelve hours ago was dead.

Ethan's stomach dropped. A cold sweat prickled at the base of his spine. He forced himself to breathe, to maintain eye contact, to not look guilty. Because he wasn't guilty. He was only doing his job. He had followed protocol. But sitting here, in this airless room, surrounded by people who had already decided he was a problem, guilt and innocence were merely abstract concepts.

Harris leaned forward slightly, his hands clasped on the table. "You were the last known person to speak with him."

The implication hung there, unspoken but obvious. Last person to speak with him. As if Ethan had driven to Latham's apartment, pushed him in the bathroom, and walked away. As if blocking a wire somehow led to murder.

Ethan's expression didn't change. He'd learned that much from years of navigating corporate politics—never let them see you sweat. "Then you already know what we discussed."

Heller's tone sharpened, cutting through the tension like a blade. "Ethan, this isn't the time for attitude. A senior executive is dead. His client accounts are under investigation, and your name is on all internal reports connected to it."

All internal reports. Ethan tasted the words like physical blows. They'd been building a file on him. Documenting his questions, his holds, his investigations. Turning his diligence into evidence of something darker. He had thought he was protecting the bank. Instead, he had painted a target on his own back.

"I did my job," Ethan uttered quietly, the words barely audible over the hum of the air conditioning. It sounded weak even to his own ears. Defensive. The kind of thing guilty people revealed.

The second government man—the one without the notepad, the one with the dead eyes—looked up. When he spoke, his voice was ice cold, too sinister for a government man. It was the voice of someone who operated outside normal chains of command, someone who answered to people whose names never appeared on organizational charts. "What exactly is your job, Mr. Cole?"

Ethan met his eyes, refusing to look away even though his instincts screamed at him to drop his gaze, to submit, to make himself small. "To protect this institution from exposure. To make sure we aren't moving money for criminals or governments we're not supposed to."

The man's lips curved into something that wasn't quite a smile. "And yet," he replied, each word dropping like a stone into still water, "you blocked a transfer that powerful people in the upper echelon of the bank wanted to see go through."

Ethan didn't answer. He knew that nothing he could say would improve his situation. The room was most definitely shrinking, the walls closing in, the air growing thinner, he sensed the conference table was actually moving. He sensed his career disintegrating before his eyes, he could see the future collapsing—terminated for cause, reputation destroyed, unemployable in finance. The career he had built for the past decade erased in a single morning.

Harris leaned forward slightly, his voice dropping to something almost conversational. "Do you have any idea how large that network of transactions is? How many jurisdictions it touches?"

Ethan hesitated. This was a trap. Everything in this room was a trap. But lying would be worse. "I reviewed a few related wires last night. There were... patterns."

"What kind of patterns?"

He paused, calculating. How much to say? How much did they already know? "Repeated routing through offshore correspondent banks. Layered entities designed to obscure ultimate beneficial owners. It's sophisticated—algorithmic."

Harris nodded slowly, as if confirming something he already knew. As if Ethan had just walked into whatever trap they'd set. "And you did this research from home?"

"Yes."

"On a personal device?"

"Yes."

Heller's voice sliced in, sharp and final. "You violated security protocol, Ethan."

There it was. The official charge. Not that he'd uncovered something corrupt. Not that he had tried to stop illegal activity. But that he had broken protocol in the process. That was how they would do it—bury him under technicalities, make him the problem, protect whoever was really behind the Apex wires.

Ethan turned to her, and for the first time since entering the room, he let his anger show. "You locked my access this morning. Someone cleared the wire."

That landed. He saw it in Donovan's face—the way his jaw tightened, the muscle jumping beneath the skin. In Heller's eyes, a flicker of something that might have been guilt or might have been calculation. Even Harris shifted slightly in his chair.

The room fell silent. The air conditioning hummed. Someone's phone buzzed in the hallway outside, muffled by wall and distance. Ethan could hear his own heartbeat, rapid and uneven, the sound of a man standing at the edge of a cliff.

Harris closed his notepad with a soft snap. "Mr. Cole, we will need you to remain available. Don't travel, don't access restricted systems, and don't discuss this matter with anyone outside authorized personnel."

Ethan heard it for what it truly meant: part warning, part threat. Stay quiet. Stay still. Wait while we decide what to do with you. His hands sat clenched on the table now, knuckles white. He forced himself to relax them, to breathe, to not show how terrified he actually was.

He gave a short nod. "Authorized by whom?"

Neither man answered. The silence was answer enough.

Heller stood, the movement sharp and final, signaling the meeting had concluded. "Ethan, take the day. We'll be in touch."

Take the day. As if this were a minor inconvenience, a scheduling conflict, not the systematic destruction of each and everything he had worked for. As if his career weren't bleeding out in real time on the conference room table.

Ethan rose slowly, his legs unsteady beneath him. He could feel the eyes of all four people following him to the door—measuring him, judging him, already drafting the reports that would define his guilt or innocence. Through the glass walls, he saw colleagues in the hallway quickly look away, pretending they hadn't been watching, pretending they didn't know.

But they knew. Of course they knew. In corporate America, proximity to scandal was guilt by association. It didn't matter if Ethan was innocent. It didn't matter if he'd been trying to do the right thing. He'd become radioactive, and by tomorrow morning, no one would return his calls.

When he stepped into the corridor, the world was off—colors a shade too pale, sounds too distant. The fluorescent lights overhead were too bright, washing the hallway in a harsh glare that made his eyes ache. The carpet muffled his footsteps as he walked back toward his office, each step was painfully slow, like he was moving through molasses.

Faces turned away as he passed. Conversations stopped mid-sentence. Keyboards clicked with renewed vigor as people pretended to be absorbed in their work. The office had become a minefield, and Ethan served as the live grenade his coworkers wanted to avoid.

Before he reached his desk, Donovan caught up with him, his footsteps heavy and purposeful.

"Cole," Donovan whispered quietly, his voice low enough that no one else could hear. "Word of advice—stop digging. Whatever this is, it's way above your pay grade."

Ethan met his stare. Something flickered in Donovan's eyes—not hostility, but something closer to pity. Or maybe fear. "That's the thing, Bill. I don't think it's about pay grades."

Donovan didn't answer. He just turned and walked away, his broad shoulders disappearing around the corner, leaving Ethan standing alone in the middle of the hallway.

Ethan stood there for a long moment, the murmur of distant phones and keyboards barely reaching him. The office hummed with ordinary life—people making deals, sending emails, drinking coffee, planning lunches. The machinery of finance grinding on, indifferent to the fact that one of its parts had just been marked for removal.

He looked through the glass toward his desk—the empty screen, the missing file, the space where the truth had been erased overnight. His workspace looked exactly as he'd left it yesterday, but his life had inexplicably changed. The nameplate with his title seemed like a joke now. The framed diploma on the wall, the industry awards, the photographs of him shaking hands with executives at bank functions—all of it straight up hollow and meaningless.

He'd built his career on integrity, on asking the tough questions, on protecting the institution from the shadows that lurked in international finance. And now those same shadows had turned their attention to him.

Latham was dead. The Apex wire was long gone. The government was inside the building, and he served as their scapegoat.

Ethan walked to his desk, sat down in his chair, and stared at the blank monitor. His reflection stared back at him from the black screen—pale, exhausted, trapped. He looked like a man who had just realized he was playing a game whose rules he didn't understand, against opponents he couldn't see.

And he was losing.

16

Break In

"I downloaded it because the numbers were lying...and the people behind them weren't supposed to be seen."
—Ethan Cole

Manhattan, New York City— 12:17 p.m.- Day 2

By the time Ethan left the Bank, the sky had turned the color of steel, heavy and oppressive, pressing down on the city like a lid. Manhattan traffic crawled along sluggishly, horns blaring like distant alarms—urgent, meaningless, part of the white noise that normally faded into background. But today sounds were amplified...threatening. A car backfiring three blocks away made him flinch. A police siren in the distance sent ice through his veins.

He didn't remember descending the elevator or crossing the marble lobby—just the blur of faces avoiding his eyes, the freezing air hitting him as the revolving door spat him out onto the street, the sick weight in his stomach like swallowed stones.

Ethan took the long way home, circling blocks without reason, checking reflections in store windows, pausing at intersections to see if anyone stopped when he stopped. He endured car mirrors like reflections that lingered too long. Pedestrians who glanced his way seemed to be memorizing his face. He could still hear Heller's voice, flat and final: don't discuss this matter with anyone. And beneath it, Harris's quiet threat: remain available.

Available for what? Arrest? More interrogation? A convenient accident in a bathroom, like Latham?

When he finally reached his apartment building, he realized his hands trembled. The door attendant—Rafael, who worked at the front desk for six years and knew Ethan by name—gave him a tight nod but didn't smile. Didn't ask how his day was. Only looked at him with something that might have been sympathy or might have been the careful neutrality of someone who had been told to notice things.

The elevator ride seemed endless, like he would never arrive at his floor. The numbers climbing too slowly. His reflection in the polished brass doors appeared haggard—dark circles under his eyes, jaw tight, skin pale. A man who had aged five years in five hours.

When he reached his floor, the hallway was empty. Quiet. The kind of quiet that made his ears ring. He could hear the hum of the building's ventilation system, the distant murmur of a television through someone's door, the click of his own shoes on the tile.

His apartment door was locked. The lights were off. His place looked normal.

But the moment he stepped inside, he knew.

The air was wrong. Too still. Too neat. Like a movie set dressed to look lived-in but missing the chaos of actual life. The smell was wrong too—not his usual scent of coffee and old books, but something sterile, chemical. The faint trace of latex gloves and methodical intrusion.

Someone had been here. Someone might still be here.

Ethan stood frozen in the doorway, his muscles tensed, ears listening. Nothing but silence. Except for the slightest of ticks of the wall clock in the kitchen, the soft humming from the refrigerator, the creak of the building settling. But beneath it all, he could feel the violation—invisible, pervasive, like fingerprints on glass.

He forced himself to move, to breathe, to check the apartment room by room even though some primal part of his brain screamed at him to run. The living room looked untouched—couch, coffee table, bookshelf. But the throw pillow was positioned differently, its corner pointing toward the window instead of the wall. The TV remote was on the left side of the table when he always left it on the right.

Insignificant things. Tiny displacements. The kind of details most people would never notice.

But his father had taught him to notice.

He noticed it first in the kitchen: the coffee pot on the counter had been set back exactly on its ring, but the little dent in its rim was aligned with the stove knob instead of angled away. Someone had moved it, examined it, replaced it. Someone had moved through the place with care, with precision, trying to leave no trace. But precision was its own tell. Life wasn't that neat.

His bedroom was worse. The closet door was slightly ajar—he always closed it completely. The dresser drawers weren't quite flush. His bed was made perfectly, hospital corners tight, the kind of precision he never bothered with. They'd searched his place thoroughly. Touched everything. Invaded the private spaces in his life.

His sanctuary had been violated, catalogued, dissected. The strong walls that protected him had evaporated. He longed for that protection once again.

In his home office, a framed photo on the desk had been moved—just slightly, but enough. It showed him and Lukas at Princeton graduation, both grinning, arms slung over shoulders. Brothers in all things except blood. The frame had been lifted, the desk beneath it checked, then replaced two inches to the left. Ethan stared at Lukas's face in the photo, those pale eyes that never quite smiled even when his mouth did, and a chill went down his spine he couldn't quite place.

They were looking for something. They thought he had something.

Then he saw the desk drawer—the one he never closed all the way, always left a quarter-inch open because the track was warped. It was shut flush. Someone had opened it, searched it, closed it properly.

His laptop sat on the desk, exactly where he'd left it, but when he touched the trackpad, the screen lit up with a login prompt. He entered his credentials. Access denied. He tried again, more carefully this time, making sure each character was correct. Access denied. A third time.

The screen flashed red:

ACCESS REVOKED - CONTACT SYSTEM ADMINISTRATOR.

His stomach tightened, a knot of fear and rage twisting in his gut. They'd locked him out of his own computer. They'd been inside his home, touched his things, searched his life, and now they were cutting off his access to the bank. His career, his data, his ability to prove what he'd found.

He was being erased.

His father's voice echoed in his memory—one of those camping trips in North Carolina when he was twelve, James teaching him and Daniel to read a campsite for signs of intrusion. "Always know your baseline, boys. How you left things. If something's moved even an inch, someone's been there. Most people don't notice. You need to notice."

James had made them practice, moving objects in each other's tents, seeing who could spot the changes fastest. Daniel had been good at it—the soldier's instinct. But Ethan had been better, more methodical, documenting each detail before they went to sleep so he could spot even the smallest displacement. His father had called it paranoia. Daniel had called it overthinking.

Now Ethan understood it was preparation. His father had known something they didn't. He had understood that the world was full of people who came in the night and moved your things and left traces that only the paranoid would see.

He opened the pantry, scanning the shelves with new eyes. Cereal boxes lined up too perfectly. Canned goods rotated so labels faced forward—something he never did. Tins stacked by size. Papers on the counter in neat stacks when he always left them scattered. Photo frames on the shelf straightened, aligned. They'd been methodical. Professional. Searching for something specific.

His hand moved almost automatically to the bag of coffee beans on the top shelf, an absurd impulse, checking the one place he'd hidden something precisely because it was mundane, overlooked, unremarkable. He pulled the bag down, raised it up and down, feeling its weight—too heavy. His fingers found the zipper, opened it, reached inside past the beans.

The hard edge of plastic pressed against his fingertips.

He closed his hand around the flash drive and pulled it free, staring at it in the dim kitchen light. Small. Black. Innocuous. The kind of thing you'd use to transfer vacation photos or backup documents. But this drive contained evidence of financial networks spanning continents, shell companies, offshore accounts, the digital trail of something vast and criminal.

The files he'd downloaded two nights earlier when instinct had overtaken protocol—when some part of him had known that official channels were compromised, that he needed insurance, that the truth would be buried if he didn't preserve it.

He'd hidden it in plain sight. And somehow, impossibly, they'd missed it.

Or had they? Had they found it, copied it, left it behind as bait? Was this drive now a tracker, a way to follow him wherever he ran?

Ethan stared at it, pulse steadying to that familiar, controlled rhythm his father had taught him. Breathe. Assess. Act. Don't panic. Panic gets you killed.

He didn't plug it in. Didn't verify the files. That would mean turning on a device, leaving a digital trail. Instead, he slipped the drive into the inner pocket of his jacket—the same pocket he'd used when he first downloaded the files—and stood absolutely still in his ransacked kitchen, feeling the weight of it against his chest like a second heartbeat.

The evidence. The network. The two things they would kill for to bury.

Then the phone rang.

The sound was shockingly loud in the silence, making him jump. He stared at his phone on the counter, watching it vibrate and flash. The caller ID read: Dad.

He hesitated, paranoia flooding through him. Were they listening? Had they tapped his phone? Was this call itself a trap?

But it was his father. And if anyone knew what to do, it was James Cole.

He answered. "Dad."

"Ethan," his father's voice came through—calm, gravelly, the voice of someone who had lived through things that were supposed to be forgotten. The voice of a man who'd worked in dark places for dark reasons and learned to survive them. "You all right?"

"Why?" Ethan put forward carefully, his throat tight.

"I got a call from an old friend," his father commented. "Told me your name came up on a Treasury task list. That's not where you want to be, son."

A Treasury task list. Official government attention. The kind of attention that came with surveillance, asset freezes, travel restrictions. The kind of attention that ended careers and lives. Ethan noticed his knees weaken and he sank onto the couch, the springs creaking beneath his weight.

"It's not what it looks like," Ethan added, hearing how defensive he sounded, how weak. "I did what I was supposed to—I stopped a transfer. Now they're acting like I killed someone."

There was a pause on the other end, long enough for the city noise to fill the silence. Sirens in the distance. The rumble of traffic. A helicopter passing overhead, its rotors beating the air like a mechanical heart.

His father finally voiced, "When the system turns on you, it's already too late to fix it from inside. You listening?"

Ethan nodded, though his throat had gone dry, though he couldn't speak. The walls of the apartment seemed closer now, pressing in from all sides. The ceiling lower. The air thinner.

"You've got something they want, don't you?"

Ethan looked down at the faint outline of the drive in his jacket, barely visible through the fabric. "Maybe."

"Then listen to me," his father voiced quietly, his voice dropping to something urgent, paternal, afraid. "Don't go back to the office. Don't talk to anyone. Get out of that apartment and disappear for a while. Whatever you do—run first, explain later."

Run. The word hung in the air like smoke. Ethan closed his eyes, seeing his life collapsing around him—his career, his reputation, his apartment, his identity. All the things he had built for the past decade dissolving like sugar in water. "Dad, I didn't do anything wrong."

"I know," the old man asserted, and there was something in his voice—a weight, a knowledge, a history of having made similar choices in similar moments. "But right now that doesn't matter. You just became a liability in somebody else's equation. You need to stay alive long enough to understand why."

The call ended with no goodbye. Just a click and dead air.

Ethan stood in the dark apartment, phone still pressed to his ear, listening to nothing. The silence was absolute. The weight of the flash drive pressed against his chest through his jacket, heavy as a stone, heavy as guilt, heavy as the evidence that would either save him or destroy him.

He looked around the apartment—slow, methodical, cataloguing. The photos on the wall. His diploma from Princeton. The bookshelf filled with financial texts and thrillers he'd never gotten around to reading. The coffee maker they'd examined. The couch they'd searched. The bedroom they'd invaded. All of the surfaces touched by strangers' hands, drawers rifled through, private moments exposed and examined.

And he realized it wasn't his anymore. This place that had been his sanctuary, his refuge from the pressures of work and the city—it was compromised now. Contaminated. A crime scene. They knew where he lived. They'd been inside. They could come back anytime.

The walls were completely closing in. The ceiling pressing down. There was no safe space anymore. No corner of his life they hadn't touched.

He grabbed a backpack from the closet—black nylon, anonymous—and moved through the apartment with purpose now, no longer caring about being quiet or careful. He tossed in essentials: clothes, toiletries, his passport, cash from the emergency fund he kept in a shoebox. Chargers. A burner phone still in its package, bought months ago on a whim and never used. The flash drive he slipped into a zippered inner pocket of the backpack, wrapping it in a t-shirt for padding.

Then he paused, staring at the bag. If they'd searched once, they could search again. If they were watching, they'd see him leave with luggage. The flash drive was too important, too dangerous. He needed a better hiding place, at least temporarily.

He went back to the kitchen, pulled down the coffee beans, and slid the drive back inside for a heartbeat, feeling the absurdity of hiding it in the same place twice. Then he removed it again and tucked it into the lining of the backpack, finding a small tear in the fabric and working the drive through until it was invisible, nestled between the outer shell and inner padding.

Good enough. It would have to be.

He took one last look around the apartment. At the life he was leaving behind. At the man he'd been this morning—confident, principled, naive enough to think that doing the right thing would protect him.

Then he left without turning on the lights, pulling the door shut behind him with a soft click that sounded like a coffin closing.

The hallway was still empty. Still quiet. The elevator descended in silence, the numbers dropping like his life expectancy. In the lobby, Rafael was on the phone, didn't look up. Ethan walked past him, through the doors, onto the street.

Outside, headlights smeared across wet pavement. The rain had started again, cold and steady, soaking through his jacket in seconds. Somewhere above the skyline, a siren wailed—distant, mechanical, like the sound of a world closing in. The city stretched out around him, millions of people in millions of apartments, but Ethan had never been more exposed, more hunted, more alone.

He kept walking, head down, backpack slung over one shoulder. He didn't know where he was going yet. Just away. Away from the apartment. Away from the bank. Away from the life that had imploded in the space of a morning.

His father was right.

It was time to run.

Because if he stayed, if he tried to explain, if he trusted the system to protect him, he'd end up like Latham. Dead in a bathroom. An accident. A statistic. Another inconvenient person who had posed the wrong questions and paid the ultimate price.

The rain fell harder. The sirens grew louder. And Ethan Cole disappeared into the city, a ghost in his own life, carrying secrets that men would kill for and evidence that might be the only thing keeping him alive.

The walls had closed in completely. Now he had to find a way through them.

Elsewhere-Kessler

Thousands of miles away, in a private study overlooking Lake Geneva, Kessler sat in a leather chair worn soft by decades of use. The room was dark save for a single lamp casting amber light across papers and maps and the detritus of empire.

A knock at the door. Soft, precise. His assistant entered without waiting for acknowledgment, crossing the room in three silent steps to place a single sheet of paper on the desk.

Kessler picked it up, reading the intercepted transcript with the patience of a man who had learned long ago that urgency was the enemy of control.

COLE, ETHAN - OUTGOING CALL - 14:47 EST RECIPIENT: COLE, JAMES - CONFIRMED DURATION: 2:34 CONTENT: [SEE ATTACHED SUMMARY] STATUS: SUBJECT HAS VACATED RESIDENCE. CURRENT LOCATION UNKNOWN.

He set the paper down, his fingers lingering on the name. James Cole. A ghost from another era, a man Kessler had once considered a friend. James had been the one who got away, the asset who Kessler forced into retirement when he wouldn't be recruited, the soldier who walked into the North Carolina wilderness and never looked back.

Until now.

Kessler smiled—a thin expression that didn't reach his eyes, the smile of a chess player watching his opponent finally move a piece that had sat dormant for decades.

"Welcome back to the game, my old friend," he murmured, his voice barely above a whisper in the empty room. "I wondered how long it would take."

He folded the paper once, twice, and fed it into the shredder beside his desk. The machine hummed briefly, then fell silent.

Outside, the rain continued to fall on Geneva, on Manhattan, on all the hidden places where powerful men made decisions that shaped the lives of millions. And in that quiet study, Kessler reached for his phone, already composing the next move in a game that had just become far more interesting.

The son had stumbled into the web. Now the father was stirring.

And Andreas Kessler had been waiting for this reunion for an extraordinarily long time.

17

Stillness Before The Shot

"The world won't slow down for you, son. So you learn to slow your-self—until the moment chooses you."
—James Cole

Appalachian Mountains— 6:42 a.m.-Late Fall 2010
Wilderness always had a way of stripping things down to truth. Ethan remembered that sound — the wind threading through long pines, the hush between distant bird calls. It was a silence so complete that even a single breath seemed loud.

He was fourteen the first time his father took him and his older brother, Daniel, deep into the Carolina back country. No phones. No roads. Just two boys, a canvas tent, and the man who'd spent a lifetime learning how to listen to danger before it spoke.

His father, James Cole, stood at the edge of the creek bank, still as carved stone. The morning light caught the gray at his temples, but the rest of him looked unbreakable. He held a rifle like an extension of himself — calm, deliberate, never wasted in movement.

"You see the deer?" he raised quietly.

Ethan squinted through his rifle scope across the creek. "Yeah. Just past the fallen log."

"Patience," his father added, settling into the particular stillness that Ethan would later recognize as operational awareness. "Most people think hunting is about the shot. It's not. It's about the wait. About being so still that you disappear into the background. About breathing so shallow that nothing hears you coming."

Ethan took in a slow breath and on the exhale, pulled the trigger.

Daniel was already restless, but Ethan absorbed it, watching how his father's body settled, how his breathing slowed, how his eyes tracked movement without his head turning.

Years later, hiding in Istanbul alleyways from men with guns, Ethan would remember this moment. The lesson wasn't about hunting. It was about becoming invisible when visibility meant death.

James nodded. "You want to catch something that matters, you wait. Patience earns you what panic can't."

Daniel rolled his eyes. "He's talking about hunting again, not life, right?"

James didn't look up. "Sometimes they're the same thing."

Ethan smiled despite himself. He always understood his father better than his brother did. Daniel had his mother's fire — the restless need to move, to fight, to win. Ethan had inherited the quiet part of her — the way she could see the storm coming before anyone else even felt the wind.

They set up camp by sundown, a small fire cracking in the hollow. The smell of cedar smoke mixed with pine needles and river mist. Daniel was field dressing the deer Ethan shot while Ethan sharpened the old hunting knife — his father's knife, the handle worn smooth from decades of calloused hands.

When James finally spoke again, his voice was low, almost lost beneath the fire's hiss.

"You boys ever wonder why I bring you out here?"

Daniel grunted. "Because you don't trust the world."

"Because the world doesn't deserve trust," James maintained simply. "It's not built for that. It's built for leverage. You learn to read people the way you read wind. It's how you stay alive."

He glanced at Ethan, and for the briefest second, there was something softer in his eyes. "Brains or brawn — doesn't matter. What matters is knowing when to move and when to wait. Ethan—" he paused, choosing his words. "You see patterns no one else sees. That's your weapon. Don't ever let someone convince you it's not."

Ethan nodded, absorbing each syllable. He didn't realize it then, but his father was building him — one lesson, one silence, one hunt at a time.

Daniel tossed another branch onto the fire. "And what about me?" James smiled faintly. "You'll keep your brother alive when thinking won't do the job."

The three of them sat there until the stars swallowed the horizon. The river whispered against the stones, the fire dimmed to embers, and somewhere far off, a lone wolf howled — a sound Ethan would remember the rest of his life.

Years later, when he sat alone in a dark Manhattan wire room tracing billions through shadow accounts, he'd hear that same howl in the silence of the servers — that warning from the woods.

Patience. Awareness. The stillness before the shot.

And he would understand, finally, what his father had meant: The world doesn't reward the loud. It rewards the ones who listen.

18

Sparrow's Flight

Kessler — Private Diary (Zurich-0 Archive: Unclassified)
"Fly as far as you like, my Sparrow. It will make your return to me all the more... inevitable."

Vienna, Austria — Fall 2017
Vienna rain never fell straight. It drifted sideways through the narrow streets, catching the glow of café lights and embassy cars, turning the air into gold dust. Selin watched from the second-floor window of a modest flat above a pastry shop, a glass of red wine in her hand, a small stack of passports spread on the table beside her laptop.

Turkish. Austrian. British. Two forged, one real.
She wasn't sure which name belonged to her anymore.

On paper, she was **Leyla Kara**, *Cultural Attaché for the Republic of Turkey.* In practice, she served as the invisible thread between three competing worlds — European security agencies, Helios Defense intermediaries, and the last vestiges of Kessler's intelligence network.

She told herself she'd left him. But the truth was more complicated. You didn't leave men like Kessler. You drifted away from their gravity — slowly, painfully — always aware they could pull you back.

The flat appeared tasteful, yet impersonal: neutral walls, travel books, a single framed photo of a Vienna skyline that meant nothing to her. She lived like a ghost.

Each morning she walked to the Turkish Cultural Mission, exchanged pleasantries in four languages, attended meetings about art exhibitions and economic partnerships — all cover for information exchanges conducted over coffee and charm.

Selin had mastered the art of listening without appearing to. Her colleagues called her *the quiet one*. In a world addicted to noise, silence served as her greatest weapon.

That night, she met a British diplomat at Café Landtmann. He appeared soft around the edges, weary, talkative. He thought she served as just another ambitious attaché — intelligent, flirtatious, harmless. Over espresso, he mentioned something offhand: a transport manifest rerouted through the Balkans under a Helios subsidiary. She smiled, touched his arm, and made him feel clever.

By midnight, she'd memorized the details. By morning, she'd sent them — encrypted — to a contact she thought belonged to an anti-Helios consortium operating out of Brussels. She believed she was fighting against Kessler.

She couldn't have been more wrong.

Two weeks later, an explosion tore through a refugee convoy in southern Serbia. Forty-three dead, all civilians. The manifest she'd passed along had contained the coordinates of their route.

Selin sat alone in her apartment, staring at the news footage — smoke, fire, bodies. She read the report three times, heart numb, until she found the telltale pattern in the metadata: *authored by a Helios-affiliated news syndicate*. The story had been shaped before the incident even happened.

Her breath caught. Kessler had orchestrated it — a false flag, designed to shift blame toward rival interests and justify new security contracts. He had used her as a ghost courier. The girl he had trained to see through lies had become one.

That night, she packed a single suitcase, burned her remaining passports in the sink, and left the apartment just as dawn broke over the Danube.

She didn't know where she was heading — only that she had to disappear before he found her again.

For months, she drifted through safe houses — Athens, Naples, Tangier. Each stop stripped another layer from her: language, identity, certainty.

By the time she reached Zurich, she no longer introduced herself as anyone.

It was there, in a narrow café off Bahnhofstrasse, that a man slid into the seat across from her without asking. Gray suit. American accent. The kind of presence that didn't need introduction.

"You've been sending ghosts into the wrong machines," he observed.

She didn't reply.

He slid a folded paper across the table — a contract, unsigned, but official enough to feel heavy.

"The Agency wants you to work for us. You can keep running, or you can start fighting the right people."

Selin looked at him, weighing the offer. She knew there was no "right" side — only degrees of corruption. But something inside her — maybe guilt, maybe defiance — whispered that fighting Kessler from the inside remained the only way to break the cage he had built.

She picked up the paper. "What's the cover?"

He smiled. "Consultant. Economic analysis. Washington will love you."

Paris — Two Years Later

Selin walked along the Seine River at dawn, coat pulled tight, the freezing wind tugging at her hair. She'd just finished transmitting a Directorate intercept to Langley — one that confirmed what she already suspected:

Kessler had never lost track of her.

He'd been feeding her data, shaping her intel streams, using her to launder his disinformation through American channels.

He'd made her his double agent, and she hadn't even known it.

For the first time since Vienna, she stopped walking. The river moved slow beneath her — dark, indifferent, endless. She took the phone from her pocket, tossed it into the water, and whispered, "You don't own me anymore."

As the ripples spread, something loosened inside her. Not freedom — not yet — but the first breath of it.

Present Day

Selin's voice faltered as she finished telling Ethan the story.

He didn't speak. There was nothing to say that wouldn't sound small.

Finally, she commented, "He taught me to lie so well I don't even trust the truth anymore."

Ethan met her gaze, voice low. "Then maybe that's what makes you dangerous to him now."

She smiled faintly — the kind of smile that held both gratitude and sorrow.

For the first time, he saw the cost of her strength: each of her identities burned to ash until only purpose remained.

19

Legacy

"A man's legacy isn't written by the world he's born into, but by the line he refuses to cross—no matter the cost."
—James Cole

North Carolina — Christmas Eve 2020

Fire crackled inside the Cole cabin, while fresh snow fell outside, blanketing the pine forest in the kind of silence that only comes to mountains in winter. Inside, the fire crackled, throwing orange light across knotted pine walls hung with family photographs spanning four decades—James Cole in uniform, younger and harder; his late wife Sarah, dark-haired and laughing; the boys at various ages, growing from children to men in progressive frames.

Daniel Cole stood by the fireplace, beer in hand, studying those photographs with the particular attention of someone who understood that memory remained the only immortality most people achieved. He was thirty years old, already carrying the weight of Helmand in his shoulders, though he never talked about it. Not even here, especially not here.

Ethan emerged from the kitchen carrying a bottle of bourbon—the good stuff, the kind their father only brought out for important occasions. He was twenty-eight, working his fifth year at International Mercantile Bank, still believing the financial system could be understood through logic and reformed through diligence.

"He's taking forever with that turkey," Ethan claimed, pouring three glasses. "You think we should check on him?"

"He's fine. You know that Dad does everything on his own timeline." Daniel accepted his glass. "Remember that buck he tracked for three days? Could have taken the shot on day one, but he wanted to be certain."

"Life is a metaphor with him."

"Life a lesson. There's a difference."

They heard footsteps on the porch—heavy, deliberate, the tread of someone who'd spent a lifetime moving through terrain that required respect. James Cole entered, stamping snow from his boots, carrying an armload of split firewood despite being fifty-seven and having two grown sons perfectly capable of the task.

"Don't even start," he contended, reading Daniel's expression. "I'm not an invalid."

"Nobody implied you were," Daniel replied. "But there's a reason we're here. You could delegate occasionally."

"I could. Won't." James stacked the wood with practiced efficiency, each log placed with the precision of someone who understood structure. "Besides, you two spend too much time in cities. Good to remember what actual cold feels like."

He brushed bark from his hands and accepted the bourbon Ethan offered. For a moment, the three of them stood in silence—a tableau of masculine affection, the kind that lived in gesture rather than language.

"To Sarah," James toasted finally, raising his glass toward her photograph. "Who would've hated this maudlin bullshit but tolerated it because she loved us anyway."

They drank. The bourbon burned clean and warm—Kentucky craft distillery, the kind James's military pension barely afforded but which he bought anyway because some things mattered more than money.

"Sit down, both of you," James expressed, lowering himself into the worn leather chair that had been his throne for thirty years. "I need to tell you something I should've told you a long time ago. Something I only recently learned myself, and it's been eating at me."

Daniel and Ethan exchanged glances—the brothers' silent language, born from two decades of shared experience. Something in their father's tone carried weight beyond the usual holiday gravitas.

James took a long sip, his hands not quite steady. "You both remember Otto Reinhardt. My friend from the service. The man whose family you spent summers with, Ethan. The man I trusted enough to let his son become like a third brother to you boys."

Ethan noticed his stomach tighten. He hadn't thought about Lukas in years—not since Cho Oyu, not since that severed rope and the questions that still haunted him.

"Of course we remember," Ethan answered carefully. "You and Otto served together in Eastern Europe. Joint operations, off-the-books work. You saved each other's lives."

"We did." James's expression darkened. "Or at least, I thought we did. I thought I knew who he was. I thought..." He stopped, gathered himself. "Three months ago, I received a package. No return address, unmarked, delivered to a PO box I haven't used in a decade. Inside was a dossier—intelligence documents, photographs, operational files."

"From whom?" Daniel queried, his operator instincts immediately alert.

"Old colleagues. People from my service days who are still in the game, still paying attention to shadows most people never see." James pulled a manila folder from beside his chair, set it on the table between them. "They sent me proof that Otto Reinhardt—the man I called my closest friend for thirty years—never existed."

The words landed like physical blows.

"What do you mean 'never existed'?" Ethan leaned forward, his analytical mind already racing through possibilities.

"I mean Otto Reinhardt served as an alias. A legend, in intelligence terms—a complete fabricated identity built to infiltrate joint NATO operations." James opened the folder, pulled out a photograph. Not the one from his mantle, but a different image: the same man, younger, in a different uniform. "His real name is Andreas Kessler. Former Swiss intelligence, yes, but he went rogue. Built something in the shadows. Something big enough that people I trust are scared to even speak about it."

Daniel took the photograph, studied it. "Jesus, Dad. How long have you known?"

"Three months. Three goddamn months of realizing that my best friend—the man I trusted with my life, with my family, with my sons—was playing a role the entire time." James's jaw tightened. "And now I'm wondering if that heart attack that forced my retirement was even real." The brothers went still.

"What do you mean?" Ethan positioned carefully.

"I mean I was young enough, in perfect health. Ran five miles every morning, clean bill of health at each physical. Then unexpectedly, without notice, a heart attack. The doctors couldn't explain it—no blockages, no family history, no underlying conditions. They called it a medical mystery." James's voice turned bitter. "But the dossier mentions something called 'biological intervention.' Compounds that can induce a heart attack. Untraceable, undetectable, perfect for forcing someone out of service without raising suspicions."

"You think Kessler poisoned you?" Daniel's voice hardened. James met his sons eyes—"I think it's awfully convenient timing. I had just been promoted to a position with expanded intelligence access. NATO joint operations oversight. The kind of role where I might have eventually seen something that exposed Kessler's network." James met their eyes.

James continued—"Two months after I took that position, I had the heart attack. Six months of recovery, forced medical retirement. And who stood there the whole time, visiting me in the hospital, helping Sarah manage the house? Otto Reinhardt. My best friend, so concerned about my health."

"Jesus Christ," Ethan breathed.

"Maybe I'm paranoid. Maybe it was just bad luck." James's expression got across he didn't believe that for a second. "But now that I know who Kessler truly is, what he's capable of, I can't stop thinking about how perfectly it worked out for him. I get sidelined right when I might become a problem, but I don't die—no investigation, no questions, just a tragic medical event. And my best friend is right there to comfort me, to make sure I don't get suspicious, to keep me isolated and grateful."

James's voice cracked slightly. "Do you understand what that means? Each summer Ethan spent with Lukas, the winters they went climbing in Switzerland. I thought I was giving my son a brother and a connection to a man I respected—I was sending him into a viper's nest without even knowing it."

Ethan's mind reeled. The summers in Appalachia, Lukas teaching him how to read terrain. The winters in Switzerland, Otto showing them survival techniques. The trip to Cho Oyu where Lukas had—

"Lukas," Ethan added quietly. "The rope. On Cho Oyu."

James's eyes met his. "I don't know. That's the hell of it—I don't know if that was intentional, if Lukas is like his father, if Otto—Kessler—sent his son to..." He couldn't finish the sentence.

"To what?" Daniel's voice was hard. "Kill Ethan?"

"To test him. To assess him. To determine if he posed a threat or could be turned into an asset." James stood, paced to the fireplace. "I don't know which, and that uncertainty is worse than knowing. Because it means I sent my son into danger without even realizing it. It means every moment of trust, each bond I thought was real, were no more than pure manipulation."

Ethan thought back to that mountain. Lukas's calm in the storm. The rope, cut too cleanly. The way Lukas had smiled before going out into the blizzard: *The mountain doesn't wait, Ethan. Neither should we.*

"Why?" Ethan demanded. "Why would Kessler spend thirty years playing Otto Reinhardt? What was he after?"

"Access. Information. Credibility." James ticked them off on his fingers. "As Otto Reinhardt, decorated Swiss intelligence officer, he had clearance to joint operations, access to NATO channels, relationships with American operators like me. He could see how we worked, who we trusted, where our blind spots were. And the whole time, he was building his own network—something outside official channels, something that could operate invisibly because we all thought he was one of us."

"The Directorate," Daniel mentioned quietly.

James turned. "You've heard of it?"

"Whispers. In contractor circles. People talk about an organization that handles problems no government wants to touch. Wet work, intelligence gathering, political manipulation. But it's all ghost stories—nothing concrete, nothing provable."

"It's real. And Kessler built it." James returned to his chair, at once looking all of his fifty-seven years. "The dossier contains fragments—enough to confirm it exists, not enough to expose it completely. But what I can piece together is that Kessler used his Otto Reinhardt identity to recruit assets, identify talent, build networks across multiple intelligence services. He was playing a thirty-year game, and I was one of his pawns."

"Or you were the mark," Ethan answered. "Maybe the whole friendship was designed to get access to us. To your family."

James's face went pale. "I've thought about that. Pretty much each and every day for three months, that's what keeps me up at night. The idea that he might have been cultivating you boys. That Lukas spending all those summers with you wasn't about friendship—it was about assessment. Determining if you had value to his father's operations."

"Ethan works in international banking," Daniel commented, the implications dawning. "The kind of banking that processes transactions for people who need discretion."

"Exactly." James met Ethan's eyes. "You're in a position to see financial flows that most people never access. To flag or ignore anomalies. To be either an asset or an obstacle."

"And I'm former Delta, now doing contract work," Daniel added. "The kind of skill set Kessler's organization would want to recruit or eliminate."

"Yes." James's voice hung heavy with guilt. "I served my country for thirty years. Thought I built something good, something worth defending. And all the while, I was being used by a man who saw people as resources, relationships as transactions, friendship as another tool of control."

The fire popped, sending sparks up the chimney. Outside, wind sighed through pines.

"There's more," James voiced quietly. "Three weeks ago, I received a message. Encrypted, untraceable. Only four words: *Old friends stay retired.*"

"A threat," Daniel added flatly.

"A reminder. That Kessler knows that I know. That he's aware I received the dossier. That he's watching to see what I do with the information." James reached into the folder, pulled out another photograph—this one recent, grainy, obviously surveillance footage. It showed James leaving the cabin, walking to his truck. "This came with the message. Proof that he can reach me whenever he wants."

Ethan shivered ever so slightly, like ice suddenly in his veins. "He's going to kill you."

"Eventually. Men like Kessler eliminate problems permanently." James's voice sounded steady, resigned. "I've made my peace with that. What I haven't made peace with is the idea that I put you both in danger by trusting the wrong man. By being blind to what he was."

"That's not your fault," Ethan observed. "If he was that good at maintaining cover for thirty years—"

"It is my fault. I'm the one who trained you to read people, to trust instincts, to see patterns. And I missed the biggest pattern of my life because I wanted a friend badly enough that I ignored the signs." James pulled out the old photograph from the mantle—the one showing him and "Otto" in their youth. "Look at his eyes. Really look."

Ethan took the photo, studied it in the firelight. At first he saw camaraderie, brotherhood. But then, as he focused on Kessler's expression, he saw something else: calculation. Assessment. The eyes of a man measuring value even in a moment of supposed trust.

"He was always this," Ethan whispered. "Even then."

"He was always exactly what he became. I simply just did not want to see it." James took the photo back. "That's my failure. And now I need you both to understand something: Lukas is Kessler's son. He was raised by this man, trained by him, shaped in his image. I don't know if he is evil like his father. I don't know if that rope on Cho Oyu was an accident or something else entirely. But I know we can't take chances."

"You think Lukas might come after us?" Daniel questioned.

"I think if Kessler decides we're threats, he'll use all assets available to him. Including his son." James looked at Ethan with anguish in his eyes. "I'm so sorry. I thought I was giving you a brother. I might have been giving you an enemy. I'll never forgive myself for that."

"Dad—" Ethan started.

"No. Let me finish." James's command voice emerged. "I need you both to hear this: if anything happens to me—if it looks like an accident but feels wrong—question it. Question everything. Don't trust the official story. Don't assume natural causes. And for God's sake, don't trust anyone connected to the Reinhardt name, no matter how much history we shared."

"You think he would actually kill you over this?" Daniel's voice carried the flat affect of someone who already knew the answer.

"I think he's already killed people for far less. The dossier contains fragments of operations—Maribor, which I'll tell you about. But also dozens of others. Assassinations dressed as accidents. Whistleblowers who died in convenient timing. Investigators who stopped investigating." James's hands were shaking now. "Kessler has built an empire in the shadows, and empires don't tolerate threats. I became a threat the moment I learned who he truly was."

"Then we expose him," Ethan replied. "We take that dossier, we find proof, we—"

"You can't. Not yet." James cut him off. "The dossier is incomplete—fragments, implications, nothing that would stand up to scrutiny. Going public now would absolutely get you killed faster. What you need to do is survive. Document and build a case so thorough that even Kessler's protection can't save him. But first, you survive."

He retrieved the small wooden box from the mantle, opened it. Inside: the old photograph, a USB drive, and a small key.

"This drive contains everything from the dossier. The key is to a safety deposit box in Richmond—there's more there, documents I've been collecting since I learned the truth. If I die, this is your inheritance: the knowledge to fight a war I couldn't win." He placed the box in Ethan's hands. "I'm trusting you with this because you're an analyst. You see patterns. Use that."

He turned to Daniel. "And you're a soldier. You understand operational security, how to stay ahead of threats. Use that."

"You're asking us to finish what you started," Daniel voiced.

"I'm asking you to be smarter than me. Don't trust the wrong people. Don't mistake performance for friendship. And don't underestimate what Kessler is capable of." James's voice broke slightly. "I sent you to spend winters with his son. I vouched for his character. I called him my best friend. Every moment of that was built on a lie I was too blind to see. Don't make the same mistake."

The weight of it settled over the cabin—betrayal layered on betrayal, thirty years of friendship revealed as manipulation, memories poisoned by truth.

"Lukas," Ethan stated again, testing the name. "You don't know if he's like Kessler, do you?"

"I don't know. That's what terrifies me most." His father met his eyes. "Lukas might be another victim of his father's manipulation. Or he might be a perfectly trained weapon, sent to befriend my son and determine his value to the Directorate. I'll never know. But I know you can't take the chance of finding out the hard way."

"The rope," Ethan voiced quietly. "On Cho Oyu. It looked cut to me. Too clean, too deliberate. But there was a storm, and I was exhausted, and I convinced myself I was imagining things."

"Trust your instincts," James replied firmly. "If you sensed something wrong, it probably was. Kessler's son would have been taught to make eliminations look like accidents. Mountains are perfect for that—so many ways to die that no one questions."

"But Lukas didn't die. He disappeared." Ethan frowned. "Why stage his own death?"

"Maybe to break the connection to you. Maybe because his father decided the friendship had served its purpose. Or maybe—" James's expression darkened "—maybe to make you think you survived something together, to forge a bond of shared trauma that he could exploit later if needed."

The implications were dizzying. Ethan's memories of Lukas now carried the weight of suspicion. The lessons, confidence, moments of brotherhood—all of it potentially calculated, performed, false.

"I'm sorry," James professed again, and this time his voice broke completely. "I'm so goddamn sorry. A father's job is to protect his children. And I sent you into the hands of a monster's son because I was too trusting, too blind, too desperate to believe in friendship that couldn't be real."

Ethan crossed the room, embraced his father. "You didn't know. You couldn't have known."

"I should have known. I trained to see through cover stories, to identify threats. And I missed the biggest one of my life because I wanted it to be real." James held his son tight. "Promise me you'll be smarter. Promise me you won't trust the wrong people like I did."

"I promise."

Daniel joined the embrace, the three Cole men standing together in the cabin's warm light, bound by blood and the terrible knowledge that some betrayals ran so deep they poisoned memory itself.

"I love you both," James expressed thickly. "The things I did—the choices I made, the missions I went on, my failures—were meant to build a world where you both could live without this weight. If I failed at that, at least I succeeded in raising sons who might finish what I started."

They stayed like that for a long moment—a family portrait of strength and vulnerability, of legacy passing from one generation to the next, of fathers preparing sons for wars they shouldn't have to fight.

Finally, they broke apart. James wiped his eyes unselfconsciously. "Alright, enough maudlin bullshit. Let's eat. That turkey isn't going to carve itself, and your mother would haunt me if I let good food get cold."

They moved into the kitchen, the conversation shifting to safer topics—Daniel's contracting work, Ethan's career trajectory, whether the Panthers would ever have a winning season. The easy rhythm of family, the comfortable lies people tell when truth is too heavy for normal dinner conversation.

But later, after Daniel had gone to bed and Ethan sat with his father by the dying fire, James spoke one more time:

"Lukas. If you ever see him again—if he survived that mountain, if he reappears in your life—don't trust him. No matter what he says, no matter how real it feels. Trust is what Kessler's people weaponize. It's how they get close enough to destroy you."

"What if he's not like his father?" Ethan submitted. "What if he's a victim too?"

"Then I'm sorry for him. Truly. But you can't afford to find out." James placed a hand on Ethan's shoulder. "Some people are born broken. Others are made that way. Kessler is both. And if he raised his son, if he trained him from childhood like I suspect he did, then Lukas Reinhardt is either dead or deadly. There's no third option."

Ethan held the wooden box, feeling its weight—not physical, but historical. "If something happens to you—"

"When something happens," James corrected gently. "Not if. I've seen how these stories end. I need you prepared for it."

"I will be."

"Good." James stood, placed a hand on his son's shoulder. "Get some sleep. Morning comes early, and your brother snores like a chainsaw. You'll want rest before that starts."

Ethan smiled despite the heaviness in his chest. "Goodnight, Dad."

"Goodnight, son."

James Cole climbed the stairs to his bedroom, each step deliberate, measured. At the landing, he paused, looked back at Ethan sitting in the firelight with that wooden box in his hands.

He wanted to say more. To explain the full scope of what Kessler had become, the network he had built, the lives destroyed in service of an ideology that treated humanity as disposable. But some knowledge proved too dangerous to share—it made you a target, turned understanding into liability.

So James nodded once—a gesture that meant *I'm proud of you* and *I'm sorry* and *Be careful* all at once—then disappeared into the darkness upstairs.

Ethan sat alone by the fire for another hour, studying the photograph, memorizing Kessler's face, trying to see the monster beneath the mask of his father's best friend. When he finally went to bed, he placed the box in his bag, nestled between clean shirts and the banking regulations manual he'd been studying.

He didn't know it then, but that box would be the last gift his father ever gave him. And the warning it contained—question everything, trust nothing, fight when you have to—would become the foundation of survival when his world collapsed into chaos and betrayal.

Outside, snow continued to fall, blanketing the cabin in white silence. The fire burned down to embers. And somewhere far away, in a glass tower overlooking Lake Zurich, the man who had spent thirty years pretending to be Otto Reinhardt sat in darkness, planning moves in a game most people didn't know they were playing.

The Cole family didn't know it yet, but the war had already begun. Had been ongoing for decades, patient and relentless.

They'd been recruited to a side they didn't know existed, by an enemy who'd spent three decades earning their trust before revealing the truth.

And in wars like that, legacy became weapon, family became liability, and love—even the love between a father and his sons—became the most dangerous vulnerability of all.

20

Flight

"I will stand between him and the darkness that hunts him—until my last breath." —Selin Yilmaz

Midtown, New York City— 5:35 a.m.- Day 4

Ethan woke before dawn to the sound of a distant siren. For a moment, he thought it was in his head—another echo from a night of fractured sleep—but then it came again, closer this time.

He lay still on the edge of the bed in the cheap Midtown hotel he'd checked into under a false name. The television flickered silently across the room, its glow washing him in pale light. The news ticker crawled along the bottom of the screen:

"Federal authorities investigating possible internal breach at International Mercantile Bank."

They didn't reveal his name. Not yet. But he knew it that was coming. The cord had begun to tighten around his neck.

He had left his apartment two days prior, circling through side streets, changing direction, watching reflections in glass. Twice, he spotted the same gray sedan in traffic—but each time, it slipped away.

He checked his phone again: No signal. The SIM card had been disposed of; he had snapped it in half and flushed the pieces. The phone was a decoy now, for anyone tracing pings. His real communication device remained a disposable burner he previously picked up from a bodega after he left his apartment.

On the small table, he spread out what he had: a driver's license under an old alias from a student finance research project, $1,200 in cash, and the black flash drive—still sealed in a paper napkin, taped flat against the lining of his pack.

He stared at it for a long moment. It didn't look like something people killed for.

A thud sounded in the hallway. A cleaning cart rolling past. He waited, counting the seconds. No knock, no voices. He exhaled and zipped the pack.

By 6:00 a.m., he walked out onto the street, moving fast. The early rain had left the pavement slick, reflecting the pulse of traffic lights. He kept his head down, hood up, backpack tight across his shoulders.

He caught a cab toward Penn Station, but halfway there, changed course. "Grand Central," he added. "West side entrance."

The driver glanced in the mirror. "You sure? Penn's closer."

"Not anymore," Ethan muttered.

The cab turned down Forty-Second. Ethan watched the rearview. No sedan. No tail. He'd lost them—for now.

He had the driver drop him three blocks from Grand Central, paid cash, and walked the rest of the way through the morning commuter crowds. The terminal's main concourse already filled up with the early rush—businesspeople checking departure boards, tourists photographing the constellation ceiling, the smell of coffee and pastries from the market vendors.

Ethan bought a ticket to Boston at one window, then immediately bought another to Philadelphia at a different window. He had learned from his father that creating false trails formed the foundation of basic tradecraft. He had no idea if it actually worked, but he convinced himself that doing something was better than doing nothing.

He found a corner near the Oyster Bar entrance where he could watch the main concourse, his back to the wall. The backpack was heavy against his spine—not from weight, but from what it contained. That flash drive represented thousands of transactions, millions of dollars, connections that threaded through governments and corporations across continents.

And he had no idea what to do with it.

His father would have known. James Cole had spent in special operations and intelligence work before retiring to the North Carolina mountains. He'd taught Ethan to notice patterns, to trust instinct over assumption, to understand that the world ran on hidden machinery most people never saw. But his father was retired. Ethan wasn't looking to bring him into this.

Daniel—his older brother, somewhere in Eastern Europe on contract security work. Ethan had tried calling, texting, emailing. Nothing. Daniel had gone dark.

Which meant Ethan stood alone.

He checked the burner phone. No messages. No calls. The screen showed 7:43 a.m.

He'd give it until eight, then catch a train somewhere. Anywhere that wasn't New York.

At 7:52, someone sat down next to him.

Ethan's hand went instinctively to the pepper spray in his jacket pocket, but the woman raised one hand slightly—palm out, casual but clear.

"Don't," she contended quietly. "I'm not here to hurt you."

She looked younger than he expected—late twenties, maybe thirty at most. Dark hair pulled back in a sleek ponytail that looked effortless but probably wasn't, dark eyes that catalogued weaknesses in a single glance. She wore dark jeans, leather jacket over a plain black shirt, minimal jewelry—a small silver pendant, nothing else. Athletic build obvious even sitting still. Beautiful in a way that made Ethan's brain momentarily forget he was running for his life—sharp cheekbones, full lips, skin that suggested Mediterranean or Middle Eastern heritage, the kind of face that was striking and memorable—definitely not safe.

"Who are you?" Ethan kept his voice low, aware of the crowds moving past them. "How did you find me?"

"My name is Selin. Selin Yilmaz." She didn't offer a hand. "And I found you because finding people is what I do. You're not as good at disappearing as you think you are."

"That's not an answer."

"It's the only answer you're getting right now." Her eyes never stopped moving—scanning the concourse, cataloguing faces, exits, threats. Professional surveillance behavior. "You have about twenty minutes before they realize you're here. The men following you aren't subtle, but they're persistent."

"What men? Who are you talking about?"

"Focus, Ethan Cole." Her voice sharpened slightly. "Right now, you're deciding whether to run from me or listen to me. I'm telling you that running is pointless. They've already flagged your credit cards, your ID, probably your face in half the security cameras in Midtown. The only reason you're still free is because they're being cautious—they want to see who you contact, where you go, what you plan to do with what you found."

"I don't know what you're—"

"The flash drive in your backpack. The one containing transaction records from International Mercantile Bank. The one that shows financial flows between defense contractors, intelligence services, and shell corporations across fourteen countries." She turned to look at him directly for the first time. "The one you downloaded from the Bank's encrypted server right before Richard Latham was murdered and made to look like an accident."

Ethan's blood went cold. "How do you know about that?"

"Because I know who killed him. Because I know why they killed him. And because right now, you're next on the list unless you start making better decisions." She stood smoothly. "Come with me. Or stay here and find out if the three men who just entered from the Lexington Avenue entrance are actually commuters."

Ethan followed her gaze. Three men in business casual, moving with the wrong rhythm—too coordinated, too aware, scanning faces methodically.

"Shit," Ethan breathed.

"That's the first smart thing you've said to me." Selin was already moving, not toward the exits but deeper into the terminal, toward the lower-level food court and track access. "Stay close. Don't run. Running attracts attention."

Ethan grabbed his backpack and followed, his heart hammering. She moved through the crowds like water, finding gaps that seemed to open for her, changing direction without obvious effort. He struggled to keep up, nearly losing her twice before she glanced back and slowed slightly.

They descended stairs to the lower concourse, past Shake Shack and Junior's, weaving through the morning food court crowd. Selin paused near a newsstand, pretending to examine magazines while watching the stairs they'd immediately just descended.

"Two of them followed us down," she whispered quietly, not looking at him. "The third stayed topside. Basic three-man surveillance. Not exceptionally creative."

"Who are they?"

"Later. First we lose them." She moved again, this time toward the track gates. "Do you have a ticket?"

"Boston. And Philadelphia. I bought both to—"

"To create a false trail. Cute. Ineffective, but cute." She pulled out her phone, tapped something quickly. "We're taking the 8:15 to New Haven. Track seventeen. Stay with me."

They flashed tickets—she had them somehow, though Ethan hadn't seen her buy anything—and descended to the platform. The train already had started boarding, morning commuters settling into seats with coffee and newspapers.

Selin led him to a car near the middle, chose seats facing backward so she could watch the platform through the window. Ethan sat across from her, backpack between his feet, trying to process what was unfolding.

"Okay," he stated once the train started moving, Manhattan sliding past outside. "Start talking. Who are you?"

Selin studied him for a moment, her dark eyes unreadable. "I'm someone who used to work for the people trying to kill you. And I'm someone who decided I didn't want to do that anymore."

"That's incredibly vague."

"It's the truth. The specific details of my employment history aren't relevant right now. What's relevant is that I know how they think, how they operate, and how to stay ahead of them. Which makes me the best chance you have of surviving the next seventy-two hours."

"Why should I trust you?"

"You shouldn't." She added it flatly, without emotion. "Trust is for people with time and options. You have neither. But you can make a calculated risk assessment: I found you when their people hadn't. I'm getting you out of Manhattan when staying there would get you killed. And I'm about to explain what you've actually uncovered, which is more than anyone else is offering."

Ethan leaned back, trying to read her. She had it correct—he didn't trust her. But he also didn't have better options. "Fine. Talk."

Selin glanced around the train car. A few business commuters, headphones in, focused on laptops. No one paying attention to them.

"The flash drive you're carrying," she began, voice low enough that only Ethan could hear, "contains evidence of a financial network called the Directorate. It's not a government agency, despite the name. It's a clandestine intelligence and security organization that operates in the spaces between legal oversight. They provide services—wet work, intelligence gathering, political manipulation, corporate espionage—to clients who can afford them and don't ask questions about methodology."

"That's conspiracy theory bullshit," Ethan came out with, but his voice lacked conviction.

"Is it?" Selin's expression didn't change. "You have worked at International Mercantile Bank since college. You have seen the anomalies—transactions that don't make sense, money flowing through shells with no visible business model, defense contractors billing for services that don't exist in public records. You noticed. However, you didn't have the context."

She had it right. Ethan had noticed. That's why he started investigating in the first place.

"The Directorate formed about thirty years ago by former intelligence officers from multiple countries—CIA, MI6, Mossad, FSB. People who understood how the world actually worked and decided they could monetize that understanding." Selin's voice remained clinical, almost academic. "They recruit assets—people like me—from vulnerable populations. Street kids, refugees, orphans. People no one would miss. Train them from childhood. Deploy them wherever clients need problems solved quietly."

"You're telling me there's a shadow organization recruiting child soldiers?"

"I'm telling you I *am* one of those children." Her eyes met his, challenging him to look away. "Recruited at twelve from the streets of Ankara. Trained in Vienna. Deployed at twenty. I spent over eight years doing things I'm not proud of for people I'm glad are mostly dead now."

Ethan stared at her. The casual way she came out with it—people I'm glad are mostly dead—sent a chill down his spine. But something in her eyes looked far from casual. Something that looked like old pain, carefully controlled.

"Why tell me this?"

"Because you need to understand what you're up against. The Directorate isn't like traditional criminal organizations. They're structured like a legitimate business—corporate hierarchy, performance metrics, global infrastructure. But they operate completely outside legal frameworks. They have assets in governments, law enforcement, media. They can make evidence disappear, make people disappear, make entire investigations lose momentum and fade away."

"Then why did Latham have evidence against them?"

"Because Richard Latham was their banker." Selin's voice softened slightly. "And bankers keep records. It's what they do. The Directorate uses International Mercantile Bank to launder money, move funds, provide financial architecture for their operations. Latham managed those flows for years. But recently, he developed a conscience. Started keeping records he wasn't supposed to keep. Building insurance in case they decided he knew too much."

"And they decided he knew too much."

"They decided he posed a liability to the Directorate. So they eliminated him. Made it look like an accident. Clean, professional, untraceable." She paused. "You figured out the transaction patterns and they proposed for Latham to reach out to you as a last ditch effort to get you to back down. And when you didn't...they took out Latham."

Ethan thought about the data he had analyzed. The sudden transfers Latham had made in the weeks before his death—amounts designed to escape attention, spread across multiple accounts, buried in routine business noise. But patterns remained patterns, and Ethan had always been good at seeing them.

"So he was trying to escape them," Ethan noted slowly.

"He tried to buy his way out. It didn't work." Selin glanced out the window as the train emerged from underground tunnels, sunlight flooding the car. "Now you have his insurance. The complete financial architecture of the Directorate—who they work for, where money goes, which operations they've funded. It's enough to destroy them. Which is why they'll do anything to get it back or make it disappear."

"Including killing me."

"Including killing all the people you have ever met if that's what it takes." She mentioned it matter-of-factly, without drama. "The Directorate doesn't take chances with exposure. They can't afford to. Their entire business model depends on operating invisibly."

Ethan's hands shook slightly. He clasped them together, trying to process. What she said sounded insane—conspiracy theory nonsense that did not belong in real life.

But Latham was dead. His brother was not to be found. And danger was following him through Grand Central.

And this woman—this beautiful, dangerous woman who had somehow found him when he clearly thought he was being careful—told him it all proved real.

"I don't believe you," he claimed, but even he could hear it was a lie.

"Yes, you do." Selin's voice turned gentle now, almost kind. "You believed it the moment you saw those transaction patterns. You believed it when Latham died and the police labeled it an accident. You've been believing it for some time now. I think you didn't want to admit it. Because admitting it means accepting that the world doesn't work the way you thought it did."

"So what do I do?" Ethan heard the desperation in his own voice. "Go to the FBI? The press? Upload what we have to WikiLeaks?"

"All of those things will get you killed faster." Selin leaned forward slightly. "The Directorate has assets in the FBI. They own journalists. They monitor WikiLeaks and all the other leak platforms constantly. The moment you try to go public, they'll know. And they'll stop you before the information spreads far enough to matter."

"Then what's the point? If I can't use this, if I can't expose them—then what?"

"I'm not saying you can't expose them. All I am saying is you can't do it stupidly." She pulled out her phone, checked something, put it away. "You need leverage first. You need protection. You need to build a network of people who can help, who have their own reasons for wanting the Directorate destroyed. And you need to stay alive long enough to put all that together."

"How?"

"By coming with me. By trusting that I know how to navigate this world because I lived in it for eight years. By accepting that survival right now is more important than justice." She paused. "And by focusing on the task at hand instead of staring at me like you're trying to decide if I'm real."

Ethan felt as if his face was heating up. He hadn't realized he had been staring. But she was right—part of his brain still processed that this striking woman with dark eyes and an accent he couldn't quite place was sitting across from him, casually discussing shadow organizations and murder like other people discussed the weather.

"I wasn't—"

"You were. It's fine. Adrenaline does strange things to perception." But the faintest hint of amusement surfaced in her voice. "I'm flattered. But right now, I need you to focus on staying alive, not on whether you find me attractive."

"I don't—"

"Ethan." She stated his name firmly, like a teacher calling a distracted student. "Focus. People are trying to kill you. That's the priority. Anything else—including whatever you're feeling right now—is background noise."

She remained all business. Professional. And she had clearly dealt with this before—men getting distracted by her appearance when they should be focusing on survival.

Ethan forced himself to look away, to concentrate on the problem instead of the person presenting it. "Okay. Fine. So we go to New Haven. Then what?"

"Then we disappear properly. New identities, new route, new plan. I have resources—safe houses, contacts, money. I've been preparing for this since I left the Directorate two years ago."

"Why did you leave?"

"Because I looked at my life and didn't like what I saw." Her voice went flat again, emotionless. "Because I killed people for money and called it service. Because I followed orders without questioning them, and innocent people died because of my obedience. And because eventually, I couldn't pretend anymore that I was one of the good guys."

The raw honesty in her voice cut through Ethan's skepticism. She wasn't performing. She wasn't trying to manipulate him. She was telling the truth.

"I'm sorry," he mouthed quietly.

"Don't be sorry. Be smart." She stood as the train began slowing. "We're coming into Stamford. We're getting off here, not New Haven. The tickets to New Haven were misdirection in case anyone checked our destination. Come on."

Ethan grabbed his backpack and followed her off the train. The platform buzzed with morning commuters all focused on their own destinations. Selin led him through the station, out to the street, to a parking garage three blocks away.

She stopped next to a nondescript Honda Civic, unlocked it, gestured for him to get in.

"Whose car is this?" Ethan questioned.

"Mine. I keep vehicles staged in several cities for situations exactly like this." She started the engine. "Buckle up. We have about a four-hour drive ahead of us."

"To where?"

"Somewhere they won't look for you. Not immediately, anyway." She pulled out of the garage, merged into traffic. "And somewhere you can start learning how to fight back instead of only running."

Ethan watched the city skyline recede in the side mirror. What he had known and built—his apartment, his job, his routine life—lay well behind him now. Gone. Maybe forever.

And sitting next to him was a woman who claimed to be a former assassin, who'd somehow found him when professional killers couldn't, who was either his best chance at survival or an elaborate trap he was too stupid to see.

"Why are you helping me?" he posed. "What's in this for you?"

Selin was quiet for a moment, eyes on the road. "Redemption, maybe. Or revenge. I haven't decided which." She glanced at him briefly. "The Directorate took eight years of my life and turned me into something I'm not proud of. If your flash drive can destroy them, I want to be there when it happens. I want to watch the whole corrupt structure burn to the ground."

"That's not a great reason to risk your life."

"It's the only reason I have." She turned back to the road. "Besides, you remind me of someone I used to know. Someone who thought the world made sense, who believed in systems and rules and justice. Someone the Directorate killed, not with bullets, but by teaching her that none of those things were real."

"Who?"

"Me. Before Vienna. Before Kessler. Before I learned how to kill without hesitation." Her jaw tightened slightly. "I'm not trying to save that person—she's gone. But maybe I can keep you from becoming what I became. Maybe that counts for something."

They drove in silence for a while, Connecticut countryside rolling past. Ethan's mind was spinning, trying to organize what he had uncovered and learned, trying to decide if he was making the right choice.

But what choice did he truly have?

"Okay," he noted finally. "I'm in. Whatever this is, whatever we're doing—I'm in."

"Good." Selin's voice was approving. "First rule: trust your instincts. If something feels wrong, it probably is. Second rule: don't trust anyone completely, including me. Verify what you see, hear or read. Third rule: stay alive long enough to make their lives difficult. Anything else is negotiable."

"Those are terrible rules."

"They're survival rules. There's a difference." She allowed herself a small smile. "You'll learn."

Ethan settled back in the seat, exhaustion finally catching up with him. Outside, America passed by—strip malls and gas stations, houses and churches, people living ordinary lives that all of a sudden seemed impossibly distant.

He'd left that world behind. Stepped through some invisible barrier into a place where shadow organizations existed, where banks laundered money for assassins, where beautiful women with dark eyes rescued economists from train stations and talked about redemption and revenge in the same breath.

It was terrifying.

But also—and Ethan wasn't quite ready to admit this yet—it was the first time in weeks that he had noticed that he wasn't alone.

He tried to convince himself that maybe, just maybe, he had a chance.

21

Shadows on the Platform

[INTERNAL COMMUNICATION – INTERNATIONAL MERCANTILE BANK]
SUBJECT: EMPLOYEE HELLER, MARGARET (ID #44219)
"Action authorized under Asset Containment Protocol. Subject demonstrated abnormal retention of privileged operational data during systems review. Termination executed via external contractor to ensure non-attributable outcome. Incident classified as accidental fatality within transit system. No further attention required. Maintain narrative."
— IMB Risk Directorate / Compliance Suppression Unit
(Handwritten notation, scanned in margin:)
"Ensure all logs referencing Heller's access to Wire Event anomaly are purged."

Subway Platform, New York City — 5:47 p.m. -Day 4
Margaret Heller stood at the far end of the Lexington Avenue subway platform, the din of evening commuters swelling and fading like a restless tide. She always preferred this end — fewer people, fewer eyes, fewer chances for someone to bump into her. At fifty-eight, her perception was the world was sharper than it used to, the edges less forgiving.

She had worked at International Mercantile Bank for twenty-seven years. Invisible in a way that kept her employed but also kept her second in charge of her division, always the deputy, never the chief. Tucked into the anonymous folds of corporate machinery. Her evenings were quiet when she wasn't at a conference: a well-kept apartment in Murray Hill, and a stack of work from the office.

Tonight, though, she sensed something different.

The weight of the past few weeks pressed down on her as she waited for the train. Richard Latham's customers. Those wire transfers. The numbers that didn't add up no matter how many times she ran them through her head. She'd been in compliance long enough to recognize when something was wrong—and everything about the Apex account screamed wrong.

It had started six months ago, maybe longer. Massive wire transfers—fifty million here, eighty million there—flowing through accounts that had no business moving that kind of volume. The beneficial owners were buried under layers of shell corporations in jurisdictions that existed specifically to hide beneficial owners. Cyprus. Liechtenstein. The Caymans. She'd flagged them quietly at first, sending memos to Latham, expecting the standard review process to kick in.

Instead, Victor Krane had called her into his office.

"Margaret," he'd stated, his voice carrying that particular smoothness that powerful men used when they wanted something buried, "these are legacy clients. Long-standing relationships. The documentation is in order. Clear the wires."

She'd wanted to push back. Twenty-seven years of instinct told her to push back. But Krane's eyes had held something she'd never seen before—not anger, not impatience, but warning. The kind of look that asserted: *this is not a discussion.*

So she'd cleared the wires. Every single one. And each night since, she'd lain awake in her Murray Hill apartment, wondering if she'd become complicit in something she couldn't name.

Then Latham had died. "accidental fall at his home," they indicated. "Slipped in the bathroom," they claimed. But Margaret had seen Richard Latham in a video conference call three days before his death, and the man hadn't looked stressed—he'd looked terrified. Jumpy. Checking over his shoulder during their meeting, speaking in half-sen tences, avoiding specifics. She had grilled him, pushing to see if he was alright. He'd smiled that tight, unconvincing smile and maintained, "Just tired, Margaret. Just tired."

Three days later, he was dead. And Margaret Heller didn't believe in coincidences anymore.

She had started keeping records. Copies of the wire authorizations. Screenshots of the account structures. Notes about dates and amounts and the pattern she could see emerging—money moving in synchronized waves across continents, always under the thresholds that would trigger automatic regulatory review. She'd hidden the files on a personal flash drive, carried it in her purse everywhere she went. Insurance, she told herself. Protection.

And then came Ethan Cole.

Margaret had known Ethan for years. In her book, he stood out as one of the good ones. Principled. Careful. The kind of young man who still believed that doing the right thing mattered, that the system worked if you worked within it. She had watched his career with quiet approval, seen him rise through compliance with the methodical integrity that the profession should embody.

When they had brought him in for interrogation—and that's what it amounted to, despite the euphemisms—she had felt sick to her stomach. The government men treated Ethan like a criminal when all he had done matched up exactly to what compliance officers should do: ask questions when the numbers didn't make sense.

She sat in that conference room, watching them pressure him, threaten him, twist his diligence into something sinister, and she'd wanted to stand up. To say: *He's right. I've seen the same things. The wires are wrong. Latham's customers are wrong. All of it is wrong.*

But she hadn't. She'd sat there in silence, complicit again, watching a good man be sacrificed because he'd stumbled onto the same truth she'd been too afraid to speak.

That marked the moment when she made her decision.

Tomorrow morning, she would call the Federal Reserve. She had contacts there from her years in the industry—people who still believed in oversight, in accountability. If the Fed wouldn't listen, she'd go to the FBI. The Financial Crimes Enforcement Network. The SEC. Someone, somewhere, would care that billions of dollars flowed through International Mercantile Bank in patterns that looked less like commerce and more like something else entirely. Money laundering. Sanctions evasion. Maybe worse.

She had been silent long enough. Latham was dead. Ethan was being hunted. And Margaret Heller had enough of being invisible.

Tomorrow, she told herself. Tomorrow this all changes.

She clutched her purse—the flash drive heavy inside it—and glanced over her shoulder.

A man in a charcoal coat stood twenty feet back, half-hidden behind a column. She had noticed him upstairs near the turnstiles. At first, she chalked it up to coincidence—New York remained a city of patterns and overlaps—but when she stepped left, he shifted. When she stepped right, he mirrored.

Stop it, she scolded herself. *You always imagine things when you're tired.*

But the feeling crawled higher up her spine.

A faint announcement crackled overhead, indecipherable under the weight of screeching steel from an incoming train on the opposite track. A strong wind funneled through the tunnel, brushing Margaret's hair forward. She swallowed hard. Her heart tapped against her ribs.

She reached into her purse for her phone. Maybe she'd call her sister in Boston to hear a familiar voice. Her fingers brushed against the flash drive—the evidence, the proof, the insurance she'd been too cautious to use. Maybe she should have gone to the regulators sooner. Maybe she shouldn't have waited.

But before she could unlock the screen, the hairs rose on her arms—a primal warning she had no words for.

She turned.

The man in the charcoal coat stood closer now. Much closer. His face had an unremarkable appearance, expression flat, like a store mannequin carved to resemble a human. He didn't smile. He didn't blink.

Margaret stepped back, inching toward the yellow line.

The headlights of the oncoming train appeared down the tunnel—a blooming white glare that swallowed the darkness around it.

"Can I help you?" Margaret proposed, voice brittle.

The man didn't answer.

The rush of the train grew louder—a thunderous churn, the rails vibrating.

Margaret opened her mouth to speak again.

A hand touched her elbow—lightly, almost politely.

Then shoved.

She pitched forward, arms flailing, a scream tearing from her throat and vanishing under the roar. She hit the tracks hard, the cold metal slamming into her ribs. In the final half-second, she looked up and saw only light.

Then the world went dark.

On the platform, the man in the charcoal coat stepped backward into the crowd as they surged toward the edge, frantic voices rising. Someone yelled for help. Someone else vomited. Someone screamed that they had seen her fall.

But the man who pushed her had already vanished, swallowed by the city like he had never existed.

In the chaos, no one noticed him bend down to retrieve a purse that had skidded across the platform—black leather, unremarkable, containing a flash drive that would never reach the Federal Reserve or the FBI or anyone else who might have cared about its contents.

And Margaret Heller—unassuming, unnoticed, unprotected—was erased with clinical precision. Another casualty of a conflict she never knew she played a part in.

Tomorrow, she had told herself. Tomorrow everything changes.

But for Margaret Heller, tomorrow would never come.

22

Ping from the Past

"Look, Noah... I don't care where you came from. You're the only person here who doesn't pretend. That's why you're my friend." —Ethan Cole

I-95, Outside Stamford, Connecticut — 10:37 a.m.-Day 4

Rain drummed against the Honda's windshield as Selin merged onto I-95 South, the wipers beating a steady rhythm that matched Ethan's pulse. The New York City skyline had disappeared behind them long ago, swallowed by gray clouds and distance. Only highway stretched forward before them—trucks and commuters, rest stops and toll plazas, the endless American corridor stretching toward destinations Ethan had never imagined running to.

"You should try to sleep," Selin commented, eyes on the road. "We've got about three hours to Philadelphia, then we'll switch. You'll need to be alert when it's your turn to drive."

"I can't sleep." Ethan stared out at the rain-blurred landscape. "Each time I close my eyes, I see Latham. Or my father. Or—"

"Then don't close your eyes. Just rest." Her voice carried the practiced calm of someone used to functioning on minimal sleep. "We're going to be driving for the next twenty-four hours if we want to make Miami in time. Adrenaline will only carry you so far."

"Miami?" Ethan turned to look at her. "I didn't tell you we were heading to Miami."

"You didn't have to. You kept checking your burner phone every ten minutes since we got in the car. That's someone waiting for a response, which means you reached out to someone. Given your limited network of people who might help and your complete lack of experience going underground, I'm guessing it's someone from your past. Someone with technical skills." She glanced at him briefly. "And Miami is far enough to feel safe but close enough to reach quickly. It's where I'd suggest if you had raised it."

Ethan discerned a mix of admiration and unease at how easily she had read him. "His name is Noah. Noah Rivera. We went to Princeton together, I graduated, he dropped out."

"What does he do?"

"Officially? I have no idea. Unofficially? He's a hacker. Works in the shadows—cryptocurrency, encrypted communications, digital security for people who need to stay hidden." Ethan paused. "He went dark a few years ago after some federal investigation got too close. I haven't talked to him since."

"But he answered your message."

"Yeah. He answered."

Selin fell quiet for a moment, processing. "Tell me about him. I need to know who we're meeting, how we can trust a criminal, what his vulnerabilities are."

"Noah's not a criminal. He's complicated." Ethan watched the road, remembering. "We met at Princeton. I was trying to understand the 2008 financial crisis—digging into it, not the textbook version. He showed me how."

Princeton, New Jersey — Spring 2014

The economics library was never truly empty, but at 2 a.m. on a Wednesday it came close. Ethan hunched over a mountain of printouts—Fed reports, currency flow data, a half-eaten sandwich fossilizing beside his laptop. He was chasing a pattern he couldn't quite name, something in the way capital moved during the crisis that the textbooks didn't explain.

"You look like you're trying to prove God's a banker."

Ethan glanced up. The kid looked thin, maybe nineteen, with unruly dark hair and eyes that darted around the room like he expected campus security to burst through the door. He wore a hoodie two sizes too big with a faded Anonymous mask printed on the front.

"Noah Rivera," the kid announced, sliding into the chair across from him without invitation. "Computer science. You're Ethan Cole. Econ. You put a question to Professor Harmon about offshore tax havens last week that made him sweat through his oxford shirt."

Noah sat, pulled out a battered laptop, and within seconds had bypassed the university's firewall to access databases Ethan had no idea existed. His fingers flew across the keyboard. "You want to know why the system broke? I'll show you."

For the next few hours, Noah walked Ethan through a shadow architecture of the 2008 financial crisis—algorithmic trading patterns, shell corporations born and dissolved within hours, automated transfers that moved capital microseconds before news broke.

"It's not a conspiracy," Noah asserted finally, leaning back as dawn light crept through the windows. "It's architecture. Someone designed the system to do exactly what it did. And they convinced the masses it amounted to chaos."

Ethan stared at the data, seeing patterns he'd missed for months. "How do you know all this?"

Noah's expression shifted—something raw breaking through the technical brilliance.

"You want the real answer?" He pulled out his wallet, removed a worn photograph. A girl, maybe twelve, gap-toothed smile, holding a second-place science fair trophy. "That's Lily. My sister. She died two and a half years ago because we couldn't afford her leukemia treatment."

Ethan's chest tightened. "I'm sorry."

"Everyone's sorry. Sorry doesn't audit the books." Noah's voice went flat, but his hands trembled slightly. "After she died, I spent six months tracking the accounts that foreclosed on our house. Followed the mortgage through seven different shell companies. You know where it ended up?"

"Where?"

"A server farm in Luxembourg owned by a corporation that didn't exist six months before the crisis. The same corporation that held 47,000 other mortgages. All foreclosed within a three-week window." He took the photo back, looked at his sister's face. "My father killed himself two months after we lost the house. My mother stopped talking. Lily and I ended up in different foster homes."

"Jesus, Noah—"

"The hospital had the medicine. The insurance had the money. But the system—the beautiful, efficient system—flat told us no. Insisted her life wasn't actuarially valuable enough." Noah closed his laptop. "So I learned how the system works. How to read its source code. And I decided if I ever got the chance, I'd use that knowledge to burn it down."

Ethan sat in silence, understanding that he'd just met someone dangerous—not because Noah was violent, but because he had nothing left to lose except purpose.

"I can't bring her back," Noah whispered quietly. "But I can make sure the next Lily has a chance. I can expose the architecture. Make them see what they've hidden."

"That's what I want too," Ethan avowed. "I just... I've been trying to work within the system."

"The system doesn't reform itself. It has to be hacked." Noah stood, shouldering his backpack. "If you're serious about understanding how money moves—how true power works—I can show you. But you have to be willing to see things that will make you uncomfortable."

"I'm in," Ethan professed.

Noah nodded once, something like relief crossing his face. "Then we'll change it together. For Lily. For all the people the system decides aren't worth saving."

He walked toward the exit, then paused. "Fair warning: once you look behind the curtain and see how this works, you can't unsee it. It will change how you look at the world."

"Good," Ethan added. "I'm tired of pretending the world makes sense."

Noah smiled—the first genuine smile Ethan had seen from him. "Then welcome to the truth, brother. It's going to ruin you."

Interstate 95 — Present

"So, he's motivated by personal loss," Selin contended when Ethan finished. "That's good. Makes him loyal but also potentially reckless. People driven by grief make choices based on emotion rather than strategy."

"He's brilliant," Ethan countered. "Whatever else he is, he's one of the smartest people I've ever met."

"Smart people die all the time. Usually because they overestimate their intelligence and underestimate their enemies." She changed lanes to pass a slow-moving truck. "But if he's stayed hidden this long, he must be good at what he does. We'll see."

They drove in silence for a while. Rain continued falling, turning the world outside into a gray blur. Ethan's mind kept returning to the flash drive in his backpack, to all the things Selin had told him about the Directorate, to the impossible situation he'd somehow stumbled into.

"Can I ask you something?" he finally positioned to her.

"You're going to anyway."

"Why did you leave? You told me it was because you didn't like what you saw, but that feels...incomplete. People simply don't walk away from organizations like that. Not without a trigger."

Selin's jaw tightened slightly. "There was an operation. Serbia, eight years ago. They tasked me with providing intelligence on a refugee convoy—routes, timing, security presence. Standard surveillance." Her voice went flat, carefully controlled. "I suspected the briefing was off. Too urgent, too clean. But I didn't question it. I passed the intelligence up the chain like I was trained to do."

"What happened?"

"The convoy was attacked. Forty-three people died. Men, women, children. Refugees who'd already survived one war, trying to reach safety." She kept her eyes on the road, but Ethan could see the tension in her shoulders. "I found out later that my intelligence had been used to target them. The Directorate had been paid to ensure they never reached their destination. Paid by people who wanted to send a message about accepting refugees."

"Jesus Christ" —Ethan interjected.

"I told myself it wasn't my fault"—Selin continued. "That I was following orders, gathering information. That I couldn't have known." Her knuckles turned white on the steering wheel. "But that's bullshit. I did know. I suspected. And I chose not to look too closely because looking would have complicated my life."

"That's not—"

"Don't." Her voice sharpened. "Don't tell me it wasn't my fault. Forty-three people are dead because I was a coward. Because I prioritized my safety over their lives. That's a fact. The only thing I get to control now is whether I let it happen again."

Ethan fell quiet, processing. Understanding a little better why she had risked her life to pull him out of Grand Central, why she was driving him toward Miami when she could have easily disappeared.

"That's why you're helping me," he phrased. "It's not only about revenge against the Directorate. It's also about the people in that convoy."

"Maybe. Or maybe I'm trying to feel like less of a monster." She glanced at him briefly. "Does it matter? The result is the same—I'm helping you, and together we might actually accomplish something that matters."

"It matters to me."

"Why?"

"Because it means you're not what Kessler made you. It means there's something he couldn't kill." Ethan surprised himself with the words, with how much he meant them. "That matters."

Selin didn't respond immediately. When she did, her voice turned quieter. "We'll see. Redemption is a luxury you earn, not something you declare. Right now, I'm focusing on surviving and taking them down as well. The rest is... complicated."

They continued south, the miles accumulating. Around noon, they stopped at a rest area outside New Haven. Selin filled the tank while Ethan bought sandwiches and coffee from the food court, both of them moving with the paranoid awareness of people who knew they were being hunted.

Back in the car, Selin handed him the keys. "Your turn. I need a few hours of sleep. Stay on 95, keep it at the speed limit, don't do anything that draws attention."

"I know how to drive," Ethan protested.

"You know how to commute. That's different than operational driving." But she already settled into the passenger seat, pulling her jacket up like a blanket. "Wake me if anything feels wrong. And I mean anything—cars that stay behind us too long, rest stops that feel off, cops that look at us twice."

"You think they're still tracking us?"

"I think assuming they're not not tracking us is how we die." She closed her eyes. "Three hours. Then we switch again."

Ethan pulled back onto the highway, hands gripping the wheel tighter than necessary. Behind him, Selin's breathing gradually slowed, deepened. Asleep in seconds—another skill she'd learned from her years in the field.

He drove through Connecticut, into New York, across into New Jersey. The rain lessened, then stopped, leaving gray skies and wet roads. Trucks rumbled past. Families in minivans headed to destinations that straight away seemed impossibly normal—vacations, visits to relatives, the ordinary movements of ordinary lives.

Ethan had left that world behind. Maybe forever.

Three hours later, as they approached Philadelphia, Selin woke without prompting. One moment sleeping, the next fully alert.

"Any problems?" she put to Ethan, like a good defense attorney grilling a state's witness.

"No. It's been quiet."

"Good." She stretched slightly, working out the stiffness of sleeping in a car. "Pull off at the next exit. We'll grab food and switch drivers. I want to push through to Virginia before we stop for real rest."

They found a diner off the highway—the kind of place where nobody asked questions and the coffee tasted like burnt optimism. Ethan slid into a booth in the back corner while Selin ordered at the counter, both of them automatically choosing positions where they could watch the entrance.

Ethan's burner phone was a cold weight in his pocket. He pulled it out, checked for messages. Nothing yet from Noah beyond that initial response: Havana Street. Sunset. Alone.

Except Ethan wouldn't be alone. He'd be bringing Selin.

He hoped Noah would understand.

The diner's TV was tuned to a news station, volume low but audible. Ethan half-listened to a story about traffic when the broadcast shifted.

"...breaking news out of Manhattan tonight."

Ethan's attention snapped to the screen.

The anchor's voice was calm, professional, practiced in tragedy. "A woman identified as Margaret Heller was struck and killed by a southbound train at the 68th Street station during the evening commute."

Ethan froze.

"Witness accounts vary, but several bystanders claim she appeared startled moments before the incident. Police have not ruled out the possibility of a medical event. At this time, investigators believe there is no indication of foul play."

A second voice chimed in—the network's transit correspondent. "Heller was a long time employee of International Mercantile Bank. According to early statements from the NYPD, surveillance footage is currently 'inconclusive' due to a malfunctioning camera on the platform."

Ethan's jaw locked.

"We'll continue to update this developing story as more information becomes available."

Selin returned to the table with coffee, took one look at his face, and slid into the booth. "What happened?"

"Margaret Heller. She worked in compliance at the bank. She..." Ethan's voice was hollow. "She tried to warn me. She pulled me aside. Told me to be careful who I trusted. That there were people at the bank was who weren't who they claimed to be."

"And now she's dead."

"Pushed in front of a train. They're calling it an accident. Malfunctioning surveillance camera." His hands trembled. "How many people, Selin? How many people must die because of this damn flash drive?"

"As many as they deem necessary." Her voice turned hard. "Whoever saw the data, anyone who helped you or who might testify. The Directorate doesn't leave witnesses. That's how they've operated invisibly for thirty years." She pushed the coffee toward him. "Margaret Heller is dead because she tried to help you. The question now is if her death means something, or whether her death is simply another name on their list."

"How do I make it mean something?"

"By surviving. By getting that data to people who can use it. By making sure the Directorate can't kill their way out of exposure." She glanced at the TV, then back to him. "Margaret knew the risks. She chose to warn you anyway. Honor that choice by finishing what you started."

Ethan stared at the pattern of raindrops still clinging to the diner's windows, his mind making connections he didn't want to make. Margaret had access to wire records. She had been in compliance for twenty-seven years. She would have seen the Apex transactions, would have recognized the patterns.

She had been eliminated. Professionally. Precisely. Like Latham.

"How many more?" he posed quietly. "How many more people die before this ends?"

"I don't know. But I can promise you this: The Directorate gets more exposed and vulnerable each time they kill to hide their actions. Because eventually, they'll kill a person connected to someone powerful who won't accept the official story. Someone who'll start asking the questions they can't answer." Selin's expression was fierce. "That's how empires fall—not from external attack, but from internal rot finally becoming visible."

"That's not much comfort to Margaret."

"No. But it's all we have." She stood. "Finish your coffee. We need to keep moving."

Ethan drained the cup, left cash on the table, and followed her back to the car. This time Selin drove, merging back onto 95 South with practiced ease.

"Tell me about Miami," she requested as they crossed into Delaware. "What's the plan when we get there?"

"Meet Noah at sunset. Havana Street—I'm guessing it's a bar or restaurant, somewhere public but not too exposed. He'll want to see the data, verify it's real. Then..." Ethan shrugged. "Then we figure out what to do with it. How to expose the Directorate without getting killed in the process."

"Public meeting is smart. Harder for them to move against us with witnesses." She glanced at him. "But you realize Noah is now a target too, right? The moment we make contact, the moment he touches that data, he's marked. Same as you, same as me."

"He knows the risks. He's been living with them for years."

"Has he?" Selin's voice carried doubt. "Being a hacker living underground is different than being actively hunted by an organization with unlimited resources and no moral constraints. One is inconvenient. The other is lethal."

"Noah's smart. He'll understand what he's getting into."

"Let's hope so. Because if he doesn't, we'll be attending his funeral within a week."

They drove in silence for a while, the afternoon stretching into evening as they pushed south through Maryland and into Virginia. They switched drivers again outside Richmond, Ethan taking the wheel while Selin dozed.

Around midnight, somewhere in North Carolina, Ethan's burner phone buzzed.

Selin snapped instantly awake. "What is it?"

Ethan checked the screen. A new message from Noah: Change of plans. Not Havana Street. Too exposed. Will send new location. Come alone.

"Fuck," Ethan muttered, showing her the message.

"He's smart," Selin conveyed. "Changing the meet location at the last minute, not committing to a specific place until the last moment. Basic counter-surveillance." She paused. "But 'come alone' is a problem."

"I'm not leaving you behind."

"I wasn't suggesting you should. But we need to handle this carefully. If Noah sees me and spooks, if he thinks you're compromised, he'll disappear and we'll lose our best technical resource." She thought for a moment. "I'll stay close but out of sight. Let you make initial contact alone. Once he's satisfied you're not being followed, I can join. But it has to be his decision."

"He'll understand once I explain."

"Maybe. Or maybe he will see a former Directorate operative and assume you've been turned." Selin's expression was serious. "Trust is hard, Ethan. Especially for people like Noah who have learned that the system is designed to betray you. You will need to convince him that I am on your side, and that's not going to be easy."

"Then I'll convince him."

"Let's hope so. Because if we can't bring Noah on board, your options for analyzing that data and building a case against the Directorate become limited real quick."

They continued south through the night, trading off driving every few hours, stopping only for gas and bathroom breaks. By dawn, they reached the Georgia state line. By mid-morning, they'd crossed into Florida.

"We're making good time," Selin offered as they passed Jacksonville. "We'll hit Miami by early afternoon. That gives us time to scout the area, find somewhere safe to wait, prepare for the meeting."

"And if it's a trap?" Ethan put forward. "If the Directorate got to Noah, turned him, used him to lure us in?"

"Then we die. But I don't think that's the case. If they'd compromised Noah, they would have kept the original meeting place. Changing it suggests he's still operating independently, still taking precautions." She glanced at him. "Besides, at this point, what choice do we have? We need technical expertise to weaponize that data. Noah's our best option."

"Our only option," Ethan corrected.

"True. But let's call it 'best' and pretend we have alternatives. It's better for morale."

Despite the darkness and death surrounding him, Ethan smiled. There was something about Selin's dark humor, her refusal to pretend their situation was anything other than desperate, that he found oddly comforting.

"What?" she implored, catching his expression.

"Nothing. Just... thank you. For this. For helping me when you could have walked away."

"I told you—I'm doing this for my own reasons."

"I know. But still. Thank you."

Selin was quiet for a moment. Then: "You're welcome. Now focus on the road. We've got about four more hours of driving, and I don't want to die in a dumb car accident after surviving what we have been through."

They drove on toward Miami, toward Noah, toward whatever came next. Behind them, Margaret Heller's death joined a growing list of casualties. Ahead, the Directorate's machinery turned, hunting them with patient precision.

But for now, they were on the move. Remaining ahead of the hunter. Still alive.

And sometimes, Ethan had learned, that was all you could ask for.

PART TWO—OLD SCORES

23

Moral Hacker

[CLASSIFIED: EYES ONLY/DIRECTORATE / NODE: CY-BER-12]

"Subject NOAH BYRNE exhibits asymmetrical morality — theft justified through ethical abstraction. Refrain from neutralization; potential for conversion remains high."

—Helios Digital Countermeasures Directorate, Asset Assessment Memo

Lisbon, Portugal — Summer 2023

The apartment above the pawn shop smelled like burnt solder and regret. Noah Byrne—he'd stopped using Rivera after the Interpol warrant—sat in the blue glow of three monitors, watching money move like blood through the body of the world.

On screen one: a corporate earnings call. The CEO of Cordovan Industries—a defense contractor—announced layoffs. Thirty-seven thousand workers. "Efficiency measures," he called it, smiling behind his podium.

On screen two: Cordovan's stock price. Up 8% in after-hours trading.

On screen three: the CEO's personal account. A $4.2 million bonus, wired from a Cayman subsidiary, scheduled to hit in fourteen hours.

Noah cracked his knuckles and got to work.

The fortress around Cordovan's financial systems looked impressive—military-grade encryption, triple-redundant firewalls, behavioral monitoring that flagged anomalous access patterns. The kind of security that cost more than most people earned in a lifetime.

But Noah wasn't most people.

He had spent three weeks mapping the network's topology, identifying the single contractor who serviced their HVAC systems and happened to have remote access for "environmental monitoring." It took Noah twelve minutes to clone the contractor's credentials and slip into the building management system.

From there, it was almost beautiful.

He threaded through the air gap between environmental controls and the financial network—a gap that existed only because someone assumed climate sensors couldn't be weaponized. He spoofed authentication tokens, borrowed processor cycles from idle workstations, and built a ghost pathway that existed only in the spaces between legitimate traffic.

By 3 a.m., he obtained root access to the core system.

The CEO's bonus sat in an internal escrow account, ready for transfer. Noah diverted it through a cascade of temporary wallets—seventeen jurisdictions in forty-five seconds—each layer adding encryption and anonymity. The money dissolved like sugar in water.

Then he reconstituted it.

Not to himself. Never to himself.

He split the $4.2 million into 3,700 micro-transactions of exactly $1,135.13 each. Each one routed to the personal accounts of the workers who'd been laid off. Not enough to be suspicious. But enough to be noticed.

A gift from nowhere.

A glitch in the system.

By the time the sun rose over Lisbon, the money was gone. Untraceable. Redistributed.

Noah leaned back in his chair, exhausted and wired. On screen two, confused posts already appeared on social media:

"Did anyone else get a random deposit this morning? $1,113.51? WTF?"

"Same here! Some kind of mistake?"

"My buddy who got laid off from Cordovan got it too. All of us did."

Noah allowed himself a small smile. Not from satisfaction—he'd stopped feeling that years ago. The smile was from confirmation. The math worked. The system could be bent, if you knew where to apply pressure.

He closed the terminal windows and opened a photo file buried in an encrypted partition.

Lily.

Twelve years old in the picture, gap-toothed, holding a science fair trophy. Second place for her project on water filtration. She had been furious about second place, even though Noah told her it was incredible for a sixth-grader.

"Second place is first loser," she had offered, scowling.

"Then next year we'll build something that wins," he had promised her.

There was no next year.

Richmond, Virginia — Fall 2012

The hospital room smelled like antiseptic and the kind of despair that settles into beige walls. Lily lay in the bed—small, pale, connected to machines that beeped with mechanical sympathy.

"Acute lymphoblastic leukemia," the doctor had conveyed. Clinical. Professional. "Aggressive, but treatable. The survival rate with proper treatment is quite good."

"How good?" Noah's mother had implored, her voice paper-thin.

"Over 80% with the full protocol. Chemotherapy, possibly radiation, and if needed, a bone marrow transplant."

"And the cost?"

The doctor's expression hadn't changed, but something in his eyes shifted. "Your insurance should cover most of it. There will be some out-of-pocket expenses."

Some turned out to mean $47,000.

Their insurance—the catastrophic-only plan his father's construction job provided—covered 60% after the deductible. The hospital offered a payment plan. The bank offered nothing.

They lost their house six months earlier when his father's hours were cut. They lived in his aunt's basement—him, Lily, their mother. His father had already started drinking away the shame, disappearing for days at a time.

Noah was nineteen years old. Sophomore year at Princeton, working nights at a data entry firm, learning to code from library books and pirated software. He had $1,800 in savings and a student loan debt that grew faster than he could comprehend.

It wasn't enough.

Nothing was ever enough.

Lily lasted six months. The hospital did what they could with the budget they had, but chemotherapy costs money, and insurance companies have actuaries who calculate the cost-benefit ratio of a twelve-year-old's life with decimal precision.

She died on a Tuesday, in the morning, while Noah worked a job entering insurance claims into a database for $11 an hour.

The irony wasn't lost on him.

Berlin Germany— Present Day

Noah closed the photo file. His hands didn't shake anymore when he thought about her. That had taken years.

The Cordovan hack wasn't revenge. Revenge was what his father had tried—drinking himself to death in a motel room, leaving a note that blamed everyone but himself and fixed nothing.

This was something else.

Redistribution. Rebalancing. Proof that the system wasn't immutable—that walls could be climbed, vaults opened, and most important —lies exposed if you proved patient and precise enough.

He called himself *Cipher Robin* as a joke, but the mythology fit. Take from the hoarded coffers, give to the dispossessed. Never keep a penny. Never take credit.

Stay invisible.

The problem with invisibility was loneliness. Three years on the run meant three years without real conversation, without trust, without anyone who knew his name—his real name, not the dozen aliases he burned through like matches.

Until tonight.

His phone—a encrypted device he checked twice a day from rotating VPNs—pinged with a message on a channel he had assumed died long ago.

"Noah. It's E. I need to see you. Off-grid. Miami. 24 hours."

Noah stared at the screen.

E. was Ethan Cole.

They had met at Princeton—two kids from nowhere trying to understand their broken world. Ethan had the intellect and the institutional access. Noah had the rage and the skills.

They stayed in touch after Noah dropped out and Ethan graduated, trading encrypted research notes, comparing findings. Ethan went to work for International Mercantile Bank, promising he would be an insider who could document the corruption.

Noah had gone underground.

Three years ago, Noah told Ethan he planned to disappear—that federal investigators were closing in on him, and anyone connected to him would become collateral damage. Ethan had tried to argue, but Noah cut the call.

He convinced himself it was safer for both of them.

Now Ethan was reaching out to him. Using their old emergency protocol.

Which meant two things—Ethan faced serious trouble. And Ethan still trusted him.

Noah's fingers moved across the keyboard, routing his reply through seven proxy servers.

"Havana Street. Sunset."

He hit send and immediately began preparations. Clean up protocols for the Berlin apartment, he would not be back. Exit route through the city. New identity documents. A charter flight to Miami under a German passport that would evaporate the moment he landed. Before he left, he stopped at the photo of Lily one more time.

"I know," he whispered quietly to the empty room. "I should stay hidden. Play it safe."

The picture offered no advice.

"But he came when I needed him once. At Princeton. When I felt alone and angry and didn't know what to do with either." Noah closed the laptop. "Maybe people like us don't get to play it safe. Maybe that's not what we're for." Noah had one more thing to do in Berlin before he left. It was critical to accomplish before he met Ethan. Noah did not feel pressure, in fact he detected a renewed sense of purpose.

He slung his go-bag over his shoulder and walked out. The Berlin twilight enveloped him—one more shadow in a city of shadows.

But this time, he was running *toward* something.

24

Fragments

"When it gets dark, and I'm scared, I think about lights. The kind that help people find their way home. Like lighthouses, or stars. I think that's what we should be. Lights for people who are lost. Even small lights matter in the dark." -Lily Grace Rivera

Richmond, Virginia—Fall 2012

Lily Rivera's hospital had the environment of a marked place where people came to slowly die. Noah Rivera sat beside his sister's bed, watching the IV drip clear fluid into her thin arm, counting each drop because counting proved easier than thinking.

Lily was twelve. She'd been fighting acute lymphoblastic leukemia for eight months. The first round of chemo had seemed promising—hair loss, nausea, exhaustion, but shrinking tumors. Hope.

Then the relapse. More aggressive. Resistant to treatment.

The doctor had used words like "options" and "protocols" and "aggressive intervention"—clinical language designed to obscure the simple truth that his baby sister was dying because the family couldn't afford to save her.

"Noah?" Lily's voice was paper-thin, barely there. She was awake, which was good. The morphine dosing meant she spent more time asleep than conscious lately.

"Right here, Lil." He leaned forward, taking her hand ever so gently. It was impossibly fragile—like tiny little bird bones wrapped in translucent skin, veins visible like rivers on a map.

"Did you bring the book?"

He had. *A Wrinkle in Time*—her favorite. They were reading it together, a chapter each night when she was lucid enough to follow the story. They had now reached chapter nine. Meg and Charles Wallace searching for their father across dimensions. Family refusing to give up on family.

The irony wasn't lost on Noah.

"Want me to read?" he gently put forward.

She nodded weakly. "But first—" She struggled to sit up. Noah adjusted the pillows behind her, trying not to notice how frail she had become, how little space she occupied in the hospital bed designed for adult patients.

"First what?"

"Tell me about the thing you're building. The code thing."

Noah smiled despite what Lily was going through. Even dying, Lily wanted to understand his work. She'd always been like that—curious about the world, asking questions until she understood not only the what but the why.

"It's called a cryptocurrency," he answered, settling back. "Digital money that nobody controls. Not banks, not governments, nobody. Just people helping people."

"Like how?"

"Okay, so—" He pulled out his notebook, started sketching. "Imagine money is like... puzzle pieces. Each piece has a number on it that proves it's real. When you want to send money to someone, you give them your puzzle piece, and there are people watching to make sure the trade is fair."

Lily's eyes brightened—that unique spark that meant she was following, understanding. "So nobody can cheat?"

"Nobody can cheat. And nobody can say you're not allowed to trade. The system treats all of us the same."

"Even people like me?" Her voice went quieter. "People who can't pay?"

Noah noticed something crack in his chest. "Especially people like you Lil. That's the whole point, building something that doesn't care if you're rich or poor. It works."

She fell quiet for a moment, her gaze lingering on his sketches with a mix of admiration and uncertainty. Then: "Will you finish it?

"I'll finish it."

"Promise?"

"I promise." He took her hand again. "One day, when you're better, I'll show you the whole thing. All the lines of code. Each transaction. You'll be the first person to truly understand it."

Lily smiled—that gap-toothed grin that had been melting his heart since she was born. "I'd like that."

But they both knew she wouldn't be better. The doctors had stopped pretending three weeks ago. Now they moved to using used words like "comfortable" and "quality of life" and "making memories."

"Read to me please Noah".

Noah opened the book, found their place. Meg and Charles Wallace and Calvin, fighting against the darkness, refusing to abandon Mr. Murry even when everything seemed hopeless.

He kept reading as Lily's breathing became slow and even, her hand loosening its grip on his. The steady sound of the heart monitor gently eased her into dreams softened by morphine, where hopefully her pain faded and death no longer hovered near.

Noah continued reading anyway, hoping Lily might hear his voice even in her sleep. The words were important, whether or not she could understand them. Stopping would feel like surrender—and Noah was determined not to give up on Lily.

The nurse came in around midnight—Michelle, the night shift regular who'd been kind when other staff had been merely professional.

"You should go home, honey," she mentioned softly. "Get some rest. We'll call if anything changes."

"I'm staying."

"Noah—"

"I'm staying." His voice sounded firm but not angry. Absolute and certain. "She wakes up scared sometimes. I need to be here."

Michelle nodded, understanding. "I'll bring you a blanket. And some terrible hospital coffee."

She left. Noah set down the book, looked at his sister's face in the dim light from the monitors. She looked peaceful now. The pain medication did that—smoothed away the tension, made her look more like the Lily from before cancer had carved her down to bone and will.

His phone buzzed. Text from his mom: *Any change?*

He typed back: *Sleeping. Comfortable. You should rest.*

Can't. I'll be there in the morning.

His mother had been sleeping at the hospital more nights than not. But tonight she had gone home—forced by exhaustion and the visiting rules that limited overnight stays to immediate family, one at a time.

Noah's father was...somewhere. Supposedly working. But the family knew he had been disappearing into bottles since the diagnosis, unable to face the slow horror of watching his daughter die. Noah tried not to hate him for it. Tried to understand that people processed grief differently.

He mostly failed at the understanding part.

Around 2 a.m., Lily stirred. Her eyes opened, unfocused at first, then finding Noah's face.

"You're still here," she whispered.

"Always."

"Liar. You have to leave sometime."

"Then I'll always come back. How's that?"

She smiled. "Better." A pause. "Noah? I'm scared."

He moved closer, brushing hair from her forehead. "I know, Lil. Me too."

"Not about dying." Her voice sounded remarkably steady for someone twelve years old discussing her own mortality. "About being forgotten. About not... mattering. Like I was here and then I wasn't and nothing changed."

Noah made out that his tears were burning but he pushed them back. She needed him strong right now. Falling apart could happen later. "You matter," he asserted fiercely. "You matter more than anything. And I'm going to make sure the world remembers."

"How?"

"The thing I'm building. It's going to be called AURORA. After the lights."

"The northern lights?" Lily had seen pictures in a National Geographic at the dentist's office, had been fascinated by them. "Why?" —Lily asked.

"Because you told me they looked like magic. Like hope painted on the sky." He swallowed hard. "And because what I'm building is about hope too. About making sure nobody else dies because the system decides they're not worth the cost."

Lily's eyes closed again, morphine and exhaustion pulling her back under. "That's good," she murmured. "I like that. AURORA. Pretty."

"You're pretty," Noah expressed with deep love for his baby sister, tears welling up and his voice cracking despite his efforts.

She smiled one last time. "Liar."

Then the morphine and sleep took her again.

Noah sat back, watching her breathe—in and out, in and out, each breath a small victory against the cancer eating her from the inside. He pulled out his laptop, opened his code editor, and began to work.

Lines of code appeared on the screen. Algorithms designed to resist central control, to distribute power so thoroughly that no single entity could stop the flow of resources to people who needed them.

He coded through the night, fingers flying across keys, building something that might outlast him, outlast her, might change a system that had decided his sister's life wasn't worth saving.

As dawn broke through the hospital window, Lily stirred one more time. She looked at Noah, at the laptop screen covered in code she couldn't read but somehow understood.

"You're going to do it," she insisted.

"I'm going to do it"—Noah replied.

"Good." She closed her eyes. "Good."

Lily died three days later. Peacefully, the doctors affirmed. As peacefully as anyone could die at twelve, drowning in their own failing lungs, surrounded by machines that beeped and hummed but couldn't save her.

Noah was holding his baby sister's hand when she passed. He sensed the exact moment when her beautiful presence became silent absence, when his sister became a memory.

At the funeral, people stated things like "She's in a better place" and "God has a plan" and "At least she's not suffering anymore." Empty platitudes that meant nothing, words people spoke because silence proved too honest.

Noah stood beside the casket—closed, because the disease had made Lily too thin for viewing, the medical interventions too visible—and he made a promise to her.

"I'm going to finish it, Lil. I'm going to build AURORA. I'm going to make them pay for the deaths like yours. Pay for families broken because the system decides love isn't cost-effective. I'm going to burn the whole damn system down and build something better in its place."

He wiped his eyes. "And when I do, everyone will know I did it for you. You won't be forgotten. I promise. You won't ever be forgotten."

The burial was brief. Small gathering—their mother, a few aunts and uncles, some of Lily's classmates who didn't know what to say. His father was there but not, eyes glazed with alcohol and grief in equal measure.

Afterwards, Noah went home, locked himself in his room, and coded for sixteen hours straight.

He built the first version of AURORA that day. Crude, incomplete, but functional. A system designed to do one thing: redistribute wealth from people who had too much to people who didn't have enough.

Robin Cipher as algorithm.

Justice as code.

His sister, immortalized in mathematics.

Berlin Germany— Noah-Present Day

Noah stared at Lily's photograph—the one taken at the science fair, second place trophy in her hands, gap-toothed smile wide enough to split the world in half.

He'd carried this photo for thirteen years. Through eighteen countries, four near-captures, and countless nights when giving up would have been easier than continuing.

But he couldn't give up. Because giving up would mean Lily died for nothing. Would mean the system that killed her continued unchanged, continued calculating which lives were worth saving and which counted as acceptable losses.

"I kept my promise," he whispered to her frozen smile. "AURORA is real. Three million users. One billion dollars redistributed. Fifty-three countries. People are getting treatment now, Lil. People like you. The system shut the door on us, and AURORA opened it, and lives are being saved."

He set the photo down gently, returned to his laptop. The code scrolled past—beautiful, elegant, perfect. A weapon built from grief and love in equal measure.

On screen, another request appeared: Medical funding for a twelve-year-old in Bolivia. Leukemia. Family couldn't afford treatment.

Noah approved it without hesitation. $26,000 in Bolivian currency transferred instantly.

"That's for you, Lily," he noted. "That one's for you."

Somewhere in Bolivia, a family would get a call saying the money had appeared. They would probably cry. Wonder if it was a mistake. But the treatment would go forward. The child would have a chance.

The chance Lily never got.

Noah looked at the photograph one more time. "I'm coming to the end, I think. Kessler's closing in. Ethan needs me for something big. I might not make it out."

He wiped his eyes. "But if I don't—if this is it—know that I kept my promise. AURORA is alive. It's growing. It's saving people. You mattered, Lil. You mattered more than anyone."

His encrypted phone buzzed. Message from Ethan: *"Noah. It's E. I need to see you. Off-grid. Miami. 24 hours."*

Noah typed back: *"Understood. Will be there and ready to go. For Lily."*

He closed the laptop, picked up the photograph, held it close.

Somewhere in Richmond, Virginia, in a cemetery he hadn't visited in years, a gravestone bore simple words:

LILY GRACE RIVERA

Beloved Daughter & Sister

She Believed in Magic

And in an unassuming warehouse, her brother had built that magic into code, line by line, transforming grief into justice, loss into legacy.

AURORA wasn't only cryptocurrency.

It was a twelve-year-old girl who had died asking if she would be forgotten.

It was her brother's promise that she wouldn't be.

And it was working.

25

Ghost Entente

"They think I'm here to steal something. I'm here to remind them their empire runs on lies...and lies always leave a backdoor." —Robin Cipher

Directorate Node Berlin, Germany—2:14 a.m. local time- Day 5

Rain fell like static over Kreuzberg— steady, cold, cleansing the streets of sound and witnesses. The kind of rain that made people pull their collars up and hurry home, that emptied sidewalks and created shadows. Perfect weather for breaking and entering.

Noah Byrne, known in Dark Web circles as Robin Cipher, adjusted the collar of his gray maintenance jacket and approached the biometric gate of the Helios Systems European Data Integration Center.

The building was a sprawling concrete bunker squatting in an industrial district, deliberately unremarkable, designed to be invisible. No corporate logos. No signage beyond a small placard with an address. Smooth concrete walls, narrow windows with reinforced glass, and the quiet hum of serious money protecting serious secrets.

Six floors above ground, three below. One of the crown jewels of the Directorate's European operations, disguised as a corporate data center. Every transaction, shell companies, and all encrypted communications in the eastern hemisphere flowed through the servers buried in its basement. A billion lives reduced to machine language, all of it controlled from here.

And Noah was about to walk through the front door.

He carried a plastic toolbox in his left hand and an old-fashioned analog multimeter dangling from his belt—props for the part, but functional enough to pass inspection. The badge clipped to his chest read "J. Keller — Systems Cooling Contractor," complete with a grainy photo that looked enough like him to fool a tired security guard but not enough to survive facial recognition software.

The name would hold if anyone checked. Helios's contractor database had been quietly edited forty-eight hours ago by Noah himself, backdooring through their payroll system using credentials stolen from an actual HVAC company in Munich. J. Keller had permits, insurance, work history. On paper, he was legitimate.

On paper was all that mattered until you got caught.

The outer gate ran completely automated—RFID scanner, card reader, biometric backup. Noah swiped the cloned badge and pressed his thumb to the reader, holding his breath. He'd lifted the fingerprint from a beer glass two days ago, photographed it, printed it onto a thin latex membrane now pressed over his own thumb. Old-school tradecraft, but it worked.

The scanner beeped. Green light. The gate clicked open.

First hurdle cleared.

Noah stepped into the outer courtyard, a kill zone of open concrete lit by sodium lamps that turned courtyard into the color of jaundice. Security cameras tracked him from three angles—he could feel their lenses following his movement, digital eyes feeding footage to monitors somewhere in a basement control room. He walked slowly, deliberately, like a man who belonged here. Like a contractor called in for an emergency repair at two in the morning, tired and annoyed but professional.

He had spent two weeks studying this place. Shift schedules, access logs, security rotations. He knew that Camera 3 had a dead zone near the northeast entrance. He knew the guards rotated every four hours and were least alert during the 2-4 a.m. window. He knew they drank Lavazza espresso with two sugars and got sloppy when they were bored.

Espionage wasn't about brilliance. It relied heavily on patience. About knowing your enemy better than they knew themselves.

A glass vestibule formed the main entrance, leading to a security checkpoint—airport-style scanners, metal detector, X-ray conveyor. Two guards sat behind bulletproof glass, both in their thirties, both carrying Glock 19s in hip holsters. The one on the left looked like a zombie, focused intently on his phone—more than likely on social media. The one on the right watched Noah approach with professional disinterest.

Noah set his toolbox on the conveyor belt and stepped through the metal detector. It beeped—the multimeter on his belt. He unclipped it, held it up, smiled apologetically.

"Forgot this thing," he articulated in German, his accent deliberately rough—working-class Berlin, not educated Hamburg. "Been a long night."

The guard waved him through without looking up. "Service elevator's down the hall, left at the end."

"Danke."

Noah collected his toolbox and walked deeper into the building, heart rate climbing but breathing steady. Through the metal detector. Past the guards. Inside the perimeter. Each step he took was now on borrowed time.

The interior had the appearance of sterility—white walls, LED strips, polished floors that reflected the ceiling lights in perfect symmetry. The air was refrigerated to sixty-two degrees, cold enough to preserve the quantum servers that formed the Directorate's digital empire, cold enough to make Noah's breath visible in brief puffs.

He counted cameras as he walked. One every twenty feet, overlapping fields of view, no dead zones. Motion sensors in the corners. RFID readers on the doors. This wasn't a corporate office. This was a vault.

The service elevator required another badge swipe. Noah used it, and the doors opened with a pneumatic hiss. He stepped inside and pressed the button for Sub-Level 3—the lowest accessible floor, where the core servers lived. The elevator descended in silence, the digital display counting down: 1... G... -1... -2... -3.

The doors opened onto a corridor of white light, narrow and clinical, like the inside of a hospital or a submarine. The temperature dropped another ten degrees. The hum of cooling systems filled the air, a constant mechanical drone that made his ears ring. Overhead, pipes ran along the ceiling—water cooling, fiber optic, power conduit. Unmarked concrete made up the walls, no decoration, no humanity. Pure function.

At the end of the corridor was a sealed glass door, reinforced and triple-paned, with a placard that read: CORE NODE ACCESS — AUTHORIZED PERSONNEL ONLY.

Beyond it, Noah could see the glow of server racks—row after row of blinking lights, blue and green, pulsing like a digital heartbeat.

He set his toolbox on the floor and knelt beside the access panel mounted next to the door. Standard electromagnetic lock, keycard reader, and a backup biometric scanner. Three layers of security. Any one of them could stop him.

Noah pulled a small fiber-optic jack from his sleeve—custom-built, no bigger than a USB drive—and slid it into the maintenance port hidden beneath the panel's faceplate. On his wrist terminal, a coded interface blossomed, lines of script cascading in green phosphor. He typed quickly, fingers flying across the virtual keyboard, exploiting a firmware vulnerability he'd discovered weeks ago.

"Come on, sweetheart," he whispered. "One more favor."

The system resisted. Encryption layers peeling back slowly, security protocols fighting him at every step. Sweat beaded on his forehead despite the cold. Somewhere above him, cameras recorded his movements. Somewhere, an algorithm might be flagging his behavior as anomalous.

Ten seconds. Twenty. Thirty.

Then—a muted click. The electromagnetic lock disengaged. The glass door slid open with a soft hiss.

Noah exhaled and stepped inside.

A cathedral of circuitry formed the core chamber. Server racks towered on both sides, fifteen feet high, their panels glowing with the quiet arrogance of absolute control. The air hummed with electromagnetic fields. The floor sat raised, cables running beneath it in organized chaos. Overhead, cooling ducts snaked across the ceiling, condensation dripping from their joints.

This formed the nerve center. The brain. All transactions, encrypted directives, even digital fingerprints of the Directorate's global operations lived here.

Noah approached the nearest console—a terminal workstation with four monitors, all displaying diagnostic readouts and system logs. He inserted a wafer-thin drive into the USB port and initiated the extraction protocol. On the screen, directories began to unfold: HELIOS DEFENSE SYSTEMS. GLOBAL NEWS SYNDICATE. EIC COMPACT. MERIDIAN STRATEGIC SOLUTIONS.

Names, ledgers, encrypted directives. Corporate structures. Shell companies. Wire transfers spanning continents. The architecture of the Directorate unfolded in silence before him, each directory more damning than the last.

For a moment, Noah forgot to breathe. He wasn't only stealing data. He was holding proof that the world's chaos did not happen randomly—it unfolded by design. Orchestrated. Profited from.

Then a soft alarm chirped.

He froze, eyes snapping to the monitor. A red thread of code pulsed across the screen—a counter-trace program, an adaptive watchdog sniffing for intruders. It had detected the data extraction, backtracking through the network, hunting for the source.

"Shit."

The progress bar on his extraction reached seventy-two percent. Not enough. He needed to reach one hundred percent. But the alarm continued escalating, cycling through warning levels, about to trigger a full lockdown.

Eighty percent. Eighty-five percent.

Then he heard it: footsteps echoing down the corridor. Not the casual shuffle of a security guard. Deliberate. Synchronized. Military precision.

Internal Response. The Directorate's private security force.

Ninety-three percent. Ninety-seven percent.

The extraction completed with a soft chime. Noah ejected the drive, shoved it into his pocket, and wiped the cache, initiating a false maintenance log to mask his entry. Then he killed the terminal and looked around frantically for an exit.

The glass door he'd come through remained the only way out. But voices were approaching—close now, ten to fifteen seconds away at most.

Noah looked up. The ventilation duct.

He grabbed a chair, climbed onto a server rack, and pried open the vent cover with his multimeter. The duct was narrow—barely two feet square—was he small enough? No time for hope. He pulled himself up, metal edges scraping his shoulders, and dragged the vent cover back into place precisely at the moment the corridor lights snapped on.

Through the slats, he saw three men in tactical gray sweep into the core chamber. They moved like operators—weapons low, eyes scanning corners, checking angles. Two carried H&K MP7 submachine guns. The third had a tablet, tracking something.

One spoke quietly into his comm, voice flat and professional. "We have a phantom signature. Node breach confirmed. External source."

Another replied, "Lock the grid. Nobody leaves the compound. Initiate isolation protocol."

As the guards proceeded with their sweep, Noah crawled deeper into the duct, moving as quietly as possible, lungs burning from shallow breathing. Below him, he heard the tactical team spreading out, checking terminals, reviewing logs. One of them stood directly beneath him now, close enough that Noah could hear his radio crackle.

"Console was accessed four minutes ago. Data extraction in progress until—" The man paused. "Extraction completed. Files copied to external drive."

"How the hell did he get in?"

"Maintenance access. Cloned credentials. He's good."

"Not good enough. Find him."

Noah kept moving, reaching the far end of the duct where it branched into two directions. Left led back toward the main building. Right led toward the mechanical rooms. He went right, dropping down into a maintenance tunnel lit by emergency lighting—red bulbs every twenty feet, casting the tunnel in a hellish shadow.

Behind him, he heard the sound of systems shutting down, servers going dark one by one as the facility entered lockdown mode. Power rerouted. Doors sealing. The entire building was quickly transforming into a cage.

He sprinted through the tunnel, boots echoing on concrete, following the exit signs toward the emergency stairwell. Somewhere above, alarms began to wail—a low, mechanical shriek that built in intensity, filling the entire structure.

He reached a junction and saw the stairwell door ahead, marked with a glowing green sign. He slammed through it and started climbing, taking stairs three at a time. Sub-Level 3 to Sub-Level 2. Sub-Level 2 to Sub-Level 1.

At the ground level, he burst through the door into a corridor—and came face-to-face with a security guard.

The man appeared young, surprised, hand dropping toward his holster. Noah didn't give him time to draw. He closed the distance in two strides, drove his palm into the guard's solar plexus, followed with an elbow to the temple. The guard dropped like a puppet with cut strings.

Noah grabbed the man's radio and badge, then kept moving. The main corridor lay straight ahead, but he could hear boots pounding on tile—more guards responding to the alarm. He veered left, following a secondary hallway marked LOADING BAY.

A concrete cavern formed the bay, with three roll-up doors, all closed. A delivery truck sat idle, engine off. Noah looked around frantically—no obvious exit, no way out except through those doors.

He ran to the control panel beside Door 2 and swiped the stolen badge. Red light. Access denied. He tried Door 1. Same result. The system had completely locked down the building, nothing getting in or out.

Behind him, voices echoed in the hallway. Close. Maybe ten seconds.

Noah looked at the delivery truck. Keys in the ignition—a small miracle. He climbed into the cab, fired the engine, and slammed it into gear. The truck lurched forward, tires screeching on polished concrete.

He aimed for Door 2 and floored the accelerator.

The truck hit the roll-up door at thirty-five miles per hour. Metal screamed. The door buckled, tore free from its track, and collapsed outward in a shower of bolts and aluminum panels. The truck plowed through, emerging into the courtyard in an explosion of debris.

Alarms shrieked. Floodlights snapped on, turning night into day. Noah kept driving, smashing through the outer gate, the truck's bumper tearing through chain-link like tissue paper.

Then he reached the street, accelerating into Kreuzberg's empty industrial avenues. Behind him, the Helios building was a blaze of lights and sirens, security teams spilling out like ants from a kicked mound.

Noah drove three blocks, abandoned the truck in an alley, and ran. His lungs burned. His hands shook from adrenaline. He had escaped. Barely. But he was alive and that was what mattered.

He tossed the maintenance jacket into a dumpster, peeled off the latex fingerprint, and merged into the sparse crowd of late-night commuters heading for the U-Bahn station. By the time he boarded the nearly empty train, his breathing had steadied, his heart rate dropping back to normal.

The rain hit the windows in sheets as the train pulled away from the platform. Noah sat in a corner seat, watching the city lights blur into streaks of color. The stolen drive sat in his pocket—weightless, yet heavy as guilt, heavy as proof.

Across from him, a digital billboard flickered with breaking news: GOVERNMENT CRISIS IN EASTERN EUROPE. MARKETS IN FREEFALL. The chaos he'd seen orchestrated inside that building was now playing out on public screens, millions of lives disrupted by algorithms and offshore accounts.

Noah looked down at his reflection in the window, water dripping from his hair, face pale with exhaustion. He had done it. He had actually broken into the Directorate's nerve center and walked out with their secrets.

But in the reflection, he caught something else: another passenger, three seats back, watching him. Young, pale, intense. For a heartbeat their eyes met in the glass. Then the passenger looked away, pulled out a phone, and typed a message Noah couldn't see.

The train descended into the tunnel, and when it emerged at the next station, the passenger had vanished.

Noah smiled faintly, though his hands were still shaking. He bought himself a head start. Maybe twelve hours before they connected all the dots. Maybe less.

He had to get to Miami and meet Ethan. He needed to make sure these files reached someone who could use them before the Directorate erased him from existence.

He muttered to himself, watching Berlin disappear into rain and darkness, "You bastards think you own the signal. Let's see how you handle the noise."

He pushed himself deeper into the night, away from the burning wreckage of his infiltration, toward whatever came next. Tonight, he had shown what he was truly made of—not only a hacker, not simply an analyst, but an operator. Someone willing to walk into the lion's den and take what he needed.

Now he had to stay alive long enough to use it.

26

Response

Kessler — Private Diary (Zurich-0 Archive: Unclassified)
"Usefulness is a season, not a promise. Yours has passed Mein Lieber Freund."

Directorate Signal Operations Geneva—6:07 a.m. local time-Day 5

Computer monitors glowed in shades of blue and red — each pulse a warning, each warning a heartbeat skipping toward cardiac arrest. Rows of analysts in soundproof headsets stared at cascading lines of code that moved faster than thought, faster than prayer, tracking digital ghosts across continents.

The Geneva Node occupied three floors of an anonymous office building near the lake, its entrance marked only by a brass plaque reading "Helvetic Data Services AG"—a company that appeared legitimate on the public registry but existed solely as camouflage for the Directorate's European signal operations hub. Inside, twenty-three hundred active nodes across sixty-two countries pulsed with data, all transactions monitored, every anomaly flagged, each threat assessed and catalogued.

This forged the nervous system of the empire. And tonight, someone had driven a knife into its spine.

Viktor Hess, section chief and former Swiss military intelligence officer, walked the operations floor with the rigid posture of a man who understood that failures at this level had permanent consequences. The last division head who'd allowed a breach had "committed suicide" by falling from a Lucerne hotel window—seventeen floors, no note, closed casket funeral. Hess had attended. Had seen the widow's face, carefully composed. Had understood the message.

In the Directorate, there were no accidents. Only consequences.

"Status on Berlin?" Hess demanded, stopping at the primary console where a Croatian hacker named Josip—offered employment instead of prison three years ago—was pulling up breach timelines.

"Initial penetration at 02:37 local Berlin time," Josip remarked, his accent thick, fingers flying across the keyboard. "Manual access via maintenance subnet, bypassed three security protocols using what appears to be... insider knowledge."

"Appears to be?" Hess's voice dropped dangerously low. "Either they had insider knowledge or they didn't."

"They did, sir. No question. They knew exactly where to look, which systems to access, how to mask their digital signature until extraction was complete. Professional work. Top end professional."

Hess sensed his stomach tighten. Professional meant training. Training meant connections. Connections meant this didn't come from an opportunistic hacker, but a targeted operation by someone who understood the Directorate's architecture.

"What did they take?"

"Core financial records. Operational directives. Corporate structures. All records and data linking shell companies to active operations. Essentially—" Josip swallowed. "Everything."

The operations floor fell silent. Even the keyboards stopped clicking. Twenty analysts held their breath, waiting for Hess's response, knowing that this breach—this catastrophic failure—would ripple upward through the organization until it reached the top.

Until it reached Kessler.

Hess crossed the floor to a secured terminal at the far wall—the kind reserved for communications that didn't officially exist, that left no logs, no traces, no evidence of having occurred. He entered a sixteen-digit code, waited for the click that meant the system had jumped across three encrypted relays and one undersea fiber cable.

The line opened. Static hissed for three seconds. Then a voice came through—calm, precise, unmistakable. European accent polished smooth by decades of operating in shadows.

"Report," Kessler requested.

Hess had heard that voice only twice before—once during his recruitment, when Kessler had offered him money and purpose, and once during a disciplinary review when another division had failed to contain a leak. Both times, Kessler had spoken with the same clinical detachment, as though discussing weather patterns rather than human lives. No anger. No concern. Simply the expectation of compliance.

Hess delivered the briefing with military precision, omitting nothing. In his experience, men like Kessler punished incompleteness more severely than failure itself. When he finished, silence filled the encrypted line. Hess could hear his own heartbeat, the soft hum of servers, the distant click of keyboards. Somewhere in that silence, judgments were being rendered.

"The Berlin Director," Kessler vocalized finally, his voice unchanged, "is Hans Volker, yes?"

"Yes, sir."

"Married. Two children—a daughter, fourteen, and a son, eleven."

Hess all of a sudden was cold, like ice water was flowing in his veins. "That's correct, sir."

"Get him on the line. Conference call. I want the second-in-command present as well."

"Sir—"

"Now, Viktor if you would please."

Hess's hands moved automatically, patching through to the Berlin node's emergency line. Two rings. Three. Then a breathless voice: "Volker."

Hans Volker, fifty-two, twenty-three years with the Directorate, a meticulous bureaucrat who'd risen through ranks by never making mistakes. Until tonight.

"Director Volker," Hess stated, his voice tight. "You're being conferenced with Geneva central command. Stand by."

Another click. "Deputy Director Richter on the line." Klaus Richter, thirty-eight, former GSG-9, Volker's second-in-command. Ambitious. Competent. Waiting for his chance to move up.

"Gentlemen," Kessler's voice cut through like a scalpel. "I trust you understand the severity of tonight's events."

"Sir, I—" Volker began, his voice shaking slightly. "I take full responsibility. We're implementing new security protocols, reviewing all personnel files, conducting integrity sweeps—"

"Hans," Kessler interrupted, his tone almost gentle. "May I call you Hans?"

"Of course, sir."

"Hans, do you know what I find most interesting and unique about our organization?" Kessler paused, but it wasn't a question that required answering. "We have built something magnificent. A machine that operates with such precision that the world doesn't even know it is being controlled. Markets rise and fall at our direction. Governments collapse or flourish based on our decisions. We are, in an exceedingly real sense, the invisible hand of history."

Volker added nothing. In Geneva, Hess watched his own hands grip the edge of the console, knuckles white.

"But such a machine," Kessler continued, his voice taking on a professorial quality, almost pleasant, "requires absolute precision. Each component must function perfectly. A single gear that slips, a single bolt that loosens—it threatens the entire mechanism. You understand this, yes?"

"Yes, sir," Volker managed.

"Your daughter," Kessler announced, and the shift in topic was so sudden, so jarring, that Hess actually flinched. "Emma, isn't it? Fourteen years old. Excellent student. Plays violin. Quite talented, I'm told."

Silence on the line. Then Volker's voice, barely above a whisper: "Sir... please..."

"And your son, Gerhardt. Eleven. Enjoys football. Plays striker for his school team. Promising athlete." Kessler's tone remained conversational, almost warm. "You're a family man, Hans. That's admirable. In our line of work, it's rare to maintain such... connections. Such vulnerabilities."

"Please," Volker muttered again, and now naked terror came up in his voice. "Whatever you want, whatever you need—I'll fix this. I'll find whoever—"

"Hans, Hans, Hans," Kessler voiced while smiling, and something almost paternal emerged in his voice, a teacher disappointed by a promising student's failure. "You misunderstand. I'm not here to negotiate. I'm here to teach. You see, failure in our organization isn't merely a professional setback. It's a philosophical problem. It demonstrates incompetence. And incompetence demonstrates... a lack of usefulness."

The silence stretched. Hess could hear Volker's ragged breathing over the line, could imagine the man's face pale and sweating, his world collapsing around him.

"So I am going to give you a choice," Kessler added pleasantly. "A simple choice, actually. You have two children. I need you to tell me which one should die for your incompetence."

The words hung in the air like poison gas.

"No," Volker replied immediately, the word torn from his throat. "No, no, please, God, no—"

"Your daughter or your son, Hans. Choose."

"I can't—I won't—please, sir, they're children, they have nothing to do with—"

"They have everything to do with it," Kessler replied, his voice hardening slightly, while still smiling. "They are the leverage that keeps you useful. The reason you work so diligently, so carefully, to maintain your position. But you have failed, Hans. The machine has been compromised because of your incompetence. So now we must recalibrate. Choose."

Volker continued sobbing, harsh gasps that came through the encrypted line like static. "Please... please don't make me..."

"Your daughter, Emma, with her violin and her bright future? Or your son, Gerhardt, with his football dreams? Which one must die, Hans? You have ten seconds."

"I CAN'T!" Volker screamed. "I can't do it, I won't, you can't make me—"

"Five seconds."

"Kill me," Volker begged, his voice breaking. "Please, just kill me, leave them alone, they're innocent—"

"Three seconds."

"I CAN'T CHOOSE!" Volker screamed and sobbed simultaneously now, the sound of a man's soul tearing apart. "Don't make me choose, please God, don't make me—"

"Time's up," Kessler announced, and his voice returned to that calm, clinical tone. "Deputy Director Richter, are you still on the line?"

A pause. Then: "Yes, sir." Richter's voice was steady, controlled. If he was disturbed by what he'd just heard, he didn't show it.

"Congratulations on your promotion to Berlin Director, effective immediately."

"Thank you, sir."

"Your first order of business is to eliminate Director Volker. I trust you're armed, yes?"

"I am, yes sir."

"Then please proceed. Hans, I want you to understand that this is a teaching moment for the entire organization. Failure is not merely disappointing—it is fatal. Director Richter, you may execute the order."

"No—" Volker's voice, desperate, pleading. "Klaus, please, we've worked together for seven years, you know me, you know I—"

Two sounds came through the line in rapid succession: the metallic click of a pistol slide, then a single gunshot. A heavy thud followed—a body hitting the floor.

Silence.

In Geneva, Hess realized he'd stopped breathing. Around him, the operations floor sat frozen, the ashen faced analysts staring at their screens or the floor or anywhere but at each other.

"Director Richter," Kessler verbalized, his voice unchanged, as if nothing had occurred. "Are we clear?"

"Yes, sir. Target neutralized."

"Excellent".—Kessler responded, almost gleeful. "Now, regarding Director Volker's family—his wife and two children. Do you have assets positioned to handle this matter?"

Hess's stomach lurched, like clutch being released too quickly. Not the children. Surely even Kessler wouldn't—

"I can have a team at the residence within fifteen minutes, sir," Richter replied.

"Well done. Now listen carefully, Klaus—and this applies to everyone on this call. What happened tonight in Berlin amounted to failures by former Director Volker. Most definitely not a failure of the organization. Director Volker's family had no involvement in his incompetence. They are not assets, they are not threats, they are simply... irrelevant."

Kessler paused, and when he continued, his voice carried a different weight—not mercy, exactly, but calculation. "However, they can still be useful in the future. The wife is an attorney. The children are students. All three are German citizens with clean records. We can't have bodies appearing that might draw investigation. That would be... inefficient."

"Understood, sir."

"Here is what you will do. The wife will receive notification that her husband died of a heart attack at his office tonight. Tragic, but not suspicious. She will be given his pension and a generous compensation package. The children will continue their education undisturbed. But—" Kessler's voice hardened.

"They will be watched. If the wife shows any signs of curiosity about her husband's actual work, if she contacts journalists or lawyers or anyone asking questions, then we revisit this conversation. If the children, when they grow older, show any indication of investigating their father's death, we revisit this conversation. Are we clear?"

"Crystal clear, sir."

"Excellent. This way, they remain useful—as leverage against anyone who might be tempted to follow Director Volker's example. A living reminder is far more effective than corpses."

Kessler's voice softened again, becoming almost philosophical. "You see, Klaus, this is the difference between brutality and precision. Brutality is emotional. Precision is eternal."

"Yes, sir. I understand completely."

"I'm sure you do. That's why you're now the Berlin Director. Now, regarding tonight's breach—I want a complete after-action report within twelve hours. Every single entry point, each compromised system, each and every second of the intruder's presence. Viktor, you're coordinating from Geneva. Klaus, you're implementing new protocols in Berlin. And gentlemen—" Kessler paused for emphasis. "There will be no further failures. The next person who fails will not be given the luxury of a bullet. Am I understood?"

"Yes, sir," both men conveyed in unison.

"One more thing, Klaus. The intruder who breached our systems tonight—this was professional work. Someone trained, someone with access to our protocols. I want you to consider the possibility that this wasn't an outside attack but an inside operation. Someone within our organization may have provided assistance."

"I'll begin internal audits immediately, sir."

"Do that. But Klaus?" Kessler's voice took on an almost friendly quality. "When you find them—and you will find them—don't kill them immediately. I want them brought to me. I want to meet someone bold enough to steal from the Directorate. Such audacity deserves a personal conversation before it's... corrected."

"Understood, sir."

"Wonderful. Then I believe we've covered all important matters. Gentlemen, do make sure tonight's lesson isn't lost on your teams. Failure equals incompetence. Incompetence equals a lack of usefulness. And there is no room in our organization for those who aren't useful. Good night."

The line clicked dead.

Hess stood frozen at the console, the handset still pressed to his ear even though it was now only dead air and static. His hands trembled. Around him, the operations floor remained silent, twenty analysts who had been silent witnesses to the spectacle, who now understood exactly what kind of organization they worked for.

Slowly, he returned the handset to its cradle. His hands wanted to shake but he wouldn't let them—couldn't let them—not in front of his team. He had survived three years in this position by projecting absolute certainty even when terror clawed at his spine.

"You heard the man." Hess's voice was somehow steady. "Full audit. Personnel files, communication logs, travel records, financial transactions. Cross-reference Directorate assets with access to Berlin node protocols. I want psychological profiles updated within six hours. Someone got sloppy. Someone always does."

The analysts bent to their terminals, hunting one of their own. But their fingers moved slower now, more carefully, as if each keystroke might be the one that drew Kessler's attention.

Hess walked back to his private office and closed the door. Only then did he allow himself to sit, to breathe, to let his hands shake. He had heard stories about Kessler—everyone in the Directorate had. The man stood as a legend in intelligence circles, a ghost who had orchestrated regime changes and market collapses, and made empires dance to his tune.

But tonight, Hess had heard something else in Kessler's voice. Not cruelty for its own sake, but something colder: absolute control. The ability to make a man beg for his children's lives, then spare them not out of mercy but because living witnesses served his purposes better than corpses.

That marked the difference between a monster and an expert. Monsters killed because they enjoyed it. Experts killed because it was efficient.

And Kessler was both.

Hess pulled up the surveillance footage from Berlin, watching the grainy images of a man in a maintenance jacket moving through the facility with professional precision. Somewhere out there, this person was running, probably thinking they'd gotten away clean.

They had no idea what was coming for them.

On the wall of screens behind his desk, red indicators pulsed: **BERLIN NODE - COMPROMISED. TRACE ACTIVE. RESPONSE INITIATED.**

The machine was awake. And it was hunting.

Daggers From Above

"Men like me don't walk away from war. We just carry it somewhere new." —Marcus Vale

Turkish-Syrian Border—9:40 p.m. local time- Day 5

Burnt coffee and cigarette smoke smells permeated the safe house. Marcus Vale sat hunched over a laptop in the corner, its blue glow reflecting off his weathered face as rain hammered against the corrugated metal roof. Outside, the Turkish-Syrian border stretched out past the horizon as a black void—no lights, no movement, only the occasional rumble of distant artillery.

He had been out of Delta for over eight months now. In Delta, he went by the name Daniel Cole. After his exit from Delta Force, he emerged as Marcus Vale. Many days he had trouble remembering who he was.

The official story of his exit from Delta was medical retirement after Helmand—traumatic brain injury, recurring headaches, the standard cover for operators who had seen too much. The truth was messier. Someone higher up had noticed Daniel asking questions about the mission that killed half his team. And it was decided those questions made him a liability. So he was forced out.

Then came the recruitment. A man in an expensive suit, meeting him at a Washington hotel bar. No name, only a business card with a phone number. "We have work for men with your talents. Work that matters. Operations the official channels can't touch."

Marcus had assumed CIA—Special Activities Division, maybe, or some other three-letter outfit working in the shadows. The missions certainly appeared Agency: surgical strikes against high-value targets in Syria, Iraq, Yemen. Men who needed killing, or so they told him. The intelligence always arrived pristine, the support seamless, the money deposited in accounts with Swiss routing numbers.

He stopped asking questions. That formed the basis of the first rule they taught him: complete the mission, collect the payment, move on to the next target. Don't look at the bigger picture. And don't start asking questions.

But tonight, the bigger picture had found him.

The target had been Hamid Al-Rashan, a Syrian warlord turned terrorist financier operating out of a compound near Aleppo. Vale's team had hit it hard and fast—three vehicles, eight operators, in and out in eleven minutes. Al-Rashan died in the first room, two bullets center mass before he could reach the AK propped against his desk.

Standard work. Clean. Professional.

Except Vale had grabbed the laptop from Al-Rashan's desk. Protocol required him to leave electronics for the cleanup team, but something had nagged at him—the same instinct that had kept him alive through Fallujah, Helmand, Sangin, and a dozen other hellholes. He stuffed it in his pack and mentioned nothing.

Now, in the safe house, he was breaking all the rules in the book.

The laptop's encryption had been child's play—Al-Rashan had used his daughter's birthday as the password. Inside were financial records, operational plans, communications logs. At first glance, it was what Vale expected: wire transfers from Saudi donors, weapons shipments from Turkish smugglers, payroll for a network of fighters.

Then he found the folder labeled "Patron."

Vale opened it, and the room seemed to shrink around him.

Wire transfer receipts. Millions of dollars flowing through a maze of shell companies—Heliostrat Defense Holdings, Bridger Capital Group, Meridian Strategic Solutions. The money originated from accounts in Luxembourg and Geneva, routed through intermediaries in Panama and the British Virgin Islands before arriving in al-Hashimi's accounts in Beirut and Dubai.

But it wasn't the money that made Vale's blood run cold. It was the operational summaries attached to each payment.

Operation Carthage - Libya, 2014. $4.7M. Objective: Destabilize transitional government, eliminate pro-Western ministers.

Vale remembered that one. He was a member of the team that had taken out a Libyan general in Benghazi. They had been told the general facilitated arms shipments to Boko Haram. The intelligence had come from "allied sources."

Operation Nightfall - Ukraine, 2014. $6.2M. Objective: Support separatist actions, undermine NATO expansion.

He hadn't been on that one, but he knew operators who had. Trainers sent to "moderate rebel groups" in eastern Ukraine. They'd come back with stories that hadn't made sense—arms shipments that disappeared, militia leaders who seemed to be playing both sides.

Operation Sandstorm - Yemen, 2015. $3.1M. Objective: Escalate regional conflict, increase weapons market demand.

Daniel's hands began to shake. He'd been in Yemen six weeks ago, part of a team supporting Saudi strikes against Houthi positions. The intelligence officer who'd briefed them had been smooth, professional, American. "Strategic necessity," he'd voiced. "Countering Iranian influence."

He clicked deeper into the files. More operations, more money, more bodies. Operations spanning three continents, orchestrated with surgical precision. And under each one, buried in the metadata, sat authorization codes and handler designations.

Vale's cursor hovered over a PDF labeled "2015-Q1-Authorization-Matrix.pdf." He opened it.

The document read like a corporate org chart—clean, professional, sanitized. At the top rested a single entity: "The Directorate." Below it, a web of subsidiaries and front companies, each connected by lines showing financial flows and operational oversight.

And there, in the right column, under "Strategic Coordination - European Theater," laid out a name that made Daniel's breath catch in his throat:

A. Kessler - Deputy Director, Special Operations

Kessler.

The name hit Vale like a gut punch. He'd heard it before—5 years back when he was Daniel Cole, in a conversation with his brother and father at the Cabin. Dad had spoken about Kessler. Formerly Otto Reinhardt, a ghost operating in the shadows of European finance, pulling strings that reached into governments, intelligence agencies, multinational corporations.

At the time, Daniel had chalked it up to Dad's tendency toward conspiracy theories. The man saw patterns that no one else saw, connections that existed only in his head. Ethan had been skeptical too, though he'd listened carefully, filing the information away in that analytical mind of his.

But now, staring at that name on the screen, Marcus Vale realized his father had been right. Kessler was no phantom. He was real. And he was at the center of something vast and terrible. And Kessler had gotten way too close—too involved—with his family.

Vale kept reading. The document laid out a network of operations spanning years—regime changes, arms deals, assassinations disguised as accidents or insurgent attacks. The Directorate did not support terrorism; it orchestrated chaos. Creating instability, then profiting from the aftermath. Weapons sales. Reconstruction contracts. Resource extraction.

And the operations Vale had been running? He wasn't fighting terrorism. He was enabling it. Each target he'd eliminated, the missions he'd completed—they had all been pieces of the Directorate's grand design. He had been their weapon, wielded by Kessler and men like him, pointed at anyone who threatened their profits or their plans.

The recruiter in Washington. The pristine intelligence. The Swiss bank accounts. It had never been the CIA. It had been them. The Directorate had pulled him out of Delta, cleaned him up, and turned him into an asset.

Vale's vision blurred. He thought about the men he'd killed—how many had actually been terrorists, and how many had simply been inconvenient to the Directorate's agenda? He thought about Helmand, about the mission that had gone sideways, about the brothers he'd lost in that valley. Had that been the Directorate too? Had they been sacrificed to tie up loose ends, to silence men who'd seen too much?

His hands curled into fists. Rage, white-hot and pure, surged through him.

He copied everything—each file, document, down to the last scrap of data—onto three encrypted thumb drives. Then he wiped the laptop's hard drive, smashed it with the butt of his rifle, and burned the pieces in the sink.

When the plastic stopped smoking, Daniel pulled out a satellite phone from his pack—not the one his handlers had given him, but a backup unit he'd acquired in Istanbul, routed through a series of proxies that would make it nearly impossible to trace. He dialed a number he'd memorized but never used.

The line clicked and hissed, bouncing through relay stations across three continents. Then, a voice:

"Secure line. Go ahead."

"Ethan," Vale announced, his voice rough. "It's me."

There was a pause—Ethan almost didn't recognize the voice. When Ethan spoke again, his tone had shifted—sharper, more focused. "Daniel? Jesus, where are you? I haven't heard from you in months. I thought you were—"

"I'm alive. That's all that matters right now." Daniel's jaw tightened. "Listen to me carefully. I don't have much time, and this line might not stay clean. You remember the conversation we had with Dad? About Kessler?"

Another pause. "Yeah. I remember."

"He was right. About all of it." Daniel's voice dropped. "I've been working for them, Ethan. The Directorate. They pulled me out of Delta, made me think I was running ops for the Agency. But it was them. Kessler. The missions I've run since Helmand have been for them."

"My God." Ethan's voice dropped barely to a whisper. "Daniel, are you sure?"

"I've got the files. Financial records. Operational summaries. Corporate structures. Kessler's name is all over it. Libya, Ukraine, Yemen—dozens of operations designed to destabilize governments and escalate conflicts. They're not terrorists, Ethan. They're profiteers. And I've been their triggerman."

Ethan was silent for a long moment. Daniel could almost hear his brother's mind working, processing the implications, running through scenarios. Finally: "Where are you now?"

"I can't say on this line. But I can't stay here. They'll know I grabbed the laptop by morning. Maybe sooner."

"Can you get to Europe?"

"I can get anywhere. But I need to know this is real, Ethan. I need to know you're in this fight."

"I'm in the fight." Ethan's voice had turned to steel. "Noah and I have been tracking the Directorate. We've got a lead on their operations in Europe—a woman named Selin who's been gathering intelligence on their networks. If what you've found is real, it could be the key to taking them down."

Daniel closed his eyes as he began to shift back to his Marcus Vale persona. "Then I'm coming. But we do this smart. No heroics. These people have reach—CIA, Pentagon, probably half the governments in Europe. If we move too fast, we're dead."

"Agreed. Get to Athens. I'll have someone meet you there and bring you in. But Daniel—" Ethan's voice softened slightly. "Watch your six. If they know you've gone rogue, they'll send everything in their arsenal after you."

"I know." Vale glanced toward the window, where the rain had turned to sleet. "I've been running from ghosts my whole life. At least now I know what they look like."

"Stay alive, brother."

"You too."

The line went dead.

Vale sat in the darkness for a moment, the weight of what he'd discovered pressing down on him like a physical force. Every step he'd taken since leaving Delta—the missions, the kills—had been orchestrated by the very people he had given his life to fight against. The Directorate had used him like a tool, pointed him at targets that served their interests, and he had never questioned it.

But now he understood. And understanding changed the lens through which he saw the world. This changed everything.

He packed quickly, methodically. Three encrypted thumb drives in separate pockets. Fake passport and travel documents. Cash in multiple currencies. A Glock 19 with two spare magazines. All other items were left behind—burned or buried or scattered to the wind.

By the time the first gray light of dawn touched the eastern horizon, Marcus Vale was gone. The safe house stood empty, rain pooling on the floor where the laptop had burned, a ghost dissolving into smoke.

But the war had just begun.

And this time, he knew who the real enemy was.

[CLASSIFIED – EYES ONLY / DIRECTORATE INTERNAL MEMORANDUM]

Subject: Security Breach –Vale, M.

Summary:

Asset Marcus Vale (former SOCOM, current contract operator) has compromised operational security by extracting classified materials from Target prior to sanitization. Recovered devices contain financial transaction records, operational summaries, and organizational charts linking Directorate operations to strategic destabilization campaigns.

Vale has gone dark. Last confirmed position: Gaziantep safe house (Site T-19). Communications intercepts indicate contact with civilian networks, including potential reach-out to family members. Threat level: CRITICAL.

Directive:

• Initiate BLACKOUT protocol for all materials related to Asset M. Vale across official and unofficial channels

• Deploy hunter teams to probable exfiltration routes

• Monitor known associates, particularly brother Ethan Cole (International Mercantile Bank) and former team members

• Authorize full-spectrum response up to and including terminal action if retrieval is not feasible

Note for Kessler:

"Your instinct about the Cole brothers was correct. The connection is now active. Vale has the files and has made contact with his brother. We have a containment opportunity, but the window is closing. Authorization is yours."

— Schmidt, Strategic Operations

28

Debt

[CLASSIFIED – DIRECTORATE / NODE: WASHINGTON DC-3]

Subject: Recruitment Authorization — Agent Harris, J.

Summary:

Subject identified as a compromised intelligence asset exhibiting high utility potential. Spousal medical vulnerability presents optimal leverage.

Directive:

– Approve funding for oncological clinical trials (Geneva Research Wing).

– Extend provisional immunity and clearance under Helios umbrella operation.

–Condition: Full operational compliance within Directorate parameters.

Bethesda, Maryland — Winter 2021

Fluorescent lights hummed overhead with a frequency that made Johnathan Harris's teeth ache. He had been sitting in this vinyl chair for six hours, watching his wife die by increments, and the institutional brightness of Walter Reed's oncology ward slapped him like an insult—as if the world should be darker, grayer, more honest about what actually transpired in these rooms.

Agent Johnathan Harris. CIA, Eastern Division. Three commendations for operations that officially never happened. Seventeen years of faithful service to a country that was now letting his wife slip away because their insurance had a clause about experimental treatments and their savings account had a bottom.

Rebecca slept fitfully in the hospital bed, her breathing shallow and mechanical, assisted by oxygen tubes that hissed with each inhalation. Stage IV pancreatic cancer. Six months since the diagnosis, delivered in the clinical monotone of a doctor who'd learned not to feel what he verbalized, not to make eye contact when hope died.

Harris had memorized the details of Rebecca's room: the beige walls that tried to be calming and failed. The digital monitors tracking pulse and blood oxygen in numbers that meant everything and nothing. The smell—industrial cleaner trying to mask something organic and wrong, the scent of bodies breaking down despite the hospital's best efforts. And beneath it all, the medicinal sweetness that lived in cancer wards, in hospices, and in places where death waited patiently for paperwork to be filed.

He held onto her through the diagnosis. Through the first round of chemo that left her retching for days. Through the second round that stole her hair. Through the third round that the oncologist had called "our last aggressive option" with a tone that declared what he couldn't: this isn't working.

Harris remembered the conversation with Dr. Patel three weeks ago, remembered it with the perfect clarity of trauma. The doctor had sat across from them in an office decorated with framed credentials and family photos—evidence of normal lives, of futures that extended beyond quarterly scans.

"There's a new trial," Dr. Patel had remarked, his hands folded on the desk like a priest delivering benediction. "Mayo Clinic, in partnership with a Swiss pharmaceutical consortium. Early results show a 12% success rate in extending survival by eighteen to twenty-four months."

Twelve percent. Harris had run operations with worse odds, had bet his life on intelligence that proved out flimsier than that. At the end, twelve percent was better than zero.

"What's the cost?" Harris had craved, though he had already known what the answer would be. Anything involving the words "experimental" and "Swiss pharmaceutical" was too costly for his paycheck.

Dr. Patel had slid a piece of paper across the desk. A single number, printed with bureaucratic precision: $340,000.

Harris stared at it until the digits blurred. Rebecca had squeezed his hand. "John," she'd uttered quietly, "we can't—"

"Your federal insurance will cover approximately 60% of conventional treatment," Dr. Patel had continued, his voice taking on that careful neutrality that doctors used when discussing money. "But this trial isn't classified as conventional. It's considered experimental, which means coverage is... limited."

"How limited?" Harris demanded.

"They'll cover the diagnostic work. The rest—the trial enrollment, the medication, the monitoring—that's out-of-pocket."

Three hundred forty thousand dollars. More than Harris made in four years. More than their house would fetch if they sold it. More than existed in any reality where they planned for retirement and college funds for grandchildren they would never have.

He had liquidated their savings that afternoon—$47,000, built over fifteen years of careful budgeting and federal salaries. He had taken a second mortgage on their house in Arlington, leveraging twenty years of equity for $80,000 that would bury them in debt even if Rebecca survived. A GoFundMe had been started that Rebecca hated, that made her cry with humiliation, watching strangers type "Thoughts and prayers" and donate twenty dollars here, fifty there, twelve thousand total from colleagues and people who had seen the campaign shared on social media.

It wasn't enough. The math was merciless. $139,000 raised. $201,000 short. And Rebecca was dying.

Now, in the vinyl chair that squeaked each time he shifted his weight, Harris watched his wife sleep and did calculations in his head. They could sell the house, maybe clear another $120,000 after paying off both mortgages. Still short. He could cash out his pension early, take the penalties, maybe get $50,000. Still short. He could—

Rebecca's eyes opened, glassy from morphine but still focused on him with that intensity that had first attracted him thirty-one years ago at a college party where neither of them had wanted to be.

"John?" Her voice sounded papery, worn razor thin.

He took her hand—fragile now, all bone and translucent skin, veins visible like rivers on a map. "I'm here, Bec. Always here."

"How bad is it?" She always had been direct. No euphemisms. Thirty years married to an intelligence officer had taught her to read between lies.

He couldn't lie to her. Had never been able to. "We're still $200,000 short. The hospital says they'll continue palliative care, manage your pain, but without the trial drug—"

"Then it's over." Matter-of-fact. The way she'd announced pregnancies and promotions and the death of her mother. Facts remained facts.

"No." His voice came out harder than intended. "No, I'll find a way. I can—there are options. I can talk to my section chief, maybe there's hardship funding, or I can—"

"John." She squeezed his hand with what little strength she had left. "Stop."

"I won't stop. I can't—"

"Listen to me." Her eyes held his, brown and deep and still full of the woman he'd fallen in love with even as her body betrayed her. "Promise me something."

"Anything."

"Don't do something stupid to pay for this. Don't... compromise yourself. I know how your mind works. I know you're thinking about corners you could cut, favors you could call in, lines you could cross."

She paused, breathing labored. "I'd rather go with dignity than have you live with something that destroys who you are. Promise me."

Harris noticed his throat closing. "Don't," he barely managed. "Don't plan your funeral while I'm sitting here."

She smiled faintly, that crooked smile that had undone him at twenty-two and undid him still. "Someone has to be practical. You always were the stubborn one."

But they both knew. The math was merciless, and math didn't care about love or vows or thirty-one years of breakfast conversations.

One Month Later — Georgetown

Harris sat alone in a hotel bar that catered to lobbyists and staffers, nursing a bourbon he couldn't taste. Rebecca had been moved to hospice that morning—a transition the social worker had called "ensuring comfort in the final phase," which meant they'd given up pretending treatment remained possible.

Dr. Patel had been apologetic. "Without the trial drug, we're looking at palliative care only. I'm sorry, Mr. Harris. We did everything we could within the parameters available."

Parameters. As if Rebecca's life was a budget item that had exceeded its allocation.

"How long?" Harris pleaded.

"Two months. Maybe three with good pain management."

So Harris sat in a bar at three in the afternoon, watching ice melt in whiskey, contemplating a world where two months was considered generous.

"Agent Harris?"

He looked up. A man in an immaculate gray suit had materialized across from him—no approach seen, no warning given, instantly present like a magic trick. European features, indeterminate accent that could have been Swiss, Austrian or Belgian, the kind of face that belonged to no particular country but looked at home in all of them.

Harris's training kicked in automatically, cataloging details: late fifties, expensive suit but not ostentatious, no visible weapons, confident posture suggesting either diplomatic immunity or dangerous stupidity. "I don't know you," Harris observed flatly.

"No." The man smiled, settling into the booth with the ease of someone who'd been invited. "But I know you. Johnathan Peter Harris. Seventeen years at CIA, Eastern Division. Specialist in financial intelligence, asset recruitment, operational security. Currently assigned to countering Iranian sanctions evasion networks." The smile widened slightly. "And currently $201,000 in debt attempting to keep your wife alive for what—two more months? Three?"

Harris's hand moved instinctively to where his service weapon would be if he were on duty. "Who the hell are you, and how do you know—"

"How do I know?" The man tilted his head with amused curiosity. "Because knowing things is what I do. It's my... calling, you might say. Your wife is Rebecca Anne Harris, Fifty-two years old. Stage IV pancreatic cancer with metastasis to the liver and lymph nodes. Dr. Rajesh Patel at Walter Reed recommended the Mayo Clinic trial three weeks ago. Cost: $340,000. You've raised $139,000 through savings, mortgages, and a quite touching GoFundMe campaign that your wife finds humiliating." He paused. "She made you promise not to compromise yourself. Sweet gesture. Futile, but sweet."

Harris all of a sudden went cold, like he was in a walk in freezer. This level of detail wasn't public record. This definitely was surveillance. This was— "What do you want?"

"Want?" The man spread his hands in a gesture of openness. "I want to help you. Such a simple thing. A man sits in a bar, drinking away his despair, while his wife dies from a treatable condition because the system he's served faithfully for seventeen years has decided she's not worth saving. This offends me. Deeply."

He slid an envelope across the table—cream-colored, expensive paper, the kind used for wedding invitations or condolence cards.

"Inside this envelope is a cashier's check for $500,000," the man continued, his voice taking on a professorial quality. "Enough for Rebecca's treatment. Enough to clear your second mortgage. Enough for you to sleep at night without calculating how many months of her life you can afford. Yes?"

Harris stared at the envelope like it was a live grenade. "Nothing's free. What do you want?"

"Information. Such a small thing, really." The man's tone remained pleasant, conversational. "Nothing that compromises national security—I'm not asking for nuclear codes or NOC lists or the identities of covert assets. Simply... early awareness. Trade flows. Regulatory changes. The kind of intelligence that helps certain financial instruments move more efficiently through global markets."

"You want me to leak classified economic data."

"Leak?" The man made a dismissive gesture. "Such an ugly word. I prefer 'share.' You share insights that help markets function more smoothly. In return, I ensure your wife receives the care she deserves. The care the system has denied her. Fair exchange, yes?"

Harris observed his hands trembling. "If I do this—"

"If you do this," the man interrupted gently, "you do it once. One simple exchange. You provide quarterly briefings on emerging sanctions frameworks—nothing catastrophic, nothing that endangers lives—and I ensure Rebecca gets into the Mayo trial. After that, we never speak again. You return to your dutiful service. I return to my work. And your wife... she lives." He paused, letting the word hang in the air. "Lives, Agent Harris. Isn't that worth one small compromise?"

Lies. Harris knew they amounted to lies. Once you crossed that line, you were owned. He had run enough assets to know the pattern: one favor becomes two, two becomes ten, ten becomes a career of compromised loyalty until you wake up one day and can't remember who you used to be.

But Rebecca's face filled his vision—gaunt, brave, slipping away from him by degrees. Her voice asking him to promise. Her hand squeezing his with what little strength remained.

Two months. Maybe three.

His hand moved toward the envelope.

"Excellent," the man remarked, standing smoothly. "You'll receive contact protocols within 24 hours. Encrypted channels, of course. Highly secure and utmost professional. Welcome to a new phase of your career, Agent Harris."

"I don't even know your name," Harris stated, still staring at the envelope in his hands.

The man paused at the edge of the booth, his smile enigmatic. "In my world, names are... negotiable. Provisional. Subject to context. But you can call me Kessler." He tilted his head. "And we are going to do wonderful work together."

Then he disappeared, dissolved into the crowd of Georgetown professionals, leaving Harris alone with an envelope that weighed nothing and everything.

Six Months Later — Hospice Room, Arlington

Rebecca died on a Tuesday morning, the same week the Mayo Clinic trial failed its Phase III review. Turns out the Swiss pharmaceutical consortium had fabricated half their data, and the experimental drug she'd received—purchased at extraordinary cost through Kessler's network—had bought her six extra months. Six months of pain, hope, and slow dissolution.

Six months to say goodbye. Six months to hold hands and watch sunsets through hospice windows. Six months to pretend the ending might be different.

Harris sat beside her body for an hour after the monitors flatlined, holding her hand even as it grew cold, whispering apologies she couldn't hear. Apologizing for not being enough. For not having enough money. For compromising his integrity which she had pleaded for him not to do for her sake.

The funeral was small. Colleagues came, spoke platitudes about service and sacrifice, left. Nobody put forward to him as to how he'd afforded the treatment. Nobody wanted to know. In the intelligence community, unexpected money was a conversation nobody had.

That night, alone in the house that still smelled like her perfume—lavender and something uniquely Rebecca—his encrypted phone buzzed. A message from an unlisted number:

"I'm sorry for your loss. Rebecca was a remarkable woman. But our arrangement continues. You've been useful, and useful men don't retire. Expect new instructions within 48 hours. — K"

Harris stared at the screen, rage and grief warring in his chest. He had sold his integrity for six months. Six months that ended in the same place as if he had done nothing. Six months that proved Kessler had been right: the system didn't care. Money was the only language it spoke.

He wanted to throw the phone against the wall. He would reach out to his case officer tomorrow morning, confess it all, accept whatever consequences came. Prison, probably. Definitely the end of his career.

But he didn't.

Because Kessler had been right about something else: once you cross the line, you can't uncross it. The debt had stopped being financial in nature. It had become existential. He had become the kind of man he used to hunt—the compromised asset, the traitor, the insider who sold secrets for personal gain.

And if he stopped now, if he confessed and went to prison and accepted his punishment, then Rebecca had died for nothing. Those four months became meaningless. The compromise became pointless suffering.

After the passing of his wife, Jonathan Harris had been Kessler's man inside Langley for five years—a ghost within the machine, invisible to the Agency that believed it owned him. The recruitment had been basic and straightforward: money for his wife's entry into clinical cancer trials, payoff his mortgage, and a Swiss account that grew with each service rendered.

In return, Harris delivered. Intelligence summaries that gave the Directorate weeks of advance notice before CIA operations. Asset identities that allowed Kessler to turn or terminate sources across three continents. And when information wasn't enough, Harris provided other services—the kind that required steady hands and moral flexibility. A journalist in Prague who'd gotten too close to Helios Defense contracts. A forensic accountant in Geneva who'd noticed patterns in wire transfers. A retired NSA analyst who'd started asking questions about signal intercepts. Each one handled quietly, professionally, their deaths attributed to accidents or suicides or the random violence of an indifferent world.

Richard Latham had been his most recent work—a simple job, once you knew the man's routine and had access to his residence. Harris had gained access to Richard Latham's residence, waiting in the darkness until Latham had come home. Then made it look like an accidental fall in the bathroom. Easy work for a professional. Now Kessler had sent new instructions: Ethan Cole. Contain, control, and if necessary, eliminate. Harris didn't ask why. He never did. He simply opened the dossier and began to learn all the details about the man he might have to kill.

Not because he believed in Kessler's vision. Not because he'd been seduced by ideology or power. But because the alternative was admitting that the choices he had made were wrong. That Rebecca had suffered an extra four months for his weakness. That he'd sold his soul for time that had run out anyway.

The debt couldn't be paid. It could only compound, growing heavier with each compromise, each order followed, each line crossed.

Present Day — Manhattan

Harris stood in a hotel bathroom, washing blood from his hands—blood that wasn't his, blood that belonged to a man who had tried to help Ethan Cole. Someone who had known too much, talked too freely, needed to be silenced.

His reflection stared back from the mirror: graying hair, hollowed eyes, lines carved deep by grief and guilt. Unrecognizable from the agent who'd once believed in clean operations and clear morality. An agent who had thought there were lines that couldn't be crossed.

He thought of Rebecca's last coherent words, spoken three days before the end: "Promise me you didn't compromise yourself for this. Promise me you're still the man I married."

He had lied to her then. Held her hand and lied.

"Too late," he whispered to the mirror now, watching water and blood swirl down the drain. "Too late for everything."

His encrypted phone buzzed. Kessler's message was brief, clear, final:

"Cole is becoming problematic, Locate him and terminate. No witnesses. No traces. Make it clean. — K"

Harris dried his hands slowly, mechanically. He stared at his own reflection until it stopped meaning anything. The debt was infinite now. The only way out was through.

Or so he told himself.

Because the truth—the truth he couldn't face even in the privacy of his own mind—was simpler and more terrible: he'd become exactly what Kessler needed him to be. Not a believer. Not a convert. But something worse.

A man who had lost it all and now had nothing left to lose.

And men with nothing left to lose were the most dangerous weapons of all.

29

Notice

[CLASSIFIED: EYES ONLY – DIRECTORATE / NODE: OPERATIONS-4]

Subject: DONOVAN, WILLIAM (BILL) — **Status:** Limited-use asset. **Directive:** leverage existing access to secure target neutralization and operational cover. Compliance required; deviation constitutes liability. **Contingency:** immediate termination authorized under Protocol Black if subject becomes compromised or in the event of public exposure risk.

—Operations Mandate, Helios Field Command (Priority: Immediate / Redacted)

East River, New York City — 8:42 a.m.- Day 5

Abandoned warehouses lined the East River like tombstones, their windows broken or bricked over, their loading docks empty except for pigeons and rust. This building had been a shipping company once—back when the docks still mattered, when cargo moved through New York instead of around it. Now it housed private suites for men who needed anonymity more than comfort, rooms that didn't appear on any municipal records, that changed hands through shell companies registered in Delaware and Luxembourg.

Third floor, corner unit. No sign on the door. No cameras in the hallway. Only a room that pretended to be a boardroom: long table scarred by cigarette burns and coffee rings, low-wattage bulbs casting the walls in an amber shadow, venetian blinds drawn tight against the afternoon glare. Outside, the East River moved sluggishly past, brown and indifferent, carrying industrial runoff toward the Atlantic.

Bill Donovan waited at the far end of the table, standing because sitting would have implied he'd been kept waiting, which would have implied weakness. In spite of nearing sixty years of age, he still carried himself like the Marine and FBI agent he'd been long ago—shoulders back, spine straight, hands loose but ready. His uniform was civilian now but the discipline remained: pressed charcoal trousers with a military crease, white shirt with the sleeves rolled exactly two turns, buzz-cut going gray at the temples. The kind of man who still shined his shoes each morning and called it maintenance.

His face was weathered granite, all hard angles and sun damage from years in the field, first with the Bureau and now with the bank's internal security division. Deep lines bracketed his mouth—not from smiling but from decades of jaw-clenching, of swallowing things he wanted to say to superiors who wouldn't have listened anyway. His eyes were pale blue, quick and assessing, the eyes of someone who'd spent a career reading people for threats and weaknesses.

He'd been told the meeting was urgent and off the record. He had not been told who would be there. That made him nervous. In his experience, unnamed meetings in unmarked buildings ended one of two ways: with a promotion or with a body bag.

The door opened.

Agent Richard Harris stepped in alone, and Donovan's instincts immediately sharpened. CIA. Twice in one week. Definitely not a coincidence. Donovan had first met him when he was in the FBI at inter-agency task force briefings, the kind of meetings where alphabet agencies pretended to share intelligence while guarding their turf like dogs over bones. Harris was late forties, compact and wiry, with the coiled energy of someone who'd spent too many years running assets and not enough sleeping.

His face was all angles—sharp cheekbones, pointed chin, hollow cheeks that suggested he forgot to eat when he was working, which was always. His eyes were what you noticed. Dark, intense, haunted by something that lived behind them and looked out at the world with barely controlled rage. He wore his tie slightly too tight, as if the discomfort kept him focused.

Harris looked exhausted. Not only tired—exhausted. The bone-deep weariness of someone who'd been compromised and knew it and couldn't see a way out except forward into deeper compromise. His hands trembled slightly as he took a seat, and he pressed them flat on the table to hide it.

Donovan had seen that look before, on agents who'd been undercover too long, who'd forgotten which lies were cover and which were truth. Harris was a man on the edge, held together by routine and necessity and nothing else.

Harris pulled out a cell phone—not his Agency-issued device, but something else. A burner, probably. Encrypted. He placed it in the center of the table and pressed a button. The speakerphone activated with a soft click.

"Mr. Donovan."

The voice that came through the speaker was European—Swiss or Austrian, something Alpine and precise, with an accent polished smooth by decades of operating in shadows. Calm. Measured. The voice of someone who had all the time in the world because time answered to him, not the other way around.

Donovan sensed his spine tingling. He hadn't had that feeling since his time in the FBI—he almost had forgotten that feeling. He couldn't see the man behind the voice, but that somehow made it worse. The disembodied quality—the sense of speaking to a ghost, to someone who existed everywhere and nowhere.

"You were recommended," the voice continued. "Quiet. Efficient. People at the bank trust you because you project competence and discretion. The Bureau trusts you by convenience—you were one of them once, yes? That makes you valuable. You exist in the space between institutions. You can move without attracting attention." A pause, letting the words settle. "You will continue to be useful. This is not a request."

Harris's jaw muscle jumped. He looked like he wanted to be anywhere else, doing anything else. But he sat there, hands pressed flat on the table, saying nothing.

Harris cleared his throat, the sound harsh in the quiet room. His voice came out strained. "We need Ethan Cole located. Quickly. Quietly. The bank is... compromised. There are threads connecting to things that can't be allowed to unravel. Cole has information—documentation, evidence—that threatens operational security at the highest levels. He is a liability that needs to be contained."

Donovan's training supplied the right response, the bureaucratic answer that would buy him time to think. "We'll run the usual channels. U.S. Marshals, local task forces, coordinate with FBI field offices. We'll open a containment operation and—"

"No."

The word from the speaker was gentle, almost regretful, which somehow made it more terrifying.

"Not the usual channels. Not public. Not bureaucratic. Nothing that creates records or requires approvals or involves people asking questions we don't want answered." The voice paused. "Clean, quiet, fast. You find him before other people find him. Or you ensure he cannot be used as a witness or a liability. You do understand the difference?"

Donovan noticed the air in the room change direction. "Was the temperature dropping?"—Donovan thought to himself. This wasn't a briefing. This was a contract. Most definitely the kind that came with consequences for failure.

"Agent Harris," the voice added calmly. "Please show Mr. Donovan."

Harris reached into his jacket with visible reluctance, as if the act itself disgusted him. He produced a thin manila envelope and slid it across the table toward Donovan, the sound of paper on wood obscenely loud in the silence.

Donovan opened it. Inside rested a single photograph, printed on glossy paper, professional quality. It showed him at a soccer field some years back—maybe five, maybe six—standing in summer sunlight, laughing with a woman he recognized as his ex-wife. She wore the blue sundress she had loved, the one that she had worn to their anniversary dinners before their lives fell apart. Behind them, partially visible at the edge of the frame, sat a child. Small, eight years old. Face unclear but presence undeniable—his granddaughter.

Donovan's throat went dry. He flipped the photo over. On the back, written in elegant script that didn't need flourish to convey menace: We like to keep things tidy. Failure is not an option.

His hands wanted to shake. He didn't let them. Instead he put the photograph back in the envelope and set it on the table, his movements deliberate, controlled. When he spoke, his voice came out smaller than he intended, raspier. "You don't get to threaten me."

The voice from the speaker carried a hint of amusement now. "Threaten? No, Mr. Donovan. We don't threaten. Threats imply negotiation, imply that you have choices. We inform. We clarify the reality of your situation."

A pause. Donovan could sense the smile in the next words.

"Life is expensive, yes? It can be made more comfortable. You help us. You leverage what you know inside the bank—access codes, surveillance footage, personnel files. You pull strings without drawing attention. You produce Mr. Cole to us, or you produce proof that he has been neutralized in a way that looks accidental. Either way, the problem ends."

Harris leaned forward, his voice dropping to something confessional, almost pleading. "And if you fail, Bill—if Cole surfaces somewhere we can't control, if he talks to the wrong people, if this becomes public—we will assume you were part of the problem. That you were complicit. And paperwork will appear in places that understand how to make careers disappear. How to make people disappear." He paused, those haunted eyes locking onto Donovan's. "It's thorough."

Donovan's training argued—this amounted to coercion, this was illegal, and precisely what he had spent a career fighting against. His morality argued—you don't cross this line, you don't become what you hunted. But the photograph in his mind, the image of his ex-wife and his granddaughter—they could certainly be found if these people wanted to find them. That made all the arguments irrelevant.

The world they were describing left no room for nuance, no space for principles. Purely survival. Compliance. The slow death of the morals that had once defined him.

He looked at Harris and saw his own future staring back: a good man compromised, a decent agent turned into something else, held together by fear and habit and the knowledge that the only way out was through.

"How do you want this handled?" Donovan finally sought, his voice hollow.

"Invisible," the voice from the speaker noted, and there was almost warmth in it now, approval. "No headlines. No messy complications. We prefer quiet solutions. We prefer things that look like misfortune—a mugging gone wrong, a car accident, a fall from a hotel window." A pause. "If misfortune is not possible, then make it look like the result of poor choices. Drug overdose. Suicide. People understand these narratives. They require no investigation."

Donovan forced his mouth into something approximating a smile, though it didn't reach his eyes, didn't reach anywhere near his eyes. "I'll do what needs doing."

"No." The voice turned cold, precise. "You will do more than that. You will be efficient—thorough—so that we never have to speak again. Because this conversation, Mr. Donovan? It never happened. This room doesn't exist. I don't exist. And if you force me to exist again, to return to this problem, then you become the problem. Am I clear?"

"Yes," Donovan responded, the word tasting like ashes.

Harris stood, his movements sharp and mechanical, a man going through motions he'd perfected through repetition. "We will coordinate through encrypted channels. You will have access to whatever resources you need—discretionary funds, surveillance equipment, travel arrangements. But understand this clearly: failure will cost you everything that matters. And I mean everything. Your career, your life will be over. It will be thorough and it will be permanent."

He reached down and ended the call. The click was soft but final, like a door closing.

Donovan closed his hands into fists under the table, nails digging into palms, using the pain to stay focused. He imagined the ledger of his life—the cases he'd solved, the people he'd protected, the principles he'd upheld—and saw a gloved hand erasing entries one by one until nothing remained but compliance and compromise.

He'd spent a career keeping people safe. Now he had a decision that would make him a different kind of keeper. The kind who ensured silence rather than justice.

Harris picked up the phone, pocketed it, then pushed the manila envelope closer to Donovan. "Keep it," he stated quietly. "As motivation. As context. As a promise of what happens if you disappoint them."

He walked to the door, paused with his hand on the knob, and looked back over his shoulder. His expression held something that might have been pity or recognition or shared damnation.

"For what it's worth," Harris mentioned quietly, "I'm sorry. I know what this costs."

"Do you?" Donovan's voice had turned bitter.

"Yeah." Harris's laugh sounded hollow, self-deprecating. "I do. I was once in the spot you are in. Before..." He trailed off, shook his head. "Find Ethan Cole. Make it clean. And maybe you get to keep something of who you were. That's the best you can hope for now."

Then he turned and left, shoulders squared, moving with the mechanical precision of a man who had already crossed all ethical lines and trained himself to sleep afterward.

Donovan stayed until the corridor hummed back to ordinary sound, until the venetian blinds threw the afternoon sun into straight, surgical lines across the scarred table. He sat there in the amber light, an aging

Marine who'd once believed in duty and honor and the rule of law, holding a manila envelope that contained a photograph and a threat and the end of the principles he'd tried to live by.

Outside, the East River moved past, brown and indifferent. Traffic hummed on the FDR Drive. The city continued its afternoon routine, oblivious to the small transaction occurring in this unmarked room, to another good man being turned into a weapon.

Finally, Donovan stood. His knees protested—old injuries from carrying too much weight for too many years. He picked up the envelope, slid it into his jacket pocket where it sat against his chest like a tumor, and walked out.

In the hallway, he made one call on a burner phone he kept for occasions like this. Polite, professional, to a contact who could make certain things invisible—surveillance requests, travel records, the kind of administrative details that could derail an investigation if someone knew to look.

Then he returned to his office at the bank and began to sketch, in the dry, efficient way of an investigator under pressure, a plan that would allow him to find Ethan Cole and present a result that would satisfy people from whom there could be no appeasement.

The photo stayed in his pocket. He could feel it there all afternoon, heavier than paper should be.

I95 South-Florida-Simultaneous

Highway stretched ahead like a promise of distance, gray asphalt shimmering in afternoon heat. Ethan drove with the windows cracked, letting humid air that smelled of pine and exhaust fill the rental sedan.

They'd ditched the Honda and picked up the rental car in Richmond using cash and a fake ID that Selin had produced from somewhere in her bag, the kind of tradecraft that made Ethan wonder exactly what she'd done before Istanbul.

Selin sat in the passenger seat, sunglasses on, dark hair pulled back in a practical ponytail, watching the landscape blur past with the focused alertness of someone who'd spent too many years checking mirrors for tails. She was beautiful in that effortless way that made men stupid—sharp cheekbones, full lips, olive skin that suggested Mediterranean heritage. But it was her eyes that gave her away: chestnut brown, intelligent, constantly assessing. The eyes of someone who'd seen violence and learned to navigate it.

She had insisted on coming. When Ethan had told her the plan—get to Miami, meet Noah, figure out the next move—she simply nodded and came out with, "Then we go to Miami." No argument. No hesitation. Simply acceptance of shared danger, as if it were the most natural thing in the world.

"You should tell me about this Noah," Selin requested, breaking the silence that had lasted since the last rest stop. Her Turkish accent was subtle but present, softened by years of international work. Her English was perfect, precise, with that slight formality that came from learning languages in military intelligence rather than classrooms.

Ethan kept his eyes on the road. "Noah Rivera. We met at Princeton—he was comp sci, I was economics. Became friends because we were both outsiders in separate ways. He's brilliant. Best hacker I've ever known. Works in cybersecurity now, freelance, mostly corporate clients who need their networks stress-tested."

"You trust him?"

"With my life. Which is convenient, since that's apparently what I'm doing."

Selin smiled slightly. "Does he know I'm coming?"

"No. I sent him a two-word message: 'Need help.' Nothing else. Figured the less information in transit, the better."

"So he will be surprised."

"Probably. Noah doesn't surprise easily, but showing up with a trained assassin might qualify."

Selin's smile widened. "Former assassin. Important distinction."

"Is there such a thing as 'former' assassin?"

She laughed, a sound like wind chimes—unexpected, musical, at odds with the tension coiled in her posture. "You've been reading too many spy novels. Yes, people leave. I left. It's possible. However it's... complicated."

They drove in silence for another hour, the landscape shifting from Virginia pine to Carolina lowlands, gas stations and fast food chains giving way to sprawl and swamp. The sun dropped lower, painting the sky in shades of copper and rust.

Miami emerged slowly—first the suburbs, then the sprawl, then the city itself rising from the flat terrain like a promise or a threat. Palm trees instead of oaks. Spanish tile instead of brick. A different kind of America, one that looked south instead of north, that spoke in accents from Cuba and Colombia and Haiti.

Noah's neighborhood sat farther south than the glossy postcards showed—old warehouses converted to live-work lofts, tangled alleyways, server farms masquerading as artist studios. The kind of place where people minded their own business because they all had something to hide.

Ethan parked three blocks away, old habit from his father's training: never park directly at your destination, always leave yourself an escape route. They walked the remaining distance, Selin moving with that casual awareness that marked professional training—checking windows, noting cameras, cataloguing exits.

Noah's building was a converted textile warehouse, five stories of brick with narrow windows and a fire escape that looked like it hadn't been maintained since the Reagan administration. The entrance was unmarked except for a buzzer panel with numbers instead of names.

Ethan pressed 4B. Static, then: "Yeah?"

"It's me."

Pause. Then the door buzzed open.

They climbed four flights of stairs that smelled like machine oil and takeout food, their footsteps echoing in the concrete stairwell. At the top, a steel door stood slightly ajar, blue light spilling out into the hallway.

Ethan pushed it open.

Noah's loft appeared exactly as Ethan had remembered: a vast open space with exposed brick walls, concrete floors, and enough computing equipment to run a small server farm. Monitors lined one wall, displaying scrolling code and security feeds and data visualizations. The air hummed with the sound of cooling fans and hard drives, smelled of coffee and electronics and the particular ozone scent of machines running hot.

Noah stood in the center of it all, backlit by monitor glow, looking almost exactly as Ethan remembered: early thirties, rail-thin from forgetting to eat, with unruly black hair and a beard that caught the light in patches. He wore a faded t-shirt from some tech conference and jeans that had seen better decades. But his eyes had a sharp appearance—dark, intelligent, missing nothing.

"E," Noah voiced, and a dry, surprised smile crossing his face. "I figured you'd send something more dramatic than a two-word ping." Then his eyes shifted to Selin, and the smile faltered. "And you brought a friend."

Selin stepped forward, extending her hand with easy confidence. "Selin Yilmaz. I've been helping Ethan stay alive. And you must be Noah. I've heard good things."

Noah took her hand, his expression shifting from surprise to assessment to something like appreciation. "Noah Rivera. And judging by the way you move and the fact that you spotted both security cameras on the way up here—" He gestured to monitors showing hallway feeds. "I'm guessing you're not merely a concerned friend."

"Former spy and assassin," Selin claimed simply. "Currently freelance. Currently keeping your friend from getting killed."

"Former spy and assassin," Noah repeated, his eyes widening slightly. "Jesus, E. You really know how to pick your allies."

Ethan let out a breath that was half-laugh, half-relief at seeing his friend alive and safe. "I had nothing dramatic left," he stated. "Only a two-word message and desperation. I need you, Noah."

Noah's smile faded into something more serious, more focused. "You always did. Come in. Both of you. Coffee's fresh. Then you can tell me about whatever mess has you running to Miami with a former spy and assassin".

Ethan stepped inside, Selin following, and closed the door behind them. The locks engaged with solid clicks—multiple deadbolts, electronic and mechanical, the kind of security that contended Noah took his privacy seriously. Outside, the Miami heat pressed against the windows. Inside, surrounded by scrolling code and humming machines, there was the possibility of understanding, of fighting back, of not being alone.

Noah poured coffee from a French press that looked older than Ethan's car, handed them both cups, then leaned against his workstation with his arms crossed. "All right. Start from the beginning. What the hell did you stumble into?"

They sat—Ethan on a worn couch that had seen better decades, Selin in a desk chair—and he told the story. All of it. The Apex wire. Latham's death. His apartment being searched. His father's murder disguised as a heart attack. The encrypted files. The Directorate. Kessler. The men hunting him.

Noah listened without interrupting, his expression unreadable, fingers drumming against his coffee mug in a nervous rhythm. When Ethan finished, silence filled the loft. Only the hum of machines and the distant sound of traffic from the street below to break the stillness.

Finally, Noah leaned back and rubbed his eyes. "So let me make sure I understand. You found a wire network moving over $100 billion through offshore accounts and shell companies. You flagged it. And now men with government credentials are hunting you with orders to kill."

"That's the summary, yes."

Noah remained quiet for a long moment, his dark eyes distant. "And you want my help because...?"

"Because you're the only person I trust who can prove it's real. Who can trace the architecture, follow the money, map the network." Ethan hesitated. "And because you understand why this matters. Why it's worth the risk."

Noah walked to a small shelf in the corner of the loft, reached up, and pulled down a worn shoebox—cardboard faded to brown, held together with packing tape. He opened it carefully, reverently, and removed something small and fragile.

A hospital bracelet. Pink plastic, faded by time and touch.

"Lily Grace Rivera," he read aloud, his voice soft. "October 2012."

He handed it to Ethan, who handled it like a sacred object. The name was printed in ballpoint pen, barely legible after years of Noah holding it, running his thumb over the letters.

"After she died," Noah voiced quietly, "I spent three years trying to find someone to blame. Some insurance executive, the hospital administrator, a policy decision where if they had made a different choice, she would still be alive. You know what I found?"

"What?"

"That there was no one villain or mastermind. Only a greedy and monstrous system designed to extract optimal profit from maximum human suffering, operating exactly as designed. The real criminal was the architecture. Millions of tiny decisions made by computer algorithms, bureaucrats and order takers following incentives, all amounting to a machine that kills without malice or conscience." He took the bracelet back, holding it gently. "No one pulled a trigger. But she died anyway."

He looked at Ethan, then at Selin, his dark eyes intense. "Your network? Apex? The Directorate? That's the same architecture. Different scale, same disease. Money weaponized, made invisible, turned into a tool for control. People die—not from bullets, but from algorithms and shell companies and financial instruments designed to extract wealth and concentrate power." He paused. "So yes. I'll help."

"You'll help," Ethan repeated, something unclenching in his chest.

Noah set the bracelet back in the box with something like reverence, closed the lid carefully. "Not because I think we'll win. The house always wins—that's how it's designed. But because Lily deserved a world that wasn't engineered to kill her for profit." He met Ethan's eyes. "And maybe your father did too."

Selin spoke for the first time since they'd arrived, her voice quiet but firm. "And because sometimes the house can be burned down. The architecture can be exposed. It requires leverage, information, and people willing to risk everything." She looked at Noah. "Ethan says you're the best. Are you?"

Noah's smile turned sharp, almost feral. "Yeah. I am." He turned to his workstation, fingers already moving toward keyboards. "Besides, I've been waiting years for someone to hand me the keys to the kingdom. And you brought me the blueprints."

He cracked his knuckles—a sound like small branches breaking—and his monitors came alive with lines of code, data streams, the digital scaffolding of the world's financial system. "Let's see what monsters you've found, E. And then let's figure out how to burn their house down."

30 |

Lines in the Water

Kessler — Private Diary (Zurich-0 Archive: Unclassified)
"They believe distance equals safety. How charming. No city is large enough to lose me... not even this chaotic little circus by the sea."

Miami, Florida—10:23 a.m.-Day 6

Noah studied Ethan for a long beat, his dark eyes moving between him and Selin, taking in the exhaustion, the tension, the barely controlled fear. "You brought it here, didn't you? The files."

Ethan's eyes flicked to the array of monitors. "Part of it. I need to trace something—fast, quiet. I can't go to anyone official."

"That's usually your opening line before I get arrested." Noah poured coffee for all three of them, the kind that could wake the dead. "Tell me what we're tracing."

Ethan hesitated, glancing at Selin, who gave a slight nod. "Money. Big money. I found movement patterns—structured trades across blind exchanges, feeding sovereign accounts. Somebody's laundering billions through defense contractors and private equity shells. It connects to a black account that shouldn't exist."

Noah's brows lifted. "And you stole it."

"I copied it. For insurance."

"Same thing," Noah observed. "You're radioactive."

"Yeah." Ethan looked toward the window—a sliver of sunlight breaking through blinds. "You're the only one I trust."

Noah took that in quietly. "That's a short list."

Selin set down her coffee cup, her voice cutting through the moment with professional efficiency. "We are wasting time. Each and every minute we spend here increases exposure. If they tracked Ethan this far, they'll find this location. We need the information now."

Noah nodded, already moving to his workstation. "She's right. Let's move."

They went to work. The glow from the monitors pulsed across their faces, green code crawling like veins. Noah routed connections through three layers of proxies—Bogotá, Reykjavik, Vilnius—then slipped into an offshore ledger Ethan had pulled from his encrypted drive.

Selin stood behind them, not watching the screens but watching the windows, the door, the street below. Her posture appeared relaxed but ready for action, weight balanced on the balls of her feet, one hand resting casually near the compact Glock 43 she had acquired in Richmond and kept hidden beneath her jacket.

Within minutes, data started to bloom on-screen. Account trees. Transfer schedules. Shell names.

Noah leaned back from the screen, his voice flat. "This isn't only laundering, Ethan. It's narrative construction."

Ethan frowned. "Explain."

"Look at the timing—these wire clusters align with all the major headlines from the past six months. Wars. Market crashes. Riots. They're not funding chaos; they're funding the illusion of inevitability."

"Who are they?" Ethan whispered quietly.

Noah tapped the folder labeled The Directorate. "The same few names—Helios, Atlantic, Global News—show up across each sector. Defense, media, logistics. They're not hiding money. They're building consent."

Ethan leaned closer. "Find who's authorizing it."

Noah tapped a key, then froze. "Already trying. But whoever this is, they've buried the trail deep." He looked up, his face pale. "Ethan. You tripped a silent trace the moment you opened this file. They know someone's looking."

Ethan suddenly felt cold chills run down his arms. "You can stop it?"

"Not completely. I can make it harder. But they'll find the source eventually."

Selin's voice cut through, sharp and urgent. "How long?"

"Minutes. Maybe an hour if we're lucky."

"Then we assume minutes." Selin moved to the window, peered through the blinds at the street below. "Ethan, check that fire escape. Noah, can you work mobile?"

Ethan stood, scanning the room—the walls, the vents. He instantly perceived the eyes that were watching him, surveilling him. His mind raced, connecting dots, seeing patterns. If the Directorate had found him here, if they'd traced the files, then they knew everything. They knew about Noah. About Selin. About—

Daniel.

The thought hit him like a punch to the gut. His brother was out there somewhere, had been for months since Helmand, running operations that Ethan now understood were probably connected to all of this. If the Directorate had files on Ethan, they had files on Daniel. If they knew about their father, they knew about both sons.

"I need to find my brother," Ethan mouthed all at once, the words surprising even him.

Selin turned from the window. "What?"

"Daniel. My brother. He was Delta Force. He has been dark since Afghanistan. But if they are tracking me, then they are tracking all of us, including Daniel and my Dad—" Ethan's voice cracked slightly. "Daniel needs to know. He needs to know what he's been working for."

Noah looked up from his screens. "You think he's been compromised?"

"I think he's been used. Like I was. Like all of us." Ethan ran his hands through his hair. "Dad trained us both. Taught us to trust the system, to serve. What if Daniel's still out there, still running missions, not knowing he's working for the people who killed our father?"

Selin's expression softened slightly. "After we survive the next hour, we'll find him. I promise. But right now—"

She stopped mid-sentence, her body going still in the way trained operators did when they sensed something wrong. "Car. Street level. Idling too long."

Ethan moved to the window, staying back from the glass. A black SUV sat across the street, windows tinted, engine running. "Could be nothing."

"It's something for sure." Selin was already moving, her entire demeanor shifting from casual to combat-ready. She pulled the Glock from her waistband, checked the chamber with practiced efficiency. "Noah, how many exits?"

"Front door, fire escape, roof access." Noah was backing away from the monitors, hands raised in that universal gesture of someone who had realized they had gotten in way over their head. "Jesus, are they really—"

"Yes." Selin's voice presented as calm, authoritative. "Ethan, you know how to shoot?"

"My father taught me. Basic handgun training."

"Good enough." She pulled a second weapon from an ankle holster—a compact .380—and handed it to him. "Safety's here. Point and pull. Don't think, but you have to react. Noah, get behind that desk and stay down."

"Selin, I don't think—" Ethan started.

"Kill the lights," she commanded, her voice brooking no argument.

The room went dark except for day light coming through the shades and the glow of a single monitor. In the sudden change of light, Ethan could see Selin moving with fluid grace toward the door, checking angles, calculating fields of fire. She had definitely done this before. She was a pro.

Noah whispered from behind the desk, "You think they're going to—"

The first shot came through the window—a quiet, practiced thud from a suppressed weapon. The monitor exploded in sparks, glass and plastic flying across the room.

"Down!" Selin's voice cut through the chaos.

Ethan hit the floor, his heart hammering, the weight of the .380 feeling sturdy in his hands. He heard Noah scrambling behind the desk, heard the sound of more rounds impacting—methodical, professional, walking a pattern across the loft's windows.

Selin returned fire, three precise shots through the window at angles calculated to suppress rather than expose her position. "Ethan! Fire escape! Move!"

Ethan crawled toward Noah, grabbed his friend by the collar. "Come on!"

"My equipment—" Noah started.

"Is replaceable. You're not. Move!"

They crawled toward the back of the loft where a metal door led to the fire escape. Behind them, Selin provided covering fire, her movements controlled and deliberate. She wasn't panicking. She was working.

"Two shooters," she called out, her voice calm despite the chaos. "Both suppressed rifles. Professional team. They're not trying to kill us yet—they're herding us."

"Herding us where?" Ethan shouted back.

"Doesn't matter. We're not going." Selin fired twice more, then sprinted across the loft in a low crouch, joining them at the fire escape door. "Out. Now. I'll cover."

Ethan kicked the door open, and humid Miami air rushed in. The fire escape was questionable, made of old metal and covered in rust, but it beat staying in a loft that was rapidly being turned into Swiss cheese.

Noah went first, his movements clumsy compared to Selin's practiced efficiency. Ethan followed, and then Selin backed out, still facing the interior, her weapon trained on the front door that was now being kicked in by whoever had been shooting through the windows.

"Go! Go! Go!" she barked, and they descended the fire escape in a controlled fall, metal clanging under their feet, rust flaking off in showers of orange dust.

At the bottom, Selin took point, weapon up, scanning the alley with professional precision. "Clear left. Ethan, watch right."

Ethan raised the borrowed .308 pistol, hands steadier than he expected, training from his father kicking in despite years of disuse. The alley sat empty except for dumpsters and shadows.

"The car's three blocks north," Ethan declared. "Can we make it?"

"Not directly." Selin was already moving, checking corners, using cover. "They will have the street covered. We have to go through buildings, come out somewhere unexpected."

She led them through a warren of back alleys and service corridors, moving with the confidence of someone who'd done urban evasion a hundred times before. Noah struggled to keep up, his breath coming in ragged gasps, but Ethan stayed close, his mind racing.

Daniel would know what to do. Daniel had trained for this—urban combat, escape and evasion, surviving when the enemy had superior numbers and firepower. Daniel would—

"Ethan!" Selin's voice snapped him back to the present. "Focus. Your brother isn't here. But we are. And we need to survive the next ten minutes before we can worry about finding anyone."

She was right. But as they ran through Miami's back streets, Ethan couldn't stop thinking about his brother. About the last time they had spoken—months ago, a brief phone call where Daniel had sounded tired, distant, carrying the weight of things he couldn't talk about.

About how their father had always insisted the two of them needed to stick together. That family remained the only thing you could trust when everything else fell apart.

About how he had failed to protect Dad, but maybe—maybe—he could still protect his brother.

If he could only find Daniel. If he could warn him before it was too late.

They reached the rental car fifteen minutes later, approaching from an unexpected direction, Selin checking for surveillance before allowing them to get in. Ethan drove, Noah in the back seat looking shell-shocked, Selin in the passenger seat with her weapon in her lap, scanning constantly for threats.

"Where to?" Ethan solicited, pulling into traffic.

"Somewhere public. Airport, mall, somewhere with crowds and cameras. They won't risk exposure in a high-traffic area." Selin glanced at him. "And then we figure out how to find your brother."

"You think he's still alive?" The question escaped before Ethan could stop it, the fear he'd been suppressing finally finding voice.

"If he's as good as you say, yes. Men like that—operators, soldiers—they're hard to kill." She paused. "But they're also exactly the kind of men the Directorate recruits. We need to consider the possibility that your brother isn't a victim. He might be working for them."

"No." Ethan's voice became firm. "Not Daniel. He's not—he wouldn't—"

"We have to be smart about this" —Selin commented gently. Your brother has been dark for months. He could be compromised. He could be turned. Or—" She met his eyes. "He could be exactly who you think he is, and he's in as much danger as we are."

Ethan drove in silence, processing. She was right. He knew she was right. But the thought of Daniel working for the people who had killed their father, who'd hunted Ethan across state lines, who tried to murder them in Noah's loft—

No. He couldn't accept that. Wouldn't accept that.

"We find him." Ethan's jaw tightened. "Whatever it takes. We find Daniel, and we bring him in. He deserves to know the truth about what he's been fighting for."

Selin nodded slowly. "Agreed. But we need to be extremely careful and methodical."

From the back seat, Noah finally spoke, his voice shaky but determined. "I can help with that. If your brother's been active militarily, there'll be digital traces. Deployment records, financial transactions, communication patterns. Give me a few hours and some decent internet, I can find him."

"A few hours we might not have," Ethan asserted.

"Then I work fast." Noah leaned forward, color returning to his face, the shock of being shot at replaced by the familiar comfort of having a problem to solve. "Your brother's out there. We'll find him."

Ethan nodded, gripping the steering wheel tighter, navigating Miami traffic while his mind raced ahead to the next problem, the next move, the next impossible thing they'd have to do to survive.

But underneath all the tactical thinking, all the survival instinct, simmered a much simpler thought: Daniel, where are you?

Elsewhere — Washington D.C.

In Washington, Bill Donovan watched a satellite feed shimmer into clarity on a classified monitor. The Miami grid came alive—cell triangulations, traffic cams, and airport check-ins painting a digital picture of the city in real-time.

Harris stood beside him, coat off, sleeves rolled, the look of a man who had decided how many lives were acceptable losses. The look of a man who'd made that calculation so many times it no longer registered as a moral question.

Kessler stood behind them both, perfectly still, hands clasped behind his back, watching the monitors with clinical interest. He'd arrived an hour ago without announcement, as he always did, materializing like a ghost with expectations that would be met or punished.

"Cole's in Miami," Harris voiced, pointing at the screen. "We picked up his trace through a flagged SIM pull. He's using old tradecraft—clever, but not invisible."

Donovan added nothing, his jaw tight, the photograph of his family burning a hole in his pocket even though it wasn't physically there.

Harris continued, his finger tracing routes on the screen. "That's his last known position. Two cameras caught movement. He's in a warehouse district now. He has one known associate there—Noah Rivera. Former MITRE contractor, got canned for data skimming. Perfect profile for hiding a fugitive."

"And the woman?" Kessler's voice cut through, precise and interested. "The Turkish operative. Selin...Selin Yilmaz. She's with them, yes?"

Harris nodded. "Confirmed. Former Mossad liaison, freelance now. Dangerous. Extremely dangerous. She's the reason Cole's survived this long."

"Fascinating." Kessler tilted his head, sounding almost gleeful. "A banker, a hacker, and an assassin. Like something from a film. Though the ending will be rather less entertaining for them."

Donovan's throat went dry. "You planning surveillance?"

Harris looked at him, measured. "No. Containment. Orders are clean. No arrests, no paperwork. We neutralize all three. The hacker's collateral—he chose to help a fugitive. The woman's a known intelligence operative on U.S. soil without clearance. Both are legitimate targets."

Donovan's stomach turned. "Rivera's a civilian analyst, not a threat."

"Anyone who helps Cole becomes part of the breach. That's the directive." Harris's voice sounded flat, bureaucratic, the tone of someone reciting policy they'd long ago stopped questioning.

Kessler stepped forward, placing a hand on Donovan's shoulder—light, almost friendly, but carrying the weight of ownership. "Mr. Donovan. You seem troubled. This concerns you, yes?"

Donovan forced himself to meet those pale eyes. "I'm concerned about exposure. Miami's not exactly subtle. Three bodies will draw attention."

"Ah, but you see, that's the beauty of it." Kessler smiled that enigmatic smile. "A banker wanted for financial crimes. A hacker with a criminal record. A foreign intelligence operative working illegally. If they die resisting arrest, who will question it? The narrative writes itself. Yes?"

He patted Donovan's shoulder once more before stepping back. "Besides, the alternative is allowing Cole to continue spreading his version of events. And we can't have that. Your family—lovely woman, your ex-wife. I saw recent photos. Still quite beautiful. And your daughter, what is she now, fifteen? Sixteen?" The smile widened. "We must ensure they remain safe. That nothing unfortunate happens to them, yes?"

"Yes. I understand." Donovan was caught in the trap.

"Very good. I knew you would see things appropriately." Kessler returned his attention to the monitors. "Agent Harris, when do we proceed?"

Harris checked his watch. "Two teams are already in play. One local contract team. One offshore asset moving into position. We'll clean it within the hour."

"Excellent. Mr. Donovan, you'll coordinate cleanup. Make sure all evidence points to the appropriate narrative. Can you do that?"

Donovan stared at the map again, watching the red dot that represented Ethan Cole blink like a heartbeat. Somewhere in that dot was a man who had only tried to do his job, who stumbled into something he shouldn't have seen, and was now marked for death because he had voiced the wrong questions.

Just like when Donovan was in the Marines, he had targeted enemy soldiers for death when he had believed in the mission, believed in the system, and that the people giving orders had some higher purpose that justified the collateral damage.

Now he understood: there was no higher purpose. Simply put, it was power striking out to protect itself.

He nodded once. "When?"

"Now," Harris replied, pressing a button on his console. Static filled the speakers, then a voice: "Teams in position. Authorization to engage?"

Kessler leaned forward, speaking directly into the microphone with that calm, pleasant voice. "Engage. All targets. No survivors."

"Copy. Engaging."

The satellite feed showed movement—heat signatures converging on the warehouse, muzzle flashes in the infrared spectrum, then dispersal as the targets moved to the fire escape.

"They're rabbiting," Harris observed. "The woman's good. She got them out before the breach."

Kessler made a sound that might have been approval. "As I contend. Dangerous. But ultimately, it only delays the inevitable. They're running. Running creates mistakes. Tired people make mistakes. Desperate people make fatal mistakes." He turned to Donovan. "Which is why you'll be ready when they do. When they surface again, you'll ensure they don't surface again."

"Yes, sir," Donovan heard himself say, his voice hollow, automated, the voice of a man who'd stopped fighting and started obeying.

Somewhere in Miami, three people were running for their lives, believing they could outmaneuver the machinery hunting them. Donovan knew better. The machine always won. The only question that remained was how many pieces the machine would leave behind.

And with that, the net pulled one notch tighter.

31

Death of Marcus Vale

[CLASSIFIED: EYES ONLY -- DIRECTORATE / NODE: PERSONNEL-BLACK]

SUBJECT: Asset Reclassification - VALE, MARCUS (True Identity: COLE, DANIEL)

Status: COMPROMISED - Subject demonstrating unpredictable resistance patterns

Background: Former U.S. Army Delta Force, recruited post-Helmand incident, deployed

across seventeen operations with acceptable performance metrics until recent behavioral anomalies

Recent Activities:

- Unauthorized intelligence gathering on Directorate operations
- Communications with civilian brother (COLE, ETHAN - flagged as primary security threat)
- Suspected data theft from Syrian operation (Deir ez-Zor facility breach)

Assessment: Subject no longer reliable. Personal loyalty override professional commitment. Recommend immediate termination before operational knowledge compromises network integrity.

Authorization: Asset termination approved. Stage as training accident. Create sufficient documentation to discourage investigation.

Executor: Assigned to HANDLER-7 (Athens station)

Albania, Near Theth — 8:23 a.m. local time- Day 6

Mountains rose like broken teeth against a slate-gray sky, peaks shrouded in mist that moved like living things through the valleys below. This far north, where Albania pressed against Montenegro and Kosovo, the land belonged to smugglers and ghosts—people who worked in the shadows, moving contraband and asking no questions—who knew the goat trails and cave systems.

The same ghosts who remembered when these mountains had hidden partisans fighting empires.

The old military compound sat in a valley carved by glaciers and forgotten by governments. Soviet-era construction, concrete bunkers and rusted fencing reclaimed by wild grass and scrub pine. What remained—a shooting range, underground storage, a command building with walls two feet thick—served the Directorate's purposes perfectly. Remote enough for deniability. Brutal enough for the work they did here. Close enough to Greece that bodies could disappear across borders without paperwork.

Daniel Cole knew it was a trap the moment he received the mission briefing.

Not obviously. Never obviously. The Directorate was too professional for that. Small inconsistencies that accumulated like hairline fractures in steel: a "training exercise" that required his specific skill set but specified no team support. A handler he'd never worked with requesting face-to-face contact in a location three hours from the nearest town. Mission parameters that would put him in a confined space where superior numbers trumped superior skill.

He'd been expecting this. Ever since Syria, ever since he'd pulled those files off the terrorist's laptop and seen the names, the accounts, the operations. Ever since he'd understood that the chaos he'd been fighting wasn't enemy action—it was profit margin. Ever since he'd made the mistake of having a brother who'd become inconvenient to powerful people.

The Directorate didn't fire employees who knew too much. They erased them. Made it look like training accidents or equipment malfunctions or tragic mistakes in hostile territory. Then they sealed the files, paid the death benefits, and moved on.

Daniel arrived at the compound at dawn, driving a rental 4x4 that handled the dirt track like it was paved with razors. The vehicle was registered to Marcus Vale—the identity he'd been using for four years, the ghost name that let him move through the Directorate's operations without triggering the flags that still surrounded Daniel Cole's actual service record.

Twenty-seven operations across four years. Syria, Yemen, Libya, Ukraine. Wet work that was never acknowledged, kills that were never counted. And this would be the last. Not because he'd planned it, but because someone else had.

He parked fifty meters from the main building, left the engine running—old habit from too many extractions that required speed over stealth. The compound looked abandoned: broken windows, weeds growing through cracked pavement, rust staining everything the color of dried blood. But Daniel's instincts were screaming. The place was occupied. Watched.

His handler waited by the command building, smoking in the thin mountain air. Code name Novak. Mid-forties, barrel-chested, with the weathered face of someone who'd spent decades in places that killed soft men. He wore surplus military gear—Serbian camo, maybe Croatian—and carried himself with the particular economy of movement that came from real combat experience.

"Mr. Vale," Novak stated in accented English, not offering his hand. His eyes were flat, assessing. "Good drive?"

"Uneventful." Daniel stepped out of the vehicle, leaving the door open, and scanned the compound with the systematic precision his father had beaten into him. Two other vehicles—a van with Albanian plates and a black sedan that screamed rental. At least three additional personnel somewhere in the buildings. More than a training exercise required. Far more. "What's the exercise?"

"Close-quarters building clearance. Hostage scenario." Novak gestured toward the bunker complex with his cigarette, ash falling onto cracked concrete. "We've set up targets, timing systems. Standard recertification. You breach alone, neutralize threats, extract the hostage. Evaluated on speed and accuracy."

"Alone?" Daniel let skepticism color his voice, playing the role of a professional asking professional questions.

"Budget cuts." Novak's expression suggested he knew Daniel didn't believe him and didn't care. "Can't deploy full teams for recertification. Besides, you're one of the best. Should be routine for a man with your record."

"Rules of engagement?"

"Treat all unknown contacts as hostile. Hostage is marked with blue tape. Anyone else is a target." Novak walked to the van, opened the rear doors, and pulled out a tactical vest and weapon—a Glock 19, worn but functional. "Standard loadout. Proceed when ready."

Daniel took the weapon, dropped the magazine, racked the slide. Training rounds, but filed down—the brass visible where someone had worked it with a grinder. Under stress, in darkness, these rounds would perform like live ammunition. Someone would examine the bodies later, see the filing marks, conclude a terrible accident. Training ammunition catastrophically failed. Operator and evaluators all killed. Tragic but explicable.

He'd used this exact method himself. Twice. On targets who'd become problems for the people who signed his checks.

Now he was the problem.

"Give me five minutes," Daniel requested, sliding the magazine back with a solid click. "I like to visualize the approach before entry."

"Of course." Novak lit another cigarette, the smoke caught by mountain wind and torn to nothing. "Take your time. We have all day."

Daniel walked the perimeter of the bunker complex, ostensibly planning his breach, actually counting personnel and identifying escape routes. Four men total including Novak. All armed—he could see the bulges beneath their jackets, the way they moved with their dominant sides slightly back. All positioned to create overlapping fields of fire if he entered the bunker through the main entrance.

They'd chosen the scenario well. Put him in a confined space, limit his mobility, use superior numbers to compensate for his superior training. Kill him in the dark, arrange the scene to suggest equipment failure. File the report. Close the Marcus Vale identity. Move on to the next operation.

Daniel had maybe fifteen minutes before they forced the issue.

He pulled out his phone—a cheap civilian model, nothing tactical, exactly the kind of device Marcus Vale might carry for personal use. The mountains made satellite signals unreliable, but he'd positioned himself on high ground, and after three attempts, he got through.

He sent three messages, typing fast, fingers steady despite what was coming:

To Ethan: *"Brother. If you're reading this, I'm gone. Everything you found at the bank connects to what I found in Syria. We've been fighting the same war. Trust your instincts. Go dark. Don't trust anyone official. I love you. Tell Dad I finally understood. - D"*

To his CIA handler (the real one, buried three layers deep in Langley's bureaucracy): *"Directorate eliminating loose ends. I'm one of them. Albanian facility 42.4°N, 19.8°E. Evidence package in Athens dead drop #7. Access code: Helmand_2015. Use it or I died for nothing."*

To a number that would trigger automated protocols he'd established for exactly this contingency: *"LAZARUS PROTOCOL. Execute per standing orders. All assets activate."*

He deleted the messages from his sent folder, powered down the phone, and tucked it into a pocket he'd sewn into his vest specifically for items he needed to survive. Then he walked back to Novak, his face calm, his breathing controlled.

Not accepting death. Preparing for the performance of it.

"Ready," he voiced.

"Excellent." Novak handed him a small camera mounted on a chest rig. "Bodycam. Standard procedure. We monitor from the control room, provide real-time feedback on your technique."

Daniel attached it, knowing they wanted footage to prove he'd been alive when he entered, that his death was accident rather than execution. What came after—the gunfire, the bodies, the story—would be written by survivors.

He approached the bunker entrance, weapon in low-ready position, his senses heightened to a combat ready pitch. This was the moment. The transition from soldier to ghost, from alive to officially dead.

He took three deep breaths—his father's teaching echoing across decades, across continents, from North Carolina mountains to Albanian peaks: "When you're out of moves, make them think you've got one more. Unpredictability is its own weapon."

Daniel entered the bunker.

Darkness swallowed him like a living thing, absolute and suffocating. His eyes adjusted slowly—shapes resolving from void, revealing a corridor lined with doors, concrete walls weeping moisture, the smell of mold and rust and something older. The "hostage scenario" would be in the central room. The kill team would be positioned at choke points, waiting for him to commit to the corridor where crossfire would be inescapable, where his body would be found later with bullets from his own filed-down training rounds.

Daniel moved left instead of forward, fast and low. Kicked through a door that wasn't part of the scenario—a storage room, dusty and forgotten, filled with Soviet-era equipment rusting into archaeological ruin. Inside: a window. Narrow, barred, but the concrete around those bars showed spiderwebbing cracks from decades of freeze-thaw cycles.

He heard movement in the main corridor—boots on concrete, voices sharp with alarm. They'd realized he wasn't following the script.

Daniel removed the bodycam, placed it facing a wall transmitting nothing useful, then grabbed the bars with both hands. Pulled. His shoulders screamed, muscles tearing as he threw his full body weight—two hundred twenty pounds of operator built through years of rucking mountains and close-quarter combat—against corroded metal.

The bars shifted. Rust and neglect did what time always did: weakened what had once been impregnable.

Voices shouted in Albanian, then English. Footsteps rushed. Someone was calling coordinates into a radio.

Daniel pulled harder, veins standing out on his forearms, jaw clenched so tight his teeth hurt. The bars tore free in an explosion of concrete dust and rust flakes. The window was narrow—barely wide enough for a man his size—but Daniel had trained for confined space movement in a hundred different scenarios. He went through headfirst, tucked his shoulders, landed in wild grass outside, rolled with the impact, came up running.

Gunfire erupted behind him—not training rounds now, but real ammunition, the distinctive crack of 7.62 rounds passing close enough to feel the displacement. Someone had decided to abandon the "accident" scenario and go for direct elimination. Fine. Daniel preferred honest violence to bureaucratic murder.

He ran for the tree line, zigzagging like his father had taught him during those North Carolina summers that were a lifetime ago, using every bit of micro-terrain—rocks, dips, the ruins of old fencing. Bullets stitched the ground around him, kicking up dirt in small geysers. One of the bullets grazed his left shoulder—hot, sharp, like touching a stove—but not stopping. Not even slowing.

He reached the forest and kept running, branches tearing at his face, his tactical vest catching on thorns. Behind him, engines roared to life.

They'd pursue by vehicle, try to run him down before he reached populated areas, before witnesses made killing him complicated.

But Daniel had spent time in these mountains. He had studied the terrain during his approach, memorized individual trails and ravines visible from satellite imagery. The Albanian Alps were brutal—sheer cliffs, loose scree, rivers that appeared from nowhere and disappeared just as quickly into karst caves. Beautiful and deadly and utterly indifferent to human ambition.

The forest was his element now. The hunters had become prey.

He ran for thirty minutes, pushing his body past exhaustion into that place where physical pain became abstract, where muscle memory took over from conscious thought. Then he went to ground in a ravine thick with beech undergrowth, chest heaving, tasting blood from where he'd bitten his cheek during the sprint.

Above, he heard vehicles pass. Doors slamming. Voices calling to each other in Albanian and English—Novak barking orders, someone arguing about whether to continue pursuit or report the compromise. Slowly, reluctantly, the sounds faded.

Daniel waited until sunset, completely still, breathing shallow, listening to the forest's language. Birds returning to normal patterns. Insects resuming their evening song. Nature telling him the human predators had withdrawn.

When full dark came—moonless, absolute—he moved again. Not toward civilization, not toward roads or towns or anywhere they'd logically watch. Instead, he went deeper into the mountains, toward the goat trails he'd seen on maps, toward a cache he'd established three months ago during a "scouting trip" whose real purpose Novak had never questioned.

The cache was there, buried under a piled up heap of stones that looked naturally made but wasn't: waterproof bag containing Albanian currency, Greek drachma, fake documents in three names, a satellite phone with encrypted SIM, first aid supplies, antibiotics, and a change of clothes. Each article needed to become someone else.

Daniel stripped in the darkness, treating his shoulder wound by feel—shallow graze, painful but functional. He cleaned it with alcohol from the kit, packed it with gauze, taped it shut. The cold mountain air bit at his exposed skin, but physical discomfort was data now, information to be processed and filed away.

He changed into civilian clothes—jeans, a heavy sweater, hiking boots that had been broken in during previous operations. Buried his tactical gear and Marcus Vale's identification. That identity was burned now. Time for someone new.

The satellite phone took three tries to acquire signal through the mountain peaks, but finally connected. Two calls. Both critical.

First, his CIA handler: "I'm alive. Barely. Directorate tried to sanitize me. Marcus Vale identity is burned—let them report it however they want. I'm going deep dark, completely off-grid. Evidence package in Athens, dead drop location seven, you know the spot. Access code Helmand_2015. What you need is there. Use it."

"Jesus Christ, Cole. We thought—" The handler's voice was tight with something that might have been relief or might have been fear at the implications.

"Let them keep thinking. Marcus Vale died today in an unfortunate training accident. What comes next is someone they can't predict." Daniel ended the call before more questions came, before emotions complicated operational necessity.

Second call was harder. His brother.

Ethan answered on the first ring, voice tight with fear and hope. "Daniel?"

"Yeah. It's me. I'm okay. Mostly." Daniel's voice cracked despite his control, emotion bleeding through training. "Listen, I don't have long and this line isn't secure. They tried to kill me. I'm officially dead now—training accident, that's what the report will say."

"What are you—where—"

"Let me finish. Please." Daniel closed his eyes, seeing his brother's face in memory—younger, smiling, before any of this started. "I'm going ghost. Deeper than before. But I got your messages. I know what happened in Miami, I know they're hunting you. And I know what you found at that bank connects to what I found in Syria."

"The Directorate," Ethan remarked, understanding dawning. "You've been tracking them too."

"For months. Since I pulled those files. Since I understood what we've been up against." Daniel's jaw tightened. "We're fighting the same war from different angles, brother. And I think it's time we fought together."

"Where are you?"

"Albania. Near the border. But I'm heading south." He paused, calculating travel time, safe routes, probability of interdiction. "I can be in Greece in three days. Athens. There's a place Dad took us once, remember? That restaurant near the Acropolis, the one with the view."

"Taverna Plaka," Ethan responded immediately. "Sunday dinners. I remember."

"Meet me there. One week from today. Noon. Come careful. Bring whoever you trust." Daniel heard a sound—distant helicopter, maybe. Time to move. "I've got evidence, E. Hard evidence. Names, accounts, operations. All that we need to burn them down. But I need your financial expertise to make sense of it. I need—" His voice caught. "I need my brother."

"I'll be there," Ethan announced without hesitation. "Daniel, I thought—when Dad died, when I couldn't find you—I thought I was alone."

"You're not alone. You've never been alone." Daniel sensed something unfamiliar to him—hope, maybe. Or purpose. "We finish this together. The way Dad would have wanted."

"The way he taught us," Ethan agreed.

"Stay alive until then. That's all that matters. Stay alive and stay smart." Daniel heard the helicopter getting closer. Definitely time. "I love you, brother. See you in Athens."

"Love you too. Be safe."

Daniel ended the call, destroyed the phone, and began the long walk south toward the Greek border, toward a city where ancient philosophers had once debated the nature of power and justice, where he and his brother would soon bring evidence of modern corruption into the light.

Behind him, the Albanian mountains stood silent, keeping their secrets. Ahead, Greece waited—neutral territory, a place where he could regroup, plan, prepare for the fight ahead.

Marcus Vale died that day in those mountains. Killed in a tragic training accident, body lost in the terrain, memorial service scheduled, file sealed. The Directorate would report it internally, satisfied that another loose end had been tied off.

But the real Daniel Cole—not the ghost identity or the sanitized service record—was exceedingly alive. Wounded. Angry. Carrying evidence that would shake the foundations of an organization that thought itself untouchable.

He walked through the night, through mountain passes that had hidden partisans and smugglers for centuries, his father's voice echoing in his memory: "When you're outgunned, you don't face them head-on. You change the battlefield. You become the thing they can't predict."

Daniel had spent four years being what they wanted—the perfect operator, the blunt instrument, the man who put forward zero questions and pulled triggers on command.

Now he would become what they feared: a soldier who'd learned their secrets and refused to stay dead.

He crossed into Greece using trails that didn't appear on any map, passing through villages where people minded their own business and cash bought silence. Athens sprawled before him like a promise—ancient stones and modern corruption, a city where empires had risen and fallen, where one more conspiracy would barely register as noteworthy.

But this conspiracy would register. Daniel would make sure of it.

He found a cheap hotel in Exarcheia, the anarchist district where police rarely ventured and questions were never asked. Paid cash for a week. Cleaned his weapons. Reviewed his evidence. And waited for his brother.

One week until the meeting. One week to prepare. One week until the Cole brothers reunited and began the war their father had never known he'd started.

Daniel stood at the window, watching Athens burn gold in the evening light, and smiled grimly. The Directorate thought Marcus Vale was dead. They were right. But they'd created something worse in his place.

They'd created a ghost with purpose. And ghosts, Daniel had learned, made the most dangerous enemies of all.

Greece was waiting. Ethan was coming. And the reckoning was about to begin.

32

Spider's Web

Kessler — Private Diary (Zurich-0 Archive: Unclassified)
"Your fear does more work than I ever will."

Over the Atlantic Ocean—38,000 feet—8:18 p.m. GMT- Day 6

At near-sonic speed, The Gulfstream G650ER cut through darkness a needle of engineered perfection threading the space between continents. Outside the oval windows, nothing existed—no stars visible through the cloud deck, no lights below, only the endless black of the mid-Atlantic where civilization dissolved into pure distance. Inside, the cabin glowed with soft amber lighting, leather and brushed titanium and the particular silence that came from soundproofing worth more than most people's houses.

Kessler's private jet was less an aircraft than a flying operations center—reconfigured at enormous expense to serve as mobile headquarters for a man who treated borders as suggestions and national sovereignty as a polite fiction. The forward cabin held six seats in club configuration, currently occupied by Directorate field operatives who sat in the kind of alert stillness that marked professionals preparing for violence. They wore civilian clothes—dark jeans, tactical boots, nondescript jackets that concealed body armor and weapons. Their faces were hard, unforgettable, the faces of men who'd spent careers on missions and executing orders from their commanders with military precision.

Behind them, the main cabin had been converted into something between a boardroom and a war room. A conference table of polished walnut, surrounded by leather chairs. Bulkhead-mounted monitors showing real-time data feeds—flight telemetry, encrypted communications, satellite imagery of a forested area in North Carolina that Kessler had been studying for the past hour. Under-floor storage compartments held enough weaponry to start a small war: assault rifles, suppressed pistols, tactical gear, medical supplies, shaped charges for breaching.

And at the rear of the plane, separated by a soundproof door of bulletproof composite, was Kessler's private office.

The space was designed with the minimalist precision that Kessler preferred. A desk of carbon fiber and steel, bolted to the floor against turbulence. A single ergonomic chair. Three monitors arranged in an arc, currently displaying the faces of six people in six different countries, each representing a node in the network Kessler had spent three decades building.

Kessler sat in his chair, hands steepled beneath his chin, his silhouette backlit by the glow of screens and the soft blue running lights that traced the office's perimeter. He looked much younger than his actual age—good genetics, better surgeons, and the kind of wealth that made aging optional. His suit was Brioni, charcoal gray, perfectly tailored even at altitude. His hair was silvered at the temples in exactly the way that suggested distinguished rather than elderly. His face was unreadable, pleasant, the face of a diplomat or a priest or a professor—harmless professions for a man who was none of these things and all of them at once.

The six faces on the monitors represented considerable power in their respective spheres: a European intelligence director in Brussels, a Middle Eastern oil minister in Riyadh, a Chinese state banker in Shanghai, a Russian oligarch in Moscow, an American defense contractor in Virginia, a Saudi prince in his palace.

All owned. All compromised. All bound to the Directorate through money or extortion or the simple recognition that cooperation was more profitable than resistance.

Behind these feeds, invisible to the participants, algorithms hummed through servers mounted in the jet's belly. Trading programs monitoring markets in real-time, adjusting positions based on intelligence these people provided. Military contracts shifted. Offshore accounts pulsed with transactions. The network not only financed wars—it also harvested instability, cultivated chaos, turned human suffering into compound interest.

"Empires don't collapse by accident," Kessler spoke softly, his voice smoothed by decades of operating the world over yet belonging nowhere. "They're designed to. And when they do, we already own the pieces."

He unmuted the feeds, his expression pleasant. "Our American friends are losing discipline. Cole has obtained sensitive data, and they're attempting to contain the situation with violence. Crude. Unacceptable. It creates attention where we need none."

The European intelligence director spoke first, his French accent thick despite fluent English. "We've intercepted communications from Langley. They've authorized a neutralization operation in Miami. Your asset, Harris, is coordinating the response."

"Of course he is," Kessler responded, something like warmth in his voice. "Agent Harris has always been loyal—to the right price. Grief makes men so wonderfully pliable. His wife's death was unfortunate, but it created opportunity."

The Middle Eastern minister leaned forward, gold rings catching the light. "We've transferred the funds as instructed. Eight hundred million through the usual channels. But your network is being examined. Cole's discovery—the files he obtained—they implicate our transactions. If this becomes public—"

Kessler's hand rose, a small gesture that silenced a man who commanded armies. "Leave that concern to me. You have your weapons contracts. Your government remains stable. I have my silence. The arrangement continues. Unless you'd prefer I release certain... documents regarding the Yemen operation?"

The minister's face paled. "No. Of course not. We trust your handling of this matter."

"Excellent." Kessler turned his attention to the Chinese banker. "And you? Your party leadership grows impatient, I'm told, yes?"

The banker's expression was tight, controlled. "They ask when your end of the arrangement will be delivered. The currency markets, the promised... adjustments."

"It already has been," Kessler remarked pleasantly. "The collapse of one currency, the rise of another—all depends on who controls the levers of power, and who controls the narrative. We control both. Your economy strengthens while others weaken. Precisely as promised. Patience, my friend. Empires aren't built in quarters—they're built in decades."

The jet hit a pocket of turbulence, a brief shudder that rattled the monitors but didn't disturb Kessler's composure. Outside, somewhere in the darkness below, the Atlantic rolled in swells that no one would ever see.

He continued through the roster: the Russian oligarch nervous about exposure in London, the American contractor worried about Senate investigations, the Saudi prince demanding assurances about oil futures. Each one managed with the same calm precision, the same mixture of reassurance and implicit threat.

Finally, he muted the feeds one by one, their faces freezing mid-response, until the office was silent again except for the steady hum of engines and the whisper of pressurized air through vents.

Kessler stood, moved to the window—a small oval of reinforced glass that showed nothing but cloud and darkness. He placed his palm against it, detected the cold radiating through, the slight vibrations of the aircraft carrying him toward a reckoning that was thirty years in the making.

He thought of James Cole. His old friend. His brother in arms, once. The man who had saved his life in Kosovo and whose life Kessler had saved in Bosnia. The man who had stood with him in fire and blood and believed—genuinely believed—that they were fighting for something noble.

The man who'd finally learned the truth and become a problem that required solving.

A soft chime. The intercom.

Kessler pressed a button. "What is it?"

A voice—Novak, his Albanian handler, calling from a relay station somewhere over Greenland. "Sir. Update on the Vale asset."

Kessler's expression didn't change, but something cold moved behind his eyes. "Speak."

"The elimination was attempted as ordered. Training scenario, isolated location, minimal exposure risk. But the asset anticipated. Escaped the facility. Disappeared into the border mountains. We pursued for six hours before losing him. Weather turned. Twelve hours dark now—no sign of him at checkpoints or crossings."

"Twelve hours," Kessler repeated, his voice still pleasant, which somehow made it more menacing. "Which means Daniel Cole is across the border, gone to ground, and moving toward reunion with his brother."

"We believe so, yes, sir."

"Excellent." Kessler smiled slightly. "Report him dead. Training accident. Body lost in terrain. File closed, identity burned. But maintain surveillance on all channels he might use to contact family. When he reaches out—and he will—we will be listening."

"Understood, sir."

Kessler ended the call, then pressed another button. The soundproof door slid open with a pneumatic hiss.

Lukas sat in the main cabin, studying tactical displays on a tablet—satellite imagery, topographical maps, probability models for target movement. He looked up as his father emerged, his pale eyes reflecting the monitor glow. He was young, lean and hard, wearing dark tactical pants and a merino wool sweater that concealed a shoulder holster. His hair was cut military-short. His face was his mother's—sharp cheekbones, elegant bone structure—but his eyes were pure Kessler. Cold. Calculating. Unburdened by doubt.

"Developments," Kessler commented, settling into the chair across from his son. Around them, the field operatives maintained their alert stillness, not listening but hearing all that was spoken. "Daniel Cole is alive. Escaped the Albanian kill team. Twelve hours dark, which means he's mobile, armed, and heading toward his brother."

Lukas's expression didn't change. "So we'll have both of them."

"Eventually. First, we deal with the father." Kessler pulled up a new display on the bulkhead monitor—aerial imagery of the Cole cabin in North Carolina, surrounded by dense forest, a single access road winding through pines. "James Cole received intelligence about my identity. Anonymous package, unmarked, delivered to a dead-drop PO box. Someone—probably remnants of his old network—provided him with enough truth to become dangerous."

"You sent him the warning."

"I did. 'Old friends stay retired.' A courtesy, given our history. A reminder that silence was survival." Kessler's smile was cold. "He chose to ignore it. Contacted his sons and provided them information he should not have. Became the loose thread that has the potential to unravel our plans if we don't cut it now."

Lukas studied the imagery. "Security?"

"Minimal. The man lives alone—his wife died years ago. No close neighbors. The nearest town is twenty kilometers. He's armed, certainly. Trained. But he's old and well past the heart attack that forced his retirement." Kessler's voice took on something that might have been regret if you didn't know him better. "The heart attack I gave him, using compounds that left no trace. I should have made it fatal then, but I was... sentimental. Thought the warning would be enough. That he'd understand the boundaries and stay within them."

"But he didn't"—Lukas stated. He knew James Cole well.

"No. James Cole was always stubborn. Always believed that truth mattered more than survival. It's what made him a good soldier and a terrible intelligence operative." Kessler leaned back. "So now we correct the mistake. Permanently."

"You want it to look like an accident?" Lukas' voice was flat, professional.

"I want it to be thorough. If James has additional copies of the dossier, if he's created insurance files, if he's documented anything—we find it and destroy it. Then we make him disappear in the most mundane way possible. Old soldier dies alone in his cabin, perhaps his heart gives out or propane tank explosion. They find him in a week when he doesn't answer calls. Sad but unsurprising." Kessler's eyes hardened. "But first, we have a conversation. He and I. About old times. About Maribor. About the choices that brought us to this moment."

"You're going to kill him yourself."

"I'm going to give him the courtesy of understanding why. The same courtesy I gave your mother." Kessler's voice was calm, clinical. "James Cole was my friend once. The closest thing I had to a brother. He deserves to know that his death isn't personal—it's necessary. That empires require sacrifice. That order demands the elimination of disorder."

The jet hummed through darkness. Outside, somewhere below, the Atlantic gave way to the American coast. They were an hour from U.S. airspace now, flying under diplomatic credentials that would ensure no questions at customs, no records of entry.

Lukas returned to his tactical display. "After the father, we move on the sons."

"Yes. Ethan first—he's the immediate threat, the one with the evidence. Then Daniel, if he survives long enough to matter." Kessler's expression softened slightly. "I know this is difficult for you. These were your friends once. The Cole cabin was your refuge, your escape from my training. From me."

"That was a long time ago."

"It was. But I want you to understand something, Lukas. What we're doing—eliminating the Cole family—it's not cruelty. It's not even revenge. They know too much. They've seen too much. They're threats to an architecture I've spent thirty years building, an architecture that maintains stability across continents. Their deaths are regrettable but necessary."

"I know, Father. You've explained this."

"Have I?" Kessler studied his son. "Or have I simply trained you to accept it? There's a difference between understanding and obedience, Lukas. I need you to understand. You need you to know that when we walk into that cabin and I sit down with James Cole for the last time, it's not because I hate him. It's because I loved him once, and love is the greatest vulnerability of all."

Lukas met his father's eyes. "You killed my mother because you loved her."

"I killed your mother because she asked questions that would have destroyed us both. Because she was going to expose the Directorate to authorities. Because she chose morality over family." Kessler's voice was soft, almost gentle. "And yes—because I loved her enough to make it quick. Painless. Love informed the method, even if necessity dictated the outcome."

"The Cole family doesn't get that consideration."

"James does. The sons—" Kessler shrugged. "The sons made their choices. Ethan by digging where he shouldn't. Daniel by surviving when he should have died. They've earned harder endings." He paused. "But you, Lukas. You will be the one to deliver those endings. I must know that you can do it. That the boy who fished and climbed mountains with Ethan Cole is truly dead."

"He is." No hesitation from Lukas. "Whatever feelings I may have had for the Coles are irrelevant to operational necessity."

"Excellent." Kessler stood. "Then let us review the approach."

They moved forward into the tactical area. The field operatives straightened as Kessler approached—six men, all former military or intelligence, all blooded in operations across three continents. Kessler knew their files by heart: Volkov, ex-Spetsnaz, thirty-eight kills. Chen, Chinese Ministry of State Security, specialist in wet work. Dietrich, former GSG-9, now freelance. Morrison, ex-SAS, dishonorably discharged for excessive violence. Kovač, Serbian, war criminal from the Yugoslav conflicts. Rousseau, French Foreign Legion, court-martialed for torture.

Monsters, all of them. Carefully selected, generously compensated, absolutely loyal because they understood that loyalty to Kessler was the only thing keeping them alive and free.

"Gentlemen," Kessler announced, his voice carrying the boardroom courtesy that made him more frightening than shouting. "In ninety minutes, we land at a private airstrip in western North Carolina. From there, we convoy to a target forty kilometers away—a cabin, isolated, occupied by a single individual. Your objective is simple: secure the perimeter, establish overwatch, ensure no interference while I conduct business inside."

He pulled up the tactical display, showed the cabin's location, the access road, the terrain. "The target is James Cole, former U.S. Army Special Operations. Fifty-seven years old but still dangerous. Expect him to be armed. Expect him to resist. Your rules of engagement: contain, do not engage unless absolutely necessary. This is a surgical operation, not a firefight. We ghost in, we accomplish the objective, we ghost out. No traces. No witnesses. No evidence."

Volkov spoke, his Russian accent thick. "If he fights?"

"Lethal force is authorized. I would appreciate him being conscious and coherent for questioning prior to liquidation if at all possible." Kessler's smile was cold. "After I'm finished, you may dispose of the body as you see fit. But first, he and I have a conversation to conclude. One that's been waiting a long time."

The operatives nodded, faces hard, already running calculations, already shifting into the pre-mission mindset where humans became targets and morality became a luxury no one could afford.

Kessler turned to Lukas. "You'll take command of the perimeter team. Morrison and Dietrich with you. I want overlapping fields of fire on all approaches. Thermal optics, suppressed weapons. If local law enforcement appears—unlikely but possible—you delay them. Traffic accident, road closure, whatever's necessary. I need twenty minutes inside that cabin. Uninterrupted."

"Understood." Lukas was already pulling gear from the under-floor compartments—tactical vest, suppressed HK416. Moving with the practiced efficiency of someone who'd done this dozens of times.

Kessler watched his son prepare for violence with something that might have been pride if the man were capable of such simple emotions. Lukas had been developed into the weapon intended—a perfect instrument, sharp and cold and unburdened by the sentimentality that had once made him hesitate. The boy who'd wanted family and belonging and all those soft things that made men vulnerable was dead. Had been dying since he was eight years old, since Kessler began the training that would forge him into a weapon.

Maria would have wept to see it. Would have begged Kessler to stop, to show mercy, to let their son be something other than an extension of his father's will.

But Maria was dead. And the lesson of her death—the lesson Kessler had spent decades teaching Lukas—was simple: love was weakness. Trust was vulnerability. Family was another word for leverage.

The jet began its descent, engines changing pitch, the subtle shift in pressure that announced arrival. Through the windows, darkness was giving way to the faint glow of scattered towns below—civilization's edge, the boundary between order and wilderness.

Kessler returned to his office, closed the door, stood alone in the soft blue light. He pulled a photograph from his inside pocket—old, creased, the colors faded. It showed two young men in military fatigues, arms around each other's shoulders, smiling in the way men smile when they've survived something together. James Cole and Otto Reinhardt, before the world learned there was no Otto Reinhardt, before Maribor, before the world fractured.

"You should have stayed retired, my friend," Kessler murmured to the photograph. "Should have understood that some truths are too expensive to reveal. But you didn't. You started asking questions. You sent your sons into my world. You made yourself a problem."

He tucked the photograph away, checked his reflection in the darkened monitor. The face that looked back was calm, pleasant, unremarkable—the face of a man who could walk through airports and board meetings and diplomatic receptions without anyone suspecting what he was.

A monster who'd learned to wear humanity like a well-tailored suit.

The intercom chimed. The pilot: "Sir, we're beginning final approach. Landing in fifteen minutes."

"Excellent. Thank you, Captain."

Kessler opened the door, moved back into the main cabin. The operatives were suited up now—tactical gear, weapons checked, faces painted with camouflage that made them into shadows. Lukas was briefing them on approach routes, fields of fire, extraction procedures. Professional. Precise. Every inch his father's son.

The jet descended through cloud layers, broke into clear air. Below, the Appalachian Mountains rose in dark ridges, forests covering the land in a dark blanket, the occasional light marking human presence in the wilderness. Beautiful in its way—ancient, enduring, indifferent to the small violences humans inflicted on each other in its shadow.

Somewhere down there, James Cole was sitting in his cabin, probably cleaning weapons, probably knowing what was coming. Cole was too good an operator not to feel it—the pressure change that preceded violence, the way the world held its breath before death arrived.

Kessler sensed a feeling. "*Was it nostalgia?*" —he thought to himself. Most definitely not. They had shared so much once—operations in Eastern Europe, missions in the Balkans, the brotherhood that came from trusting someone with your life. Real friendship, or as close to real as Kessler had ever allowed himself.

Before Maribor.

Before James Cole saw what Kessler truly was.

The wheels touched down with a slight bump, the engines reversed, the aircraft slowing on a private runway that didn't appear on any aviation charts. A black convoy was already waiting—three SUVs, diplomatic plates, tinted windows that concealed whatever needed concealing.

The jet taxied to a stop. The door opened with a pressurized hiss.

Kessler stood and turned to his team. Six hardened killers and his son, all looking at him with the particular focus that violence required.

"Gentlemen," he stated pleasantly, "we have an old friend to visit. Let's not keep him waiting."

He descended the stairs into cold North Carolina air, breathed deep, smiled slightly.

Somewhere ahead, through dark forests and darker roads, James Cole was waiting.

And Kessler—who had spent thirty years pretending to be someone else, built empires in shadows, and eliminated each person that threatened his careful architecture—was going home.

Not to the Switzerland where he kept his office and his wealth and his carefully constructed legend.

But to the mountains where he'd once had a friend. Once believed in something other than power. Once been young enough to think that brotherhood meant something more than tactical advantage.

"I'm excited to see my old friend again," Kessler murmured to Lukas as they walked toward the waiting convoy. "It's been far too long. And we have so much to discuss. Maribor. His sons. The choices that brought us to this moment." He smiled, cold and certain. "It will be good to have closure. To finish what should have ended long ago."

Lukas added nothing further. With the focus of an experienced operator, he checked his weapon and climbed into the lead vehicle.

The convoy rolled into darkness, headlights cutting tunnels through the forest.

Behind them, the jet's engines cooled, ticking in the frigid air.

And ahead, in a cabin surrounded by silent trees, an old soldier loaded his rifle and waited for ghosts to arrive.

The war had been waiting—simmering.

Now it was finally coming home.

33

Firing Line

"Congratulations Ethan. In ten minutes, you've surpassed the legal insanity threshold for Miami drivers."- Noah

Miami, Florida—5:35 p.m.- Day 6

DRIVE! Selin's voice cut through the chaos like a whip crack.

Ethan stomped the accelerator, the car's engine screaming as they fishtailed out of the warehouse district, tires smoking on wet pavement. Behind them, a black SUV rounded the corner, its grille filling the rearview mirror like a shark's mouth.

"Left! Go left!" Selin had twisted in the passenger seat, her Glock raised, tracking the pursuing vehicle through the rear window. "Next intersection—NOW!"

Ethan yanked the wheel, the sedan's suspension protesting as they careened through a yellow light turning red. Horns blared. A delivery truck locked its brakes, missing them by inches. In the back seat, Noah was braced against the door, his laptop somehow still balanced on his knees, his face pale green.

"Jesus Christ, E!" Noah shouted over the engine noise. "You drive like you learned from video games! Bad video games! The kind with terrible physics!"

"Shut up and hold on!" Ethan snapped back, cutting across two lanes toward the highway on-ramp.

"Airport," Selin commanded, her voice eerily calm despite the violence of their movement. "Crowds, cameras, security. They won't risk exposure in a public space. Get us there. Fast."

The SUV was gaining, its engine far more powerful than their rental. Ethan could see two figures in the front seats, maybe more in the back. Professional hitters, moving with coordinated precision.

They hit I-95 doing seventy, weaving through traffic. Miami at rush hour was a special kind of hell—aggressive drivers, tourists who didn't understand lane discipline, and enough brake lights to look like Christmas in July. Ethan used it all, slipping between cars with inches to spare, using the tiniest of gaps.

"Right lane, three cars ahead," Selin observed, her tactical mind processing the battlefield. "Old man in a Cadillac. He's going to brake all of a sudden. Use him as a screen."

Ethan obeyed without questioning, cutting right at the moment the Cadillac's brake lights flared. The SUV swerved but couldn't avoid clipping the Cadillac's bumper, sending both vehicles into a spin. Behind them, metal crunched and tires screamed.

"Yes!" Noah pumped his fist. "That's—oh shit, there's another one!"

A second SUV had appeared from an on-ramp, merging into traffic behind them. These weren't only following—they were coordinating, boxing them in, forcing them toward a kill zone.

"They've got comms," Selin observed, scanning constantly. "Multiple teams. Professional operation. Ethan, next exit. We need to get off the highway before they can set up ahead of us."

The exit came up fast—LeJeune Road, cutting through Coral Gables. Ethan took it at sixty, the sedan tilting dangerously, Noah yelping as his laptop nearly flew out of his hands.

They plunged into surface streets, the afternoon sun casting long shadows through palm trees that lined the road like sentinels. Miami was showing off—art deco buildings painted in pastels, outdoor cafes full of beautiful people who had no idea a three-car chase was screaming past their mojitos.

The second SUV was still on them, closer now, its driver clearly more skilled than the first team. Ethan could see the passenger leaning out the window with what looked like a compact submachine gun.

"Gun!" Selin barked. "Ethan, when I say drop, you drop below the dashboard. Noah, get ON THE FLOOR!"

"I'm trying! There's no room! Your seat is—"

"NOW!"

The rear window exploded in a shower of safety glass. Selin returned fire, three quick shots that spiderwebbed the SUV's windshield. The vehicle swerved, clipped a parked car, recovered.

"This is insane!" Noah shouted from the footwell. "This is absolutely insane! I'm a hacker! I sit in front of computers! I don't do car chases!"

"You're doing one now!" Ethan yanked them through a right turn, narrowly missing a food truck that was...parked in the middle of the road. Because this was Miami.

Then, ahead of them, the most perfectly Miami thing possible: a flatbed truck loaded with freshly cut palm trees, their fronds dragging on the pavement like some kind of tropical parade float, was attempting to make a left turn from the right lane while the driver shouted into a phone, completely oblivious to traffic.

"You've got to be kidding me," Ethan muttered.

"Go around! Go AROUND!" Selin pointed to a gap between the truck and a strip mall.

"That's a sidewalk!"

"It's Miami! Anything is a road if you're brave enough! GO!"

Ethan jerked the wheel, mounting the curb, scattering pedestrians who dove out of the way with the practiced reflexes of people who'd seen worse. They flew past the palm tree truck, one of the fronds scraping their roof with a sound like fingernails on a chalkboard.

Behind them, the SUV wasn't so lucky. It tried to follow but clipped the truck's rear end, sending palm trees sliding off the flatbed like giant green missiles. The SUV's windshield disappeared under fifty pounds of tree, the driver swerving wildly before slamming into a fire hydrant.

Water exploded into the air, creating an impromptu fountain that drenched nearby sunbathers who barely looked up from their phones.

"HA!" Noah's head popped up from the footwell. "Did you see that? Did you SEE that? We got them with a PALM TREE! That's the most Florida thing that's ever happened!"

"We still have one on us," Selin voiced grimly, pointing at the rearview mirror where the first SUV—somehow repaired or re-placed—had rejoined the chase. "Airport. Now. Before they regroup."

Ethan pushed the sedan harder, engine whining as they rocketed through Coral Gables toward the airport. His hands were white-knuck-led on the wheel, his father's voice in his head: "Fear is information. Process it. Use it. Don't let it use you."

They passed a guy on a bicycle towing a full-size couch. A woman walking three iguanas on leashes. A lifted truck with truck nuts and a "Florida Man" bumper sticker. Miami was Miami-ing at maximum ca-pacity, and somehow that made the violence feel even more surreal.

"There!" Selin pointed ahead. Miami International's terminal build-ings rose like concrete mountains, planes screaming overhead at thirty seconds intervals. "Departures level. Drop us and get to long-term park-ing. We'll meet you at the pre-established checkpoint—the abandoned warehouse on 7th. You remember?"

"I remember," Ethan stated, threading through airport approach traffic.

"When we get out, you keep driving," Selin instructed. "Lead them away. Give us time to disappear into the crowd. Then you dump this car, steal another—"

"I'm not stealing a car!"

"Fine. Rent one. Whatever your American conscience requires. But lose this vehicle and meet us at the checkpoint in three hours. Not be-fore. Understood?"

Ethan nodded, pulling up to the departures curb where the so called "parking police" were already yelling at them about no stopping. Selin and Noah were out in seconds, blending into the river of travelers hauling luggage and screaming at children. Ethan caught one last glimpse of Selin's dark hair disappearing into the crowd, Noah limping slightly behind her, then he was accelerating back into traffic.

The SUV was still behind him, but now hesitating—too many witnesses, too many cameras, too much security. Ethan saw them slow, saw the passenger speaking urgently into a phone, saw them fall back.

He kept driving, leading them away from the airport, deeper into Miami's sprawl. His heart was hammering, adrenaline making the world too sharp, too bright. Noah's complaint echoed in his head: "You drive like you learned from video games."

His father had actually taught him to drive on the back roads of North Carolina, teaching him and Daniel to handle vehicles like they were extensions of their bodies. "Driving isn't about speed," James had observed. "It's about control. Options. Always knowing your next move."

Ethan checked his mirrors, saw the SUV falling further back, finally peeling off toward a side street. He'd bought them time. Not much, but enough.

Three hours until the meet. Three hours to dump the car, acquire a new one, and make it to the checkpoint without being followed.

He could do that. He had to do that.

Behind him, Miami sprawled in the evening light, beautiful and chaotic and completely indifferent to the small dramas playing out in its streets. Just another Tuesday in paradise.

Simultaneous — Washington D.C.

Donovan watched the mission feed from a dim motel room on the edge of D.C., the kind of place that rented by the hour and asked no questions. His laptop glowed in the darkness, the only light source, casting his face in blue-white pallor that made him look like a corpse.

The audio feed from Harris's team came through clean—too clean, professional-grade equipment that shouldn't exist outside government channels. He'd listened to the Miami chase in real-time, heard the gunfire, heard the coordination. Heard men who sounded like him discussing the elimination of targets with the same clinical detachment he'd once used for mob bosses and cartel enforcers.

The difference was: Ethan Cole wasn't a mob boss. He was a bank analyst who'd put forward questions. The wrong questions, sure. Questions that threatened powerful people. But questions that deserved answers, not bullets.

Donovan had spent most of the night replaying a single image: Ethan Cole's personnel file on the screen. The kid's evaluations—all excellent. His academic record from Princeton—top ten percent. His compliance history—spotless, meticulous, the kind of employee an institution would purport to want until that employee actually found something wrong.

He wasn't a traitor. He was right. And they were going to kill him for it.

Donovan rubbed his temples, his stomach vainly attempting to push down a feeling he hadn't noticed in years: shame. He'd spent thirty years in law enforcement, first as a Marine MP, then FBI, then private security. He'd told himself he was one of the good guys, that he protected people, that the badge meant something.

When had that stopped being true?

His phone buzzed. Text from an unknown number: "Status update required. Confirm Cole containment."

Donovan stared at it, fingers hovering over the keyboard. He could lie. Could say Cole was down, operation successful, problem solved. Buy the kid time to run, to hide, to maybe survive.

But they'd know. They always knew. And then the photograph would become reality—his ex-wife, his daughter, both paying for his moment of conscience.

He typed: "Still in pursuit. Subject proving elusive. Will advise."

The response came back immediately: "Inadequate. Report to secure line in 10 minutes."

Donovan immediately sensed something was off. That wasn't Harris. That was someone higher up the chain. Someone who wanted to hear his voice, assess his loyalty, decide if he was still useful or had become another problem requiring elimination.

He knew what would come next. The voice on the phone would be calm, reasonable, reminding him of what was at stake. Family. Future. The choices he'd already made that bound him to this path. And then, if Donovan showed any hesitation, any sign of growing a conscience, he'd become the next target.

His hand moved to open the secure line, then stopped. On the laptop screen, a new message had appeared in his secure email—not from Harris or Kessler's people, but from an encrypted account he didn't recognize:

"Bill—I know what they're making you do. I know about the photograph. I know about your family. But there's another way. When you're ready to stop running, we'll be ready to help. A friend."

Donovan's blood ran cold. Someone was watching him. Someone knew about the leverage, the threats, the choices he'd made. But who? And why reach out now?

The secure line was ringing. He had to answer. Had to make a choice.

He looked at the photograph from his wallet—his granddaughter, smiling at a school dance, whole life ahead of her. She didn't know what her grandfather had become. Didn't know he'd sold his soul to keep her safe.

But was she actually safe? Or was he simply telling himself that to justify the choices he'd made? Because men like Kessler didn't honor deals. They used leverage until it stopped being useful, then they eliminated loose ends. All of them.

The phone kept ringing.

Donovan closed his eyes, made his decision, and answered.

"Mr. Donovan," he answered, his voice steady despite the fear crawling up his spine.

The voice that came through was Kessler's—that pleasant, measured tone that made threats sound like observations. "Mr. Donovan. Tell me about your day?"

"Cole escaped. He's got help—professional help. Former intelligence, probably. They're good. But we're tracking them."

"Are you, though?" Kessler's voice carried amusement. "Because from where I'm sitting, it appears Cole has outmaneuvered two professional teams. With a hacker and a woman. That suggests either Cole is far more capable than we assessed, or—" He paused. "Or someone is helping him in ways we haven't anticipated. You wouldn't know anything about that?"

Donovan's mouth went dry. "No, sir."

"Interesting. Because I'm looking at your communication logs right now. You attempted to access Cole's file this morning. You tried to send an encrypted message to an external address. The message was blocked, but the attempt was noted." Kessler's voice dropped. "So I'll ask again: are you helping Mr. Cole?"

"I was doing research. Trying to understand his network, his resources. You can't hunt someone if you don't know who they might contact."

"Plausible. Reasonable, even." Kessler sounded thoughtful. "But unconvincing. You see, Mr. Donovan, I've been doing this an exceptionally long time. I've watched men struggle with their consciences. Watched them decide that the price of compliance is too high, that saving their souls matters more than saving their families. It's always tragic. And it always ends the same way."

"Sir, I—"

"Your granddaughter. Jennifer, yes? Such a pretty girl. Sixteen. Applying to colleges soon, I believe. Georgetown is her first choice. Ambitious. She has your eyes, I'm told." The voice remained pleasant, conversational. "It would be terrible if something happened to interfere with her future. An accident. A scandal. A grandfather arrested for conspiracy. These things ruin young lives, don't they?"

Donovan noticed rage beginning to surge through him, white-hot and pure. "You leave her out of this."

"That's entirely up to you, Mr. Donovan. You finish this job—you find Cole, and you eliminate the problem cleanly—and your granddaughter most definitely goes to Georgetown. She lives her life. And you remain the hero who protected his country and his family. But if you hesitate, if you develop a conscience at this late stage—" Kessler's voice hardened slightly. "Then I'll ensure that both you and your dear Jennifer understand the cost of disloyalty. I do certainly hope I am being clear, Mr. Donovan."

This was it. The moment. The choice between being a good man and being a safe man. Between protecting his daughter and protecting his soul.

Donovan thought about the Marines who'd taught him that honor meant something. About the FBI agents who'd believed in justice. About the man he'd been before the compromises started, before each small corruption led to the next, until he'd become unrecognizable to himself.

"Crystal clear," he heard himself say.

"Very well. Then we understand each other perfectly well. Find Cole. Finish this. And Mr. Donovan—" Kessler's voice softened again, almost kindly. "Don't try to be clever. Don't try to be a savior. Men who attempt to be such end up saving no one, especially themselves. You would agree, yes?"

"Yes," Donovan uttered, the word tasting like ashes.

The line went dead.

Donovan sat in the darkness, staring at his daughter's photograph, feeling the weight of all the choices that had led him here. He'd become exactly what he'd spent his career fighting against: a man who used violence to protect power. A man who justified evil with family. A man who'd chosen survival over principle so many times he'd forgotten there was a difference.

The encrypted email was still on his screen: "When you're ready to stop running, we'll be ready to help."

But he wasn't ready. Not yet. Maybe not ever.

He closed the laptop, pocketed his phone, and walked out into the D.C. night to finish becoming the monster he'd promised himself he'd never be.

Back in Miami — Two Hours Later- 7:35 p.m.

The abandoned warehouse on 7th Street looked like the other condemned buildings in Miami's industrial district—rusted corrugated metal, broken windows, chain-link fence adorned with NO TRESPASSING signs that nobody respected. Graffiti covered each available surface, ranging from impressive murals to simple tags. The place had been their backup plan, scouted two days earlier when Selin had insisted on establishing multiple fallback positions.

Ethan arrived first, parking the "borrowed" Toyota Corolla three blocks away and approaching on foot. He'd dumped the rental in a long-term lot at the airport, walked through the terminal to confuse any surveillance, then caught a bus to a strip mall where the Toyota had been sitting with keys in the ignition. A Miami resident's questionable parking choices had become Ethan's salvation.

He slipped through a gap in the fence, moving with the careful deliberation his father had taught him: check corners, stay in shadows, assume hostile until proven otherwise. The warehouse interior was vast and empty, shafts of evening light cutting through the gloom in dusty columns.

"You're late," Selin's voice came from the shadows to his left.

Ethan didn't jump—barely—and turned to find her emerging from behind a stack of pallets, weapon lowered but ready. Noah was with her, looking exhausted, his wounded arm in a better sling now, probably courtesy of an airport pharmacy.

"By three minutes," Ethan added. "I had to make sure I wasn't followed."

"Were you?"

"No. Dumped the car, took three buses in random directions, walked the last mile. If they're still on me, they're better than I can detect."

Selin nodded approval. "Good. Noah managed to save most of his equipment. We've got connectivity, we've got encryption, we've got—" She paused. "We've got a problem."

"Besides the obvious?" Ethan moved closer, keeping his voice low despite the apparent emptiness.

Noah held up his laptop, screen glowing in the dim warehouse. "While we were being shot at—which, for the record, was absolutely terrifying and I never want to do again—I managed to finish parsing the data you pulled from the bank. Ethan, this is bigger than we thought. Way bigger."

"How much bigger?"

"The Directorate isn't purely one organization. It's a network. Hundreds of companies, shell corporations, front groups. They're embedded in governments, militaries, intelligence services. And the man at the center—" Noah turned the screen. A photograph. Silver hair, pleasant face, expensive suit. "Andreas Kessler. Swiss national, officially retired banker. Unofficially? He's the architect of the whole thing."

Ethan stared at the face, feeling ice in his veins. "You're sure?"

"His name appears in ledgers going back thirty years. He's connected to arms deals, regime changes, market manipulations. And Ethan—" Noah hesitated. "There's a connection to your father. Old operations. Classified stuff I shouldn't have access to but managed to find anyway because I'm actually good at my job despite people shooting at me."

"I know, he told me a few years back about their connection. I never thought—"

Noah interrupted— "Kessler worked with your father. Back in the nineties. Some kind of joint operation—CIA and European intelligence. But something went wrong. The files are heavily redacted, but your dad's name appears in reports investigating corruption, unauthorized operations. He was asking questions."

Ethan sensed the world tilting off its axis.

"We need to move," Selin whispered quietly. "This location is compromised the moment we've been here more than four hours. Standard protocol. We regroup, we plan, we decide next moves. But we can't stay in Miami. Too hot, too many resources they can deploy here."

"Where do we go?" Ethan quizzed.

Selin and Noah exchanged looks. Then Noah muttered quietly, "Your brother. We need to find Daniel. If Kessler was working with your father, he knows about both of you. Daniel's in danger. And—" He paused. "According to the chatter I'm picking up, there's been a training accident in Albania. Casualty reported as Marcus Vale. One of Kessler's contract operators."

Ethan sensed his chest tighten, the vice tightening on him. "Marcus Vale is Daniel. That's his operational identity."

"I know," Noah maintained gently. "But the weird thing? No body recovered. Report filed, but no confirmation. If your brother is half as good as you say he is—"

"He got out," Ethan finished. "He survived. And he'll be coming."

"Coming where?" Selin questioned.

Ethan thought about his brother, about the years of training, about the places their father had taken them that held meaning only to the family. "Greece. Athens. There's a place we used to go as kids. Daniel knows I'm in trouble, and he'll head there. He'll expect me to figure it out."

"Then that's where we go," Selin insisted. "We leave tonight. Before they can regroup. Before they can predict our next move."

Outside, Miami hummed with evening life—clubs opening, tourists flooding the beaches, the city preparing for another night of beautiful chaos. Inside the warehouse, three fugitives prepared for a journey that would either end in justice or death.

Ethan looked at Noah's screen again, at Kessler's pleasant face. The architect. The spider at the center of the web.

"We're coming for you," Ethan whispered to the photograph. "All of us. And this time, you won't see us coming."

Two days prior — Geneva, Switzerland

Kessler stood at his window, watching dawn break over the Alps, when the call came through. The aide's voice was carefully neutral—they'd learned not to show emotion when delivering potentially problematic news.

"Sir, we've confirmed a secondary contact. The younger Cole has been communicating with someone using old military encryption protocols. We backtraced it through three proxies before the trail went cold. But we caught fragments of the conversation."

"And?" Kessler's voice remained calm, but his fingers tightened slightly on his coffee cup—the only tell that he was interested.

"A retired American operator. Former CIA. The father." The aide paused. "James Cole. He's alive. The heart attack was... he survived it. And he's been in contact with his son Ethan Cole."

A stillness came over Kessler at hearing about the American operator. Then, slowly, a smile spread across his face—genuine pleasure, the first real emotion he'd shown in months. "James. My old friend James" he said aloud.

"Sir?"

"Do you know how rare it is," Kessler remarked, ignoring his aide's question, turning from the window, his eyes bright with something that looked almost like joy, "to have a worthy opponent? Someone who understands the game? Who knows the rules well enough to break them creatively?"

He walked to his desk, sat down, and pulled up a file he'd kept for thirty years—photographs, operation reports, classified briefings. All featuring a younger James Cole. "We worked together, in the late 90's. He was American special forces, I was... well, I was representing certain European interests. We had compatible objectives. Our sons were fond of one another. For a while."

"What changed?"

"He developed a conscience," Kessler asserted, his voice warm with nostalgia. "Started asking questions about where the money was going, who benefitted from our operations. He thought we were serving our countries. I knew we were serving ourselves. When he threatened to expose certain irregularities, I had to... make arrangements."

"The heart attack."

"A mild heart attack, actually. Sufficient to force his retirement, insufficient to actually kill him. A modest miscalculation on my part." Kessler's smile widened. "But perhaps a fortunate one. You see, I've spent the past several years wondering whether my old friend James had forgotten about me, about what he'd learned. Whether he'd decided to let sleeping dogs lie."

He stood, paced to the window, hands clasped behind his back. "But he didn't forget. He's been watching. Probably investigating. Gathering evidence. Training his sons to continue the work if something happened to him. How wonderfully paranoid of him."

"Orders, sir?"

Kessler turned, and his expression had transformed from pleasant to predatory. "Finish the sons first. Both of them. Eliminate them cleanly, publicly if possible, in a way that sends a message. But James—" His eyes gleamed. "James is mine. We have unfinished business, he and I. Conversations we never got to complete."

"That's risky, sir. If he's been planning—"

"Risk is what makes life interesting." Kessler's voice took on an almost giddy quality. "For thirty years, I've been playing chess against bureaucrats and fools. Men who think money is the only currency that matters. But James? James understands the deeper game. He knows that ideas are more dangerous than bullets, that truth is more valuable than gold." He paused, savoring the moment. "He's the only opponent worth having. And I'm going to enjoy every minute of destroying him."

The aide shifted uncomfortably. "Sir, with respect, if Cole has been gathering evidence for decades—"

"Then we'll take it from him. Along with his dignity, his hope, and finally, his life." Kessler walked back to his desk and continued—"I know James. He'll be holed up in his old cabin, I know exactly where he will be. The younger Cole will likely be heading to Greece, most likely to meet up with his brother. Athens has always been one of James' favorite cities—all that history about democracy and justice and the other myths we tell ourselves."

He zoomed in on a map of Athens, studying it with the intensity of a general planning a campaign. "Position assets there. Surveillance, interdiction teams, all assets we have available. When the Cole brothers reunite—and they will reunite, family is their weakness—we'll be waiting."

"And if Ethan Cole has already shared the evidence? If there are backup copies, dead drops, insurance files?"

Kessler's smile became razor-thin. "Then we will find those too. And we will eliminate any person that Ethan Cole has shared evidence with. This is our purpose. To create order from chaos. To silence the voices that threaten stability. James Cole thought he could hide from history, thought he could train his sons to fight battles he'd lost. But history always comes around again. And this time—" He picked up his phone, dialed Lukas's number. "This time, we will finish what we started long ago."

The phone rang once before Lukas answered. "Father."

"Lukas. New development. Your dear Uncle James survived our little heart attack and has been orchestrating his sons' resistance. We need to pay him a visit. The brothers can be eliminated in any manner you see fit, but we need to pay James a visit and finish what I started long ago. Understood?"

"Understood. This complicates things."

"On the contrary," Kessler noted, his voice bright with anticipation. "This makes it especially interesting. We are not hunting children anymore. We are hunting a professional. Someone who taught his sons everything they know and who has had decades to prepare for this moment." He laughed softly. "Finally a challenge worthy of our attention."

Kessler ended the call and stood at the window, watching the Alps catch the morning light, feeling more alive than he had in years. James Cole. His old friend. His worthy adversary. Coming out of the shadows for one final confrontation.

"I wondered when the past would wake up," Kessler murmured to himself, repeating words he'd voiced years ago. "And now it has. Now we'll see who learned the better lessons, James. You with your principles and your family. Or me with my pragmatism and my machine."

He turned back to his desk, pulled out a bottle of cognac he'd been saving for a special occasion, and poured himself a glass. Raised it toward the mountains.

"To old friends," he added softly. "And to the game we're about to play."

He drank, savoring the burn, savoring the anticipation, savoring the knowledge that somewhere out there, James Cole was doing exactly the same thing—preparing for a reunion a long time in the making.

And when they finally met again, when all the pieces were in position and all the secrets laid bare, only one of them would walk away.

Kessler intended to make sure it was him.

34

Call Home

"Kessler wants my life? Fine. But he'll have to come and take it. And I won't go down easy."—James Cole

Miami Florida- 7:46 a.m.- Day 7

Silence enveloped the warehouse except for the low hum of the re-frigerator-sized generator Noah had scavenged from the dock. Ethan and Selin took turns taking quick cat naps. While Selin was keeping watch, Ethan sat on an overturned crate near a cracked window, watching the horizon fade from indigo to gray. Miami was waking — unaware that its newest fugitives were hiding two floors above the waterline.

Ethan finally pulled the burner phone from his pocket and turned it over in his hands. His father's number was burned into memory, but he hadn't called in months. Maybe longer. The last time they'd spoken, Ethan had brushed him off — I'm fine, Dad. I'm not living in your world. But now, his world had found him.

He took a breath and dialed.

Three rings. Then a click. The voice that answered was gravel and calm, the kind that sounded like it had seen too much and stopped flinching.

"Ethan?"

"Hey, Dad." A pause, long enough to say what was needed.

"I know you're in trouble, son."

Ethan closed his eyes. "Yeah."

He could almost hear his father's jaw tighten through the line.

"Talk to me."

"I can't. Not over this. But Dad, I need you to know something." Ethan glanced across the warehouse at Selin, who was checking the window sight lines, her profile backlit by the rising sun. "There's someone with me. A woman. Turkish intelligence officer named Selin Yilmaz."

His father's voice changed — softened almost imperceptibly. "Turkish? How'd you manage that?"

"Long story. She saved my life. Multiple times now." Ethan paused, surprised at what he was about to say. "I think... I'm falling for her, Dad. I know it's insane given the whirlwind of events that are happening, but—"

"It's not insane." His father's voice carried something Ethan hadn't heard in years — warmth beneath the steel. "That's the only sane thing in all of this. You find someone who has your back when the world's trying to kill you, you hold onto that."

"You sound like you're my best man at a wedding I'll never have."

A soft laugh, rough with emotion. "Your mother would've liked her. Anyone crazy enough to run with a Cole boy has to have something special." The humor faded. "What's she like?"

Ethan watched Selin move through the shadows with practiced efficiency — lethal and graceful in equal measure. "Smart. Tougher than me. She doesn't take my shit, and she..." He struggled for words. "She makes me want to be better than I am."

"Then she's perfect." His father's voice grew thick. "Listen to me, son. When this is over — and it will be over — you marry that woman. You hear me? You don't wait. You don't let fear or timing or anything else get in the way. Life's too goddamn short for that kind of cowardice."

"Dad—"

"I mean it, Ethan. I'm proud of you. More than I've ever told you. You and Daniel both — you turned out better than I had any right to expect. Better men than me."

"That's not true."

"It is. I made mistakes — trusted the wrong people, put you in danger I didn't see coming. But you... you've got something I never had. You know when to trust your instincts. When to let someone in." A pause, heavy with things untold. "Your mother saw that in you when you were a boy. She told me you had her heart, not mine. She was right."

"Why in the hell are you talking like this?" —Ethan questioned while his throat began to itch. An itch that couldn't be scratched.

"Because I should have said it years ago. I should have told you and your brother each and every day." His father's voice wavered, just slightly. "I love you, son. I am so proud of the man you've become. And I want you to know — whatever happens next, you didn't fail. You hear me? You did good."

"Dad, what's going on? What aren't you telling me?"

A long exhale, like a man preparing for something inevitable. "They came for you already. Professionals. That means they know what you found. And if they know what you found, then they know you talked to me."

"Then get out. Leave the cabin. Go to Daniel—" "Can't do that." His father's voice was calm, resolved. "Some debts come due, Ethan. I've been running from my debts for too long. Time to settle accounts."

"This is about Kessler, isn't it?"

The silence was confirmation enough.

"Ethan, you listen to me carefully. You don't go to the cops. You don't call your office. You take that woman who's watching your back, and you disappear. You find your brother. You survive." His father's voice hardened. "And you don't come looking for me. Promise me that."

"I can't promise that." "Yes, you can. Because I'm telling you to. Last order from your old man — you let me handle this my way."

Ethan could picture him now — standing in that cabin in North Carolina, the battered flag on the wall, the long shadows across the floorboards, the rifles laid out like a museum of discipline. Loading weapons with the same methodical precision he had taught his sons. Preparing for an enemy he'd known would come eventually.

"Dad, there has to be another way—" "There isn't. Not anymore." A pause. "You still carrying the blade I gave you?"

Ethan touched his boot — the old K-BAR tucked inside. "Always." "Then remember what I taught you. You move first. You finish what you start. And Ethan..." His voice cracked, just slightly. "You tell that Turkish girl how you feel about her. Don't keep secrets from someone you love. I kept too many from your mother, thought I was protecting her. All I did was waste time I could've spent being honest."

"Dad—"

"And you tell Daniel..." His father stopped, gathered himself. "You tell your brother I was proud of him too. That watching him become the man he is... that was the greatest honor of my life. You both were."

"Please don't do this", Ethan pleaded.

"It's already done. Has been for thirty years — Only I didn't realize it until now." The sound of a rifle bolt sliding home. "I'm sorry I brought this to your door. Sorry I trusted the wrong man and dragged you into his world. But I'm not sorry for the life I gave you, or the men you and your brother became. You remember that."

Through the phone, Ethan heard wind through trees, the distant bark of his father's dog. With increasing senses, they felt to Ethan as if they were last sounds.

"You take care of yourself, Ethan. You build the life I didn't get the chance to build with your mother. You be happy — that's how you win. Not by fighting wars in shadows, but by living your life in the light."

"Dad, I love you—"

"I know you do, son. I love you too. More than I have words for." A pause. "Your mother used to say love was the only thing that lasted. The only thing worth the cost. She was right about that too."

"Dad—"

"Goodbye son."

Then silence and the line went dead.

Simultaneous- The Cole North Carolina Cabin

The phone slipped from James Cole's hand onto the table beside a field map marked with positions — old tactical thinking, old habits. His vision blurred for barely a moment as he stared at the photographs on the mantle: Sarah, beautiful and gone. Daniel in dress uniform. Ethan on graduation day, smiling like the world still made sense.

James Cole had taught his sons everything he could. Taught them to fight, to think, to survive. Told them he loved them — finally, after too many years of letting silence speak where words should have lived.

It would have to be enough.

He walked to the window and stared out at the tree line. The woods were quiet. Too quiet. The kind of quiet that came before contact. Before violence. It was then he noticed his dog had stopped barking.

He reached for the M4 leaning against the wall and thumbed the safety. His hands were steady — old muscle memory, the calm that came from accepting outcomes rather than fighting them.

"I should've killed you in Maribor," he whispered to the empty room. "Should've seen what you were before you destroyed the world."

Outside, shapes moved between the trees. Professional spacing. Co-ordinated approach. Three... no, four men. Moving like they'd done this before, like they'd done it dozens of times. James Cole chambered a round and moved away from the window.

His last thought before the door exploded inward was of his wife Sarah, so many years ago, laughing in morning light. Telling him that love was the only thing worth dying for. She had been right about that too.

Back in Miami

Ethan lowered the phone and sat in silence, the weight of the call set-tling like lead in his chest. His hands were shaking. His father's voice still echoed in his ears — proud, resigned, saying goodbye without saying the words. Selin crossed the warehouse and knelt beside him. She didn't ask what was wrong. Didn't offer empty comfort. She simply placed her hand over his, steady and warm.

"My father," Ethan uttered quietly. "He's going to die. Maybe already dead."

"You don't know that", Selin remarked.

"I do." Ethan met her eyes. "He was saying goodbye. Telling me he loves me. Telling me to trust you."

Selin's expression softened, ever slightly. "Smart man."

"He added I should tell you how I feel. Not keep secrets. That he wasted too much time with my mother being careful instead of honest."

"Then tell me"—Selin demanded.

"I'm terrified." The words came out raw, unfiltered. "I'm terrified that everyone I love is going to die because I found those files. My father, Daniel, Noah. You. I'm terrified that I'm going to fail all of you the way he thinks he failed me."

"You won't." —Selin softly responded.

"How do you know?"-Ethan posed, his tone becoming more controlled.

"Because you're still fighting. Because you called your father even knowing it might be the last time. Because you're not running away from this — you're running toward answers." She squeezed his hand. "That's not failure. That's courage."

Ethan wanted to believe her. Wanted to believe that love and courage could be enough against men who killed for profit, who turned friendship into weapons, who built empires in shadows. But his father's voice kept echoing: *Some debts come due.* Noah watched them from the other side of the room, his arm freshly bandaged. "That your old man?"

"Yeah."—Ethan replied.

"What'd he say?"

Ethan stood slowly, his father's final words burning in his memory like a brand. "He told me to run." He looked at Selin, then at Noah. "But he also told me to finish what I start. So that's what we're going to do."

"Finish what?"-Noah stated, more statement than question.

"Find Kessler. Expose the Directorate. Burn it all down."

"And your father?"-Noah raised.

Ethan's jaw tightened. "If he's alive, we save him. If he's not..." He touched the K-BAR in his boot. "Then we make sure the men who killed him don't get to walk away."

Selin stood beside him, her expression hard and determined. "Then we move now. Before they consolidate. Before they clean up loose ends."

"Agreed."

Outside, Miami continued waking — oblivious to the three fugitives in a warehouse, planning war against an enemy most people didn't know existed. In North Carolina, in a cabin surrounded by silent woods, James Cole's war was ending. In Miami, his son's war was only beginning.

And in the space between — in the terrible distance between a father's last words and a son's first act of vengeance — love and legacy collided with the only truth that mattered: Some debts could only be paid in blood. And the Cole family had been in debt for a long time.

35

Ghosts of Maribor

"James, you see tragedy, while I see necessity. That is why you will always suffer in this world, and why I will always shape it."
—Andreas Kessler

Miami Florida—7:26 a.m.- Day 7

Back in Miami, miles away, the phone in Ethan's hand had gone silent. He stared at it for a long moment, his father's last words echoing: "Don't look back. Don't look for me."

But Ethan couldn't stop his mind from circling back to the name his father had avoided: Kessler.

He'd heard it once a couple of years back, in a conversation he wasn't supposed to overhear. His father and an old Army buddy, Colonel Harrison, whiskey-drunk at a reunion on the cabin's back porch.

Ethan had been pretending to sleep in the upstairs room with the window cracked open. Their voices had drifted up through the humid darkness, slurred and raw with the kind of honesty that only comes when men think no one's listening. "You should've killed that son of a bitch when you had the chance," Harrison had announced, ice cubes clinking in his glass. "I know," his father had replied.

"But I thought he was one of us."

"Nobody's one of us after Maribor, James. That place changed him. Or maybe it showed you what he always was." Silence then. The sound of bourbon being poured. Then his father's voice, quieter, haunted: "I watched him execute an unarmed man in cold blood. Smiled while he did it. And I did nothing."

"You were following orders."

"Orders from ghosts. Orders that came through back channels I couldn't verify. And Otto—" His father had stopped himself. "Kessler. He knew exactly what he was doing. He wanted me to see it. Wanted me to understand that he'd gone somewhere I couldn't follow."

Ethan tried to unhear what he'd heard. Trying to forget the way his father's voice had cracked on that last sentence. He'd never questioned what Maribor meant. Now, standing in a Miami warehouse with his father's goodbye still burning in his ears, Ethan understood: the war his father had fought wasn't over. It had been waiting. Hibernating in shadows and silence. Gathering strength.

And now it had come home.

Operation Black Frost — Eastern Europe, Winter 2012

The snow fell in silence—thick, slow, suffocating. Each flake a small death drifting through darkness, covering the world in white erasure. James Cole moved through the forest like a shadow made of muscle and discipline, his breath steady despite the cold biting through the seams of his gloves, through the gaps in his collar, through the layers of gear that were supposed to keep him human in this frozen hell.

Here he was. Major, U.S. Army Special Operations. Six tours across three continents. Decorated. Trusted. Excellent his job. Still believed the work meant something. The radio whispered in his ear—coded static from the base camp twelve kilometers away, voices reduced to numbers and brevity codes.

Alpha Team holding position. Extraction window closing. Weather deteriorating. All the bureaucratic poetry of men trying to control chaos from a distance. His partner moved ahead through the trees—Otto Reinhardt, Swiss intelligence liaison, pale eyes that caught moonlight like ice. He moved with the kind of fluidity that made Cole think of wolves, of predators who understood terrain as instinct rather than training. Lean and controlled, Each motion economically precise, the faint shimmer of his rifle optics catching silver light as he ghosted between birch trees that stood like bones against the darkness.

They had been working together for three years. Joint NATO operations, the kind that happened in margins and footnotes, the kind that official histories would never record. Cole had saved Reinhardt's life in Kosovo. Reinhardt had returned the favor in Bosnia. They'd been drunk together, trained together, bled together. Brotherhood forged in the spaces between nations, where flags meant less than competence and trust was the only currency that mattered.

James Cole had trusted him. Trusted him completely. The forest opened into a clearing where the old monastery sat like a wound in the snow—Orthodox, abandoned since the Yugoslav wars, walls pocked with bullet holes and artillery scars. Windows gaped empty, stained glass long since shattered into memory. The copper dome had collapsed inward, revealing wooden ribs beneath like a carcass picked clean by time and violence. Beautiful, in the way ruins are beautiful. Honest about what the world does to faith.

Their target was inside: Dimitri Volkov, arms broker, go-between for weapons flowing from Russian arsenals into the Balkans. Small-time operator with big-time connections. The kind of man who knew where the bodies were buried because he'd helped negotiate the shovels. The mission parameters were clear: extract, interrogate, deliver to NATO custody. Standard black-bag operation. In and out before dawn, before the local police or—worse—the Croatian paramilitaries realized anyone had been there.

Cole signaled: two fingers, then a fist. *Hold position. I'll secure the perimeter.* Reinhardt nodded, those pale eyes reflecting nothing, giving nothing away. Professional. Controlled. Cole moved along the monastery's eastern wall, checking angles, clearing sightlines. The snow muffled his footsteps, his breath, even his thoughts. In the silence, he could hear his heartbeat, steady and strong. Could hear the wind moving through broken stone like the breathing of something vast and patient.

When he rounded the corner and entered through the collapsed nave, Reinhardt was already inside. The interior was a cathedral of shadows and ice. Moonlight fell through the ruined dome in pale shafts, illuminating columns of frozen air where breath became visible, where the temperature had dropped low enough that moisture crystallized midflight. The floor was buried under snow that had drifted through broken windows, smooth and undisturbed except for their boot prints and a dark shape in the center.

Dimitri Volkov knelt in the snow like a penitent, hands zip-tied behind his back, head bowed. Forty-something, balding, wearing a leather jacket too thin for the cold. His breath came in ragged clouds. Blood crusted one side of his face—probably from the grab, from being yanked out of whatever warm hole he'd been hiding in and dragged here to answer for his sins.

He looked up as Cole approached, eyes wide with the particular terror of men who've spent their lives trafficking in violence and now find themselves on the receiving end.

"Please," Volkov muttered in broken English. "Please, I have children—" "Shut up," Reinhardt responded quietly. Not cruel, not kind. Just matter of fact. The voice of a man stating a condition of reality. Cole moved to the extraction point—a side door that opened onto the forest trail where their exfil vehicle waited half a kilometer away. He checked his watch: 0347 hours. Forty-three minutes until the window closed. Plenty of time.

"We're clear," Cole noted, turning back. "Let's—"

Reinhardt's pistol was already raised. The moment crystallized, sharp and terrible. Cole saw it with the hyper-clarity that comes in moments of cognitive dissonance, when the brain tries to reconcile what's happening with what should be happening: Reinhardt's Sig Sauer P226, suppressor threaded on, muzzle centered on Volkov's forehead. Reinhardt's finger on the trigger, taking up slack. Reinhardt's face absolutely calm, serene even, like a priest about to deliver communion.

"Wait—" Cole started.

The suppressor hissed. Not silent—silencers never are—but muted, compressed, the sound of air being forced through a tube. A mechanical cough in the frozen dark. Volkov's head snapped back. He stayed upright for a moment, kneeling in the snow, then toppled sideways like a felled tree. Blood spread from the exit wound, black in the moonlight, steaming in the cold, melting the snow in a perfect circle that grew and grew and grew. Cole's hand went to his sidearm, instinct overriding thought.

"What the hell was that?" —Cole demanded with a furious tone.

Reinhardt holstered his weapon with the same calm precision he had come to be known by. "He was compromised. Orders changed."

"Who changed them?" Cole's voice was tight, controlled, but violence hummed beneath it—the violence of betrayal, of trust being gutted in real-time.

Reinhardt turned to face him fully. In the moonlight, his features looked carved from ice—sharp cheekbones, hollow shadows where his eyes should be, mouth a thin line of absolute certainty.

"People above your clearance, my friend. The kind who redraw maps instead of reading them."

"That's not an answer." —Cole snapped back.

"It's the only answer you're going to get—Mein Freund".

Cole stepped forward, closing the distance, putting himself into Reinhardt's space. Close enough to see the other man's pupils, to smell gun oil and cold leather, to read the micro expressions that might betray hesitation or doubt. There were none. "That wasn't justice," Cole voiced, jaw tight enough to ache. Reinhardt studied him for a long moment—not defensive, not guilty, but very... interested. The way a scientist might study a specimen.

"Justice?" He uttered the word like it was foreign, like he was tasting it for the first time and finding it curious. "Justice is a luxury for men who've never seen what happens when it fails."

"He was our prisoner. We had protocols—"

"Protocols." Reinhardt smiled, and the expression was worse than anger. It was patience. Condescension. The look of someone explaining basic arithmetic to a child. "Volkov knew the location of six weapons caches. He knew the identities of multiple NATO assets embedded in paramilitary groups. He knew operational details that, in the wrong hands, would get good men killed." He gestured at the body cooling in the snow.

"He was going to sell that information the moment we delivered him to custody. To the Russians, to the Serbs, to whoever paid first. So I solved the problem."

"By executing him?" —Cole retorted.

"By preventing a larger tragedy. By doing what needed to be done because you—"

Reinhardt's eyes hardened "—because men like you still believe in rules that our enemies abandoned years ago."

The wind howled through the broken dome, carrying the smell of cordite and copper, the wet-iron stench of fresh blood. Snow swirled through the nave like ghosts, settling on Volkov's open eyes. For the first time, Cole saw it clearly: the fracture in Reinhardt. Not a fracture—that implied something broken, something that had once been whole. No, this was architecture. This was design.

The man standing before him had been built this way, or had rebuilt himself this way, stone by stone, until nothing remained but function. Purpose without conscience. Will without doubt. A man capable of doing anything because he'd already convinced himself it was necessary.

"What are you?" Cole whispered quietly.

Reinhardt tilted his head. "I'm the man who does what you can't. What you won't."

"I won't murder prisoners." —Cole insisted.

"Then you'll lose." Reinhardt's voice was soft, almost gentle. "You'll lose because you're still fighting yesterday's war with yesterday's rules. The world has moved on, James. It's not about nations anymore. Not about flags or constitutions or the rule of law. It's about who has the will to act when action is required. Who can see the board clearly enough to make the hard moves."

He turned away, surveying the monastery with an appraising eye. "We burn this. Standard cleanup protocol. The snow will cover the rest."

"I'm reporting this." —Cole barked.

"James, James my dear friend...No, you won't." Reinhardt's eyes glimmered.

"The hell I won't—"

Reinhardt turned back, and for the first time, Cole saw something that might have been emotion in those pale eyes. Not anger. Not fear. Something colder. "You won't report this because the orders came through NATO channels. Because half a dozen people in three different countries authorized this operation. Because if you start pulling threads, you'll discover that the system you believe in has been compromised for years."

He stepped closer. "And because you're a good soldier, James. You follow orders. You trust the chain of command. That's what makes you valuable. That's what makes you...useful."

The words hit like physical blows. Not because they were wrong, but because they were right. Because Cole had spent his entire adult life believing in structure, in hierarchy, in the idea that good men doing hard things in the service of noble causes could make the world better.

And now that belief was revealed as exactly what Reinhardt mentioned it was: predictability. Weakness.

"This isn't over," Cole added.

"I would expect nothing less, James".

Reinhardt pulled a thermite grenade from his pack. "But we still have a job to finish. So let's finish it, or stand aside and let me work."

They burned the monastery that night to erase the evidence. Cole helped, because what else could he do? Walk twenty kilometers through hostile territory to report a murder to superiors who might have ordered it?

Abandon his mission, his unit, his career, over a dead arms dealer who'd been a monster in his own right? So he placed the charges. Set the timers. Stood in the snow and watched the building that had survived wars and revolutions and the slow entropy of decades go up in flames.

The fire climbed fast, hungry, feeding on centuries of dry wood and ancient tapestries and the accumulated faith of generations who'd prayed in that space for salvation. It reflected off the snow like a second sun, turning night into day, painting the clearing in shades of gold and orange and red.

The heat was intense enough that Cole had to back away, had to shield his face, even from fifty meters. Smoke rose in a pillar that would be visible for miles, a beacon announcing that something here had died.

Reinhardt stood closer to the flames than was safe, his face painted in blood light, his eyes reflecting fire. He looked like something out of medieval paintings—a saint or a demon, depending on perspective. Beautiful in the way destruction is beautiful. Terrible in the way inevitability is terrible. As the roof collapsed inward with a roar of timber and masonry, Reinhardt turned to Cole.

Snow had started falling again, catching in his hair, on his shoulders, melting against the heat that radiated from his skin. "One day, you'll understand," he voiced softly. His voice was barely audible over the fire's roar, but Cole heard each word clearly.

"The world doesn't need heroes, James. It needs control. And I have simply evolved past the handicap of conscience."

James Cole didn't answer. Couldn't answer. What do you say to a man who has revealed himself to you as something other than human? Something post-human, maybe. Something that had looked at the entirety of moral philosophy and ethical constraint and decided it was vestigial. Evolutionary baggage to be discarded in pursuit of efficiency.

As they watched the fire rise higher, the weight of something unspoken began to settle between them like a gravestone. A silent promise, though neither of them named it as such: that if they ever met again, when the stakes were different and the circumstances allowed for honesty, one of them would have to fall.

Because two men couldn't exist in the same world when one had crossed a line the other still believed in. The fire burned through the night. By dawn, nothing remained but blackened stone and ash. The snow covered most of it within hours, nature providing the final erasure that intelligence services required.

They walked back to the exfil point in silence. Loaded into the vehicle without speaking. Drove through the gray winter morning while the radio crackled with meaningless traffic and the heater struggled against cold that had nothing to do with temperature. Cole filed his report when they returned to base: ***Target eliminated during extraction. Monastery destroyed per cleanup protocols. Mission successful.***

He didn't mention the execution. Didn't mention Reinhardt's eyes in the firelight, or the way the man had spoken about conscience like it was a disease. He told himself it was because he lacked proof. Because chain of command had to be respected. Because you don't destroy a good man's career over one bad call in impossible circumstances. All of it was true. None of it was why. The real reason: he was afraid. Afraid that if he pulled that thread, the entire sweater would unravel. That he'd discover the system he'd given his life to was exactly what Reinhardt indicated it was—compromised, corrupted, a machine that ground up good intentions and produced expedient outcomes.

So he stayed silent. And Otto Reinhardt—who was actually Andreas Kessler, though Cole wouldn't learn that until later—disappeared back into the shadows of international intelligence. They worked together a few more times over the following months, always professional, never acknowledging what had happened in Maribor. Then Reinhardt rotated out, reassigned to some other theater, some other operation. Cole thought he'd never see him again. He was wrong.

Because men like Reinhardt or Kessler—whatever their names may be— don't disappear. They wait. They build. They evolve. And many years later, in a cabin in North Carolina, James Cole would receive a dossier that revealed the truth: that the man he'd trusted, the man he'd called brother, had been a lie from the beginning. That Maribor hadn't been a turning point—it had been a revelation. A moment when the mask slipped enough to show what had always been underneath.

And now, in Miami, James Cole's son held a phone that had gone silent, trying to understand a war that had started before he was born. Trying to comprehend what it meant that his father had once stood in snow and firelight, watching a man become a monster, and done nothing.

The ghosts of Maribor had waited patiently. Now they were coming home.

36

Last Light

Kessler — Private Diary (Zurich-0 Archive: Unclassified)
"Ah... James Cole. I had hoped your ghost would stay buried. But since you insisted on returning to the game...I suppose I must remind you how it ends."

North Carolina Mountains-Cole Cabin—7:46 am.- Day 7
Frozen for a moment in time, it felt as if the forest was holding its breath.

James Cole stood motionless at the window, M4 rifle steady in weathered hands, watching shapes materialize from darkness. They moved between the pines with professional spacing—three visible, which meant at least four more in positions he couldn't see. Moonlight caught the glint of optics, the dull sheen of tactical gear.

They'd found him.

Ranger growled at his feet, hackles raised, seventy pounds of German Shepherd coiled to strike. James reached down, unclipped the dog's collar.

"Go, boy. Hunt."

Ranger exploded through the dog door—a dark blur streaking across the clearing toward the tree line, teeth bared, the primal fury of an animal defending his territory.

James tracked him through the scope. The dog disappeared into shadows between pines. Snarling. A man's shout of alarm—

A single suppressed shot echoed through the forest.

Ranger yelped. Then silence.

James didn't let himself feel it. Not yet. He filed it away in the place where soldiers keep their grief until the killing is done.

The shapes in the trees had regrouped. Moving again. Closing on the cabin from three sides with the coordinated precision of men who had done this dozens of times.

James stepped back from the window, checked his rifle, and waited.

He didn't wait long.

The RPG announced itself with a whistle—that distinctive shriek of a rocket-propelled grenade cutting air. James threw himself sideways as the front door ceased to exist.

The explosion was volcanic. Four inches of solid oak vaporized into a hurricane of splinters and fire. The blast wave picked James up mid-dive and hurled him across the room like a toy. He crashed through the coffee table, hit the far wall. Sarah's photographs rained down around him—their wedding day, the boys as children, thirty years of memories shattering on the floor.

His ears screamed. A high, piercing tone that turned the world silent. Through the smoke and dust, he saw the cabin's front wall sagging inward, flames climbing the exposed timber, a jagged hole where his door had been.

He rolled onto his stomach, tasted blood, and crawled.

The bedroom. Twenty feet. An eternity.

Smoke burned his lungs. His vision swam. But his hands still worked, his legs still pushed, and he knew this cabin like he knew his own heartbeat.

He shouldered through the bedroom door, kicked aside Sarah's braided rug, and found the trap door. Iron ring handle. Three feet square. His escape route.

He yanked it open and dropped into darkness.

Just at that moment, shapes poured through the breach. Suppressed rifles. Shouting commands in languages that blurred together.

The basement swallowed him—low ceiling, dirt floor, the cold smell of earth. His hands found the supplies he had staged: flashlight, spare magazines, his backup M4 leaning against the foundation wall. He grabbed the rifle, chambered a round, and moved toward the tunnel entrance at the far end.

Fifty yards of crawl space, shored with timber, opening into a drainage culvert behind the cabin. He'd dug it himself over three weeks of midnight labor. Insurance against exactly this moment.

He emerged into wintry air, lungs burning, ribs screaming. The cabin was fully engulfed now—flames roaring through the roof, smoke billowing black against stars. His home of thirty years dying in front of him.

But he wasn't dead. Not yet.

James circled through the trees, staying low, using the trees for cover. He counted six men spread across the clearing—four covering the cabin's exits, two moving toward the tree line where they'd find his tunnel eventually.

He took the first one from behind. The suppressed M4 coughed once, and the man dropped without a sound. James was already moving, repositioning, using the chaos of the fire to mask his approach.

The second kill was messier. The man turned at the wrong moment, caught the muzzle flash, tried to bring his weapon up. James put two rounds through his chest and one through his face before he could shout a warning.

Voices now. Urgent. They'd found the bodies.

James pressed against a pine trunk, controlling his breathing despite the pain in his ribs. Two down. Four plus whoever else Kessler had brought. The math wasn't good, but math never won battles. Will did. Preparation did.

He dropped a third man as the operative crossed between trees—a clean shot through the neck that severed the spine. The body collapsed in stages, puppet with cut strings.

Then a voice cut through the night. Calm. Conversational. Carrying across the clearing with the easy authority of someone who'd never had to shout to be heard.

"James?"

Kessler.

He emerged from the tree line like a specter—silver hair catching firelight, charcoal suit somehow immaculate despite the forest, hands clasped behind his back as if he were strolling through a garden rather than a combat zone.

"That's enough if you please James," Kessler continued, his accent smoothed by decades of rootlessness. "You've made your point. Three of my men—impressive, given your age. But we both know how this ends."

James kept his rifle raised, sighting down on Kessler's center mass. Fifty yards. Easy shot. He could end this right now, put a round through the heart of the man who'd betrayed him, who'd built an empire on their friendship's corpse.

His finger tightened on the trigger.

"Before you do that," Kessler added, still walking forward with absolute unconcern, "you should know that I have a gift for you. A reunion, of sorts."

"Stop moving"—James Cole barked like an old soldier.

Kessler stopped. Smiled. That same pleasant smile James remembered from past operations, of past drinks, of moments when he'd believed this man was his brother.

"You received my warning," Kessler announced, almost warmly. "Old friends stay retired. I gave you the opportunity to remain silent, James. To live out your days in your beloved cabin, drinking bourbon and pretending the world hadn't moved on without you. But you couldn't do that, could you? You had to talk with your sons and share too much with them. Had to drag them into a war they can't win."

"They'll win." James's voice was hoarse from smoke. "They'll expose everything you've built."

"No James... of course they won't." Kessler's certainty was absolute. "Ethan is a banker who stumbled into something he doesn't understand. Daniel is a traumatized soldier running from ghosts. Neither of them has the resources or the reach to threaten what I've created. They will run for a while. Hide. Feel heroic. And then we will find them, and this unfortunate chapter will close."

"Like you're closing it with me?"

"You were my friend, James. My closest friend actually. I take no pleasure in the necessity of this visit." Kessler's expression softened—or performed softening, it was impossible to tell which. "But you put forward questions to your colleagues and superiors. You learned truths that cannot be unlearned. You became a variable I could not control. Surely you understand. You were a soldier. You know how variables get resolved."

"I know you're a monster. I know Maribor showed me exactly what you are."

"Maribor." Kessler nodded slowly. "Ah yes. The moment our friendship truly ended. I saw it in your eyes that night—the judgment, the horror. You looked at me like I had become a monster. But James..." He spread his hands with a smile that revealed his true essence. "I have always been a monster. You just did not want to see it. None of you ever do, until it's too late."

James's finger trembled on the trigger. One shot. One squeeze. End the monster right here in the ashes of his home.

"Before you decide," Kessler remarked softly, "I mentioned a reunion."

He raised one hand—a casual gesture, almost a wave.

A figure emerged from the shadows to Kessler's left.

Lean. Pale-eyed. Moving with fluid precision that James recognized instantly because he'd helped teach it, had spent summers drilling it into a boy who'd been like a third son.

Lukas.

James's rifle wavered. His breath caught. The world narrowed to that face—older now, harder, but unmistakably the boy who'd fished with Ethan in the stream behind this cabin, who'd learned to shoot on this very property, who'd called him "Uncle James" with genuine affection.

"Hello, Uncle James." Lukas's voice was charming. Professional. The voice of a stranger wearing a familiar face.

"Lukas?" James couldn't process it. Couldn't reconcile the child he'd loved with the operative standing beside his father, rifle held with casual competence. "What are you—why are you—"

"Lukas is my creation," Kessler observed simply. "He has always been my creation. The summers here, the friendship with Ethan—research. Assessment. Determining whether your boys had value to my organization." He smiled. "Lukas was never your family, James. He was always mine."

James tried to raise his rifle. Tried to center the sights on Lukas's chest. His arms wouldn't obey. All the years of training, a lifetime of combat discipline, and he couldn't shoot the boy he'd taught to tie fishing lures.

"I can't—" The words came out broken. "Lukas, you don't have to do this. Whatever he's made you, you can still—"

"I'm exactly what I was made to be." Lukas raised his rifle with smooth precision. "Thank you for the lessons, Uncle James. I've put them to good use."

He fired.

The round took James in the chest—a hammer blow that drove the air from his lungs and dropped him to his knees. He looked down, saw blood spreading across his shirt, looked up at Lukas's impassive face.

"Why?" The word was barely a whisper.

Lukas didn't answer. James Cole hit the ground hard, pine needles rough against his cheek, the burning cabin filling his vision with orange and red. He tried to move, to raise his weapon, to do anything except lie there and bleed.

His vision darkened at the edges. The ringing in his ears became a roar. The last thing he saw before consciousness fled was Kessler's polished shoes stepping into view, and the last thing he heard was that pleasant voice saying:

"Don't let him die yet. We have questions first for my old friend."

Then the world went dark.

North Carolina Mountains-Near the Cole Cabin

Pain.

James Cole came back to the world through a red haze of agony. His chest burned. His head throbbed. Each breath was like inhaling broken glass, cutting him from the inside out.

He tried to move and couldn't.

Rope bit into his wrists, binding them behind a wooden chair. More rope around his ankles, his chest, his throat—tight enough to restrict breathing but not enough to strangle. Professional work. The kind of restraints designed to keep a man conscious and cooperative.

The room swam into focus. Not the forest—somewhere else. A cabin, but not his cabin. Smaller. Rougher. Hunting lodge, maybe, or an abandoned ranger station. A single bulb hung from the ceiling, swaying slightly, casting shadows that moved like living things.

Kessler sat across from him, legs crossed, perfectly composed despite the blood on his shirt cuffs—James's blood, probably. He held a glass of amber liquid, swirling it gently, watching James with the patient attention of a predator who'd already caught his prey and was simply deciding how to consume it.

"Welcome back," Kessler professed warmly with a smile. "I was worried that Lukas had been too enthusiastic. But you have always been resilient, James. It is one of the things I have always admired about you."

James tested the ropes. Solid. No give. His weapons were gone, his vest stripped away, his body a catalog of injuries that made thinking difficult.

"Where—" His voice cracked. He swallowed blood, tried again. "Where is this?"

"A property I maintain for situations requiring... privacy. We are about twenty miles from your cabin. Or what's left of it." Kessler sipped his drink. "I'm sorry about the house, truly. I know how much it meant to you. But evidence has to be destroyed, loose ends tied. You understand now don't you?"

"Go to hell."

"Eventually." Kessler voiced calmly while setting down his glass. "But first, we must talk. You sent your sons information—files detailing my network, my operations, my identity. I need to know what else exists. What copies you made. Who else has seen these things."

"I'll tell you nothing."

"Now James. You will tell me what I need." Kessler's voice didn't change—still pleasant, still conversational—but something icy cold moved behind his eyes. "The only question is how much pain you will have to endure first. I would prefer to minimize that but your actions will decide that of course. We were friends once were we not? That should count for something."

"Friends." James spat blood onto the floor between them. "You murdered my wife. You gave me a heart attack. You sent your son to kill my dog and shoot me in the chest. That's not friendship. That's ownership."

"Sarah's death was regrettable but necessary. The cardiac event was meant to remove you from positions where you might become problematic. And tonight..." Kessler shrugged. "Tonight is simply the conclusion of a story that began in Maribor, when you first saw what I was and chose to do nothing."

"I should have killed you then."

"Yes. You should have. But you didn't, because you were a good soldier who followed orders and trusted systems that I had already corrupted. Your nobility was your weakness, James. It always has been."

James's vision blurred. Blood loss, probably. Or shock finally catching up with the adrenaline. He forced himself to focus, to keep Kessler talking, to buy time for—

For what? No one was coming. Ethan was in Miami. Daniel was God knows where. He was alone, bleeding, bound to a chair in a cabin that didn't exist on any map.

"The dossier," Kessler pressed. "Where are the copies?"

"There are no copies."

"Lie." The word was flat, certain. "You're too careful, too paranoid, to maintain only one version of something that important. You have backups. Hidden drives. Safety deposit boxes. Tell me where."

"Even if I knew, I wouldn't tell you."

"Then you'll die slowly instead of quickly. That's your choice, James. I'm simply offering alternatives." Kessler stood, buttoned his jacket. "I'm going to give you a few minutes to reconsider. Think about your sons. Think about what happens to them if you don't cooperate. I can make their deaths painless—quick, professional, the kind of end soldiers deserve. Or I can make them suffer. Ethan first, since he's the immediate problem. We'll take our time with him. Make sure he understands exactly what his curiosity cost."

"You touch my boys and I'll—"

"You'll what?" Kessler's smile was patient, almost pitying. "You're tied to a chair with a bullet in your chest. You're in no position to threaten anyone. The only power you have left is the power to choose how this ends—for you and for them."

He walked toward the door, paused, looked back.

"You were the best friend I ever had, James. The only person I trusted, for a time. That's why this is difficult for me. That's why I wanted to handle it personally rather than delegating to subordinates." His expression might have been genuine regret, or might have been performance—with Kessler, they were the same thing. "I wish you'd stayed retired. I wish you'd accepted that some truths are too expensive to pursue. But you didn't. And now we're here."

He opened the door.

"Lukas" —Kessler called out.

The younger man appeared in the doorway, rifle slung across his chest, face as empty as it had been in the forest. He looked at James with no recognition, no warmth, no trace of the boy who'd spent summers here learning to be part of a family he'd never actually belonged to.

"Your dear Uncle James has declined to cooperate," Kessler affirmed. "We'll try again in thirty minutes, after the blood loss has had time to work on his resolve. If he still refuses..." He met James's eyes. "Finish it. Make it clean. He was my friend once. He deserves that much."

Lukas nodded. "Yes, Father."

Kessler left.

The door closed behind him with a sound like a coffin lid.

James and Lukas faced each other across the small room—the man who'd been like a father and the boy who'd been like a son, the last remains of a love that had been a lie from the beginning.

"Lukas," James offered, his voice barely a whisper. "Whatever Kessler's done to you, whatever he's made you believe—this isn't who you have to be."

Lukas pulled a chair from the corner, set it in front of James, sat down with his rifle across his knees. His pale eyes studied James's face like a scientist examining a specimen.

"You don't understand," Lukas mentioned quietly. "This is exactly who I have to be. It's who I've always been. The boy you knew—the one who fished with Ethan and learned to shoot on your porch—that was the performance. This is the reality."

"I don't believe that."

"It doesn't matter what you believe. It only matters what's true." Lukas leaned forward slightly. "My father built me for this. From the time I could walk, he was shaping me. The summers here were training exercises. The friendship with Ethan was intelligence gathering. Every moment of affection, each gesture of belonging—it was all preparation for moments exactly like this one."

"That's not a life. That's a prison."

"It's purpose." For a moment, something flickered in Lukas's eyes—something that might have been doubt, or might have been anger, or might have been nothing at all. "My father gave me purpose when the world would have given me nothing. He made me strong when kindness would have made me weak. I owe him everything."

"You owe him nothing. He used you. He's using you now"

"And you loved me?" Lukas's voice carried an edge now. "You treated me like a son? You taught me and fed me and let me sleep under your roof—but you didn't know me at all. You loved a fiction. A mask I wore because my father told me to wear it." He stood abruptly, the chair scraping against the floor. "That's the difference between us. You see the world as you wish it were. My father sees it as it is. And in a world like this, only one perspective survives."

He walked to the door, paused with his hand on the handle.

"When I come back, you will tell us what we need to know. The location of the copies. The names of anyone who has seen the files. All information we need." His voice was flat, certain. "You will tell us because you love your sons, and because you know what my father and I will do to them if you don't. That love—that weakness—is the only leverage we need."

He opened the door. Frigid air rushed in, carrying the smell of pine and smoke and the particular emptiness of forests at night.

"Thirty minutes, Uncle James. Use it wisely."

The door closed.

James Cole sat alone in the swaying light, blood dripping slowly onto the wooden floor beneath him, rope biting into wrists rubbed raw by futile struggling.

Thirty minutes.

In thirty minutes, Lukas would return. And when he still refused to talk—because he would refuse, because some things mattered more than survival—the boy he'd loved would put a bullet in his brain and walk away without looking back.

This was how it ended.

Not in glory. Not in victory. Only a broken old soldier in a forgotten cabin, soon to be a body that wouldn't be found.

But James Cole, the broken old soldier, held out the desperate yet steadfast hope that his sons would survive long enough to finish what he'd started.

James closed his eyes and thought of Ethan. Of Daniel. Of Sarah, waiting for him somewhere beyond the pain.

"*I love you*", he thought. "*All of you. I'm sorry I couldn't do more.*"

The light swayed. The blood dripped. And somewhere outside, Lukas Kessler checked his watch and waited for the time to pass.

37

Cost of Command

*"Kessler—you sent me a picture of my father bloody and in chains. Let me send you one back—of everything you built—burned to the fucking ground." —*Daniel Cole

Exarcheia, Athens Greece—4:25 p.m. local time- Day 7
Like a creature shaking off a long morning of revolution, the anarchist district woke slowly in the afternoon sun.

Daniel Cole sat by the window of a third-floor hotel room, watching Exarcheia come alive below. The neighborhood was a contradiction painted in spray paint and defiance—elegant neoclassical buildings covered in layers of graffiti, their ornate facades transformed into canvases of political rage. Tags in Greek, English, Arabic, and a dozen other languages competed for space: ACAB scrawled across a pharmacy shutter. NO BORDERS on a crumbling wall. The anarchist circle-A repeated like a heartbeat across any available surface.

The streets were narrow, claustrophobic, designed for a city that existed before automobiles. Motorcycle shops with hand-painted signs sat beside bookstores selling Bakunin and Kropotkin. Cafés spilled mismatched chairs onto cracked sidewalks where young people with septum piercings argued philosophy over thick Greek coffee. A burned-out car—relic of last month's riot—sat at the corner like a monument to permanent resistance.

This was the heart of Athenian counterculture. The district that riot police feared to enter without overwhelming force. The place where the government was the enemy and solidarity meant something more than a hashtag.

Perfect for a ghost.

Daniel had checked in two hours ago under a German passport that identified him as Klaus Weber, freelance photographer. The hotel was a converted apartment building, its lobby a single desk staffed by a woman who did not question and accepted cash with the practiced disinterest of someone who'd seen a thousand men fleeing a thousand different demons.

His room was sparse—single bed, wooden chair, a window overlooking Exarcheia Square where the morning market was setting up. On the nightstand: a bottle of Jameson, half-empty. Beside it: a photograph he shouldn't still carry, its edges worn soft from years of handling.

Lieutenant Oliver Shaw. Twenty-six years old. Married. Kid on the way. Dead because someone in Washington decided air support was "politically inadvisable."

Daniel poured himself another whiskey despite the early afternoon hour. The amber liquid caught the gray light filtering through unwashed glass. He'd been awake for thirty-six hours, running on adrenaline and the particular exhaustion that came from crossing too many borders with too many identities.

Below, a group of teenagers in black hoodies gathered around the burned car, passing around a joint and arguing in rapid Greek. An old woman in widow's black crossed herself as she walked past them, hurrying toward the Orthodox church at the corner. A dog—skinny, feral—trotted down the center of the street like it owned the place.

Exarcheia didn't care about his past. Didn't care about Helmand or the faces that haunted him. It was a neighborhood that had seen too much history to judge a man for his scars.

Daniel had spent years trying to outrun those scars. Years doing black ops work for people who didn't officially exist, telling himself he was serving a higher purpose. Precision strikes against terrorist cells. Targeted assassinations of men who trafficked in human misery. Extractions of assets too valuable to abandon.

But the faces never left. Shaw. Martinez. Kowalski. Each man he had failed to bring home.

His encrypted phone buzzed. Message from Ethan:

"D—I'm in Miami. Noah is with me and someone new. Her name is Selin Yilmaz. Turkish intelligence. Long story. We're coming to you. Dad told us both about Kessler before—you know. We need to finish this together. Where are you?"

Daniel stared at the message, his brother's words carrying weight beyond their simple syntax. Someone new. Turkish intelligence. His little brother had apparently stumbled into an international conspiracy and picked up allies along the way. That was either impressive or catastrophic, depending on perspective.

He typed back: *"Greece. Exact location when you get in country. When can you get here?"*

The response came quickly: *"Noah is getting us out. Not sure how he did it but he has access to a private charter flight and Selin has contacts who can get us through without flagging systems. 18-20 hours maybe. Stay dark until we arrive. They're hunting all of us now."*

Daniel almost smiled. Stay dark. Like he hadn't been a ghost for three years, like he needed his banker brother to teach him operational security.

"Copy. Be careful. Trust no one you haven't vetted personally."

"Selin's solid. She saved my life twice. Noah too. We're a team now."

A team. Daniel thought about what that word meant—what it had meant in Helmand, what it meant now. A team was people who would die for each other. People who trusted absolutely, who moved as one organism, who understood that individual survival was less important than collective success.

He'd had that once. Had lost it in the dust and blood of Afghanistan, in the silence where air support should have been.

"I'll be here," he typed. *"We'll figure this out when you arrive."*

He set the phone down and returned to watching Exarcheia wake. A café owner was hosing down the sidewalk, sending rivers of water into the gutter. A delivery truck squeezed through streets never designed for it, horn blaring at a cyclist who responded with an elaborate hand gesture. The teenagers by the burned car had dispersed, replaced by an old man feeding pigeons from a paper bag.

Normal life. The kind Daniel had forgotten existed.

He thought about Ethan coming here—his little brother who'd spent his career in glass towers analyzing numbers, now running from killers across continents. When had the world tilted so badly that a banker and a burned operative were humanity's best hope against men like Kessler?

His phone buzzed again. Different tone—the backup device he kept for contacts who shouldn't have this number.

An unlisted number. Unknown sender.

He opened the message, and his blood turned to ice.

A photograph. His father—James Cole—bound to a chair in a dim room. Blood soaked the front of his shirt, spreading from wounds in his chest. His face was battered, one eye swollen shut, but his expression was defiant even in captivity. Even facing death.

Below the image, a single line of text:

"The son should know what became of the father. —K"

Daniel's hands began to shake. Not fear—rage. The kind of rage that burned clean and hot, that stripped away everything except the primal need to destroy.

Kessler.

The man who'd worn his father's friendship like a mask for thirty years. The man who'd orchestrated their lives from the shadows, who'd treated the Cole family like pieces on a chess board.

He'd shot his father. Bound him. Photographed him like a trophy.

And sent it to Daniel like a taunt.

Daniel stood abruptly, nearly knocking over the whiskey bottle. He paced the small room, muscles coiled, combat instincts screaming for action. He wanted to put his fist through the wall. Wanted to find Kessler and tear him apart with his bare hands. Wanted to—

He forced himself to stop. To breathe. To think.

This was what Kessler wanted. Rage made men stupid. Rage made them act without planning, strike without precision, walk into traps that cooler minds would see.

His father had taught him that. Had spent years drilling it into both his sons: *Anger is fuel, not steering. Let it power you, but never let it drive.*

Daniel picked up his phone, typed a message to Ethan:

"Kessler sent me a photo. Dad tied to a chair. Shot. Beaten. Kessler's taunting us. He wants us angry and stupid. Don't give him that."

The response from Ethan came after a long pause: *"Is Dad alive in the photo?"*

Daniel looked at the image again, forcing himself to study it with tactical detachment. His father's chest wound was bloody but didn't appear to be arterial—no bright red spray, no pooling that would indicate immediate death. The defiance in his eyes suggested consciousness, awareness, life.

Daniel typed back—*"Looks like it. But I don't know when this was taken. Could be hours old. Could be a trophy shot after."*

After a pause, Daniel received—*"We'll assume he's alive until we know otherwise. That's how Dad would want it."*

Daniel shook his head. He knew better. While their father had never accepted defeat, and wouldn't stop fighting until the last possible moment, he was likely dead. But Daniel wanted to give his brother hope.

Daniel typed back—*"Agreed. Get here fast. We plan this properly, then we take the fight to them."*

"18 hours. Stay safe, D."

"You too, E. And tell your new friend—this has become...personal."

He set the phone down and returned to the window. Exarcheia had fully awakened now—the market in the square buzzing with vendors selling vegetables, bootleg DVDs, revolutionary literature. A group of riot police stood at the district's edge, watching but not entering, respecting the unwritten boundaries that kept the neighborhood's fragile peace.

Daniel thought about the photo. About his father's blood-soaked shirt and battered face. About the monster who'd done this, who'd spent thirty years pretending to be family before revealing the knife he'd always held behind his back.

Kessler wanted to break them. Wanted to use James as leverage, as psychological warfare, as proof that no one the Cole brothers loved was safe.

Instead, he'd made a mistake.

Because Daniel had spent eight years learning to channel rage into precision. Had spent a career turning grief into purpose, loss into determination. Shaw and Martinez and Kowalski—they hadn't taught him to surrender. They'd taught him to fight smarter, harder, more ruthlessly than the men who'd abandoned them.

He pulled out the photograph of Shaw, set it beside his phone where the image of his father still glowed. Two men. Two betrayals. Two reasons to keep fighting when any rational calculation would certainly push him to run.

"I couldn't save you," Daniel whispered to Shaw's frozen grin. "Couldn't save any of them. But I swear to God, I'm going to kill that son of a bitch Kessler and burn his motherfucking world to the ground."

He sat back down, began cleaning his weapons with the methodical precision of ritual. The Glock 19 first—field strip, inspect, oil, reassemble. Then the combat knife, its edge already razor-sharp but requiring the meditation of the whetstone anyway.

Outside, Exarcheia continued its morning rhythms—coffee and arguments, graffiti and resistance, the stubborn insistence that some spaces couldn't be conquered by power or money or fear.

Ethan would soon arrive with his Turkish intelligence officer and his hacker friend. They would plan. They would strategize. They would find a way to strike at an enemy who'd been winning this war since before they knew it existed.

And somewhere—James Cole was waiting. Fighting. Refusing to break.

Daniel would not let him wait alone.

The world needed men who thought and men who acted. For the first time in a long time, Daniel Cole was ready to be both.

And if Kessler wanted to send photographs of broken fathers, Daniel would send back something far worse.

He would send Kessler an invoice for betrayal of his father.

And he would collect it in blood.

38

Diverging Currents

"If this is my last step, at least it's in the right direction." —Bill Donovan

Miami—3:49 p.m.- Day 8

Burning gold in the afternoon sun, the Miami skyline shined brightly, but the city appeared hollow, predatory. Ethan stood at the window of the waterfront warehouse that had become their temporary refuge, watching shadows lengthen across Biscayne Bay. When a boat passed by, or a car slowed on the street below, a spike of adrenaline would shoot through his chest.

Daniel's words still echoed in his mind: *"The system works exactly as it is designed to. It just wasn't designed for people like us."*

Behind him, Noah hunched over three laptops arranged in a semicircle, his bandaged arm moving carefully as he typed. Lines of code scrolled across the screens—financial algorithms, encrypted communications, the digital breadcrumbs of an empire built on blood money.

And beside Noah, cross-legged on a shipping crate with the disassembled Glock in her lap, sat Selin.

Ethan still wasn't entirely sure what to make of her. Turkish intelligence, she'd told him. MIT—Millî İstihbarat Teşkilatı. Dark hair pulled back in a severe ponytail, eyes that missed nothing and revealed less. She'd appeared in his life three days ago, materializing from the chaos of a firefight like something conjured from smoke, and had proceeded to save both his and Noah's lives with the kind of ruthless efficiency that suggested she'd done it many times before.

"You're staring," Selin observed without looking up, her hands re-assembling the pistol with practiced speed.

"Sorry." Ethan turned back to the window. "Still trying to figure out why Turkish intelligence cares about an American banker running from his own government."

"Kessler's network doesn't recognize borders." The Glock clicked back together in her hands. "Neither do the people hunting him. I've been tracking Directorate financial flows for two years. Your discovery at the bank—the accounts you found—they connect to operations in Istanbul, Ankara, across the Mediterranean. My government wants him exposed as much as you do."

"And they sent you alone?"

Something flickered in her eyes—pain or anger carefully contained. "I volunteered. This is personal."

She didn't elaborate, and Ethan didn't push. Everyone in this ware-house was running from something. They all had ghosts.

Noah looked up from his screens. "I've got transport. Private charter out of Opa-locka Executive Airport. Pilot owes me from a thing in São Paulo—don't ask. He can get you to Athens without touching any sys-tem Kessler's people monitor."

"Us," Ethan corrected. "He can get us to Athens."

Noah shook his head, his expression grim. "I can't fly. Not yet. The arm—" He gestured at his bandaged limb. "And someone needs to stay mobile on this side of the Atlantic, run interference, keep their digital eyes pointed the wrong direction."

"So what's your plan?" Selin put forward.

"Captain Morales. Cargo ship captain operating out of the port. He's taking me south by boat—Cartagena first, then deeper into South America." Noah's fingers paused on the keyboard. "I can work from anywhere with a satellite connection, and Morales has resources. Safe houses. Communication networks. People."

Ethan frowned. "Who is this Morales?"

Noah leaned back, a complicated expression crossing his face. "Part of something I've been building for three years. A network—underground, completely off-grid. People across the globe who've been destroyed by the Directorate. Anglers whose villages were destroyed for resort development. Journalists whose families were threatened. Whistleblowers who tried to expose Kessler's operations and were silenced." He met Ethan's eyes. "They're scattered across the globe. Most don't know each other exist. But they all know me. And they all want the same thing."

"Revenge," Selin voiced quietly.

"Justice." Noah's voice hardened. "Morales is one of the originals. His brother tried to fight Kessler's people legally when they took his fishing village—courts, lawyers, proper channels. They found him in the harbor a month later, weighted down. Official cause of death: suicide." He shook his head. "Morales has been moving cargo and people through the Caribbean ever since, helping anyone who needs to disappear from Kessler's radar. He's kept a dozen witnesses alive who should be dead."

Ethan absorbed this. His hacker friend had been building a resistance network, and he'd never known. "Why didn't you tell me?"

"Because you were a banker, E. You believed in the system. Believed the institutions would work if good people pushed hard enough." Noah's smile was sad. "I didn't want to drag you into this world until you were ready to see it."

"I see it now."

"Yeah." Noah closed his laptop. "You do."

Selin stood, holstering the Glock at her hip. "The plane. When does it leave?"

"Two hours. Enough time to pack what we need and get there without rushing." Noah's fingers flew across the keyboard one final time. "I'm building you clean identities now. German passports—Christian

Weber and Ingrid Hartmann. Married couple, photography enthusiasts, documenting Mediterranean architecture."

"Married?" Selin raised an eyebrow.

"Couples draw less attention than two singles traveling together. Trust me." Noah glanced between them with something that might have been amusement. "Try to act like you like each other."

Ethan ignored the implication, focused on the logistics. Daniel was waiting in Athens. His brother—the soldier, the ghost, the one member of their family who might actually know how to fight this war. Getting to him was the only thing that mattered.

Then—with the slightest of creaks—the safehouse door opened without warning.

Selin had her weapon drawn before Ethan finished turning, her body positioning itself between the entrance and Noah's computers with the fluid instinct of someone who'd done this a thousand times. Ethan grabbed the pistol from the table beside him, heart hammering—

Donovan stepped through, hands raised, palms out.

"Easy," the older man requested. "I'm not here to cause trouble."

Ethan's grip didn't waver. "How did you find us?"

"I've been in this game forty years, Cole. Finding people who don't want to be found is literally my job." Donovan lowered his hands slowly, his movements careful, non-threatening. He looked older than Ethan remembered—grayer, more worn, the weight of something heavy in his eyes. "I'm not here for Harris. I'm not here for the Bank or anyone else. I'm here because..." He paused, searching for words. "Because I'm done."

"Done with what?" Selin's weapon stayed trained on his chest.

"Done pretending I don't know what side I'm on." Donovan moved to the nearest chair, sat down heavily like a man finally setting down a burden he'd carried too long. "I've seen Kessler's operation from the inside. Watched good people disappear because they posed the wrong questions. Watched the system I believed in get hollowed out and replaced with something rotten." His voice cracked slightly. "I have a granddaughter, Cole. Soccer player. She wants to be a marine biologist.

And when I wake up in the morning I wonder if the work I've done—the things I've helped cover up—will eventually touch her."

"Why should we trust you?" Ethan grilled.

"You shouldn't. Not completely. Trust is earned, and I haven't earned it yet." Donovan reached slowly into his jacket—Selin's finger tightened on the trigger—and withdrew a small black envelope. "But this might help."

He set it on the table between them. Ethan picked it up, opened it. Inside: two passports, German, the names Jonathan Hale and Maria Richter. Clean documents. The real thing—not forgeries, but genuine credentials built through official channels.

"Backup identities," Donovan told them. "In case your existing backup identity work gets burned. I pulled them from a pipeline I've kept hidden for exactly this kind of situation." He met Ethan's eyes. "I know a guy from the Balkans—we ran intel fronts together for operations that never existed. He owes me, and he's still got access to the old networks. These documents will breathe. They'll hold up to scrutiny."

Selin slowly lowered her weapon. "What do you want in return?"

"Nothing. That's the point." Donovan's smile was tired, broken. "I've spent my whole career taking payment for loyalty. Money, advancement, the illusion that I was serving something larger than myself. But loyalty that's bought isn't loyalty—it's simply employment." He stood, moving toward the door. "When you take down Kessler—and you will, because you're too stubborn and too angry to fail—I want to know I helped. Even if no one ever knows. Even if it doesn't save me from what's coming."

"What is coming?" Ethan raised.

Donovan paused at the door. "Harris knows I've been wavering. Kessler knows too—he's always known. Men like me don't get retirement. We get closure." He looked back one final time. "Whatever happens going forward, don't trust anyone who offers help without asking for payment. In our world, generosity is the surest sign of a setup."

Ethan nodded slowly. "Then what does that make you?"

Donovan smiled—a tired, broken smile. "A man who's already out of moves. Good luck, Cole. Give Kessler hell."

The door closed behind him. The warehouse fell silent except for the hum of Noah's equipment and the distant sounds of the harbor.

An hour later, they stood in the warehouse's loading bay—three people who'd become something like family in the crucible of the past week. Outside, the Miami sun had begun its descent, painting the harbor in shades of amber and rose.

Noah had his go-bag slung over his good shoulder, a burner phone in his pocket, three laptops distributed across hidden compartments in his luggage. His rental car sat idling near the dock entrance, ready to take him to Captain Morales.

"Morales will have a sat-phone for me within six hours of departure," Noah added. "Encrypted, bouncing through seven different relays. I'll check in every twelve hours unless something goes wrong."

"And if something goes wrong?" Ethan questioned.

"Then I'll go dark and trust the network." Noah's expression was serious but not afraid. "Morales has people in each major port from Cartagena to Buenos Aires. Safe houses. Weapons caches. Medical contacts who don't ask questions. If Kessler's people find us, we'll disappear into the jungle and come out somewhere else."

Selin studied him with professional assessment. "You've been planning this a long time."

"Three years." Noah's smile was thin. "Ever since I first traced Directorate money through a shell company in Panama and realized how big this whole thing was. I knew someday it would come to war. I just didn't know when." He looked at Ethan. "Didn't know it would be you who lit the fuse."

"I didn't mean to—"

"I know." Noah stepped forward, pulled Ethan into a one-armed embrace that was fierce despite his injury. "But I'm glad you did. Some fires need to be lit, E. Some systems need to burn." He stepped back, eyes bright. "Find your brother. Build your team. And when the time comes to bring Kessler down, you call me. The whole network will be ready."

Ethan nodded, throat tight. "Be safe."

"Safe is for people who aren't fighting wars." Noah turned to Selin, extended his hand. "Take care of him. He's smarter than he looks, but he still thinks the world runs on logic."

Selin took his hand, gripped it firmly. "I'll keep him alive."

"Do more than that." Noah glanced between them with something knowing in his expression. "Keep each other alive. That's the only way any of us survive this."

He walked to the car without looking back—a slight figure with a wounded arm and a laptop bag, heading toward a cargo ship that would carry him into the unknown. The engine revved, the tires crunched on gravel, and then he was gone, swallowed by the Miami traffic.

Ethan and Selin stood in the silence he left behind.

"We should go," Selin voiced with finality. "The plane won't wait."

Ethan nodded, picked up his own bag, and followed her into the fading light.

Miami Docks — 5:15 p.m.

The cargo ship *Santa Maria* sat low in the water, her hull streaked with rust and salt, her deck stacked with shipping containers that could hide anything from refugees to weapons to men who needed to disappear. She was ugly, anonymous, exactly the kind of vessel that passed through a hundred ports without anyone remembering her name.

Captain Javier Morales waited at the bottom of the gangway, a weathered man in his sixties with hands that told stories of storms survived and borders crossed. His face was carved by sun and wind, his eyes the color of the Caribbean he'd sailed for forty years.

"You're late," he stated as Noah approached.

"Had to say goodbye."

Morales grunted, studied Noah's bandaged arm. "You'll heal on the water. Salt air's good for wounds." He turned toward the ship. "Your cabin's ready. Communications room set up as you requested. We've got two weeks to Cartagena if the weather holds."

Noah fell into step beside him. "And if it doesn't hold?"

"Then we take longer." Morales's expression hardened. "I've been running this route for twelve years, moving people the Directorate wants dead. Haven't lost one yet. Not going to start with you."

They climbed the gangway, the ship groaning beneath their weight. The deck smelled of diesel and brine, of rust and the particular metallic scent of vessels that had seen too many years and too many secrets.

"The network's been activated," Morales muttered quietly as they walked. "Word's gone out to the nodes—São Paulo, Buenos Aires, Santiago, Lima. Each person in the network knows something's happening. They're ready."

"How many?"

"Forty-seven confirmed assets across South America alone. Accountants who saw too much. Journalists who published the wrong story. Farmers whose land was stolen. Police who wouldn't take bribes." Morales stopped at a hatch, turned to face Noah. "Each one of them lost something to Kessler's machine. Each one of them has been waiting for a chance to fight back."

"And you trust them?"

Morales's eyes went distant, seeing something far away—a harbor. A brother's body. The moment when grief became purpose. "I trust that Kessler took something from every single one of them that can never be replaced. Children. Spouses. Livelihoods. Dignity." His voice dropped. "That kind of debt doesn't expire. It waits patiently for the right moment to collect."

Noah nodded slowly. "Then let's make sure that moment comes soon."

The *Santa Maria*'s engines rumbled to life, a deep vibration that ran through the deck plates. Somewhere above, a horn sounded—once, twice—and the ship began to move, pulling away from the dock.

Noah stood at the rail and watched Miami shrink behind them. Somewhere in that city, Donovan was waiting for death. Somewhere beyond it, Ethan and Selin were climbing into a plane. And somewhere across the Atlantic, the man who'd built an empire on blood and silence was moving his pieces for the endgame.

Private Jet over the Atlantic Ocean — 8:37 p.m.

The Gulfstream climbed through scattered clouds, Miami shrinking to a glitter of lights below before vanishing entirely beneath the cloud deck. Inside the small cabin, the only sounds were the steady hum of engines and the whisper of pressurized air through vents.

Ethan sat by the window, watching darkness swallow the last traces of America. His phone—the burner Daniel had sent instructions to—was heavy in his pocket. The last message from his brother still burned in his mind: a photograph of their father, bound to a chair, bloody, beaten. Kessler's signature on long ago debts finally being collected.

Selin sat across from him, her profile sharp against the oval window's light. She'd been quiet since takeoff, her eyes fixed on something beyond the glass—beyond the clouds, beyond the ocean, somewhere in a past she'd been running from for years.

"You said it was personal," Ethan claimed finally. "Kessler. The Directorate. What did they do to you?"

For a long moment, she didn't answer. When she finally spoke, her voice was different—quieter, stripped of the professional detachment she'd worn like armor since they met.

"What I'm about to tell you could get me killed. Could get you killed." She turned from the window to face him. "But if we're going to do this—if we're going to fight him together—you need to know who I am. What I truly am."

Ethan waited.

"My name was Leyla once. Before I was recruited by Kessler, I was a street kid in Ankara—stealing bread from market stalls, sleeping in alleys, surviving through speed and invisibility." Her voice was flat, reciting facts like an after-action report. "My mother was a heroin addict. She chose oblivion over me. I was on my own by nine years old."

"Nine?" Ethan couldn't hide his shock.

"Nine." She smiled without humor. "That's when Kessler found me. I was trying to steal from a military supply truck. I expected arrest. Violence. Maybe death." Her eyes went distant. "Instead, he offered me dinner. And then he offered me something I'd never had: a future."

"He recruited you. As a child."

"He recruited sixteen of us. Children from streets and orphanages and refugee camps across Europe. We were given numbers, not names. Subject 47—that's who I was at the start. We were trained in a re-purposed facility that smelled of concrete and chlorine." Her hands tightened in her lap. "Combat. Languages. Interrogation resistance. Infiltration. How to kill without hesitation."

"Jesus."

"The final test came when I was twelve." Selin's voice dropped to barely a whisper. "They gave us animals to care for. Rabbits. We fed them, cleaned their cages, watched them hop around. Three weeks of building attachment." She paused. "Then they handed us knives and told us to kill them."

Ethan sensed the room getting colder, the air more still.

"I passed. Didn't hesitate. Didn't cry afterward." Her jaw tightened. "Kessler was watching through a one-way mirror. When it was over, he came to me personally. Gave me a silver pin—a sparrow—and told me I'd earned a name. Not Leyla anymore. Not Subject 47." She touched her collar absently, as if the pin were still there. "Sparrow. That's what he called me. Small, seemingly harmless, capable of flight, and deadlier than most predators when properly deployed."

"Selin—"

"Let me finish." Her voice cracked. "Please. I've never told anyone this. Not completely."

He nodded.

"I worshipped him." The admission came out raw, ashamed. "You have to understand—I was a child who'd been abandoned. My mother chose drugs over me. The world had been nothing but pain, hunger, and fear. And then Kessler appeared, and he—" She stopped, gathered herself. "He took the time. He explained things to me. Praised me when I did well. Made me feel like I mattered, like I had purpose. For the first time in my life, someone acted like a father."

Ethan's throat tightened. He thought of his own father—James Cole, who'd actually been a father, who'd loved his sons without ulterior motive, who'd taught them to fish and shoot and be men. And who was now probably dead because of the same monster who'd stolen Selin's childhood.

"He was never a father," Ethan voiced quietly. "He was grooming you. Training you to be a weapon."

"I know that now." Tears slipped down her cheeks. "But when you're nine years old and starving and someone finally sees you—you don't question it. You become whatever they need you to be."

She wiped her eyes with the back of her hand, continued. "For years, I did whatever they demanded of me. Intelligence gathering. Asset recruitment. Information brokering. I told myself I was serving something larger than myself. That the work mattered." Her voice turned bitter. "Then Vienna happened."

"What happened in Vienna?"

"Spring 2017. I was working under diplomatic cover—Cultural Attaché, shuffling information between European security agencies and Kessler's intermediaries. I thought I'd found a way to help—passing coordinates to what I believed was an anti-Directorate consortium." Her hands were shaking now. "A refugee convoy in southern Serbia. Forty-three people. Families. Children. The information I passed was supposed to protect them."

"It didn't."

"It killed them." The words came out broken. "Kessler used me as a ghost courier. The coordinates I sent were used to target the convoy. A false flag operation, designed to shift blame and justify new Directorate contracts." She looked at Ethan with devastation in her eyes. "I killed forty-three innocent people because I trusted a monster who pretended to be my father."

The plane hummed through darkness. Outside, stars were beginning to emerge above the cloud deck—cold, distant, indifferent to the confessions being made thirty thousand feet below.

"I ran," Selin continued. "Burned my identities, disappeared into safe houses—Athens, Naples, Tangier. Stripped myself down to nothing until I didn't know who I was anymore. And then, in Zurich, the CIA found me. Offered me a chance to fight back." She laughed bitterly. "But even that was a lie. Kessler had never lost track of me. For two more years, he fed me intelligence streams, used me to launder his disinformation through American channels. Made me his double agent without me even knowing."

"When did you figure it out?"

"Paris. Two years after Zurich. I intercepted a Directorate communication and realized he'd been playing me the entire time." She met Ethan's eyes. "I threw my phone in the Seine and told myself he didn't own me anymore. But the truth is..." Her voice dropped to a whisper. "He taught me to lie so well I don't even trust the truth anymore. I don't know if I'll ever be free of what he made me."

Silence settled between them. The engines hummed. The stars wheeled past.

Ethan looked at her—deeply, past the tactical competence and the hard edges, past the secrets and the pain. He saw a woman who'd been stolen as a child. Who'd been shaped into a weapon by a man who'd pretended to love her. Who'd tried to escape and been pulled back, tried to fight and been turned against herself.

"My father is probably dead." Ethan spoke slowly.

Selin looked up, startled by the shift.

"Daniel sent me a photograph. Dad tied to a chair, shot, beaten. Kessler's work." Ethan's voice was steady, but something was breaking underneath. "My father trusted Kessler for thirty years. Called him his best friend. Invited him into our home, let his son spend summers with us. And it was all a lie. The memories I have of 'Uncle Otto' and his family—all of it was reconnaissance. Assessment. Kessler using us the way he used you."

"Your father—"

"Was a real father." Ethan's eyes burned. "He taught me and Daniel to fish, to shoot, to be honorable men. He loved us without wanting anything in return. And Kessler..." His voice cracked. "Kessler shot him—he's likely dead. Probably interrogated him first and made him suffer."

Selin reached across the space between them and took his hand. Her fingers were cold, trembling slightly, but her grip was strong.

"Kessler stole my childhood," she came out with quietly. "He stole your father. He's taken something irreplaceable from both of us."

"Yes."

"Then we both have reasons to destroy him."

Ethan squeezed her fingers. "You were a child. What he did to you wasn't your fault. The convoy—Vienna—none of it was your choice. You were manipulated from the moment he found you."

"That doesn't bring them back. The forty-three people. The families."

"No. It doesn't." Ethan leaned forward. "But destroying the man who made you pull the trigger? That's something. Making sure he can never do this to another child, another family? That matters."

"You should hate me," she whispered. "For what I was. What I did."

"I don't hate you." He held her gaze. "I see someone who survived something that would have destroyed most people. Someone who escaped a monster and is now trying to make it right. That's not weakness, Selin. That's strength."

"I don't feel strong. I feel..." She searched for the word. "Broken."

"So do I." Ethan's voice was rough. "My father is gone. My brother is a ghost I barely know anymore. What I believed about my life—my career, the system, the idea that good men could work within institutions to make things better—it's all shattered." He moved to sit beside her, still holding her hand. "We're both broken. But that's okay. Maybe broken people are the only ones who can see clearly enough to fight this."

She looked at Ethan—gazed deeply into eyes, not the tactical assessment she'd been making since they met, but something deeper. Something that recognized shared damage, shared loss, the particular bond that forms between people who've both been wounded by the same enemy.

"He took our lives from both of us," she mentioned.

"Then we take everything from him." —Ethan replied, his voice growing colder.

She moved then—a sudden motion, closing the distance between them, her head dropping to rest against his shoulder. He noticed her shaking, the silent sobs she had been holding back finally breaking free. Years of guilt and shame and loneliness pouring out in the safety of this small cabin, this liminal space between continents where neither of them had to be anything except human.

Ethan wrapped his arm around her and held on. Held on while she cried for Leyla, for Subject 47, for the girl who'd killed a rabbit to prove she could survive. Held on while she mourned the childhood she never had, the father she had wanted Kessler to be, the forty-three lives that weighed on her conscience nonstop.

And somewhere within those spaces, he sensed his own grief finally surface—for his father, for the summers that had been lies, for the world that had turned out to be so much darker than he had ever imagined.

They wept together, thirty thousand feet above an ocean that separated who they had been from who they had to become.

When the tears finally subsided, Selin pulled back barely enough to look at him. Her eyes were red, her composure shattered, and she was somehow more real than she'd ever been.

"Thank you," she told him affectionately. "For not running. For not looking at me like I'm a monster."

"You're not a monster. Kessler's the monster. You're a wonderful human being he tried to turn into a weapon." Ethan touched her face, wiping a tear from her cheek. "But weapons can be turned against the people who made them."

She smiled—fragile, uncertain, but genuine. "Maybe that's what makes us dangerous to him now."

"Exactly." He leaned his forehead against hers. "We know how he thinks. We know what he's taken. And we have nothing left to lose."

She kissed him.

It wasn't planned, wasn't calculated—simply a moment when words became inadequate and action was the only language left. Her lips were soft, tasting of salt from tears, and when he kissed her back, there was nothing tentative about it. Just two people who'd found something real in a world of lies, who'd recognized in each other the kind of damage that only Kessler could inflict.

When they finally broke apart, she rested her head against his chest, and he held her close, feeling her heartbeat synchronize with his.

"We're going to destroy him," she asserted quietly. "For your father. For those forty-three people. For all the lives he's stolen and every life he's ruined."

"Together," Ethan stated.

"Together," Selin agreed.

They sat like that as the plane carried them east—two broken people holding each other together, flying toward a war they might not survive. But for the first time since this nightmare began, Ethan noticed something other than fear. Something that might have been hope. Something that might have been the beginning of love.

Somewhere ahead, Daniel was waiting. Somewhere behind, Noah was sailing into South American waters. And somewhere in between, Kessler's machine continued to turn, unaware that the people it had damaged were finally coming for it.

Miami — The Setai Hotel — 11:47 p.m.

Donovan poured three fingers of bourbon and stood at the floor-to-ceiling windows of his suite, watching the city lights reflect off Biscayne Bay. The penthouse had been a mistake—too visible, too predictable—but after forty years of government-rate motels and surveillance apartments, he'd wanted one night of comfort before whatever came next.

He thought about his granddaughter. Emma. Her last soccer game, the way she'd looked up at him from the field with that gap-toothed smile, so certain that the world was good and safe and that her grandfather would always be there to watch her play.

He should have run. Should have disappeared into the same channels he'd given Cole, vanished into South America or Southeast Asia, somewhere Kessler's reach didn't extend. But running meant leaving Emma. Running meant never seeing that smile again.

So he'd come back to his hotel, poured his drink, and waited.

The knock came at 11:52.

Donovan didn't reach for his weapon. There was no point. If it was who he thought it was, the hallway would already be clear, the hotel security already compromised, the exits already covered.

He opened the door.

Harris stood in the corridor, two men in tactical gear flanking him. His face was expressionless, professional—the face of a man doing a job he'd done many times before.

"You tracked me to the warehouse," Harris stated. Not a question.

"Yes."

"Gave them documents. Travel papers. A way out."

"Yes."

Harris nodded slowly. "Kessler gave the order six hours ago. Made the declaration that you had become a liability. Told us to make it clean."

Donovan took a sip of his bourbon—the last sip of anything. "And you always follow orders."

"I do." Something flickered in Harris's eyes—not guilt, not hesitation, only the faintest acknowledgment that this moment meant something. "For what it's worth, I respected you. Once."

"For what it's worth, I pity you." Donovan set down his glass. "You think you're a soldier. You're just a tool. And when you're not useful anymore, Kessler will do to you exactly what you're about to do to me."

Harris's jaw tightened. Then he raised his suppressed pistol and fired twice.

Donovan collapsed against the window, his blood streaking the glass, the city lights blurring as his vision faded. His last thought was of Emma, running across a soccer field, laughing in the sunlight, beautifully unaware of the world her grandfather had helped create.

I'm sorry, he thought as his vision went dark. *I'm so sorry.*

Over the Atlantic — Kessler's Jet — 12:15 a.m.

The confirmation came through encrypted channels: DONOVAN NEUTRALIZED. CLEAN. NO WITNESSES.

Kessler read the message with a satisfaction that bordered on pleasure. He sat in the leather chair of his private office, thirty thousand feet above the Atlantic, returning from the successful resolution of the James Cole problem. Lukas sat across from him, studying tactical displays on a tablet.

"Donovan is gone," Kessler announced. "Harris performed as expected. One less variable."

Lukas looked up. "He helped Cole. Gave him travel documents. That suggests he had access to other pipelines, other networks we might not have mapped."

"Likely. But Donovan was always a sentimentalist. He didn't have the strategic thinking to build real opposition—only the guilt to make small, futile gestures." Kessler smiled. "The documents won't matter. We know Cole is heading to Athens. We know his brother is there. The trap is already set."

"And the granddaughter?"

Kessler's smile faded slightly, replaced by something more calculating. "Emma. Soccer player. Lives with Donovan's daughter in Virginia." He turned his glass slowly, watching the amber liquid catch the cabin light. "An interesting question. Donovan betrayed us—does that debt extend to his bloodline?"

"She's a child," Lukas remarked. His voice was neutral, professional, but something flickered behind his eyes.

"Children grow into adults. Adults ask questions. Questions become threats." Kessler studied his son. "Does that trouble you?"

"I'm asking about operational necessity, not morality."

"Good answer." Kessler nodded slowly. "For now, we watch. The girl knows nothing, suspects nothing. She's not a threat today. But she's leverage—potential pressure on anyone who might have helped Donovan, anyone who might be tempted to follow his example." He paused. "Have someone make contact. Assess her. Learn her patterns, her vulnerabilities, the shape of her life. If we ever need to use her, I want to know exactly how."

Lukas nodded and made a note on his tablet. The question of Emma Donovan remained undecided—a variable held in reserve, a life that existed now at the intersection of mercy and utility.

Arlington, Virginia — Three Days Later — 4:15 p.m.

The soccer field glowed green in the autumn afternoon, surrounded by maple trees beginning to turn gold and red. Parents lined the sidelines in folding chairs, thermoses of coffee in hand, cheering as their daughters chased the ball across perfectly manicured grass.

Emma Donovan played midfield with the singular intensity of a young person who took life seriously. She was tall for her age, athletic, her dark hair pulled back in a ponytail that whipped behind her as she ran. Her grandfather had been at her last game. He'd promised to come to this one too.

But her mother had gotten a phone call yesterday. Had cried for hours. Had told Emma that Grandpa wouldn't be coming to games anymore.

Emma didn't fully understand. Something about an accident. Something about his heart. Adults always spoke about things like that when they didn't want to tell you the truth.

She focused on the game instead, channeling her confusion into movement, into competition, into the simple clarity of chasing a ball and trying to score.

After the final whistle—her team had won, 3-1—Emma walked toward the sideline where her mother waited with a forced smile and red-rimmed eyes. She was halfway there when a woman intercepted her path.

Blonde, mid-thirties, wearing a university polo shirt and carrying a clipboard. Professional but approachable, the kind of person you'd trust without thinking about it.

"Emma Donovan?" The woman smiled warmly. "I'm Rachel Smith, recruiting coordinator from Georgetown. I've been watching your play—you've got real talent. Do you have a minute?"

Emma's eyes widened. Georgetown. A real college recruiter, here to see her. "Really?"

"You bet Emma. Your footwork is exceptional for your age. And that assist in the second half—great field vision." Rachel fell into step beside her, keeping the conversation light, casual. "Tell me about yourself. What position do you like best? How long have you been playing?"

They talked for five minutes—long enough for Rachel to learn Emma's schedule, her school, her favorite subjects, the names of her closest friends. Long enough to map the contours of a person's life with the precision of an intelligence operative conducting reconnaissance.

When Emma's mother approached with a questioning look, Rachel smiled and handed over a business card. "Just introducing myself. Emma's got real potential. We'll be in touch."

She walked away across the parking lot, climbed into a nondescript sedan, and pulled out a secure phone.

The message was brief: **INITIAL CONTACT COMPLETE. SUBJECT ACCESSIBLE. FULL PROFILE TO FOLLOW.**

Eight thousand miles away, over European airspace now, Kessler read the report and smiled.

"Excellent," he murmured. "Another piece on the board."

He closed the message and returned to planning the Athens operation. The Cole brothers were converging. Sparrow was a complication but manageable. The hacker was fleeing south, irrelevant for now.

The plan was unfolding according to its design.

And in Virginia, a girl walked off a soccer field, clutching a business card from a woman who didn't exist, completely unaware that she had become a variable in a war she would never understand.

The machine Kessler had built continued to turn.

And it was always hungry for new pieces.

39

Breaking Point

[CLASSIFIED: EYES ONLY -- DIRECTORATE / NODE: BALKAN-OPS-7] OPERATION NIGHTFALL - AFTER AC-TION REPORT
Date: [REDACTED]
Location: Highway E-75, Serbia-Kosovo Border Region
Objective: Refugee convoy interdiction and asset demonstration
Personnel: Local contractors (deniable), Directorate coordination (KARA, S. - intelligence provision)
Outcome: SUCCESSFUL

- 43 casualties (within acceptable parameters)
- Media narrative established: "Ethnic violence/regional instability"
- Asset KARA performed per specification
- Secondary objective achieved: Destabilization sufficient to justify increased security contracts (Helios Defense Systems awarded €47M peacekeeping deployment)

Collateral Assessment: Civilian casualties create optimal conditions for intervention narrative

Note: Asset KARA demonstrated brief hesitation during initial briefing. Monitored for loyalty assessment. Continued deployment approved pending psychological evaluation.

Kessler's Directive: *"Hesitation is the first symptom of conscience. Conscience is the disease that destroys operatives. Monitor KARA closely. If infection spreads, terminate and replace."*

Serbian Highway, Dusk — Fall 2022

Overlooking the Sava River in Belgrade, the hotel room windows were fogged from the November cold. Selin sat at the small desk, reviewing the intelligence packet she'd been given three days ago. The briefing had been standard—refugee convoy moving from Kosovo through Serbia toward the Hungarian border. Suspected human trafficking, potential terrorist infiltration, requires monitoring and interdiction.

Standard. Routine. The kind of operation she had run dozens of times before.

Except something was wrong. She hoped it wouldn't prove deadly.

She had learned to trust those instincts—the quiet internal whispers that came before disasters, the instincts that had kept her alive through six years of fieldwork. But she'd also learned that questioning orders created problems. Created doubt. Created the kind of attention that ended careers or lives.

The convoy would pass through a rural section of Highway E-75 tomorrow evening. Her job was simple: provide exact timing, vehicle descriptions, and passenger manifest to her handlers. What happened after that wasn't her concern.

Except it was her concern. Because she'd spent the last week gathering that intelligence, and nothing about it suggested trafficking or terrorism. The convoy was forty-three people—families, mostly. Children. Old people. All properly documented, all legally seeking asylum under EU regulations.

They were refugees. Not threats. Only people running from war.

Her phone buzzed. Encrypted message from her handler—a Directorate coordinator she knew only as "Athens-7":

"Confirm convoy departure time. Critical for interdiction window. Delay not acceptable."

Selin stared at the message. *Interdiction.* The word was off. It was wrong. In intel terminology, interdiction meant stopping something illegal. But these people weren't illegal. They were documented. Legal. Protected under international law.

Unless the law wasn't what mattered.

She typed back: *"Convoy appears legitimate. Recommend continued surveillance rather than direct action."*

The response came immediately:

"Your assessment noted. Orders unchanged. Confirm departure time."

Selin noticed her stomach tighten, the same feeling after she ran 10 miles on an empty stomach. This wasn't intelligence gathering. This was targeting. And she was the one painting the target.

She walked to the window, watching the river move in the darkness below. Somewhere out there, forty-three people were preparing for a journey they thought would lead to safety. They didn't know someone was tracking their every movement, calculating the optimal moment to strike.

She thought of her mother. Of being twelve years old on Istanbul streets, alone and terrified. If someone had offered her mother a convoy to safety, would Selin want an operative somewhere providing intelligence to destroy it?

Her phone buzzed again:

"KARA. Respond. Confirm departure time. This is a direct order."

Her fingers hovered over the keyboard. She'd been trained for this moment—the moment when personal feelings conflicted with operational necessity. Kessler's voice echoed in her memory: *"The mission matters more than your comfort. Execute orders. Question later, if ever."*

She'd always executed orders. That's what made her valuable. What kept her employed, protected, useful.

But something in her—some fragment of the twelve-year-old girl who'd once needed help and received none—refused to type the confirmation.

Instead, she typed: *"Need 24 hours to verify intel. Possible compromise in source data."*

"Negative. Time-sensitive operation. Confirm now or replacement operative will be assigned."

There it was. The threat. Not subtle, not hidden. Comply or be replaced. And if she was replaced, her career ended. Possibly her life ended as well, depending on how much Kessler valued her continued silence about operations she'd been part of.

But if she complied, forty-three people died.

The equation was simple. Her life, her career, her safety—all of it traded against forty-three strangers she'd never meet.

Kessler had taught her how to make that calculation. How to value strategic objectives over individual lives. How to see people as variables in equations that served larger purposes.

She'd believed him. For six years, she'd believed that what they did—the deaths, the manipulations, the calculated cruelties—served some greater good. Maintained stability. Prevented worse outcomes.

But looking at the convoy manifest, seeing names like "Amira, age 7" and "Hassan, age 68," she couldn't remember what greater good justified their deaths.

Her hands shook as she typed: *"Departure time: 18:30 tomorrow. Route confirmed per previous intel. Vehicle descriptions attached."*

She hit send before she could stop herself.

The response: *"Confirmed. Stand by for post-operation debrief. Excellent work."*

Selin closed her laptop and walked to the bathroom. She vomited—once, twice, her body rejecting what her mind had a moment ago agreed to. Then she sat on the cold tile floor, hugging her knees, trying to breathe through the understanding that she had become exactly what her twelve-year-old self would have hated.

A weapon. A tool. A person who chose safety over conscience.

The Next Evening

The explosion happened at 7:47 local time—seventeen minutes after the convoy passed the designated point. Selin watched the news coverage from her hotel room, volume muted, seeing the aftermath in images that would never fully leave her mind.

Burned vehicles. Covered bodies. A child's shoe in the road, small and red, somehow untouched by the fire that had consumed the world around it.

The news anchor spoke in Serbian, his expression appropriately grave. The subtitle translation scrolled at the bottom: *"Tragic incident on Highway E-75. Early reports suggest ethnic violence, possibly linked to regional tensions. 43 confirmed dead. No survivors."*

No survivors.

Selin sat perfectly still, watching the footage loop. Emergency responders moving between wreckage. Families gathering at police barriers, searching for loved ones who wouldn't be found alive.

Her phone buzzed. Text from Athens-7:

"Operation successful. Media narrative established. Your next assignment briefing in 48 hours. Maintain cover until relocation."

Operation successful.

Forty-three people dead, and someone—somewhere in the Directorate's machinery—had marked it as *successful* in a spreadsheet.

She thought about the intelligence she'd provided. How precise she'd been. How professional. She'd done exactly what was required, exactly when it was needed. She'd been an excellent operative.

And forty-three people had died because of that excellence.

Her laptop was still open. She pulled up the convoy manifest one more time, reading the names she'd helped kill:

Amira Kovač, age 7

Hassan Begović, age 68

Lejla Mehić, age 34 (pregnant)

The list went on. Forty-three names. Forty-three people who'd believed they were traveling toward safety, never knowing that safety had been a lie, that someone in a Belgrade hotel room had sold them to killers for the price of her own continued employment.

Selin closed the laptop and made a decision.

She walked to the window and opened it—six stories up, cold November air rushing in. For a moment, she considered the fall. How easy it would be to step out. How that would solve the problem of living with what she'd done.

But suicide was for people who'd given up. And something in her—some stubborn fragment that Kessler hadn't managed to kill—refused to give him that satisfaction.

If she died, the convoy died for nothing. But if she lived, if she found a way to stop being his weapon, hopefully their deaths could mean something.

Perhaps she could become the person who prevented the next convoy from dying.

She pulled out a separate phone—the one she had bought with cash three months ago, the one her handlers didn't know existed, the one she had told herself was paranoia but had kept anyway.

She typed a message to an email address she'd memorized from a classified briefing about compromised intelligence officers: *"I have information about Directorate operations. Human rights violations. Manufactured crises. I can prove it. But I need protection first. — Sparrow"*

She hit send before fear could stop her.

Then she packed her bag, left the hotel through the service entrance, and disappeared into Belgrade's night. She had maybe twelve hours before her handlers realized she'd gone dark. Maybe twenty-four before they sent cleaners.

She had to be gone before then. She had to become someone else. Had to find a way to burn down the toxic and evil world she had been part of building for the Directorate.

Not because she thought she could be redeemed. Redemption wasn't possible after forty-three deaths.

But because stopping Kessler from creating forty-three more deaths—that was something worth dying for.

Three Days Later — Vienna Safe House

Selin watched the news coverage of her own death. "Former Intelligence Contractor Dies in Car Accident. Belgrade Police Investigate."

The footage showed a burned-out vehicle on a mountain road—the kind of accident that happened to people who raised too many questions. The body inside was too damaged for identification, but dental records (forged) confirmed it was Leyla Kara, age 29, Turkish national, employed by various security contractors.

The Directorate had killed her. Officially. Paperwork filed, body buried, case closed.

Which meant her new identity—the identity she'd constructed over three sleepless nights using skills Kessler had taught her—could start existing.

Her encrypted email had received one response, from an address that routed through so many proxies she couldn't trace it:

"Verification required before protection offered. Prove you have actionable intelligence. Prove you're not a plant. Then we talk. — Ghost"

She typed back: *"I can give you Directorate operation codes, financial routing numbers, and names of compromised officials in six countries. I can prove the Serbian convoy was orchestrated, not accidental. I can prove the system you think maintains order actually creates chaos for profit. But I won't do any of that until I know you're not them."*

The response took three hours:

"Meet me in Zurich. Café Odeon, noon, three days from now. Wear blue. Carry a copy of Der Spiegel. Order schwarzkaffee. If you're real, I'll make contact. If you're bait, you'll never see me. Either way, come alone."

Selin smiled despite her situation. *Ghost* was careful. Good. Careful people lived longer.

She spent three days establishing Selin Yilmaz—background story, fake employment history, references that would check out under casual scrutiny. She dyed her hair, changed her wardrobe, practiced new mannerisms until Leyla Kara was someone she had known once but couldn't quite remember.

The meeting in Zurich went well. Ghost turned out to be an ex-MI6 officer who'd discovered the Directorate the hard way—through a friend's suspicious death and intel that didn't add up. He believed her story because he'd lived a version of it himself.

"You can't go back," he announced, sipping his coffee in the bright Swiss afternoon. "You know that, right? The person you were is gone. Anyone you knew in your past life is compromised. You're a ghost now. Best case, you survive. Worst case—"

"I already know worst case. I've been executing worst case for six years." Selin met his eyes. "I'm not looking for protection. I'm looking for a way to fight back."

"Against Kessler? Against the Directorate?" Ghost laughed—bitter, knowing. "You'd have better odds fighting gravity."

"Gravity doesn't murder refugees to juice defense contracts. Gravity doesn't calculate acceptable casualties for profit margins. Gravity has nothing to do with this. This is people making choices. And choices can be unmade."

Ghost studied her for a long moment. "You're either extremely brave or exceptionally stupid."

"Can't it be both?"

"Usually is." He slid a card across the table—blank except for an email address written in pencil. "This connects you to people who are building something. A network. Resistance isn't the right word—more like... collective documentation. We can't stop the Directorate. But we can record what they do. Build evidence. Wait for the right moment to expose them."

"How long until that moment comes?"

"Could be years. Could be decades. Could be never." He stood, preparing to leave. "But it's better than doing nothing. And it's better than being their weapon."

"Thank you," Selin whispered quietly.

"Don't thank me. I'm probably sending you to your death." He paused at the door. "But for what it's worth—those people on the convoy? They died because you followed orders. But each person you save by stopping the next operation? They will live because you broke those orders. The math doesn't balance. It never does. But it's better than the alternative."

He left.

Selin sat alone in the café, drinking coffee that had gone cold, watching Swiss civilians live normal lives that didn't include deciding which refugees lived or died.

She thought of Amira, age 7. Hassan, age 68. Lejla, pregnant, dreaming of the child she'd never meet.

I can't save you, she told their ghosts. *But I can try to save the next convoy. The one after that. However many I can reach before they kill me.*

It wasn't redemption. It wasn't forgiveness. It wasn't anything except the bare minimum of being human after years of being a tool.

But it was something.

And something was better than the nothing she'd been living with since that November evening when she'd typed a departure time and condemned forty-three people to death for the crime of seeking safety.

She paid for her coffee, walked out into Zurich's autumn afternoon, and began the work of becoming someone Kessler couldn't find.

Someone who'd spend the next two years gathering evidence, making contacts, building the foundation that would let her finally, truly break free.

Someone who'd eventually meet an American banker running for his life and recognize in him the same desperate need to be better than what the world had made them.

But that was later.

For now, she was Selin Yilmaz, ghost of a dead operative, walking through a Swiss city toward an uncertain future.

Carrying forty-three names in her memory like stones.

Hoping that someday, somehow, their deaths would mean something more than a line item in the Directorate's quarterly profit report.

40

Photograph

Kessler — Private Diary (Zurich-0 Archive: Unclassified)
"Maria… you asked for truth. I only gave you mercy."

Athens, Greece — Exarcheia District — 6:47 a.m. local time–Day 9

Past graffiti-covered buildings and cafés that wouldn't open for hours, the taxi wound through narrow streets still slick with pre-dawn rain,. Ethan watched the anarchist district slide past his window—a neighborhood of spray-painted revolution and stubborn resistance—and for the first time in days, he sensed something other than fear.

Selin sat beside him, her hand resting on his thigh, a small gesture of connection that was fresh and new, something she hadn't felt before. They hadn't slept on the plane—too much adrenaline, too many confessions, too much grief and hope tangled together. But somewhere over the Atlantic, holding each other in the dark, they'd crossed a threshold that couldn't be uncrossed.

The taxi stopped outside a crumbling apartment building. Hotel Nostos, according to the faded sign. Third floor, room 34—Daniel's coordinates.

They climbed the stairs in silence, Selin's hand on her weapon, Ethan's heart hammering. He hadn't seen his brother in years. Hadn't spoken to him properly since before their father's warning at Christmas.

Now they were about to reunite in a foreign city, fugitives from an enemy who'd been playing their family for three decades.

The door opened before Ethan could knock.

Daniel stood in the doorway—older, harder, eyes carrying the substantial weight of a man who had seen too much death. But when he saw his brother, something cracked in that hardened facade. Something human.

"E," he uttered quietly.

"D."

They embraced—fierce, wordless, the kind of hug that contained years of silence and distance and the shared understanding that their father was likely dead because of the same monster they'd come to destroy.

When they finally separated, Daniel's eyes moved to Selin. Assessing. Professional.

"You must be the Turkish intelligence officer Noah mentioned." His voice was flat, careful.

"Selin." She extended her hand. "I've heard about you. Former Delta. Marcus Vale. Impressive service record."

"That record is classified."

"So is mine." She smiled thinly. "We're all ghosts here."

Daniel studied her for a long moment, then nodded once—the abbreviated approval of someone who'd learned to read people in seconds. "Come in. We have a lot to discuss."

The room was sparse—single bed, wooden chair, a table covered with maps and photographs. On the wall, Daniel had pinned surveillance images, financial documents, a web of connections that traced Kessler's network across continents.

"I've been building this for three years," Daniel remarked. "Everything I could gather on the Directorate while I was working for them. Shell companies. Asset identities. Operational patterns." He gestured at the web. "But it's not enough. Not yet."

Ethan moved to the table, studied the documents. His analyst's mind was already working, seeing patterns Daniel might have missed. "Noah's running interference from South America. He's got a network—people the Directorate hurt. Witnesses, whistleblowers, victims. They're ready to move when we give the signal."

"And what's our play?" Daniel requested.

Ethan looked at Selin, then back at his brother. "We expose him. The financial flows, the assassinations, the governments he's destabilized. We build a case so complete that even his protection can't save him."

"That's a long game."

"It's the only game that ends with him destroyed instead of dead." Ethan's voice hardened. "Killing Kessler creates a martyr. Exposing him burns the whole machine to the ground."

Daniel was silent for a moment. Then: "Dad would be proud of you."

"Dad taught us both." Ethan's throat tightened. "He told me to question everything. Trust nothing. Fight when I have to." He looked at the photograph Daniel had pinned to the wall—their father, younger, standing beside a man who'd been his best friend and his greatest enemy. "We're going to finish what he started."

Selin moved to stand beside Ethan, her shoulder brushing his. "Together." Daniel looked between them—saw something in the way they stood, the way they touched, the shared damage written in their eyes. His expression softened slightly.

"Together," he agreed.

Outside, Athens was waking. The anarchist district stirred to life—cafés opening, students arguing, the eternal rhythm of a neighborhood that had learned to resist. And in a small hotel room above it all, three people who had lost to the same monster began planning how to take it all back.

Somewhere across the Mediterranean, that monster was about to receive his first warning.

Geneva — Kessler's Private Residence — 5:47 a.m. local time

Sleep had become a luxury Kessler could no longer afford. His body demanded rest that his mind refused to grant. He sat in his study, surrounded by monitors displaying global markets, security feeds, satellite imagery. The machinery of control hummed even when he didn't.

But tonight, he wasn't watching the screens.

Instead, he held a photograph—old, faded, edges worn from handling. A woman with dark hair and cautious eyes stood in front of a chalet in Gstaad, holding a small boy who stared at the camera with unsettling intensity. Behind them, a younger Kessler—forty pounds lighter, fewer lines, something almost resembling warmth in his expression.

Maria. His wife. Dead over thirteen years now.

The official story was an accident—black ice on an Alpine road, car through a guardrail, two-hundred-meter fall into a ravine. The actual story was more complicated.

She'd been asking questions. About his work, his colleagues, the discrepancies between what he claimed to do and the money that appeared in their accounts. She'd been a professor of ethics before they married—moral philosophy, the kind of academic who believed truth mattered more than convenience.

That belief had killed her.

He'd tried to warn her. "Some truths are structural," he'd observed. "They hold up buildings. You don't excavate them unless you want the buildings to collapse."

"Then maybe they should collapse," she'd replied.

Three weeks later, she was dead. An accident. Officially.

Kessler had arranged it to look natural—no explosives, no tampering, simply a well-placed sheet of ice and a phone call to distract her at the critical moment. Quick. Painless. Necessary.

Lukas had been eight years old.

The boy had posed once, years later, if his mother had truly died by accident. Kessler had looked into those pale, knowing eyes—so much like his own—and told him the truth.

"The world is structured to reward control and punish sentiment. Your mother chose sentiment. I chose control. Which one of us survived?"

Lukas had been silent for a long time. Then: "Did you love her?"

"Yes."

"Then how could you—"

"Because I loved her." Kessler's voice had been steady, surgical. "If I'd let her continue, she would have exposed things that would've destroyed us both. She would have died anyway—messily, publicly, painfully. I gave her a quick exit and ensured you survived. That's what love looks like when it intersects with reality."

Lukas had left the room without another word. He didn't speak to his father for three months after that. But eventually, he came back. And when he did, he was different. Colder. Clearer.

Ready to learn.

Now, sitting in the Geneva dark, Kessler traced his wife's face in the photograph and wondered—not for the first time—if he'd been wrong.

Not about the necessity. He still believed in that. But about the cost.

Lukas had become exactly what Kessler needed him to be: brilliant, ruthless, capable of any sacrifice. But somewhere in that transformation, the boy who'd cried at his mother's funeral had disappeared. Replaced by a weapon so finely honed it no longer questioned whose hand held it.

I made him in my image, Kessler thought. *I turned my son into a tool.*

His phone buzzed. A message from Lukas:

"Father, I've been thinking about the Cole endgame. Three men who love each other, facing a system designed to break them. Does it remind you of anyone?"

Kessler stared at the message. Smart boy. Too smart.

He typed back:

"If you're asking whether I see myself in them—yes. James was my friend once. His sons are brilliant. Under different circumstances, I'd have recruited them."

"And now?"

"Now they're lessons. Proof that brilliance without control is sophisticated chaos."

A long pause. Then:

"Sometimes I wonder if control without compassion is sophisticated cruelty."

Kessler's hands trembled—slightly, only for a moment. His son, questioning him. Using Maria's words, Maria's philosophy, as if her ghost spoke through their shared blood.

He typed:

"Your mother told me the same thing. But she's dead, and I'm not. The world rewards one approach and buries the other."

"I know. I wonder sometimes what she would think of what I've become."

Kessler closed his eyes. The honest answer—the answer he couldn't send—was this:

She'd hate you. And she'd hate me for making you this way. But we don't have the luxury of her philosophy. The world is what it is.

Instead, he typed:

"She'd be proud that you survived. Survival is the first moral obligation."

A lie. But a useful one.

"Get some rest, Father. The endgame begins soon. You'll need your strength."

Kessler set down the phone. He looked at the photograph one more time—Maria's skeptical smile, Lukas's unblinking stare, his own younger face still holding traces of the man he'd been before necessity carved him into something else.

"I'm sorry," he whispered to the woman in the picture. "I'm sorry for what I did. I'm sorry for what I made him."

But sorry didn't resurrect the dead. And it didn't undo the machine he'd built—the machine that consumed the Cole family the same way it had consumed his own.

He placed the photograph in his desk drawer and locked it.

Some ghosts belonged in the dark.

He reached for his bourbon, savoring the burn, letting the silence settle around him like a familiar shroud. The monitors hummed. The world turned. And Kessler sat alone with his thoughts, secure in the knowledge that his empire was unassailable, his enemies scattered, his control absolute.

At that same moment, the screens in his study turned red. Kessler's eyes and face froze. The monitors—all twelve of them—flashed crimson warning codes, scrolling data breaches, system alerts cascading faster than his eyes could track. A single message appeared across the displays, white text on blood-red background:

AURORA PROTOCOL DETECTED

DIRECTORATE NODE COMPROMISED

BUENOS AIRES - FINANCIAL SECTOR

His secure phone erupted—not Lukas this time, but his head of cybersecurity, voice tight with controlled panic: "Sir, we're under attack. Someone's inside the Buenos Aires node. They're not only breaching—they're extracting. Transaction records, asset identities, operational funds. Whoever this is, they know exactly where to look."

Kessler's blood went cold. The Cole brothers were in Athens. His lovely Sparrow was with them. That left— the hacker. Noah. The little architect who disappeared into South America.

"Trace it," Kessler ordered, his voice deadly calm. "Find the hacker. And mobilize our South American assets. I want him shut down and neutralized immediately."

He ended the call and stared at the crimson screens, watching his carefully constructed world bleed data into enemy hands.

The war had changed. And for the first time in thirty years, Kessler sensed an unfamiliar feeling.

Concern.

41

Aurora Rising

Cartagena, Colombia — 11:47 p.m. local time- Day 10

Aromas of humidity, coffee, and ozone from servers running too hot wafted through the safehouse—the mixture hitting the senses like freezing water on the face. Noah Rivera sat cross-legged on the concrete floor, surrounded by a constellation of laptops, each one routing through different VPN layers, each one a node in the distributed consciousness he was building.

The room occupied the upper floor of an abandoned textile factory on the outskirts of Cartagena's old city, its windows blacked out with paint and cardboard. Captain Morales had secured it three days ago—one of dozens of properties scattered across South America that served the network of survivors, witnesses, and fighters who'd dedicated their lives to destroying the Directorate.

AURORA had started as theory—currency designed to resist control. Now it was becoming something more dangerous: proof that the system could be circumvented entirely.

Noah's fingers flew across the keyboard, pulling up the target he'd been preparing for weeks: the Directorate's financial node in Buenos Aires. A nexus of shell companies, laundered money, and black-budget accounts that funneled millions to operations across three continents. Tonight, he was going to bleed it.

"You should eat something."

The voice came from the doorway. Soft, accented, carrying the special warmth of someone who'd learned to care for broken things.

Isabella Morales stood silhouetted against the dim hallway light, holding a plate of arepas and a bottle of water. She was twenty-eight, her father's daughter in any way that mattered—dark eyes that saw through pretense, hands that knew both healing and violence, a mind that processed strategy the way most people processed conversation.

"I'm not hungry," Noah announced without looking up.

"You haven't eaten in sixteen hours." She crossed the room, set the plate beside his workstation. "My father says you're smart. He also says you're going to kill yourself before you finish whatever you're building."

"Your father worries too much."

"My father buried his brother because of men like Kessler." Isabella crouched beside him, close enough that he could smell jasmine and gunpowder—an impossible combination that somehow suited her perfectly. "He knows what obsession looks like. He also knows what happens when it consumes you."

Noah finally looked at her. In the blue glow of the monitors, her face was a study in contradictions: the softness of a woman who'd trained as a nurse before the Directorate destroyed her clinic, the hardness of a guerrilla fighter who'd spent three years running medical supplies through cartel territory.

"I lost my sister," he added quietly. "Lily. She was a child. Cancer. The insurance company decided she wasn't worth saving." He turned back to the screens. "The algorithm that killed her was funded by money that flowed through accounts like the ones I'm about to crack. So yes, I'm obsessed. And no, I'm not going to stop."

Isabella was silent for a long moment. Then she reached out, touched his shoulder—not romantic, not yet, but something that acknowledged shared damage.

"Then let me help. I can't code, but I can watch your back. I can make sure you don't collapse before you finish." She squeezed gently. "And I can remind you that revenge means nothing if you're not alive to see it."

Noah met her eyes. Something passed between them—mutual recognition perhaps. The unique understanding that develops between people who have both lost their worlds and chosen to fight instead of grieve.

"Stay," he added softly with a warmth that filled the room. "But don't touch anything. What I'm about to do is going to wake up some nasty and dangerous people."

Isabella settled into a chair beside him, the plate of arepas between them. "I've been waking up dangerous people my whole life. What's one more?"

Despite what he and his friends were going through, Noah smiled.

His phone buzzed. Encrypted message from one of the hackers he'd recruited in the first weeks:

"They're scanning for your signature. Directorate cyber teams hitting the nodes we've established. Three safe houses compromised in the last week."

Noah's fingers flew across the keyboard, implementing another layer of obfuscation. Directorate searches for him generated false positives—a hundred Noah Riveras, all digital ghosts, all equally plausible targets.

"Let them search," he muttered. "I'm not hiding. I'm multiplying."

"What does that mean?" Isabella quizzed.

"It means AURORA isn't a program anymore. It's a distributed system—thousands of nodes across six continents, each one running independently, each one capable of continuing even if I'm captured or killed." He pulled up a global map, green dots scattered across far flung landmasses. "They think they're hunting one person. They don't understand I've become a process. And processes, once properly distributed, are nearly impossible to kill."

Isabella studied the map. "Those dots. Each one is a person?"

"Each one is someone the Directorate hurt. Journalists. Whistle-blowers. Accountants who saw too much. Farmers whose land was stolen. These folks volunteered to run a piece of the network because they want what I want." Noah's voice hardened. "Justice. Or at least something that looks like it."**Buenos Aires — Directorate Financial Node — Simultaneous**

Over seven thousand kilometers away, in a climate-controlled server room beneath a Recoleta office tower, red warning lights began to flash.

The facility housed one of the Directorate's sensitive financial operations—a clearinghouse for black-budget transactions that moved money from legitimate businesses into accounts that funded illicit operations, from arms deals to political assassinations. Twelve technicians worked in shifts, monitoring data flows, maintaining firewalls, ensuring that the billions of dollars passing through their systems remained invisible to regulators and law enforcement.

Tonight, the invisible had become visible.

"We're being breached," someone shouted. "Multiple entry points. They're not only reading—they're extracting."

The lead technician—a former NSA contractor named Reeves who'd sold his skills to the highest bidder—sprinted to the main console. What he saw made his blood run cold.

Transaction records streaming out through encrypted channels. Asset identities being copied. And the money—millions of dollars in operational funds—rerouting through pathways so complex his tracking software couldn't follow.

"Shut it down," Reeves ordered. "Pull the connection. Kill the power if you have to."

"We can't." The junior technician's voice was panicked. "They've locked us out of our own systems. Whoever's doing this, they're inside the architecture. They know exactly where to look."

On the main screen, a message appeared—white text on crimson background:

AURORA PROTOCOL INITIATED

YOUR MONEY NOW FEEDS THE CHILDREN YOU STARVED

ROBIN CIPHER SENDS HIS REGARDS

Reeves grabbed his phone, dialed the emergency line that connected directly to Geneva.

"Sir, we have a critical breach. Buenos Aires node. They are extracting critical data—financial records, asset identities, operational funds. We're hemorrhaging data."

The response was cold, controlled, terrifying: "Contain what you can. I'm mobilizing South American assets. Whoever's running this operation will be dead shortly."

The line went dead.

Reeves stared at the screens, watching years of carefully constructed financial architecture collapse in real time. Somewhere out there, a ghost was dismantling an empire.

And he was powerless to stop it.

Cartagena Columbia — 12:23 a.m.

Noah watched the data streams with something approaching joy. It had worked. AURORA was inside the Buenos Aires node, extracting critical Directorate data—transaction records that proved money laundering, asset identities that could expose operatives, and most importantly, forty-seven million dollars in operational funds.

"Where's the money going?" Isabella requested, watching the numbers cascade across the screen.

"Where it should have gone in the first place." Noah pulled up a distribution map. "UNICEF hunger programs in sub-Saharan Africa. Medical clinics in refugee camps. Legal aid funds for families the Directorate destroyed. Food banks in communities Kessler's companies gutted when they moved manufacturing overseas."

"Forty-seven million dollars?"

"Split into thousands of micro-transactions, each one routed through different cryptocurrency exchanges, each one completely untraceable." Noah's smile was savage. "By morning, Kessler's blood money will be feeding children in Somalia, providing insulin to diabetics in Guatemala, funding lawyers who represent whistleblowers his people tried to silence."

Isabella stared at the screen, at the cascading numbers, at the global map showing money flowing to places that desperately needed it. "This is what you've been building. Not just a weapon against them—a redistribution system."

"Robin Cipher," Noah told her quietly. "That's what the media calls me. I steal from the corrupt and give to the poor...the needy...the desperate. It's not justice—not in the actual sense. Justice would be Kessler in prison, his empire dismantled, his victims compensated. But this?" He gestured at the flowing numbers. "This is hope. And sometimes hope is enough to keep people fighting."

His second phone vibrated—the one connected to Ethan through a dead-drop protocol. He read the message:

E: *"We made it to Athens. Daniel's here. We're planning the next move. How long can you stay dark?"*

Noah typed back:

N: *"As long as it takes. AURORA is 67% distributed. Even if they find me, they can't kill it. I hit the Buenos Aires Directorate node—$47M redirected to humanitarian causes. Kessler's going to feel this one."*

E: *"They'll come for you. Harris. Directorate kill teams. All of their assets."*

N: *"I know. But Lily will have mattered. That's enough."*

He stared at his sister's photograph—the one he'd carried since Princeton, edges worn soft from handling. She'd be twenty-five now if the system hadn't decided her life was actuarially worthless.

"I'm making them pay," he whispered to her frozen smile. "One transaction at a time."

E: *"Stay alive, Noah. We need you for the endgame."*

N: *"I plan to. Besides, I've got someone watching my back now."*

He glanced at Isabella, who was studying the data streams with the focused intensity of someone who understood exactly what they were witnessing.

E: "Who?"

N: "Long story. Tell you when this is over. Stay safe, E. Give Kessler hell."

He set down the phone and returned to his screens. The Buenos Aires extraction was complete—forty-seven million dollars redistributed, transaction records copied, asset identities secured. Somewhere in Geneva, Kessler was learning that his empire had just begun to bleed.

Outside, Cartagena's streets hummed with life—vendors selling fruit, lovers walking along the old city walls, the ambient sound of a city that had survived colonialism, drug wars, and poverty through sheer stubborn resilience.

Noah understood that resilience. It was why he'd chosen Colombia. Here, survival was an art form, resistance was culture, and the line between legal and necessary had been negotiated so many times it barely existed.

His third laptop pinged—a Directorate IP attempting to penetrate one of his honeypot servers. Noah smiled, triggered the countermeasure he'd been preparing for weeks.

The attacking system abruptly found itself flooded with data—terabytes of encrypted noise that looked like intelligence but was actually random number generation masked as financial transactions. Whoever was on the other end would spend months trying to decrypt gibberish.

"Enjoy the puzzle," Noah professed strongly, closing the laptop.

"They'll trace that eventually," Isabella indicated with firm resolve. "The attack came from somewhere. They'll find the origin point."

"They'll find an origin point. Not *the* origin point." Noah stood, stretched, aching where he had been shot in Miami. The wound had healed poorly—no doctors, no hospitals, only field dressing and antibiotics bought from a veterinary supplier. "I have forty-seven decoy servers running across twelve countries. Each one looks exactly like this one. By the time they figure out which signal is real, I'll be somewhere else."

"Where?"

"Your father's boat. The Santa Maria sails for Buenos Aires tomorrow night. I want to be close when the chaos hits—when Kessler's people realize how much they've lost, when the journalists I've been feeding start publishing, when the whole rotten structure starts to shake."

Isabella stood, moved closer. "Buenos Aires is where they'll be looking for you. It's the most dangerous place you could go."

"It's also where I can do the most damage." Noah met her eyes. "I'm not suicidal, Isabella. I don't want to die. But I also won't hide while other people take the risks I should be taking."

She studied him for a long moment—the way she'd studied patients in her clinic, assessing vital signs, reading the truth beneath the surface. Then she reached up, touched his face, her fingers warm against his cheek.

"Then I'm coming with you," she insisted. "Someone has to keep you alive long enough to see this through."

"Your father won't like that."

"My father lost his brother to these people. He'll understand." She dropped her hand, but something had changed in the space between them—a recognition, a possibility, a future neither of them had dared imagine before tonight. "Besides, I'm a better shot than most of his crew. And I know Buenos Aires. I did my nursing residency there, before—" She stopped, shadows crossing her face. "Before it all fell apart."

Noah didn't ask what had happened. Each person in this network had a story like that—a moment when the Directorate touched their lives and left nothing but wreckage. The details didn't matter. The commitment to fighting back did.

"Okay," he muttered. "But if things go bad—"

"If things go bad, we improvise. That's what survivors do." Isabella picked up the plate of arepas, now cold. "Now eat something. We have a long journey ahead, and you're no use to anyone if you collapse from hunger."

Noah took an arepa, bit into it, tasted corn and cheese and something like hope. On his screens, AURORA's transaction logs continued to scroll—thousands of payments flowing to journalists in authoritarian countries, legal aid funds for refugees, medical clinics operating in war zones.

Robin Cipher wasn't a myth. It was an algorithm. And tonight, that algorithm had declared war.

Geneva — Kessler's Private Residence — 3:17 a.m.

The screens in his study still glowed crimson, like shadows drinking the light.

Kessler sat motionless, staring at the damage reports streaming in from Buenos Aires. Forty-seven million dollars—gone. Transaction records spanning three years—copied. Asset identities that had taken decades to cultivate—exposed.

And the money. The worst part was where the money had gone.

His analysts had traced the outflows: UNICEF. Doctors Without Borders. Legal defense funds. Food banks. Refugee assistance programs. The hacker hadn't just stolen from him—he'd weaponized the theft, turning Kessler's blood money into a global act of charity that would generate headlines, investigations, questions.

"Robin Cipher," he murmured, reading the message still frozen on his main display. "Clever boy."

His phone rang. Lukas.

"I've seen the reports," Lukas added. "How bad?"

"Bad enough. The financial damage is recoverable—we have reserves, contingencies. But the exposure..." Kessler's jaw tightened. "Transaction records linking shell companies to operations we've denied for years. Asset identities that should have stayed buried. If this reaches the wrong journalists, the wrong prosecutors—"

"Then we stop it from reaching them. Kill the hacker. Burn his network. Make an example."

"I've already mobilized South American assets. But this Noah is more sophisticated than we anticipated. He's distributed his system across dozens of nodes. Killing him might not be enough."

"Then we eliminate anything connected to him. Safe houses, collaborators, anyone who has ever helped him." Lukas's voice was cold, professional—the weapon Kessler had spent years forging. "We burn it all down, and we make sure the world knows what happens to people who challenge us."

Kessler was silent for a moment, thinking of Maria. Of the cost of the machine he'd built. Of the son he'd shaped in his own image, now proposing mass murder with the casual efficiency of someone ordering lunch.

"Do it," he said finally. "And be surgical. The Cole brothers are the primary threat. The little architect hacker is a distraction—dangerous, but secondary."

"Understood. I'll coordinate with Harris."

The line went dead.

Kessler stared at his screens, at the crimson warnings still flashing, at the message that mocked the system he had built:

YOUR MONEY NOW FEEDS THE CHILDREN YOU STARVED

Somewhere in Colombia, a ghost was laughing at him.

But ghosts could be killed. And Kessler had been killing ghosts for a long time.

The hunt had only just begun.

42

Gathering

Kessler — Private Diary (Zurich-0 Archive: Unclassified)
"Disagreement is welcome, of course...so long as you remember it changes nothing." —Kessler

Davos, Switzerland — 1:47 a.m. local time- Day 11
Snow fell soundlessly over the Alps, blanketing the mountain roads in ghostly silence. The conference center was empty now — the politicians, journalists, and think-tank hopefuls had all gone home. But beneath the façade of the World Economic Forum, in a private sublevel sealed off from cameras and security protocols, the true meeting was only beginning.

A long glass table stretched the length of the room, surrounded by eight figures. No placards, no flags—only people whose signatures could start wars with the same ease as opening a spreadsheet.

At the head of the table sat Konrad Voss, CEO of Helios Defense Systems. His company built the drones that enforced borders, the satellites that listened to governments, the contracts that never appeared on public ledgers. Helios was the heart of The Directorate—the syndicate that decided where the world's next crisis would be profitable.

To his left sat the Chair of The Atlantic Group, her holdings veiled through sovereign funds and shell trusts. Across from her, the Director of The European Intelligence Compact—a coalition that didn't officially exist—stirred his espresso with clinical disinterest. Further down, the CEO of Global News Syndicate adjusted his cufflinks, smiling faintly. He already knew tomorrow's headlines.

Kessler entered without ceremony. No one rose. They all knew who he was—the unseen architect, the man who made the machine breathe.

Voss looked up, his expression carefully neutral. "You're late."

"Time is a precious commodity, Konrad." Kessler took his seat with the unhurried grace of a man who knew the room would wait. "I prefer not to spend it on your frivolous ceremonies."

He placed a tablet on the table. The screen displayed a rotating map of the world—hotspots glowing red: Ukraine. Taiwan. Sudan. Caracas. Buenos Aires, now pulsing an angry crimson.

"Buenos Aires," the intelligence director voiced, leaning forward. "We've all seen the reports. Forty-seven million dollars extracted from one of our most secure nodes. Transaction records compromised. Asset identities exposed." He looked at Kessler with something approaching accusation. "This happened on your watch."

Kessler's expression didn't flicker. "The hacker calls himself Robin Cipher. Noah Rivera—a former Princeton prodigy whose sister died because an insurance algorithm decided her life wasn't worth saving. He's been building a distributed financial network called AURORA for three years. Last night, he used it to breach our Buenos Aires operations."

"And the money?" the media CEO put forward. "Where did it go?"

"Humanitarian organizations. UNICEF. Doctors Without Borders. Legal defense funds." Kessler's smile was thin, humorless. "He's not only stealing from us—he's weaponizing the theft. Making us fund our own opposition."

The Atlantic Group chair set down her water glass with deliberate precision. "This is unacceptable. Our exposure—"

"Is being contained," Kessler interrupted smoothly. "I've mobilized South American assets. Rivera will be dead within forty-eight hours, and his network will be dismantled node by node."

"You mentioned the same thing about the Cole brothers," Voss observed. His tone was mild, but his eyes held a challenge. "And yet here we are, three weeks later, discussing how a banker and his soldier brother have managed to evade the teams you've sent after them."

The room went still. Shadows, shaped like falling knives, stretched across the walls.

Kessler turned to face Voss directly, his movements deliberate, almost theatrical. When he spoke, his voice carried the distinct warmth of a man explaining something to a child.

"Konrad. You've been with us—what—twelve years now? Helios has grown from a regional contractor to a global power under our guidance. Your satellites watch governments for us. Your drones enforce borders that politicians only pretend to control." He smiled. "All of that exists because of the architecture I have built and nurtured. The relationships I cultivated. The problems I solved while you were still selling radar systems to NATO."

Voss's jaw tightened. "I'm not questioning your contributions, Andreas. I'm questioning your current judgment. The Cole situation should have been resolved weeks ago. Instead, it's metastasized. A banker who should be dead is now working with his Delta Force brother. They've connected with Turkish intelligence. And now this hacker—"

"Ah, yes." Kessler's eyes glittered. "Turkish intelligence. That brings us to another matter, doesn't it?" He tapped his tablet, and a photograph appeared on the main display: a woman with dark hair and harder eyes, captured in surveillance footage outside a hotel in Miami. "Do you recognize her, Konrad?"

Voss studied the image, his expression carefully blank. "Should I?"

"Her operational name was Sparrow. One of my most promising assets—recruited as a child, trained in our Vienna facility, deployed across three continents." Kessler's voice dropped, becoming almost intimate. "She defected in 2017 after the Serbia operation. Ran to the CIA, then went independent. And now—" He zoomed in on the image, showing

Selin standing beside Ethan Cole. "—she's helping the very people who threaten the system we have built."

"A defector." The intelligence director waved dismissively. "They happen. What's your point?"

"My point, Director, is that Sparrow—or Selin, as she now calls herself—spent three years as a Helios contractor after she left us." Kessler turned back to Voss, his smile widening. "Your company vetted her. Your people approved her clearances. Your security protocols failed to flag her psychological vulnerabilities."

Voss's face went pale. "The vetting process—"

"Was your responsibility." Kessler's voice remained perfectly pleasant, which somehow made it more terrifying. "I'm not assigning blame, of course. Mistakes happen. But it does raise questions about Helios's current reliability, doesn't it? About your judgment?"

The other board members shifted uncomfortably. The Atlantic Group chair was studying her water glass with sudden intensity. The media CEO had stopped smiling.

Voss leaned forward, his voice hardening. "Now wait just a minute here. You're trying to deflect attention from your own failures by—"

"By stating facts?" Kessler's eyebrows rose in mock surprise. "Konrad, please. We're all professionals here. I'm simply observing that the current situation involves multiple points of failure, and that intellectual honesty requires acknowledging all of them." He spread his hands. "Including my own. The Cole brothers should have been eliminated in Miami. They weren't. I take responsibility for that. The question is—" His gaze locked onto Voss like a targeting laser. "—do you take responsibility for Sparrow?"

The silence stretched. Voss opened his mouth to speak, then closed it. He looked around the table, searching for support, and found none. The other board members had retreated into careful neutrality—the exceptional stillness of predators waiting to see which way the fight would go.

"Andreas," Voss spoke finally, his voice carrying a note of forced calm, "I think we're both under significant pressure right now. Perhaps this isn't the time for—"

"For honesty?" Kessler's smile didn't waver. "On the contrary, Konrad. I think it's exactly the time. You've been questioning my judgment quite publicly for the past several weeks. Board communications. Private calls with members. Suggestions that perhaps the Directorate needs... newer leadership."

Voss went rigid. "Those were private conversations."

"Nothing is private in our world. You know that." Kessler leaned back in his chair, the picture of relaxation. "I don't blame you for being ambitious. Ambition is admirable. But ambition without competence is simply... noise." He glanced around the table. "I think we can all agree that what the Directorate needs right now is less noise and more results."

Heads nodded. The intelligence director. The media CEO. Even the Atlantic Group chair, though her expression remained carefully neutral.

Voss's face had gone from pale to flushed. He understood, finally, what was happening. This wasn't a board meeting—it was a tribunal. And he was the defendant.

"Let me be clear about what I'm proposing," Kessler continued, his voice hardening. "Helios remains a vital part of our operations. Your satellites, your drones, your surveillance networks—all essential. But it's time for a... restructuring of leadership responsibilities. Someone to oversee Helios's integration with our other assets. Ensure that failures like the Sparrow situation don't recur."

"You're talking about removing me from my own company."

"I'm talking about ensuring the Directorate's continued success." Kessler's smile was all teeth now, the warmth stripped away to reveal the predator beneath. "You'll retain your title, of course. Your compensation. Your public profile. You'll simply... report to a board-appointed oversight committee going forward." He paused. "It's quite generous, when you think about it."

Voss stared at him, and in that moment, the full weight of his miscalculation became clear. He'd thought questioning Kessler would position him as a leader. Instead, it had marked him as a threat—and threats were eliminated.

"This is a mistake," Voss muttered quietly. "I've given this organization—"

"What we required of you," Kessler agreed. "And we are all most grateful. But gratitude doesn't change where we are at Konrad. The mathematics simply say you have become a liability for the Directorate." He stood, straightening his jacket with precise movements. "The board will vote on the restructuring proposal tomorrow morning. I trust you'll accept the outcome gracefully."

He walked to the door, then paused, looking back over his shoulder.

"Oh, and Konrad? If you're thinking about reaching out to outside parties—journalists, regulators, anyone who might be interested in our operations—I'd advise against it." His voice dropped to something almost gentle. "We both know how stories like that end. Car accidents. Sudden illnesses. Tragic endings." He smiled one final time. "I would certainly hate to see you become another statistic."

The door closed behind him with a soft click.

Voss sat alone at the long glass table, the other board members already filing out, already distancing themselves from a man who had been marked for disposal. The snow continued to fall outside, silent and indifferent, blanketing the mountains in white while the darkness beneath grew deeper.

Konrad Voss had played his hand, and he had lost.

Now the only question was whether he would survive the consequences.

Athens, Greece — Hotel Nostos — 4:23 a.m.

The encrypted phone buzzed on the nightstand, pulling Ethan from a shallow, restless sleep. Beside him, Selin was already awake—she slept like a soldier now, alert to every sound, all shifts in the air.

He reached for the phone. A message from Noah, routed through seven different relays:

Buenos Aires operation complete. $47M redistributed. They know I'm coming. Heading south with Morales—will check in when we reach Argentine waters. Stay sharp. They'll be looking for all of us now.

Ethan showed the message to Selin, then swung his legs out of bed. Through the thin walls, he could hear Daniel moving in the adjacent room—his brother had been awake for hours, studying maps, planning routes, doing what soldiers did when the mission was unclear but the danger was certain.

"Noah started a fire under Kessler's entire South American operation," Ethan added. "That's going to draw attention away from us, but it's also going to make them desperate. Desperate people make mistakes—and they also stop worrying about collateral damage."

Selin pulled on a shirt, her movements efficient. "Then we need to move. Athens was a good regrouping point, but we've been here too long. If they have any assets in Greece—"

A knock at the door. Three sharp raps, pause, two more. Daniel's signal.

Ethan opened the door. His brother stood in the hallway, a tablet in his hand, his expression grim.

"We have a problem," Daniel noted, stepping inside. "I've been monitoring Directorate communications through a back channel I cultivated when I was working for them. There's chatter about Harris."

"Harris?" Selin's hand moved instinctively toward her weapon.

"Kessler's cleaner. Former CIA, went private years ago. He's the one they send when they want something done quietly and permanently." Daniel turned the tablet to show them a surveillance image: a hard-faced man with gray-flecked hair and the dead eyes of someone who'd stopped seeing people as people a long time ago. "He arrived in Athens twelve hours ago. He's not alone—he's got a four-man team with him, all former military, all Directorate contractors."

"They found us." Ethan's stomach dropped.

"Not yet. But they know we're in Greece, and Harris is methodical. He will work through every contact, each hotel and safe house until he picks up our trail." Daniel set down the tablet. "We need to leave. Tonight."

"And go where?" Ethan posed. "We came here to regroup, to plan. If we start running blind—"

"Not blind." Selin's voice was quiet but firm. "I have contacts. People I worked with before—before Kessler, before all of this. In Istanbul."

Daniel's eyes narrowed. "Turkish intelligence?"

"Some of them. Others are... independent. People who've been tracking the Directorate's operations in the Mediterranean for years. They have resources, safe houses, information networks." She met Ethan's eyes. "I wasn't sure I could trust them—wasn't sure I could trust anyone from that life. But if Harris is here, if they're closing in..."

"Then we need allies," Ethan finished. "People who know the terrain, who can give us cover while we figure out our next move."

"Istanbul is fifteen hours by road, less if we can arrange transport," Daniel replied. "But crossing the border—"

"I can get us across." Selin was already moving, pulling a bag from under the bed. "There's a fishing captain in Alexandroupoli who owes me a favor. He runs refugees across the Aegean when the coast guard isn't looking. For us, he'll make an exception."

"A smuggler," Daniel voiced flatly.

"A survivor. Like all of us." Selin met his gaze without flinching. "I know you don't trust me completely, Daniel. I was Kessler's creature for a long time. But I'm telling you—if we stay here, Harris will find us within forty-eight hours. And when he does, he won't be coming to talk."

The brothers exchanged a look—the silent communication of siblings who'd learned to read each other across years of distance and silence.

"She's right," Ethan responded after a pause. "We can't fight Harris and his team. Not here, not with what we have. But if Selin's contacts can give us breathing room, time to plan, access to resources..."

"Then Istanbul it is." Daniel nodded once, the decision made. "We leave in two hours. Pack light—only what we can carry. If Harris has eyes on the main roads, we'll need to move fast and quiet."

Selin was already on her phone, speaking rapid Turkish to someone on the other end. Ethan caught fragments: coordinates, timing, a name that sounded like Yusuf.

Through the window, Athens was beginning to wake—early morning light spilling across the rooftops of Exarcheia, the district stirring to life with the smell of coffee and bread. They'd been here less than two days, and already they were running again.

But running toward something this time, Ethan reminded himself. Not running away.

"My contact will meet us in Alexandroupoli tomorrow night," Selin remarked, ending her call. "From there, a boat across to the Turkish coast. By the time Harris figures out we've left Athens, we'll be in Istanbul."

"And then?" Daniel submitted.

"And then we meet with people who've been fighting the Directorate longer than any of us. People who know its weaknesses, its pressure points, the places where the machine can be broken." Selin's eyes hardened. "Kessler thinks he's hunting us. It's time to show him we can hunt back."

Ethan reached for her hand, squeezed it once. Something had changed between them on that flight from Miami—a connection forged in shared confession, in grief and hope tangled together. He didn't know what it would become, but he knew it mattered. She mattered.

"Together," he whispered quietly.

"Together," she agreed.

Daniel watched them for a moment, something unreadable in his expression. Then he turned away, already planning, already strategizing, the soldier in him taking over.

"Two hours," he repeated. "Then we move."

Outside, the sun continued to rise over Athens, painting the ancient city in shades of gold and rose. Somewhere to the north, Harris and his team were beginning their search. Somewhere to the south, Noah was heading towards Buenos Aires with forty-seven million dollars in stolen money and a network of survivors ready to strike. And elsewhere, Kessler was consolidating power, eliminating threats, preparing for the endgame he'd been planning for many decades.

The pieces were moving. The board was set.

And the Cole brothers, the defected Sparrow, and a ghost called Robin Cipher were about to show the Directorate what happened when victims stopped running and started fighting back.

43 |

The Hunt

"The prey that thinks it's hunting is the easiest to kill."
— Johnathan Harris

Athens, Greece — Hotel Nostos — 9:17 a.m. local time- Day 12

Morning light filtered through the cracked blinds, casting prison-bar shadows across the floor of their cramped hotel room. Ethan sat at the small desk, studying the network diagram Daniel had constructed—a web of Directorate operations, financial flows, and personnel that spread across the wall like a conspiracy theorist's fever dream. Except this conspiracy was real, and the men at its center wanted them dead.

Selin emerged from the bathroom, her dark hair still damp, moving with the coiled efficiency of someone who'd learned to be ready for violence at any moment. She'd been awake since four, cross-referencing intelligence intercepts with the data Noah had extracted from Buenos Aires.

"We have a problem," she stated firmly.

Daniel looked up from his laptop. "Define problem."

"Harris. His team checked into a hotel in Monastiraki two hours ago. Four men, all traveling on diplomatic passports that don't match any legitimate embassy personnel." She turned her phone to show them the surveillance footage she'd pulled from a contact in Greek intelligence. "They're not even trying to hide. That means they're confident."

Ethan studied the grainy image: Harris in the lobby, speaking to one of his men, his posture radiating the casual competence of a predator who knew his prey was close.

"How did they find us?" Ethan posed.

"Could be anything. Facial recognition. A compromised contact. Or—" Selin hesitated. "—they might have had eyes on us since Miami and we just didn't notice."

Daniel stood, moved to the window, scanning the street below with the practiced eye of someone who'd spent years learning to spot surveillance. "Doesn't matter how. What matters is they're here, and we have maybe six hours before they triangulate our position."

"Less," Selin replied. "Harris is methodical. He will have informants out in the streets, bribes flowing to taxi drivers and hotel clerks. The moment we step outside, someone will be watching."

Ethan perceived the familiar weight of being hunted settle into his chest—the tightening of breath, the hyperawareness of external sounds. But beneath the fear was something else now. Anger. Resolve.

"Then we don't run." He met their eyes. "We use it."

Both Daniel and Selin turned to look at him.

"They expect us to bolt for the border," Ethan continued, his mind working through the angles the way it had once worked through financial models. "Istanbul, Bulgaria, anywhere that puts distance between us and them. That's what prey does. But what if we don't act like prey?"

Daniel's eyes narrowed. "You're talking about an ambush."

"I'm talking about controlling the engagement. Right now, Harris has the initiative. He chooses when and where to strike. We need to take that away from him."

Selin was already pulling up maps on her tablet. "There's an abandoned freight yard outside Thessaloniki. Old rail depot, decommissioned ten years ago. I used it once for a dead drop when I was working the Balkans." She zoomed in on satellite imagery showing rusted warehouses, overgrown tracks, shipping containers arranged in chaotic clusters. "Plenty of cover. Multiple sight lines. If we could draw Harris there—"

"We'd have the advantage," Daniel finished. "Home field, more or less. Set up positions, control the approach routes." He studied the image, his tactical mind already mapping firing lanes and fallback points. "But how do we get him to follow? Harris isn't stupid. He won't walk into an obvious trap."

"No," Ethan agreed. "But he'll follow what he thinks is a panicked retreat. We give him a target he can't resist—one that looks like it's running scared."

"You," Selin answered quietly. "You're talking about using yourself as bait."

"I'm talking about splitting up. Making Harris divide his forces." Ethan moved to the map, traced two routes with his finger. "I head toward Alexandroupoli—toward your contact with the boat. That's the obvious escape route. Harris will have to send men after me. Meanwhile, you two head north to Thessaloniki, make it look like a desperate fallback to a secondary safe house."

"He'll send his best after you," Daniel replied. "Harris himself, probably, with at least two operators."

"Good. That means fewer guns at the freight yard." Ethan met his brother's eyes. "I can lose them in Athens. The city's a maze—I've been studying it since we arrived. All those years of pattern recognition, reading systems, finding the gaps in the structure? This is the same thing, with streets instead of spreadsheets."

"Ethan—" Daniel started.

"I'm not the soldier, D. I know that. But I'm also not helpless." Ethan's voice was steady. "Dad taught us both how to survive. Different lessons, maybe, but the same core skills. Patience. Observation. Knowing when to move and when to stay still." He paused. "You need to be at that freight yard because you're the one who can actually win a firefight. But I need to be somewhere else, drawing attention."

Selin looked between the brothers, seeing something pass between them—an old argument being settled, a hierarchy being renegotiated.

"If we do this," she told them carefully, "we need to coordinate exactly. Timing, routes, communication protocols. One mistake and Harris picks us off separately."

"Then we don't make mistakes." Ethan pulled out a burner phone, one of six they'd purchased two days ago. "We go in forty-five minutes. That gives us time to prep, plant false trails, and get eyes on Harris's team before we move."

Daniel was silent for a long moment. Then he nodded—a single, sharp gesture that carried more weight than any words.

"Forty-five minutes," he agreed. "Let's get to work."**Athens — Monastiraki District — 9:25 a.m. local time**

Harris stood at the window of his hotel room, watching the morning crowds fill Monastiraki Square. Tourists with cameras. Locals hurrying to work. Street vendors setting up their stalls. Somewhere in this city of four million people, three targets were hiding.

Not for long.

His phone buzzed. Kovacs, his second-in-command, calling from the surveillance van parked three blocks away.

"Got a hit," Kovacs voiced. "Facial recognition flagged the woman—at a pharmacy in Exarcheia twenty minutes ago. She bought bandages, antiseptic, and a prepaid phone."

"Medical supplies," Harris murmured. "Someone's hurt, or they're preparing for something." He turned from the window. "What about the brothers?"

"Nothing solid. But we've got three hotel registrations that match their profile. All in the same neighborhood."

"Exarcheia." Harris smiled thinly. A neighborhood that didn't trust police, didn't cooperate with authorities, and provided natural cover for people who wanted to disappear. Smart choice. But not smart enough.

"Pull the team together," Harris ordered. "We move in thirty minutes. I want two-man teams on each hotel, overlapping fields of surveillance. When they run—and they will run—we'll be ready."

He ended the call and checked his weapon: a suppressed Glock 19, standard Directorate issue. He'd killed seventeen people with guns like this one. Eighteen, if you counted Donovan—though that had been almost too easy. The old man had practically welcomed the bullet, as if death were a relief from the weight he'd been carrying.

The Cole brothers would be different. The banker had proven surprisingly resilient, and the soldier was Delta—trained to survive situations that would kill ordinary men. Add the Turkish woman, with her MIT training and her intimate knowledge of Kessler's methods, and you had a genuinely dangerous combination.

Good, Harris thought. I haven't had a challenge in months.

He holstered the Glock and headed for the door. The hunt was about to begin.**Athens — Exarcheia District — 10:10 a.m.**

They moved.

Ethan went first, slipping out through a service entrance that opened onto a narrow alley choked with graffiti and overflowing dumpsters. He wore a baseball cap pulled low, a tourist's daypack on his shoulder, his posture carefully adjusted to project harmlessness.

The burner phone in his pocket vibrated once. Daniel's signal: Harris's team was in position, two blocks north, waiting.

Ethan turned south.

The plan was simple in concept, brutal in execution. He would let himself be seen—a calculated exposure, barely long enough for Harris's spotters to confirm his identity. Then he would run, heading east through Athens's labyrinthine streets toward the highway that led to Alexandroupoli.

If the plan went right, Harris would split his team: half pursuing Ethan, half tracking Selin and Daniel as they moved north toward Thessaloniki.

If the plan went wrong, Ethan would be dead before noon.

He walked three blocks, stopped at a newsstand, bought a bottle of water. Normal behavior. Unremarkable. But as he turned away, he let the cap shift slightly—exposing his face to the security camera mounted on the corner pharmacy.

"Come and get me", Ethan mouthed as he stared at the camera.

He counted to thirty, then started walking faster. By the time he reached Syntagma Square, he was almost jogging.

The phone buzzed again. Selin's voice, tight with tension: "They took the bait. Two vehicles moving your direction. Harris is in the lead car."

"Good. You and Daniel?"

"Moving north now. Two more vehicles tracking us, but keeping distance." A pause. "Be careful, Ethan. Harris doesn't make mistakes."

"Neither do I." He ended the call and broke into a full run.**Athens — Plaka District — 10:25 a.m.**

The chase exploded through the ancient streets of Plaka.

Ethan sprinted past whitewashed buildings and bougainvillea-draped balconies, his lungs burning, his mind racing three steps ahead of his feet. Behind him, he could hear the screech of tires, the shouts of Harris's men as they abandoned their vehicles to pursue on foot.

He had studied this neighborhood for exactly this moment. Each alley and shortcut, the doorways that led to a courtyard that led to another street. The city was a puzzle, and puzzles were what he did.

Sharp left through an archway. Up a flight of stone steps, worn smooth by centuries of feet. Through a taverna's kitchen—startled cooks shouting in Greek—and out the back into a narrow passage that smelled of olive oil and cat urine.

He could hear them behind him. Closer now. Two sets of footsteps, moving with military precision.

Ethan controlled his breathing the way his father had taught him during hunting trips. Four counts in, hold four, four counts out. Heart rate drops. Movement stills. You become part of the shadow.

He pressed himself into a doorway, forcing his body to go still. The footsteps grew louder, then passed—two men in tactical clothing, weapons barely concealed, scanning the alley with professional intensity.

"Where the fuck did he go?" one of them muttered.

"Split up. You take the stairs, I'll check the courtyard."

They separated. Ethan waited until the closer man's footsteps faded, then moved—silent, quick, down a passage the men had already cleared.

He emerged onto a busy street, merged with a group of tourists following a guide with a red umbrella. Another anonymous face in the crowd.

His phone buzzed. Daniel: "They lost you?"

"For now. I'm heading for the secondary vehicle."

"Harris has redirected. He's coming back your way with the full pursuit team."

Ethan's stomach tightened. The plan had been for Harris to keep chasing him east, toward Alexandroupoli. If he was doubling back—

"He suspects something," Ethan vocalized. "He's trying to regroup before we can get clear."

"Can you lose him again?"

Ethan looked around, mapping escape routes, calculating odds. "Maybe. But not forever."

"You don't need forever. Just long enough for us to reach the freight yard." Daniel's voice was steady, controlled—the voice of a man who'd directed operations under fire. "Get to Alexandroupoli if you can. If not, go dark. We'll find each other after."

"Daniel—"

"You did good, E. You gave us the opening we needed." A pause. "Dad would be proud."

The line went dead.**Athens — Omonia Square — 12:17 p.m.**

Harris stood in the center of Omonia Square, his jaw tight with frustration. His men had lost the banker twice now—twice—in a city they'd been surveilling for days.

He'd underestimated Ethan Cole. That was the simple truth. The file mentioned banker, analyst, non-combatant. But the man moving through Athens's streets wasn't acting like a civilian. He was acting like someone who'd been trained to evade, to disappear, to turn the environment into a weapon.

"Sir." Kovacs approached, slightly out of breath. "We've got movement on the northern targets. The soldier and the woman are heading toward Highway 1—looks like they're making for Thessaloniki."

"Together?"

"Together. Moving fast, but not panicked."

Harris processed this. The Cole brothers had split up—that much was clear. The banker had drawn pursuit while the soldier and the Turkish woman fled north. Standard escape-and-evade tactics.

But something was wrong. The whole morning was off. The way they had been spotted at exactly the right moment. The way the banker had led them on a chase through neighborhoods perfectly suited for evasion. The way the northern group was moving toward Thessaloniki—not Istanbul, not Bulgaria, but a secondary Greek city with no obvious strategic value.

Unless it wasn't an escape. Unless it was a trap.

"Split the team," Harris ordered. "Kovacs, take Jensen and Petrova. Continue pursuit of the banker. I want him found and eliminated. The rest of you, with me. We're going after the soldier."

"Sir, if they're setting up an ambush—"

"Then we walk into it with our eyes open." Harris checked his weapon again. "These people have been running for weeks. They're tired, scared, desperate. That's when amateurs make mistakes—they think they can turn the tables, become the hunters instead of the hunted." He smiled coldly. "They forget who they're dealing with."

He climbed into the SUV, already mapping routes to Thessaloniki in his head.

If the Cole brothers wanted a confrontation, Harris would give them one.

And he'd make sure it was the last confrontation they ever had.**Athens — Kifissos Highway — 2:32 p.m.**

Ethan sat in the back of a taxi, watching Athens recede in the rearview mirror. He'd finally lost Kovacs and the others in the chaos of Omonia—slipping into a metro station, riding two stops, emerging into a different neighborhood entirely.

Now he was heading east on the Kifissos Highway, toward Alexandroupoli, toward the border, toward whatever came next.

The phone buzzed. Selin: "We're clear of Athens. Heading north on Highway 1. Harris took the bait—he's following us with three men."

"That leaves two on me," Ethan observed. "I think I lost them at Omonia, but I can't be sure."

"Get to Alexandroupoli. My contact will meet you at the harbor—Captain Yusuf, fishing boat called the Marmara Star. He'll get you across to Turkey."

"And you?"

A pause. When Selin spoke again, her voice was different—softer, more vulnerable. "We'll handle Harris. Daniel and I, together. The freight yard gives us advantages he won't expect."

"Selin—"

"Don't." Her voice hardened again. "You gave us this chance, Ethan. You drew them off, bought us time. Now let us do our part."

"I should be there."

"You should be alive. That's what matters. That's what—" She stopped herself. "Get to Turkey. We'll find you when this is over."

"When this is over," Ethan repeated. The words were hollow, like a promise neither of them believed.

"I'll call when we're in position," Selin replied. "Stay safe, Ethan."

The line went dead.

Ethan stared out the window at the Greek countryside rolling past—olive groves and white houses, a landscape that had seen three thousand years of invasions and occupations and had somehow survived them all.

Somewhere behind him, two of Harris's men were still searching. Somewhere ahead, a fishing boat waited to carry him to Türkiye.

And somewhere to the north, his brother and the woman he was beginning to love were driving toward a confrontation with a killer who'd never lost.

He checked the burner phone. No new messages. The silence was like a countdown to oblivion.**Highway 1 — North of Larissa — 4:47 p.m.**

The freight yard emerged from the afternoon haze like a graveyard of industry—rusted warehouses, abandoned rail cars, shipping containers arranged in chaotic clusters that created a maze of metal and shadow.

Selin pulled the rental car off the highway and onto a dirt road that wound through overgrown fields toward the facility's eastern perimeter. Daniel sat beside her, his weapon already in hand, his eyes scanning for threats.

"Harris is twenty minutes behind us," she stated. "Maybe less."

"Good. That gives us time to set up." Daniel studied the freight yard's layout through the windshield. "You know this place?"

"I used it once, years ago. Dead drop for a Bulgarian asset." She pointed toward a cluster of shipping containers near the yard's center. "There—those containers create a natural chokepoint. Only two approaches, both with limited cover. If we position ourselves on the elevated platforms to the east and west—"

"Crossfire," Daniel finished. "Anyone coming through the chokepoint gets caught between us."

"Harris will figure it out eventually. But by then—"

"By then, it'll be too late." Daniel opened his door. "Let's move. We need to be in position before they arrive."

They moved through the freight yard like shadows—two people trained differently but united by common purpose. Selin took the eastern platform, a rusted maintenance walkway that overlooked the chokepoint from fifteen feet up. Daniel circled west, finding cover behind a derailed tank car that provided both concealment and protection.

Selin settled into position, checked her weapon, and waited.

The afternoon sun beat down, turning the metal containers into ovens. Sweat trickled down her back. Her hands were steady.

She thought of Ethan—somewhere to the east now, moving toward the border. She thought of the night on the plane, the confessions they had shared, the kiss that had tasted of tears and possibility. She thought of all the things she hadn't given voice to, all the futures she hadn't dared imagine.

If she survived this, she would tell him. Everything.

If she didn't—

Her phone buzzed. Daniel: "Vehicle approaching. Two minutes."

Selin exhaled slowly, letting the training take over. The person she'd been—Leyla, Subject 47, Sparrow—faded into background noise. What remained was pure focus. Pure purpose.

She raised her weapon and sighted on the chokepoint.

The hunt was about to end.

But who was truly the hunter, and who the prey?

In less than an hour, they would find out.

Chapter 44—Retribution

"Harris, you should have run the moment you saw me"
—Selin

Outskirts of Thessaloniki Greece— 5:24 p.m. local time- Day 12

Rust, diesel, and the ghosts of dead industry hung in the air. The freight yard stretched before them like a graveyard of capitalism—shipping containers stacked in chaotic towers, rail cars frozen mid-journey on tracks that led nowhere, warehouses with shattered windows staring blind at the afternoon sky.

Selin pressed herself against the corrugated steel of her elevated position, weapon steady, eyes tracking the dirt road that wound through the facility's eastern approach. Fifteen feet below, the chokepoint waited—a narrow corridor between two rows of containers that any vehicle would have to pass through to reach the yard's interior.

Across the yard, she could see Daniel's position behind the derailed tank car. He was invisible from her angle, but she knew he was there, knew his weapon was trained on the same kill zone, knew that whatever happened in the next few minutes would determine whether they lived or died.

Her earpiece crackled. Daniel's voice, barely above a whisper: "Vehicle. One hundred meters."

She saw it now—a black SUV moving slowly through the overgrown access road, its tinted windows revealing nothing. It stopped outside the chokepoint, engine idling.

For a long moment, nothing happened.

Then the doors opened.

Harris emerged from the driver's side, his movements deliberate, controlled. He wore tactical black, no visible weapon, but Selin knew he'd be armed. Men like Harris were always armed.

Two more men climbed out behind him. Both carried suppressed submachine guns—MP7s, she noted automatically. Professional hardware for professional killers. They moved with military precision, scanning the freight yard with the practiced efficiency of soldiers who'd cleared a hundred hostile environments.

"They know," Daniel's voice came through her earpiece. "Look at their formation. They're expecting an ambush."

"Doesn't matter," Selin replied. "They still have to come through the chokepoint."

Harris raised his hand, signaling his men. One moved left, the other right—flanking maneuver, standard doctrine. They were going to try to circle around, find the high ground, neutralize any threats before Harris exposed himself.

"I've got the one on the right," Selin announced. "You take left."

"Copy. On your mark."

She tracked her target through the iron sights—a big man, ex-military by his bearing, moving with the careful steps of someone who knew how to clear urban terrain. He was heading toward a stack of containers that would give him a line of sight to Daniel's position.

He never got there.

"Mark."

Selin squeezed the trigger.

The freight yard erupted into violence.

Her first shot caught the flanking operative in the shoulder, spinning him sideways. Her second punched through his chest before he could raise his weapon. He went down hard, his MP7 clattering against the concrete.

Across the yard, she heard Daniel's weapon bark twice—controlled shots, the signature of a trained sharpshooter. A cry of pain, then silence.

But Harris was already moving.

The moment the shooting started, he'd dropped into a combat roll, using the SUV as cover. Now he was sprinting toward the containers—not retreating, Selin realized with a chill, but advancing. Heading straight for Daniel's position.

"Daniel, he's coming to you—"

Her warning was cut short by the crack of return fire. The operative she'd shot wasn't dead—he'd dragged himself behind a rusted crane housing and was firing blindly in her direction. Bullets sparked off the metal walkway, forcing her to duck.

She rolled to a new position, sighted on the crane housing, waited. A head appeared—for a split second, just long enough to aim. She fired once. The head disappeared in a spray of red.

But the exchange had cost her precious seconds. By the time she looked back toward the chokepoint, Harris had vanished into the maze of containers.

And Daniel was out there, alone.

The Container Maze at the Freight Yard — Simultaneous

Daniel heard the shots from Selin's position, heard her warning cut off by gunfire, and decided. He couldn't stay pinned behind the tank car waiting for Harris to flank him. He needed to move, to take the fight to the enemy before the enemy brought it to him.

He pushed off from cover and entered the container maze.

The corridors between the stacked boxes were narrow, shadowed, full of blind corners and ambush points. Each step was a calculated risk. The numerous shadows could hide a bullet with his name on it.

He moved the way he had been trained—weapon up, weight balanced, breathing controlled. Clear left. Clear right. Move. Repeat.

The operator Selin had told him to take had gone down fast—two shots to center mass, clean kills that showed Daniel hadn't lost his edge despite years away from active duty. But the engagement had depleted his position, forced him to relocate. Now he was in Harris's territory, playing Harris's game.

A sound. Metal on metal, barely audible. Coming from his left.

Daniel spun toward it—

Harris came out of the shadows like a wraith, inside Daniel's guard before he could bring his weapon to bear. A brutal strike to his wrist sent the pistol flying. A knee to his thigh dead-legged him, dropping him to one knee.

But Daniel had been fighting well before Harris was recruited by the Directorate. He rolled with the momentum, came up with an elbow strike that caught Harris across the jaw, followed by a palm heel to the chest that drove Harris back.

They faced each other in the narrow corridor, both breathing hard, both measuring the distance.

"Daniel Cole," Harris observed, rolling his shoulders. "I've been looking forward to this."

"You and your bastards killed my father." Daniel's voice was flat, but something burned beneath it—something that had been building since that photograph arrived, since he'd seen his dad bound to a chair, bleeding, broken. "You tortured him."

"We did more than that." Harris smiled—a thin, cruel expression that held no warmth. "Kessler wanted it clean, but we took our time with it. Your old man was tough, I'll give him that. Didn't beg. Didn't cry." The smile widened. "Kept asking about you and your brother. Kept saying you would come for him. Right up until the end."

Something snapped inside Daniel.

He launched himself at Harris with a roar—not the controlled violence of his training, but something older, pure raw and fury. The kind of fury that was spawned from a son who had lost his father to a monster.

Harris met him head-on. They crashed into the container wall, grappling, striking, each trying to gain the advantage. Daniel drove an elbow into Harris's ribs, something cracked loudly. Harris responded with a headbutt that split Daniel's eyebrow open, blood streaming into his eye.

They separated, circled. Daniel wiped the blood from his face, smearing it across his cheek.

"Your father was weak," Harris claimed. "Sentimental. He genuinely believed friendship, loyalty, honor. That's why he died. That's why you're all going to die."

"My father was ten times the man you'll ever be."

"Your father was a fool who trusted the wrong people." Harris reached into his jacket and drew a combat knife—seven inches of blackened steel, honed to a razor edge. "Just like his sons."

He attacked.

The knife came fast—faster than Daniel expected. Harris has been more than trained; he was expert-level, the blade an extension of his arm, each strike designed to kill or cripple.

Daniel dodged the first slash whispering just past his throat. He blocked the second with his forearm, taking a shallow cut that burned like fire. Trying to create distance with Harris relentlessly pressing forward, like an animal...a predator.

A feint, then a thrust. Daniel twisted, but not fast enough. The blade caught him across the ribs, opening a gash that immediately soaked his shirt with blood.

He staggered back, one hand pressed to the wound, the other raised in a defensive guard. His vision was blurring at the edges—blood loss, exhaustion, the accumulated damage of the fight catching up to him.

Harris circled, patient now, savoring the moment. "You know what your father told Lukas at the end? He said he was proud of you. Both of you and your brother." He laughed. "Lukas told him we would make sure to pass that along before I killed you."

Daniel's legs were shaking. The wound in his side was pumping blood with each heartbeat. He had thirty seconds of fight left in him—maybe less.

But thirty seconds was enough.

He dropped his guard, let his shoulders slump, let the weakness show. Bait.

Harris took it.

He lunged forward, knife driving toward Daniel's heart—and Daniel moved. Not back, but forward, inside the arc of the blade. He caught Harris's wrist with both hands, twisted with every ounce of strength he had left, the joint giving way with the sound of a wet crack.

Harris screamed. The knife fell.

Daniel didn't let go. He drove his knee into Harris's stomach, doubling him over, then brought his elbow down on the back of his neck. Harris hit the ground face-first, stunned but not finished.

He rolled, tried to rise, but Daniel was already on him—straddling his chest, hands around his throat, squeezing with a fury that went beyond training, beyond tactics, beyond anything except the primal need to destroy the man who'd murdered his father.

"This is for my father," Daniel snarled through bloody teeth.

Harris clawed at his hands, his face turning purple, his eyes bulging. But Daniel was past feeling, past mercy, past anything except the red rage that had been building since he'd first seen that photograph.

Then a voice, cutting through the haze: "Daniel. Stop."

Selin.

She stood at the entrance to the corridor, weapon lowered, watching him with eyes that held no judgment—only understanding.

"He needs to die," Daniel asserted, his voice ragged.

"He will. But not like this." She moved closer, crouched beside him. "Not with your hands. Not with his face the last thing you see when you close your eyes."

Daniel's grip loosened—ever so slightly, barely enough for Harris to gasp a single breath.

"He killed my father," Daniel voiced strongly. "He told me—he told me Dad asked about me and Ethan. Right until the end."

"I know." Selin's hand found his shoulder. "I know what he took from you. I know what men like him take from all of us." She met his eyes. "But this isn't justice. This is your pain revealing itself. And pain doesn't solve anything—it keeps going until there's nothing left."

For a long moment, Daniel didn't move. His hands stayed locked around Harris's throat, his body trembling with the effort of holding back, of choosing.

Then, slowly, he released his grip and stood.

Harris rolled onto his side, coughing, gasping, one hand clutching his broken wrist.

"Finish it," Daniel muttered to Selin. His voice was hollow now, emptied of everything except exhaustion.

Selin nodded once. She raised her weapon, sighted on Harris's head.

Harris looked up at her, blood and spittle streaming from his lips. "You think this changes anything? Kessler has a hundred men like me. You kill me, he sends more. You can't win. You can never—"

The shot echoed through the freight yard, silencing him mid-sentence.

Harris slumped forward, the light fading from his eyes, his last words lost to the wind and the rust and the endless silence of the abandoned place.

Selin lowered her weapon.

It was finished.

Freight Yard — 6:17 p.m.

They sat in the shadow of a shipping container, the afternoon light turning golden as it slanted through the gaps in the rusted metal. Daniel had his shirt pulled up, Selin's hands pressing a field dressing against the wound in his side.

"It's not deep," she revealed. "But you need stitches. Real ones, not the field variety."

"I've had worse."

"I know." She finished taping the dressing, let his shirt fall. "But you're not twenty-five anymore. Bodies remember damage."

Daniel almost smiled. Almost. "You sound like my father."

"Your father sounds like he was a wise man."

"He was." Daniel stared at the container wall, seeing something far away. "He taught us both—me and Ethan. Different lessons, same wisdom. How to read the land. How to wait for the right moment. How to know when to fight and when to walk away." He paused. "I forgot that last one for a while."

"You remembered when it mattered."

"Because you were there." He turned to look at her. "Thank you. For stopping me. For—" He struggled with the words. "For not letting me become him."

Selin reached out, touched his face—a brief contact, warm and grounding. "We've all been close to that edge. The difference between us and them is that we step back."

They sat in silence for a moment, letting the weight of what had happened settle.

"What now?" Selin asked finally.

Daniel stood, wincing as the movement pulled at his wound. "I'm going north. There's a contact in Bucharest—someone who used to run logistics for Kessler's Balkan operations. If anyone knows where the old man is hiding, it's her."

"You're going after Kessler directly."

"Someone has to. Harris was a symptom. Kessler is the disease." He met her eyes. "You should go back. Find Ethan. Get him to Istanbul, to your contacts. Build the network, gather the evidence. When the time comes to expose the Directorate, you'll need to be ready."

"And you?"

"I'll find Kessler. Track him, map his security, identify his vulnerabilities." Daniel's expression hardened. "When you're ready to move, I'll be in position. And this time, there won't be any escape."

Selin stood, faced him. "Ethan won't like you going alone."

"Ethan doesn't have to like it. He only has to trust me." Daniel managed a thin smile. "Tell him I'll be careful. Tell him—" He stopped, started again. "Tell him Dad would be proud of him. What he did today, drawing Harris off, giving us the opening we needed. That took courage. The kind Dad always suggested was rarer than skill."

"I'll tell him."

They looked at each other for a long moment—two people who had survived something that should have killed them, bound by blood and fire and the shared weight of what they'd done.

"Be careful," Selin voiced with a blend of strength and warmth.

"You too."

Daniel turned and walked into the lengthening shadows, moving north through the freight yard toward the highway that would take him to Sofia, to his contact, to whatever came next in the long hunt for Kessler.

Selin watched him go until he disappeared behind a row of containers. Then she pulled out her phone, dialed the number Ethan had given her.

He answered on the second ring. "Selin? What happened? Is Daniel—"

"He's alive. We both are." She paused, choosing her words carefully. "Harris is dead. His team is dead. It's over."

She heard Ethan exhale—a sound of pure relief. "Thank God. I've been going crazy out here, waiting—"

"I know. I'm coming to you. Alexandroupoli, right? Captain Yusuf's boat?"

"I'm already on board. We've been waiting for word before we sail."

"Then wait a little longer. I'll be there by morning." She looked toward the north, where Daniel had vanished. "We have a lot to talk about. And after that—Istanbul. My contacts. Everything we need to take this fight to Kessler."

"And Daniel?"

Selin hesitated. "He's going his own way. Chasing leads that might take him to Kessler directly. He remarked—" She remembered Daniel's words, the weight behind them. "He said to tell you your father would be proud. Of what you did today."

Silence on the line. When Ethan spoke again, his voice was thick. "He's going after Kessler alone."

"He's doing what he has to do. What he was trained for." She started walking toward the rental car, still hidden behind the eastern perimeter. "We all have our roles to play, Ethan. Daniel's is the hunter. Yours is the architect. And mine—"

"Yours is what?"

She thought about it—about the girl who'd killed a rabbit at twelve, the woman who had put a bullet through a man's skull without hesitation, the person she was becoming in the spaces between violence and hope.

"The bridge," she offered finally. "Between what we were and what we have to become."

She ended the call and climbed into the car. The engine turned over, the wheels crunched on gravel, and she drove south toward Alexandroupoli, toward Ethan, toward the next chapter of a war that was only beginning.

Behind her, the freight yard faded into the distance—three bodies cooling in the afternoon sun, a debt finally paid, and the first real victory in a conflict that would shake the world.

Harris was dead.

But Kessler was still out there.

And the hunt was far from over.

PART THREE-BLOOD VENGEANCE

45

City of Two Worlds

"

*Selin, I don't know how long we have, or what's waiting outside that
door...but being here with you feels like the first true thing in my life.*"
—Ethan Cole

Istanbul, Türkiye — 6:17 a.m. local time- Day 13

Like a ghost returning home, The Marmara Star slipped through the
pre-dawn waters of the Bosphorus. Ethan stood at the bow, watching
Istanbul emerge from the morning mist—a city that had straddled empires for three thousand years, where East met West in a collision of
minarets and modern towers, Byzantine ghosts and Ottoman grandeur.

The skyline unfolded before him like a fever dream of history. The
Hagia Sophia rose against the lightening sky, its massive dome glowing
amber in the first rays of sunrise. Beside it, the Blue Mosque's six
minarets pierced the clouds like stone fingers reaching toward heaven.
Ferries cut white wakes across the dark water, their lights still burning,
while fishing boats hauled in nets heavy with the night's catch.

The air carried a thousand scents—salt and diesel, roasting chestnuts
and strong coffee, the unique metallic tang of a city that had survived
conquest after conquest and emerged, somehow, more itself than ever.
Seagulls wheeled overhead, their cries mixing with the distant call to
prayer that echoed across the water from a hundred mosques.

Selin appeared beside him, her shoulder brushing his. She looked different here—more relaxed. This was her city, her world. The tension

she'd carried since Athens had eased into something that looked as close to peace as anything.

"Beautiful, isn't it?" she proposed quietly.

"I've never seen anything like it."

"Most people haven't." She pointed toward the European shore, where ancient walls gave way to modern apartment blocks. "That's Sultanahmet—the old city. Constantine's capital, the heart of the Byzantine Empire. And there—" She gestured to the Asian side, where hills rose green and residential. "Kadıköy. Where I grew up, before I was recruited."

Captain Yusuf emerged from the wheelhouse, a weathered man with kind eyes and hands that told stories of decades at sea. He'd asked no questions when Selin had contacted him, had simply prepared his boat and waited. Some debts, Ethan was learning, transcended explanation.

"We dock in twenty minutes," Yusuf announced in accented English. "My cousin will meet you with a car. After that—" He shrugged. "I see nothing, I know nothing, I remember nothing."

"Thank you, Captain," Selin expressed. "For everything you have done for me."

Yusuf waved dismissively. "Your father saved my son from drowning when we were young. Some debts take a lifetime to repay." He disappeared back into the wheelhouse, leaving them alone with the approaching city.

Ethan looked at Selin. "Your father?"

"A story for another time." She took his hand, squeezed it gently. "Right now, we need to focus on staying alive."

Beyoğlu District — 9:15 a.m.

The safe house occupied the top floor of a crumbling Ottoman-era building in Beyoğlu, the old European quarter that had once been the center of Constantinople's foreign commerce. The narrow streets below started to teem with life—vendors selling simit from wooden carts, students hurrying to university, old men playing backgammon in tea houses that hadn't changed in a century.

Selin had made three phone calls during the drive from the docks. Ethan hadn't understood the rapid Turkish, but he'd recognized the tone—professional, precise, the language of intelligence operatives arranging assets.

"My old network," she explained as they climbed the worn marble stairs. "MIT contacts who stayed loyal. They don't know about my connection to the Directorate—only that I need a place to disappear, and that I'm calling in favors I earned a long time ago."

"Can we trust them?"

"We can trust that they hate Kessler more than they distrust me." She unlocked the apartment door, revealing a space that was surprisingly modern behind its ancient facade. Clean lines, minimal furniture, blackout curtains, and enough electronic equipment to run a small intelligence operation. "The Directorate has been running operations in Turkey for twenty years. Assassinations, economic manipulation, political interference. MIT has been trying to root them out and failing. If we can give them actionable intelligence—"

"They become allies."

"They become weapons." Selin moved through the apartment, checking windows, testing locks, the habits of her training reasserting themselves. "This is about survival, Ethan. We use any resource available, or we die."

Ethan set down his bag, watched her move through the space. The morning light caught her profile—the sharp lines of her face, the dark hair that had come loose from its ponytail during the boat ride, the way her body carried both grace and lethality in equal measure.

"Selin."

She turned.

"When was the last time you slept?"

She started to answer, stopped. The question had caught her off guard—not the operational concern of a partner, but the simple care of someone who saw her as more than an asset.

"I don't remember," she admitted.

"Then we rest. Both of us." He moved toward her, took her hands in his. "The intelligence can wait a few hours. The world won't end because we stopped running long enough to breathe."

"Ethan—"

"I know. I know there's a clock, and people hunting us, and a thousand reasons to keep moving." He lifted her hands, kissed her knuckles gently. "But I also know that I've been running for weeks, and fighting, and watching people I care about get hurt. And right now, in this moment, the only thing I want is to be still. With you."

Something shifted in her expression—the armor cracking, the operative giving way to the woman beneath.

"I don't know how to do this," she whispered. "I was trained to use intimacy as a weapon. All the relationships I've ever had were either for cover or leverage. I'm not—" Her voice caught. "I'm not sure how to be real with someone."

"Then we learn together." Ethan pulled her close, her resistance dissolving as she leaned into him. "I'm not asking for forever, Selin. I'm only asking for now. For this moment. For whatever we can build in the spaces between the chaos."

She looked up at him, her eyes wet. "You should hate me. For what I was. What I did."

"I told you before—I don't hate you. I see you. The real you, underneath all the layers Kessler built." He touched her face, traced the line of her jaw. "And what I see is someone worth fighting for."

She kissed him then—not the desperate kiss on the plane, born of confession and grief, but something deeper. Slower. A kiss that tasted of possibility rather than pain.

They moved to the bedroom without speaking, drawn together by something that had been building since Miami, since Athens, since the moment they'd recognized in each other the singular kind of damage that only Kessler could inflict.

Outside, Istanbul hummed with its eternal rhythm—ferries crossing the Bosphorus, muezzins calling the faithful, vendors shouting their wares. The city that had survived a thousand empires cradled them in its ancient embrace, indifferent to their small dramas but somehow protective nonetheless.

And for a few hours, in a safe house above the chaos, Ethan and Selin stopped being operatives, fugitives, and survivors.

They were two desperate and lonely people, finding each other in the darkness that wanted to consume them. **Beyoğlu District Safe House — 2:17 p.m.**

Afternoon light slanted through the curtains when Ethan woke. Selin lay beside him, still sleeping, her face peaceful in a way he'd never seen before. The hard lines had softened, the constant vigilance temporarily suspended.

He watched her for a moment, this woman who'd been stolen as a child and forged into a weapon, who'd killed for a monster and then turned against him, who carried the weight of forty-three lives on her conscience and still found the strength to fight.

She was, he realized, the strongest person he'd ever known.

His phone buzzed on the nightstand—the encrypted burner, vibrating with an incoming message. He reached for it carefully, trying not to wake her.

Noah's identifier. He opened the message:

Made it to Buenos Aires. Isabella got us here safe—her father's cousin is one hell of a pilot. Setting up operations now. The network here is solid—people who've been tracking Directorate money flows for years. We're close to something big.

Ethan typed back:

Istanbul. Safe house arranged through Selin's contacts. Harris is dead—Daniel and Selin took him out. Daniel's chasing leads on Kessler directly.

A pause. Then:

Harris is dead? Holy shit. That changes things. Kessler has lost his best cleaner.

He'll send more. He always does.

Then we need to move faster. AURORA is 82% distributed now. The Buenos Aires operation gave us access to transaction records we didn't have before. I'm seeing patterns—money moving into political campaigns, media companies, defense contractors. This isn't only corruption, E. It's a blueprint for controlling democracies from the inside.

Can you document it? Build a case that journalists can use?

Already working on it. Isabella's been incredible—she knows the medical and humanitarian networks, which ones are legitimate and which are Directorate fronts. We're building a map of the entire system.

Isabella?

Captain Morales's daughter. Long story. She's... she's good, E. Really good. Reminds me what we're fighting for.

Ethan smiled, glancing at Selin's sleeping form.

I know what you mean.

Stay safe. We'll be in touch when we have something concrete.

He set down the phone, let out a slow breath. Noah in Buenos Aires with Isabella and the network. Daniel —God knows where hunting Kessler. Selin beside him, her contacts reaching into Turkish intelligence. For the first time since this nightmare began, they had pieces on the board that Kessler didn't control.

Selin stirred, her eyes opening slowly. She saw him watching her and smiled—a real smile, unguarded.

"How long was I asleep?"

"Several hours. You needed it."

She stretched, sat up, the sheet falling away from her shoulders. "Any news?"

"Noah made it to Buenos Aires. He's with Captain Morales's daughter—apparently she helped get them there. They're building something, connecting with local networks who've been tracking Directorate money for years."

"Good." Selin reached for her phone, checked her own messages. "My contacts have intelligence on Directorate operations in the Mediterranean. Shell companies, front organizations, a list of Turkish officials who've been compromised." She looked at him. "If we can verify it, cross-reference it with Noah's financial data—"

"We'd have enough to go public."

"We'd have enough to burn Kessler's entire network to the ground." Her eyes hardened. "But it has to be coordinated. We release all the information and data at once, through multiple channels, impossible to suppress. Otherwise he'll figure out how to contain it, discredit the sources, disappear into another layer of shell companies."

"Then we coordinate." Ethan reached for her hand tenderly. "You, me, Noah, Daniel. Each person we have connected with since this started. We build the case, we prepare the release, and when the time is right—we show the world who Kessler truly is."

She leaned forward, kissed him softly. "But first—" A mischievous smile crossed her face. "—I'm going to make us coffee. And then we're going to work."

"In that order?"

"In that order. Some things are sacred, Ethan. Even in wartime."

She slipped out of bed, and Ethan watched her go—this woman who had been Subject 47 and then Sparrow. Who had been a weapon in a monster's hand—now moving through a sunlit kitchen, making coffee, laughing at something on her phone.

The war wasn't over. Kessler was still out there, still dangerous, still hunting them.

But for the first time, Ethan believed they might actually have a chance at winning.

46

Deliverance

"This city ends their reach. AURORA begins mine." —Noah Rivera

Buenos Aires, Argentina — 9:10 p.m. local time- Day 13

Spread beneath them like a galaxy fallen to earth, the lights of Buenos Aires—millions of points of light sat arranged along the Rio de la Plata. The grand avenues radiating from the center of the lights looked like spokes of a wheel built by conquistadors and refined by generations of immigrants who'd made this city their own.

Noah pressed his face to the window of the small Cessna as it banked toward the private airfield on the city's outskirts. Beside him, Isabella was already packing up the laptops they'd been working on during the flight—six hours from Cartagena, with a fuel stop in Lima, courtesy of her father's cousin Miguel.

Miguel Morales was the opposite of his cousin Javier—gregarious where Javier was taciturn, reckless where Javier was careful. But he flew like he'd been born in the cockpit, and he'd asked exactly zero questions about why two passengers needed to reach Buenos Aires without touching any commercial airport.

"We're ten minutes out," Miguel called back from the pilot's seat. "My contact will meet you on the tarmac. After that, you're on your own."

"Thank you, Miguel," Isabella replied. "Tell my father we arrived safely."

"Tell him yourself when this is over." Miguel's voice carried a warning. "Whatever you're doing here, it's dangerous. Buenos Aires has eyes all over—cartels, intelligence agencies, Directorate assets. Don't stay in one place too long."

"We won't," Noah replied. He'd already mapped out a rotation of safe houses across the city—contacts from his network, people who'd lost family members to Directorate operations, who had their own reasons for wanting to see Kessler fall.

The plane touched down smoothly, rolling to a stop beside a hangar that looked abandoned but definitely wasn't. A car waited in the shadows—a battered Fiat that wouldn't draw attention in any neighborhood.

Noah and Isabella grabbed their bags, ducked through the prop wash, and climbed into the vehicle. The driver—a young woman with fierce eyes and a university sweatshirt—pulled away without introduction. Some questions didn't need asking.

San Telmo District — 11:47 p.m.

The safe house occupied the basement of a tango club in San Telmo, the old bohemian quarter where artists and revolutionaries had always found refuge. Above them, dancers moved to the melancholy strains of a bandoneón; below, Noah set up his workstation in a space that smelled of wine barrels and secrets.

"How much longer?" Isabella asked, watching him connect cables and boot systems.

"Until it's done. Or until they find me." He looked up at her, managing a tired smile. "Whichever comes first."

She moved closer, placed a hand on his shoulder. "Then we work fast."

Isabella had surprised him in Cartagena. He'd expected her to stay behind, to let her father's network carry him to safety while she returned to whatever life she'd been living before the Directorate had destroyed her clinic. Instead, she'd packed a bag, kissed her father goodbye, and climbed into the car without hesitation.

"Why?" he'd asked.

"Because someone has to keep you alive," she'd imparted. "And because I'm tired of watching good people lose to monsters who hide behind spreadsheets."

Now, watching her organize their supplies with the efficiency of someone who'd run medical operations in war zones, Noah understood why he'd let her come. It wasn't only practical—her knowledge of humanitarian networks, her contacts across South America, her ability to distinguish legitimate aid organizations from Directorate fronts. It was something else. Something he hadn't felt since before Lily died.

Hope. She made him feel hope.

His laptop pinged. AURORA's transaction logs scrolling across the screen—thousands of micro-payments flowing to journalists, legal aid funds, medical clinics. The money he'd stolen from Buenos Aires was already at work, redistributed to causes that undermined the same power structures that had taken his sister.

"$947 million," he voiced quietly. "That's what we've moved so far. Every dollar stolen from Directorate accounts, fragmented and redistributed before they can trace it."

Isabella looked at the numbers, her expression unreadable. "And they can't stop it?"

"Not anymore. AURORA is distributed across forty-seven countries, embedded in infrastructure they can't touch without taking down systems they depend on." He pulled up a global map, green nodes blinking across each continent from Europe through Asia and South America. "Medical records databases. Academic archives. Government servers. Any attempt to delete it creates automatic backups. I've made it immortal."

"Robin Cipher," she added softly. "That's what they're calling you. The ghost who steals from the powerful and gives to the desperate."

"I'm not a hero, Isabella. I'm just a guy who learned to code and got angry enough to use it." He stared at Lily's photograph, propped against the monitor. "She would have been twenty-five this year. Medical school, in all likelihood. She wanted to be a pediatrician—can you believe that? A kid who couldn't afford her own insulin wanted to spend her life helping sick children."

Isabella moved behind him, wrapped her arms around his shoulders. "She sounds like someone worth fighting for."

"Lily was everything worth fighting for." His voice cracked. "And she was left to die because the system decided her life wasn't cost-effective."

They sat in silence for a moment, the music filtering down from above, the weight of loss and purpose settling around them like a familiar shroud.

Then Noah's secure phone buzzed. Ethan's identifier.

"Istanbul. Safe house arranged through Selin's contacts. Harris is dead—Daniel and Selin took him out. Daniel's gone north, chasing leads on Kessler directly."

Noah stared at the message, processing. Harris—Kessler's most dangerous cleaner, the man who'd killed Donovan, who'd hunted them across two continents—was dead.

He typed back:

"Harris is dead? Holy shit. That changes things. Kessler lost his best cleaner. "

E: *"He'll send more. He always does. "*

N: *"Then we need to move faster. AURORA is 82% distributed now. The Buenos Aires operation gave us access to transaction records we didn't have before. I'm seeing patterns—money moving into political campaigns, media companies, defense contractors. This isn't only corruption, E. It's a blueprint for controlling democracies from the inside."*

Isabella read over his shoulder. "You're building a case."

"I'm building a bomb. Each transaction, every shell company and bribed official—documented, verified, ready to release." Noah's fingers flew across the keyboard, pulling up files. "When we go public, it won't be allegations. It will be evidence. The kind that can't be denied or discredited."

"And Isabella?" Ethan's next message appeared.

Noah looked at her—this woman who had left everything to follow him into a war she didn't have to fight—and typed:

"Captain Morales's daughter. Long story. She is good, E. Really good. Reminds me what we're fighting for. "

Isabella smiled, touched his face gently. "Is that what I do?"

"That's exactly what you do." He caught her hand, held it. "I'd forgotten, after Lily. I'd forgotten that there were things in the world worth saving, not destroying. You remind me."

She leaned down, kissed him—soft, unhurried, a promise rather than a demand.

"Then let's save something," she answered. "Together."

Noah turned back to his screens, Isabella settling into the chair beside him. Above, the tango played on—music of passion and loss, of a city that had survived dictators and economic collapse and emerged, somehow, more alive than ever.

Below, two people worked through the night, building a weapon that couldn't be stopped, preparing for a battle that would shake the world.

AURORA hummed in the darkness, $947 million and climbing.

And elsewhere, Kessler was about to learn what happened when the people he'd dismissed as prey finally learned to hunt.

47

Cleaner's Trail

"One down. Now I'm coming for the man who pulls the strings."
—Daniel Cole

Outskirts of Bucharest, Romania – 7:14 a.m. local time- Day 14

Daniel Cole sat in a different safehouse now—the previous one already sanitized, burned, erased from existence. Harris' blood had washed off his hands easily enough. His wounds still hurt, but they would heal. The weight of what he'd done was proving more stubborn.

Harris hadn't been the first man Daniel had killed. Wouldn't be the last. But he'd been different—Selin fired the shot that killed him—a fellow operator, someone who'd once served the same flag, fought the same wars. The fact that Harris had been corrupted, had helped murder their father, didn't make the killing feel cleaner. The fact that Selin fired the shot that easily didn't make it easier either.

And she was with his brother.

Daniel opened his laptop—the secure one, routed through channels even the CIA couldn't trace—and began his real work: reverse-engineering Kessler's network by tracking the bodies.

He'd spent three months building a database that existed nowhere officially but everywhere in pattern: each unexplained death, every convenient accident or suicide that felt off. Journalists who died in car crashes days before major stories broke. Whistleblowers who jumped from balconies. Executives who had heart attacks at forty-five with no prior health issues.

Three hundred seventeen deaths across twenty-two countries over fifteen years. All deaths officially unconnected. Each one fitting a pattern only someone trained to see patterns would recognize.

Daniel had learned pattern recognition in Delta—the art of seeing enemy networks through seemingly random attacks, identifying command structures through the signature of operations. The same skills that made him deadly in Afghanistan made him dangerous to men like Kessler.

He pulled up a map, plotting the deaths geographically. They clustered around financial centers—Zurich, London, New York, Singapore, Dubai. But there were outliers too—journalists in Bolivia, activists in Nairobi, doctors in Yemen.

What connected them?

Daniel drilled down into the financial records he had been collecting—another skill from his operator days, understanding that money was purely another form of intelligence. Each corporation paid taxes. Each death triggered insurance claims. Each funeral left a paper trail.

He found it in the insurance: seventeen different companies, all of them subsidiaries of a parent corporation registered in Liechtenstein. Helios Holdings.

"There you are," Daniel whispered.

He pulled up Helios's corporate structure—a maze of shell companies and offshore entities designed to obscure ownership. But Daniel had time and expertise and the motivation of someone whose father had been taken by the same machine.

Four hours later, he'd traced Helios back to three principal directors. One was listed as "A. Kessler." The other two were names he didn't recognize—European, private, functionally invisible.

But Kessler was the operational heart. Every death cluster correlated to his known locations within a two-week window. He wasn't simply ordering hits—he was supervising them, ensuring quality control, maintaining his empire through precision violence.

Daniel leaned back, processing the implications. Kessler hadn't just built a criminal enterprise. He had built a state within states—an organization with more operational capability than most intelligence agencies, funded by money skimmed from the global economy, protected by leverage over officials at all levels up to the top.

You couldn't arrest a man like that. Courts didn't work against people who owned judges. Exposure didn't work against people who controlled media narratives.

You could only eliminate him. And even then, you'd have to be precise.

Daniel pulled up the intelligence file he'd been building for years now—suspicious deaths, convenient accidents, all of the threads that led directly back to Kessler's network. The pattern was undeniable. Journalists. Whistleblowers. Investigators. And one name that made his chest tighten: James Cole.

His father's death had been ruled accidental. Cabin fire. Body too burned for proper identification. Dental records "consistent" but not conclusive. The kind of bureaucratic certainty that killed curiosity.

But Daniel knew fire. Knew how bodies burned. Knew the difference between accident and orchestration.

Something was wrong with the official story. He just couldn't prove it. Not yet at least.

The facility in the Caucasus mountains had appeared in his research months ago—a Directorate black site, accessible only by a single road, defended by what intelligence suggested was a small army of private contractors. Kessler's personal fortress.

Daniel had no proof his father had ever been there. No satellite confirmation. No intercepts. Purely a gnawing certainty in his gut—the same instinct that had kept him alive through a dozen operations—that Kessler knew more about James Cole's death than any official report admitted.

If Daniel could breach that facility, access Kessler's records, he might finally learn the truth. Whether his father had died in that cabin, or whether something darker had happened. Whether James Cole's last moments had been accident or execution.

This wasn't a rescue. It was an investigation that might require a body count.

But Daniel had run missions like this before—elevated risk, low survival probability, acceptable losses in pursuit of truth.

He'd spent the years since Helmand trying to atone for leaving men behind. Perhaps the way to atone was to find out what had happened to the one man who had taught him never to leave anyone behind.

Even if the answer was a grave instead of vindication.

His encrypted phone buzzed. Message from Ethan:

"Found more evidence in Turkey. The network is massive. Noah thinks we can expose it, but I don't know if exposure is enough. These people don't go to prison. They rebuild elsewhere."

Daniel typed back: *"Exposure isn't the endgame. Elimination is. I'm working on it."*

E: *"Don't do anything crazy."*

D: *"Too late. I've been crazy since Helmand. This is the first time it's useful."*

E: *"Daniel—"*

D: *"Trust me. I know what I'm doing."*

He closed the chat before his brother could argue. Ethan was brilliant—better at strategy, better at long games, better at thinking through consequences. But he'd never understood what Daniel learned in combat: sometimes the only way to win was to accept that winning and surviving were different objectives.

Daniel pulled up satellite imagery of the Caucasus facility—grainy, months old, but enough to show layout and probable guard rotations. He began planning the infiltration with the methodical precision of someone who'd done this dozens of times.

Except this time, he wasn't working for anyone else's objectives. This was personal. This was about understanding what happened to his father. This was about making Kessler answer for thirty years of bodies that included, possibly, James Cole.

And if he was being honest with himself—truly honest—there was a part of him that hoped the answer was in that fortress. That hoped Kessler had been arrogant enough to keep records, evidence, proof of what actually happened that night at the cabin.

Because not knowing was worse than any truth Daniel could imagine.

"I'll find out what you did to him," Daniel whispered to the satellite image, thinking of Kessler somewhere in that fortress. "And then I'll make you pay for it."

Outside, Bucharest hummed with evening traffic—people living normal lives, worried about normal problems, unaware that somewhere in their city, a weapon named Daniel Cole was preparing to breach one of the most secure facilities in Eastern Europe.

Not for rescue. Not for extraction. But for truth.

And in Daniel's world, truth usually came with a body count.

But some questions were worth dying to answer. And "what happened to my father" was at the top of that list.

Even if the answer was confirmation of a death he'd already mourned. Even if all he found was proof that James Cole had died exactly as the official report stated—accidentally, alone, with no conspiracy beyond bad luck and an old cabin's faulty wiring.

At least he'd know.

And knowing, Daniel had learned, was the only peace soldiers like him ever got.

48

Spirits of Vienna

Kessler — Private Diary (Zurich-0 Archive: Unclassified)
"My lovely, spirited Leyla... freedom has only ever been a story I allowed you to believe. Come home, and let us end this pretending."
—Kessler

Istanbul, Türkiye — Late Evening local time- Day 14
Selin stood on the villa's terrace, cigarette burning between her fingers—a vice she'd abandoned five years ago when Kessler taught her that addiction was vulnerability. But tonight, the old habit returned like muscle memory, her hands needing something to do while her mind processed threats she couldn't quite name.

Below, the Aegean whispered against rocks worn smooth by millennia. Above, stars emerged in the gathering darkness, indifferent to the small dramas of survival playing out beneath them.

Behind her, through the villa's glass doors, Ethan slept—finally. She'd watched exhaustion claim him in stages: first the forced calm of adrenaline crash, then the trembling that signaled deeper fatigue, finally the surrender to unconsciousness that came when the body overruled the mind's insistence on vigilance.

He trusted her. That was the problem.

Her encrypted phone buzzed, the vibration sharp against her palm. She knew who it was before looking.

Unknown: "Still playing protector? Does the Cole boy know what you are?"

Her thumb hovered over the delete button, but training stopped her. Never ignore a message from an unknown number—it might contain intelligence, might reveal the sender's location through metadata, might provide some angle of leverage.

She typed back: "I'm not yours anymore."

The response came immediately, as if he'd been waiting with his finger over send:

Unknown: "You will always be mine. I built you from the ground up. Every skill, instinct and fear you have learned to weaponize—you are my wonderful creation, Leyla."

The name hit like a slap. Leyla Kara—the girl she'd been before Kessler found her stealing food outside a military barracks in Ankara. Twelve years old, rail-thin, more animal than child after six months on the streets.

He had been wearing civilian clothes that day, had approached with the careful slowness of someone who understood wounded things. He had bought her dinner—real food, not garbage—and asked her name in Turkish so fluent it mostly masked his European accent.

She had told him. And in that moment of trust, she had given him everything.

Another message appeared: "The boy you trained with. Do you remember him? Pale hair, perfect discipline. You asked me once what happened to him."

Selin's hand trembled. She did remember—a young operative she'd trained alongside for one week in Berlin. Swiss or Austrian accent, cold eyes, clinical precision in everything he did. They had run obstacle courses together, practiced close-quarters combat, studied surveillance techniques in the frozen courtyards of that repurposed East German facility.

His name was Lukas, she remembered now. He had the kind of controlled intensity that came from discipline. They had not spoken much—Kessler discouraged fraternization among his recruits—but she definitely had sensed something in him. A hollowness. Like he had been carved out and filled with someone else's purpose.

Then he'd vanished after that week, and when she'd asked Kessler about him, her mentor had smiled that unique kind smile that meant the question answered itself if you were smart enough to see.

Unknown: "His name was Lukas. My son. He's waiting for you and the Cole brothers. When the time comes, you'll have to choose: the man you think you love, or the family you can't escape."

Selin crushed the cigarette against the railing, watching the ember die. Family. The word was a joke. Kessler had never been family—he'd been architect, sculptor, puppet master. He'd taken a starving child and shaped her into a weapon, all while making her believe it was love.

She thought of Vienna. Of the years she'd spent as his operative, believing she was helping maintain stability, prevent chaos, protect the innocent. She'd eliminated targets he'd designated as threats. Infiltrated organizations he'd marked as dangerous. Reported on colleagues who'd shown signs of disloyalty.

She'd been his perfect instrument. Right up until she'd seen the convoy.

The memory came sharp and unwanted: A Serbian highway at dusk. Forty-three refugees trying to reach safety. The intelligence she'd passed along—routes, timing, vehicle descriptions—had been used to target them, not protect them. The explosion had been visible from her hotel window, a bloom of orange flame against the purple twilight.

She'd watched the news coverage with growing horror. Kessler's media assets had shaped the narrative within hours: terrorist attack, tragic but isolated, unrelated to the broader humanitarian crisis. The truth—that it had been orchestrated to justify increased security contracts and shift migration patterns—remained buried beneath layers of plausible deniability.

That was when she'd understood. All the operations she had run, every target she had eliminated with elite precision, every piece of intelligence she had gathered—none of it had been about protection. It had all been about profit. About maintaining the architecture of control that made men like Kessler wealthy and powerful.

She'd run that night. Burned her Vienna identity. Disappeared into the network of safe houses and false papers she'd been smart enough to prepare, even when she'd believed in him.

But you never truly ran from Kessler. He'd taught her that lesson himself: the best hunters let their prey exhaust themselves, then collect them when they're too tired to resist.

Behind her, the villa door opened. Ethan emerged, hair disheveled, eyes still heavy with sleep but sharpening as he registered her posture—the tension in her shoulders, the way she held the phone like it might detonate.

"Can't sleep either?" he asked.

She forced a smile, pocketed the phone. "Old habits."

He joined her at the railing, close enough that their shoulders touched. The simple gesture—so different from Kessler's calculated affection, his touches that always served a purpose beyond comfort—made something in her chest crack.

"Want to talk about it?"

"Not really." She stared at the dark water below, watching moonlight fracture across the waves. "Sometimes the past doesn't want to stay buried."

Ethan was quiet for a moment, his presence steady beside her. Not pressing, not demanding—genuinely there. "I know enough," he replied finally. "I know you've been running from something. I know you've been hurt by someone you trusted. I know you're trying to be better than whatever made you." He turned to face her, his expression serious but open. "That's all I need to know."

She wanted to believe him. Wanted to believe that redemption was possible, that Kessler's programming could be overwritten by something as simple as genuine care. But she'd been trained too well to trust easy answers.

"Ethan," she contended quietly, the words harder than any physical training she'd endured, "there are things about me you don't know. Things I've done—"

"I know enough," he repeated, his voice gentle but firm. "You think I haven't noticed the way you move? The way you scan rooms like you're cataloging exits and threats? The fact that you can field-strip a Glock in under twenty seconds?" He reached for her hand. "I know you were trained by someone. I know you worked in intelligence. I know you've killed people."

She flinched at the bluntness, but he didn't let go of her hand.

"And I know you're here anyway. You could have disappeared in Athens, in Istanbul, anywhere along the way. But you stayed. You're helping me." His thumb traced small circles on the back of her hand. "Whatever you were, whoever made you—you're choosing to be something else now. That's what matters."

The words should have comforted her. Instead, they were like a countdown timer. Because she knew something Ethan didn't: Kessler didn't send messages as warnings. He sent them as theater, setting the stage for a performance only he could see.

And in that performance, she'd been cast as both Judas and martyr. She hadn't decided just yet which role she'd play.

Her phone buzzed again. She pulled it out, read the message:

Unknown: "I taught you everything I know except how to say good-bye. When the time comes, you'll understand that love is another form of control. See you soon my Sparrow."

The old codename—her designation during training—made her feel twelve years old again. Small. Powerless. Property.

She deleted the message and powered down the phone completely.

"Come back to bed," Ethan told her softly. "Tomorrow we keep moving."

She followed him inside, memorizing details with the desperate precision of someone cataloging what might be lost. The way he moved through the dark villa without fear. The sound of his breathing. The warmth of his hand in hers. The particular quality of his voice when he was tired but trying to stay alert for her sake.

Because she knew—had known since Vienna, since Kessler had started sending messages, since she'd made the choice to stay instead of run—that this wasn't a love story. It was a tragedy waiting for its final act.

She lay down beside Ethan, feeling the steady rhythm of his breathing gradually slow as sleep reclaimed him. In the darkness, she stared at the ceiling and made her decision.

When Kessler came—and he would come, with the patient inevitability of a predator who'd been tracking wounded prey—she wouldn't let Ethan pay for her past. Whatever sacrifice was required, she'd make it. Whatever role Kessler had written for her, she'd rewrite it.

Because perhaps Ethan was right. Maybe redemption wasn't about erasing what you'd done. Maybe it was about choosing, in one crucial moment, to be something other than what you were made to be.

Her phone, powered down and dark on the nightstand, nevertheless was alive. Watching. Waiting.

Outside, the Aegean whispered against the rocks, the same sound it had made for ten thousand years—indifferent to love, to betrayal, to all the small human dramas played out on its shores.

Selin closed her eyes and tried to sleep, knowing she wouldn't. Knowing that tomorrow they'd run again, and the day after, and the day after that.

Knowing that eventually, running stopped working.

And then you had to choose: who you were, or who you wanted to be.

She reached for Ethan's hand in the darkness, held it like an anchor, and waited for the dawn.

49

Collateral Damage

"They want a war, Ethan? Fine. Let's show them what choosing the wrong woman costs." —Selin

Istanbul, Türkiye- 6:15 a.m. local time- Day 15

At the moment the sun was barely rising over the horizon, Ethan awoke to the faint hum of engines outside the villa. Selin was already alert, eyes scanning the hills beyond the coast. Something didn't feel right.

"They're here," she announced, voice low, steady.

Ethan's heart rate spiked—not with fear, but with awareness. Kessler's reach was ruthless, and Istanbul was no longer safe. Outside, shadows moved across the villa grounds—professional, silent, predatory.

"Grab the gear," Ethan insisted, moving with the precision of someone who had been hunted his entire life. Selin followed, packing laptops, encrypted drives, and essentials. The flash drive with the wire network rested in Ethan's jacket pocket, a lifeline and a target.

They slipped down narrow stone alleys, shadows clinging to them as they moved through Istanbul's labyrinthine streets. Motorbikes appeared unexpectedly—three men, silent except for the engine's growl, cutting them off. Ethan and Selin ducked into a side street, hearts racing, steps measured but fast.

A sudden bang—Selin dove, dragging Ethan behind a dumpster as a bullet ricocheted past. "They're coordinated," she whispered. "Professional."

"They always are," Ethan muttered. He spotted a small fishing dock ahead, boats tied loosely, waiting for someone daring enough to escape.

They ran, leaping onto the nearest vessel, engine already warm. Ethan started it, the propeller kicking up water into the dawn light. The pursuers were relentless, three jet skis now in the channel, slicing through the waves with terrifying speed.

Ethan twisted the throttle, dodging ferries and low-hanging docks, weaving like a ghost through the Bosphorus. Selin fired sporadically with a small sidearm, taking out one jet ski's driver. The other two continued their approach, cutting off potential escape routes.

"Hold on!" Ethan shouted as he cut sharply around a rocky promontory. Water sprayed over the bow, salty and cold, but he didn't slow. Each maneuver was deliberate, a mix of instinct and training, the kind his father had drilled into him decades ago.

Hours later, the chase ended in a small, hidden cove. Exhausted but alive, they disembarked and pulled the boat ashore. Selin looked at him, dark hair plastered from the sea, eyes sharp but alive with adrenaline.

"You okay?" she asked, voice soft, almost intimate.

Ethan exhaled, finally letting the tension ebb. "Better than the alternative," he answered, letting a faint smile touch his lips.

They collapsed onto the sand, the Bosphorus coastline stretching infinite before them. The afternoon sun was climbing now, burning off the morning's adrenaline with Mediterranean heat.

Safe house Karaköy district – 9:15 pm local time

Selin's phone buzzed three hours later. Unknown number. She stared at it for a moment before answering, putting it on speaker so Ethan could hear.

"Sparrow." The voice was calm, European, familiar in the worst conceivable way. Kessler.

She said absolutely nothing, jaw tight.

"I think it's time we spoke. Properly. Without the theatrics of this morning's chase." He paused, and she could almost hear the smile. "Meet me tonight. Eleven p.m. Reina—you know it, I'm sure. Bring Ethan. Let's discuss terms like civilized people."

"Terms?" Selin's voice was ice. "You tried to kill us this morning."

"That was business. This is negotiation. There's a difference." Kessler's tone carried the patronizing patience of a man explaining simple concepts to children. "Reina. Eleven p.m. Come armed if it makes you feel safer. But come. Because the alternative is that I continue hunting you across continents until one of us gets tired—and I assure you, my resources exceed your stamina."

The line went dead.

Ethan and Selin exchanged a look. "It's a trap," he voiced.

"Obviously." She was already standing, mind tactical. "But it's also an opportunity. Reina is public—one of the most popular nightclubs in Istanbul. Packed on weekends. Witnesses everywhere. Even Kessler can't orchestrate a clean hit with that many eyes."

"Can't he?" Ethan pulled out his phone, searching. Reina's website showed exactly what Selin described: massive waterfront club on the Bosphorus, known for international DJs, house music that shook the foundations, crowds in the thousands. "We'd be surrounded by civilians. If anything goes wrong—"

"It will." Selin's eyes were hard. "But we can't keep running, Ethan. Eventually we need to confront him. And if he's offering a meeting, even a trap, we use it. We go in prepared, we stay aware, and we get out the moment it turns."

Ethan wanted to argue. His instincts screamed that walking into Kessler's invitation was suicide. But Selin was right—running only delayed the inevitable. And if there was even a chance to negotiate, to find leverage, to end this without more bodies...

"We go together," he responded finally. "We watch each other's backs. And at the first sign of trouble, we're gone."

"Agreed."

Reina Nightclub, Bosphorus Waterfront— 10:58 p.m. local time

The club was exactly what the website promised: sensory overload wrapped in velvet rope exclusivity. Bass so deep it was a second heartbeat, strobes cutting through smoke and darkness, bodies pressed together in the kind of beautiful chaos that only happened when music, alcohol, and the proximity of strangers collided.

Ethan and Selin moved through the entrance past security who barely glanced at the couple in dark clothing. Inside, the crowd was international—wealthy Turks, European tourists, Russians, Americans—all lost in the DJ's set, a relentless house track that built and dropped like controlled demolition.

The main floor was packed. Three levels of balconies overlooked the dance floor, VIP sections roped off, bottle service girls navigating through the mass of bodies with practiced grace. Floor-to-ceiling windows showed the Bosphorus beyond, lit by the city's reflected glow.

Selin's hand found Ethan's as they pushed through the crowd. She leaned close, lips nearly touching his ear to be heard over the music. "Stay sharp. Exits at two, seven, and ten o'clock. Balconies have stairs to the service corridors."

He nodded, scanning faces. No sign of Kessler. But that meant nothing. The man could be anywhere—VIP section, balcony, or not here at all, watching through surveillance he'd arranged.

Ethan's phone buzzed. Text message. Unknown number.

Third floor VIP. Northeast corner. Come alone.

He showed Selin. She shook her head immediately. "We stay together."

They moved toward the stairs, weaving through dancers lost in the music's trance. The crowd thinned slightly as they climbed—second floor, then third, where the VIP sections were cordoned off with velvet ropes and security who looked more professional than the entrance staff.

Northeast corner. A private booth, curtains drawn. No security visible, which was wrong. Everything about this screamed wrong.

Selin's hand moved to the small of her back where she'd concealed a pistol under her jacket. Ethan touched her arm—wait. Listen.

From behind the curtain: nothing. No conversation, no movement. Only the club's bass vibrating through the floor, the DJ building toward another drop.

Ethan pulled the curtain aside.

The booth was empty. Expensive leather couches, a table with an unopened bottle of champagne, and a phone. A burner, placed deliberately in the center.

It rang.

Ethan answered, already knowing. "You're not here."

"No." Kessler's voice was clear despite the music. "Did you actually believe that I would be? After all you've learned about how I operate?" A pause. "But my people are. Positioned throughout the club. They've been watching you since you entered. And now, they have their orders."

Ethan's blood went cold. "You would kill us in front of hundreds of witnesses?"

"I'd create chaos in which two unfortunate people got caught in crossfire between rival groups. Drug dealers, perhaps. Chechen mafia. The narrative writes itself." Kessler's tone was almost apologetic. "You've been useful, Ethan. Both of you. But utility has limits. Consider this my way of closing the ledger."

The line went dead.

For one heartbeat, nothing happened. The music pounded. The crowd danced. The lights strobed.

Then Selin grabbed Ethan's arm. "Move. Now."

She'd seen them first—three men moving through the crowd with purpose, no longer pretending to be clubgoers. Hands inside jackets. Eyes locked on the VIP section. Professional. Coordinated.

Ethan and Selin ran.

The first shots came as they hit the stairs—suppressed but still audible as sharp cracks beneath the music. Screaming started somewhere behind them. The crowd surged, panic spreading like fire through dry grass.

Selin pulled her weapon, turning to fire twice at the nearest pursuer. He went down, clutching his leg. But two more appeared from the second-floor balcony, cutting off the main stairs.

"Service corridor!" Selin shouted, pointing to a door marked 'PERSONNEL ONLY.' They crashed through it, into sudden darkness and concrete, the club's music muffled now but the bass still throbbing through the walls.

Footsteps behind them. Close. Getting closer.

Ethan spun as a figure emerged from the darkness—one of Kessler's men, weapon raised. No time to think. Just pure muscle memory from years of training with his father and Daniel. He ducked under the gun, drove his shoulder into the man's ribs, used the momentum to slam him against the concrete wall.

The man recovered fast, swinging the weapon like a club. Ethan blocked with his forearm, pain flaring but adrenaline overriding it. He grabbed the man's wrist, twisted, something popped. The weapon clattered to the floor.

The operative went for a knife. Ethan was faster—grabbed the man's head and drove it into the wall once, twice, until he went limp.

"Behind you!" Selin's voice cut through the haze.

Ethan turned. Two more coming through the door, weapons up. Selin fired—one shot, center mass. The first man dropped. The second got a shot off before she could adjust.

The bullet caught her in the upper arm, spinning her against the wall. She didn't scream, only a viper like hiss through clenched teeth, her weapon clattering from unexpectedly numb fingers.

The second operative advanced, weapon trained on Selin. Ethan moved without thinking—grabbed the knife from the first man's belt and threw it in one fluid motion. It wasn't pretty, wasn't Hollywood.

The blade tumbled awkwardly through the air and caught the operative in the shoulder rather than the chest.

But it was enough. The man staggered, weapon dropping. Ethan closed the distance, drove his fist into the man's throat, then swept his legs. The operative went down hard, skull cracking against concrete with a sickening sound.

Silence. Only breathing—ragged, desperate. And the muffled bass from the club, oblivious to the violence in its service corridors.

Ethan rushed to Selin. Blood soaked her jacket sleeve, dark and spreading. "How bad?"

"Through and through. Missed the bone." She was already moving, teeth gritted against the pain. "We need to go. There were at least six. We've taken out four."

"Can you run?"

"I can do whatever needs doing." She retrieved her weapon with her left hand, awkward but functional. "Exit's this way. Service entrance to the loading dock."

They moved through the corridor, Ethan supporting Selin, both of them listening for pursuit. Behind them, the club's music reached a crescendo, the DJ dropping the beat as a thousand people surged as one, oblivious to the bodies in the darkness beyond their paradise.

The service exit opened onto a loading dock. Cool night air, the smell of the Bosphorus, and blessed silence after the club's assault.

No sign of the remaining operatives. Either they'd been pulled back or were regrouping. Either way, the window was now.

Ethan spotted a delivery van, keys still in the ignition—some driver's cigarette break. He helped Selin into the passenger seat, then climbed behind the wheel. The engine caught on the first try.

They were three blocks away when the first police sirens started wailing toward Reina.

In the safe house, Ethan cleaned and bandaged Selin's arm. The bullet had passed through the outside of her bicep—painful, bloody, but not life-threatening. She'd been lucky. They both had.

"Four men," Selin mentioned quietly, watching Ethan work. "You took out four Directorate operatives in hand-to-hand combat."

"You took out two," Ethan corrected, tying off the bandage. "I simply cleaned up the rest."

"Still." Her eyes held something he couldn't quite read—surprise, respect, something deeper. "Where did you learn to fight like that? Bankers aren't usually trained in close quarters combat."

"My father. My brother." Ethan sat back, exhaustion finally catching up. "Daniel was Delta Force. When I was growing up, he and Dad would train me in hand to hand tactics. I thought it was bonding. Turns out it was preparation."

Selin reached out with her good arm, touched his face. "You saved my life tonight."

"You saved mine on the boat this morning. Seems we're even."

"No." Her voice was soft, serious. "We're not keeping score anymore, Ethan. This isn't about debt. This is about..." She trailed off, searching for words.

"About us," he finished.

"Yes."

They sat in the dim light of the safe house, battered and exhausted, surrounded by the evidence of Kessler's global reach. Four operatives dead in a nightclub. The police would be investigating. The Directorate would be adjusting tactics.

But for this moment, they were alive. Together. And that had to be enough.

Ethan pulled out the flash drive—the network, the evidence, the thing that had started all of this. He stared at it in the lamplight.

"Kessler's moves are faster than we expected," he offered quietly. "He's already laying traps across Europe, Asia... and South America."

Selin's hand found his. "Then we'll move faster. Together."

In Buenos Aires, Noah had uncovered new threads linking Kessler directly to multiple intelligence agencies and criminal syndicates. He sent Ethan an encrypted update, the lines of data sprawling like a spider-web over the globe.

Ethan read it under the safe house's dim light, mind racing. The network was massive, the pursuit relentless, but now, finally, they had both intelligence and allies.

Selin leaned her head on his shoulder, careful of her wounded arm. "You can't do this alone anymore," she whispered.

"I don't have to," Ethan replied, voice firm. "We fight this together—wherever it leads."

Outside, Istanbul's night sounds filtered through the windows—traffic, distant music, the call to prayer from a nearby mosque. Somewhere in the shadows, Kessler was watching. His reach was global, his patience infinite, his willingness to use overwhelming force now proven.

But Ethan had momentum, allies, and something Kessler had underestimated: the will to fight back when cornered. The nightclub had been meant to end them. Instead, it had proven they could survive his traps.

And that changed everything.

The fight had only just begun.

50

Collapse

"You brought your little Sparrow with you, Ethan. Good. Breaking a man is so much easier when he gets to watch what he loves die first."
—Lukas Kessler

Istanbul-Haydarpaşa Train Station — 7:23 a.m. local time-Day 16

Morning crowds at Haydarpaşa Station moved like rivers around them—commuters with briefcases, students with backpacks, families dragging luggage toward platforms that promised escape to somewhere else. Ethan kept his head down, baseball cap pulled low, moving through the throng with Selin a half-step behind.

They'd left the safe house before dawn, taking a circuitous route through Kadıköy's back streets, doubling back twice to check for surveillance. Selin's contacts had warned them: Directorate assets were mobilizing across Istanbul, searching for the Americans who'd killed Harris in Thessaloniki and Directorate operators in the nightclub.

The train to Bodrum left in twelve minutes. From there, Noah was arranging extraction—a private plane to get them out of Türkiye, somewhere Kessler's reach couldn't follow.

"Platform seven," Selin uttered quietly, guiding him through the crowd. "The 7:35 to Denizli. We transfer there for the coast."

"How long?"

"Eight hours, if nothing goes wrong." She glanced at him, a faint smile crossing her face. "In our experience, something always goes wrong."

They found their compartment—a private sleeper that Selin had booked under a false name—and settled in as the train lurched into motion. Istanbul's skyline receded through the window, minarets and skyscrapers giving way to industrial districts, then suburbs, then the rolling green of the Anatolian plain.

For the first time in days, Ethan allowed himself to breathe.

Turkish Countryside — 9:47 a.m.

The train swayed gently as it cut through farmland, its rhythmic steel heartbeat a lullaby beneath Ethan's boots. Selin stared out the window, watching the sun paint the fields in slow-moving gold. Ethan sat beside her, head leaned against the glass, his eyes half-closed.

A voice broke the silence. "Jesus Christ..." a man muttered in Turkish, staring at his phone.

The tone—disbelief layered with fascination—made Selin glance up.

Through the compartment's open door, she could see the small screen, a breaking-news ticker rolling in Turkish:

"INTERNATIONAL MERCANTILE BANK SEIZED BY GLOBAL REGULATORS — CEO VICTOR KRANE FOUND DEAD IN APPARENT SUICIDE."

She leaned forward, catching the next headline beneath it:

"Sources cite internal compliance breach and evidence of massive offshore transfers under investigation."

Ethan opened his eyes, sensing the shift. "What is it?" —he asked Selin.

The man in the corridor whistled softly in Turkish. "Unreal. Whole damn bank's gone under."

"Krane," Selin voiced, the word catching in her throat. "He's dead. The bank—they've seized everything. Regulators moved in overnight."

Ethan sat up, fully alert now. "Suicide?"

"That's what they're calling it." Selin's jaw tightened. "They're cleaning house. The whole bank's the cover story now. They'll bury it all—including anyone tied to it."

"Then Krane was killed."

Selin met his eyes. "Absolutely".

A little over two weeks after he had first flagged the Apex wire, the system had finally caught up with International Mercantile Bank.

The overhead lights flickered as the train entered a tunnel, plunging the compartment into momentary darkness. When the light returned, Ethan's reflection stared back at him from the glass—hollow-eyed, unshaven, carrying too many ghosts.

Then Selin's phone buzzed.

She looked at the screen, and her face went pale.

"What is it?" Ethan asked.

She turned the phone toward him. A message from an unknown number, but the content made the sender unmistakable:

"Sparrow. My reach extends to all places—trains, borders, the very air you breathe. You've had time to reconsider. Choose wisely now: return to where you belong, or die beside the American. There are no other options. — K"

Ethan went cold and turned to look at passengers. Kessler. Here. Now. Watching them even as they fled.

Selin stared at the message for a long moment. Her hands were steady, but something moved behind her eyes—the ghost of the girl who'd been Subject 47, who'd worshipped a monster because he was the only father she'd ever known.

Then she typed a single word and hit send:

"No."

She looked at Ethan, her expression fierce. "I made my choice. On that plane from Miami. In that safe house in Istanbul. Every moment since I met you." She reached for his hand. "I choose you. I choose this. Whatever comes next."

Before Ethan could respond, the compartment door slid open.

Lukas Kessler stood in the doorway.

He looked younger than Ethan remembered, same athletic build, with his father's pale eyes and something colder beneath them. He wore a business suit that didn't quite hide the coiled violence in his frame, and he smiled the way predators smiled before they struck.

"Sparrow," Lukas vocalized, his voice carrying the faint lilt of a European education. "Father is disappointed. He gave you all the opportunities to come home."

"He isn't my home." Selin was already moving, positioning herself between Lukas and Ethan. "He never was."

"No?" Lukas stepped into the compartment, closing the door behind him. "He raised you. Trained you. Made you the assassin you are. And this is how you repay him? By spreading your legs for an American banker who doesn't even know which end of a gun to hold?"

The words were designed to provoke, to make her angry, to make her sloppy. Ethan recognized the technique—he'd seen it in boardroom negotiations, in hostile takeovers, in the arena where predators circled prey.

Selin didn't take the bait. "Your father is a monster, Lukas. He stole my childhood. Turned me into a weapon. Used me to kill innocent people." Her voice was steady. "I'm done being his creature. And I'm done being yours."

Lukas moved.

He was fast—faster than Ethan had anticipated. One moment he was standing by the door; the next he was inside Selin's guard, a blade appearing in his hand like a magic trick.

Selin blocked the first strike, redirected the second, but Lukas had the advantage of surprise, position, and a wounded opponent. They crashed against the compartment wall, grappling for control of the knife, their movements a blur of violence in the confined space.

Ethan froze for half a second—the instinct of a civilian confronted with professional violence. Then something deeper took over. The lessons his father had taught him. The fury at everything Kessler had taken. The realization that the woman he loved was about to die if he didn't act.

He grabbed the metal luggage rack above his head and swung himself forward, driving both feet into Lukas's side.

The impact sent Lukas stumbling, his grip on Selin loosening just enough for her to twist free. She spun, drove an elbow into his jaw, followed by a knee to his stomach. Lukas doubled over—but he was already recovering, already bringing the knife up for another strike.

Ethan hit him again.

Not elegantly. Not with training or precision. Just raw, desperate force—a tackle that drove both of them against the compartment door, slamming it open, spilling them into the corridor.

Passengers screamed. Someone pulled an emergency cord. The train lurched, brakes squealing, throwing everyone off balance.

Lukas rolled to his feet, knife still in hand, blood streaming from a cut above his eye. He looked at Ethan with something like surprise—and something like respect.

"The banker has teeth," he declared, almost hissing the words. "Father will be interested to hear that."

"Tell him yourself." Selin was beside Ethan now, her own weapon drawn. "When we send you back in pieces."

Lukas smiled—his father's smile, cold and calculating. "Another time, perhaps. Father wants you alive, Sparrow. For now." He glanced at Ethan. "But he is expendable. Remember that."

Lukas slid with precision toward the end of the car, keeping his knife raised. The train was slowing rapidly now, the emergency stop bringing it to a shuddering halt in the middle of open farmland.

"We need to go," Selin stated to Ethan. "Now. Before the police arrive."

They jumped from the train and ran.

Anatolian Countryside — 10:34 a.m.

Like a mirage, the farmhouse appeared through the heat haze—whitewashed walls, red tile roof, an old tractor rusting beside a stone well. Ethan's lungs burned from running; the gash on his arm where Lukas's knife had caught him throbbed with each heartbeat.

They'd jumped from the train as it stopped, scrambled down an embankment, and run through fields of wheat and sunflowers until the tracks were out of sight. Selin had navigated by instinct, leading them away from roads, away from anywhere Kessler's people might be watching.

"Wait here," she insisted, approaching the farmhouse alone.

Ethan watched from behind a stone wall as she knocked on the door, spoke rapid Turkish to the elderly man who answered. The conversation went back and forth—gestures, nods, the universal language of negotiation. Finally, the farmer disappeared inside and returned with keys.

"He'll drive us to the bus depot in Afyon," Selin articulated, returning to Ethan. "From there, we can catch a coach to Bodrum. He doesn't ask questions, and I paid enough to ensure he forgets our faces."

"Can we trust him?"

"He lost two sons to political purges. He has no love for anyone in power." She touched Ethan's arm—the wounded one—and her expression softened. "Let me look at that before we go."

She cleaned the wound with supplies from the farmer's medicine cabinet, bandaged it with the efficiency of someone who'd done this many times before.

"You saved my life," she spoke to Ethan quietly, not meeting his eyes. "In that compartment. Lukas had me—I was off balance, hurt from the gunshot wound in the nightclub. He was too fast. If you hadn't—"

"I wasn't going to lose you." Ethan caught her hand. "Not to him. Not to anyone."

She looked up, and for a moment, the operative disappeared. What remained was just a woman—scarred, exhausted, afraid—who'd found something worth fighting for.

"I love you," she professed. The words came out rough, unpracticed, as if she'd never expressed them before. "I don't know if I know how to love. Kessler trained that out of me. But whatever this is—whatever I feel when I look at you—it's the closest I've ever come."

Ethan pulled her close. "That's enough. That's more than enough."

The farmer appeared in the doorway, jingling his keys impatiently. The moment broke, but something had been given that couldn't be taken back.

They climbed into his battered truck and headed south, toward Bodrum, toward whatever came next.**Bodrum, Türkiye — Two Days Later**

The villa overlooked the Aegean, white walls brilliant against the deep blue of sea and sky. Bougainvillea cascaded over ancient stone, and the air carried the scent of salt and jasmine and the peace that came from being, however briefly, beyond reach.

Noah's face filled the laptop screen, Isabella visible in the background of what looked like a Buenos Aires apartment. Daniel appeared in a separate window, his location deliberately obscured—somewhere in Eastern Europe, hunting leads on Kessler's movements.

"The plane's arranged," Noah voiced. "Private charter, leaves tomorrow night from Milas-Bodrum Airport. Pilot's been vetted through Morales's network—he's flown extraction runs for us before. He'll get you to London without touching any commercial system."

"And the nodes?" Daniel asked. His face was gaunt, shadowed—he'd been running hard since the freight yard, and it showed.

Ethan pulled up the network diagram they'd been constructing for weeks. "London and Zurich are the two major financial hubs. London oversees the European political operations—bribes to MPs, funding for media manipulation, the infrastructure that keeps their narrative alive. Zurich is the treasury—where the real money flows before it gets distributed."

"If we hit both simultaneously," Selin continued, "we can expose the full scope of the operation. Transaction records from Zurich proving the money flows, combined with political intelligence from London showing where it goes. It's a complete picture—undeniable, documented, ready for release."

"Security?" Daniel asked.

"London node operates out of a private bank in the City—Meridian Trust. Three-story building, security team of six, standard protocols." Ethan had memorized the details during their two days in Bodrum. "We go in as auditors. Selin's contacts have provided credentials that will hold up to initial scrutiny. We have maybe thirty minutes once we're inside before someone makes a call they shouldn't."

"Zurich?"

"Harder," Daniel admitted. "The node's buried in a legitimate Swiss private bank—Hoffmann & Cie. Old money, old security, and Swiss discretion that makes them resistant to outside pressure." He paused. "But I've got an inside contact. A compliance officer who's been documenting irregularities for years. She's ready to move, but she needs someone to extract her and the data simultaneously."

"Can you do it alone?" Ethan asked.

Daniel's smile was thin. "I've done harder with less. The question is timing. We need to hit both nodes within a two-hour window. If London goes first, Zurich will lock down before I can get in. If Zurich goes first—"

"London does the same," Selin finished. "We coordinate. Exactly 10:00 a.m. local time, both locations. That gives us the element of surprise and ensures they can't warn each other."

Noah was typing rapidly. "I can monitor both operations from here. AURORA's distributed enough now that I can run interference—crash their communication systems, delay their response protocols, give you extra time if things go sideways."

"And the release?" Ethan asked.

"Already staged. The moment you confirm data extraction, I push the data out—financial records, political intelligence, the whole network map—to forty-seven journalists across twelve countries. Major papers, investigative outlets, all entities who have been trying to crack the Directorate for years." Noah's eyes were bright with purpose. "By the time Kessler realizes what's happening, the story will be out. Impossible to suppress, impossible to discredit."

"What about Kessler himself?" Isabella asked—her first contribution to the conversation.

"We're working on that," Daniel replied. "My contacts have been tracking his movements. He's been moving between properties—Switzerland, Germany, Luxembourg—never staying more than forty-eight hours. But there's a pattern. After we hit the nodes, he'll have to surface, try to manage the damage." His expression hardened. "That's when I'll find him."

"And then?" Ethan asked.

Daniel was silent for a moment. When he spoke, his voice was flat. "Then I'll do what needs to be done."

No one asked for clarification. They all understood.

"Tomorrow night, then," Selin answered. "Ethan and I fly to London. Daniel moves on Zurich. And in forty-eight hours—"

"We bring down the house," Noah finished. "Each node and connection, every secret they've kept buried."

The screens went dark. Ethan and Selin sat in the fading light of the Bodrum villa, the Aegean spreading before them like a promise.

"Scared?" she asked.

"Terrified." He reached for her hand. "But I'd rather be terrified with you than safe without you."

She smiled—the real smile, the one that made her look young and hopeful despite what they have faced against Kessler and the Directorate. "That might be the craziest and romantic thing anyone's ever told me."

"Then you've been talking to the wrong people."

"I have." She leaned into him, her head resting on his shoulder. "Until now."

The sun set over the Aegean, painting the sky in shades of gold and crimson. Tomorrow they would fly to London, Daniel to Zurich, walk into danger, and try to tear down an empire that had been building for decades.

But tonight, for a few more hours, they had this: the sea, the silence, and each other.

It would have to be enough.

51

European Node

Kessler — Private Diary (Zurich-0 Archive: Unclassified)
"Ah, Daniel Cole... the loud one. Your father swung his fists too. They never changed a thing."

Zurich, Switzerland—12:20 a.m. local time- Day 16
Zurich's financial district gleamed under harsh white lights, monolithic and quiet—too quiet. Daniel moved alone through the shadows, slipping past guards and cameras with the precision his training demanded. His steps were measured; experience told him every shadow was potentially lethal. The flash drive sat in his pocket, a pulse of power and danger he couldn't ignore.

He watched the corridors using the sector scanning method his father — and later Delta had taught him—divide your field of vision into zones, sweep each zone methodically, never let your eyes dart randomly. *"Random scanning misses patterns"*, his father had mentioned during countless training sessions. *"Systematic scanning catches anomalies. The guard who walks too fast. The maintenance guy who's too interested in exits. The camera that's angled wrong."*

Noah's voice crackled through his earpiece, distant but steady from his position in Argentina. "You're clear for the next forty seconds. Security rotation heading west."

"Copy that," Daniel whispered, moving through the polished marble corridors.

He reached the secured terminal and began the extraction, his fingers flying across the keyboard. The decrypted files mapped flows from humanitarian funds to arms distributors, from media NGOs to mercenary logistics firms. Everything Ethan and Selin would need for their parallel operation in London.

"Daniel," Noah's voice carried an edge now. "I'm seeing movement on the third floor. Someone's coming in through the executive elevator. This wasn't on the rotation schedule."

Daniel's blood ran cold. "Identification?"

A pause. Then: "Tall. Blond. Moving like military. Daniel—it's Lukas."

The name hit Daniel like a physical blow. Lukas—Kessler's son. The man who never showed up unless the target was priority one. The kid who used to come to the Cole cabins so many years ago. He was dead. Replaced with the monster who killed his father, attacked his brother and Selin on the train.

"How long do I have?"

"Two minutes, maybe less. He's not alone—I'm counting four operatives with him. Get out. Now."

Daniel yanked the flash drive from the terminal and ran. His exit route was compromised—Lukas would have covered the main corridors. He diverted through a maintenance shaft, crawling through ductwork that hadn't been updated since the Cold War, the metal groaning under his weight.

Behind him, he heard the door to the server room crash open. Commands barked in German echoed through the ventilation system.

"They're tracking your heat signature," Noah warned. "You need to move faster or find a way to mask it."

Daniel dropped from the ductwork into a mechanical room, immediately dousing himself with water from a cooling system pipe. The shock of cold was brutal, but it would buy him seconds. He pushed through an emergency exit and found himself on a narrow maintenance ledge, four stories above the street.

Gunfire erupted behind him—they'd found his trail. Daniel leapt to an adjacent building's fire escape, the impact jarring his shoulder. More shots ricocheted off metal railings as he descended, taking the stairs three at a time.

He hit the ground running, weaving through Zurich's maze of alleyways. A black sedan screeched around a corner ahead of him—more of Lukas's team. Daniel reversed course, vaulting over a fence into a construction site.

"The river," Noah announced. "Fifty meters north. There's a tour boat departing in ninety seconds. Blend with the tourists."

Daniel sprinted through the site, dodging equipment and scaffolding, emerging onto the riverbank just as the boat began pulling away. He launched himself across the gap, landing hard on the deck. Tourists scattered, startled. He straightened his jacket, smiled apologetically, and disappeared into the crowd.

From the shore, he caught a glimpse of Lukas—standing motionless, watching. Not pursuing. Just watching, with the patience of a predator who knew the hunt was far from over.

Elsewhere-Kessler

Three hours later, Kessler's phone vibrated. He answered without looking at the screen.

"He escaped," Lukas affirmed, his voice flat. "Barely. But he got the data."

Kessler smiled, settling deeper into his leather chair. Through the window, Geneva's lights twinkled like scattered diamonds. "And did he see you?"

"Yes. I made sure of it."

"Excellent." Kessler's voice carried a warmth that would have chilled anyone who knew him well. "Fear is a resource, Lukas. We've just made a substantial deposit. They'll run harder now, make mistakes. Predictable mistakes."

"The London operation is still active. Ethan and the woman are moving on the secondary node."

"I know." Kessler swirled the whiskey in his glass, watching the amber liquid catch the light. "I'll oversee that one personally. It's time Ethan and I had a conversation about his father."

"And afterward?"

"Afterward, we'll let them think they've won something. Nothing motivates like false hope." Kessler's smile widened. "Everything is proceeding exactly as planned, Lukas. Every single piece is falling into place."

He ended the call and raised his glass to the city below—a silent toast to the prey who didn't yet know they were already caught.

52

Collision Course

Kessler — Private Diary (Zurich-0 Archive: Unclassified)
"I've prepared something exquisite for your arrival. Come Ethan and Sparrow...and let me savor the moment you realize you both were mine from the beginning."

London, England- 11:20 p.m. local time- Day 16
London's streets were gray and rainy, a perfect cloak for those who wanted to disappear. Mist rose from underground vents as rain hammered Victorian architecture that had witnessed centuries of secrets.

Ethan and Selin moved through Southwark simultaneously with Daniel's Zurich operation, keeping to side streets where CCTV coverage was older, grainier, less likely to feed into facial recognition systems. Noah coordinated both teams from his position in South America, his voice alternating between their encrypted channels with the precision of a conductor managing two orchestras.

"Daniel's made contact with the Zurich terminal," Noah reported. "You're clear for entry. Security rotation gives you a four-minute window."

The node they'd targeted—a Directorate financial hub embedded in a legitimate consulting firm near London Bridge—had taken weeks to identify. Nine stories of glass and steel, indistinguishable from dozens of similar corporate facades. Somewhere on the fourth floor, behind encrypted access panels and biometric locks, a server farm processed millions in illegal transactions daily.

They moved fast, bypassing security systems with the tools Noah had provided. Selin's fingers flew across keyboards while Ethan watched the corridors, his nerves alive with tension.

"Got it," Selin whispered. "European account structures, shell corporation networks—this should be everything we need."

A sound behind them. Not loud—just wrong. Ethan spun, weapon raised.

Kessler stood in the doorway, hands clasped behind his back, dressed in an impeccable charcoal suit. He was alone, unarmed, regarding them with the mild interest of a museum patron studying a moderately engaging exhibit.

"Please," Kessler remarked, his accent carrying traces of old European aristocracy. "Don't let me interrupt. You've come so far—it would be rude not to let you finish."

Ethan's finger tightened on the trigger. "One reason I shouldn't kill you right now."

"Several, actually." Kessler stepped further into the room, utterly unconcerned by the weapon pointed at his chest. "But the most compelling is that you have questions. About your father. About what he was. And I—" He smiled, the expression somehow both warm and reptilian. "—am the only one who can answer them."

Selin's hand found Ethan's arm. Warning. Caution.

"James Cole." Kessler spoke the name like savoring fine wine. "Your father and I were friends once; you did know that. Yes? Not colleagues. Not associates. *Friends.* We believed in the same things—order, stability, the careful management of chaos. He was brilliant, your father. Perhaps the finest operative I ever trained."

"You're lying."

"Am I?" Kessler tilted his head. "He taught you to scan rooms in sectors, yes? To read micro-expressions? To disappear in plain sight? Where do you think he learned those things?" He spread his hands. "From me.

From the Directorate. Your father was one of us for fifteen years before he developed... inconvenient scruples."

Ethan's grip on the weapon faltered slightly. He hated that it did.

Kessler's attention shifted to Selin. "And you, my dear. My little Sparrow." His smile widened. "Did you tell him? How I found you on the streets, starving, watching your family die? How I gave you purpose, training, a reason to live?"

"You made me a weapon," Selin contended, her voice steady despite the venom beneath it.

"I made you *magnificent.*" Kessler's eyes gleamed with something like paternal pride. "The skills you're using against me right now—I taught you. I sculpted you from grief and rage into something beautiful. And now you think you can simply walk away?" He chuckled softly. "You can't escape what you are. Neither of you can."

"We're leaving," Ethan contended. "And you're going to let us."

"Am I?" Kessler remained motionless. "Tell me, Ethan—do you believe you found that server room through skill? That your hacker friend—what was his name—Noah? —pieced together our security rotations through mere cleverness?" He shook his head slowly. "You're here because I allowed it. You've learned what I wanted you to learn. And now you'll run, and you'll think you've accomplished something, and that belief will make you predictable."

"Ethan," Selin murmured. "We need to go. Now."

Kessler stepped aside, gesturing toward the exit like a gracious host. "Please. The emergency stairs are unguarded. Your extraction vehicle is waiting three blocks north. I've ensured you'll have a clean escape." His eyes locked with Ethan's. "Consider it professional courtesy—one operative's son to another. We'll meet again, under less...cordial circumstances. But for now, run. It's what you're good at."

They ran. Through emergency stairs and side streets, into a waiting van that carried them into London's maze of traffic. Instincts honed over the last two weeks told Ethan it was too easy, that Kessler's words were poison designed to burrow into his mind.

But they had the data. They had proof. And they were alive.

In the safe house, Selin finally spoke. "He let us go."

"I know."

"Which means this is part of his plan."

Ethan stared at the flash drive in his hand—the tiny device they'd risked their lives for, everything that was supposed to bring Kessler down. "I know that too."

But what choice did they have? The trap was set, and they were already inside it.

Elsewhere-Lukas

An hour later, Kessler's phone rang. Lukas.

"They've gone to ground," Lukas reported. "Safe house in Brixton. Should I move?"

"No." Kessler stood at his window, watching the city lights. "Let them rest. Let them analyze the data. Let them think they're winning."

"And the hacker? Rivera?"

"Ah." Kessler's voice took on an edge of anticipation. "That's the next movement in our symphony. Cyber Division has triangulated his position. Buenos Aires, as we suspected. He's been coordinating both operations—Zurich and London—from a specific location. Arrogance. Youth. Our little architect thinks his digital walls make him untouchable."

"When do we take him?"

"Within the week. We'll take him alive if possible—I want to understand what he's built. But if not..." Kessler shrugged, a gesture of elegant indifference. "The message will still be delivered. They wanted to hurt us? Now they'll understand what that costs."

"Ethan and Selin will try to reach him."

"I'm counting on it." Kessler smiled into the darkness. "Everything is proceeding exactly as planned. The prey runs toward the trap, thinking it's sanctuary. By the time they realize their mistake, it will be far too late."

He ended the call and returned to his whiskey. Somewhere across the Atlantic, his people were already moving, converging on a young man who thought he could wage war on the Directorate with nothing but code and conviction.

They would learn. They always did.

53 ▍

Course Correction

Kessler — Private Diary (Zurich-0 Archive: Unclassified)

"Isn't it marvelous? I am furious with you all… and yet I worry terribly what comes next. Joy, anger, concern—such fascinating colors on the same canvas."

Unknown Location— Simultaneous with Zurich and London Operations- Day 16

Kessler's computer screen flickered to life—emergency alert, priority red, source: Cyber Division.

"AURORA breach detected. Directorate financial systems compromised. Estimated hemorrhage: $4.7 billion and accelerating. Countermeasures ineffective. Requesting authorization for extreme response."

Kessler leaned back in his chair, expression unchanged, reading the detailed analysis with the calm of someone who'd anticipated this exact scenario.

Noah Rivera—the ghost they'd been hunting for months—had finally revealed himself. Not by surfacing physically, but by attacking the one thing Kessler couldn't afford to lose: liquidity.

"Clever boy," Kessler murmured. "You learned patience from someone."

He opened a secure channel to his cyber warfare team—twelve of the world's most sophisticated hackers, all working from distributed locations, all bound to the Directorate through leverage that made loyalty irrelevant.

"Report," Kessler voiced.

A voice responded—young, Eastern European, frantic: "He's not just stealing money. He's redistributing it faster than we can trace. Each account we lock down generates seventeen new accounts automatically. The system is learning. It's becoming autonomous."

"Autonomous implies intelligence."

"Sir, I'm telling you—whatever Rivera built, it's not just code anymore. It's adapting to our countermeasures in real time. Our attempts to shut it down create new redundancies. When shut down a hundred nodes, two hundred more appear. It's exponential growth designed specifically to resist centralized control."

Kessler considered this, his mind running through scenarios, calculating probabilities, assessing options.

"Can you trace him?"

"We have seventeen possible locations across South America. He's routing through indigenous internet infrastructure—community mesh networks that don't appear on standard maps. Even if we identify the right location, he'll know we're coming before we arrive."

"And if we kill him?"

Silence on the line. Then: "The system might become completely autonomous. There's embedded code that suggests if his biometric signature stops pinging the network, it releases some kind of... I don't know what to call it. A logic bomb? A dead man's switch? Something that makes what we have seen so far look like a test run."

Kessler smiled—the expression of a grandmaster recognizing worthy opposition.

"Noah Rivera," he observed quietly, "lost a sister to our system. And he's built a sister in the code—something that will outlive him, continue his mission, achieve the revenge his death would prevent."

"Sir?"

"He's made himself irrelevant. That's brilliant. We can't threaten him because he's accepted death. We can't kill him because his creation survives him." Kessler stood, walked to his window. "This is what happens when you give a genius a cause worth dying for. You create something unkillable."

"What are your orders?"

Kessler considered. The financial hemorrhage was significant but not fatal. The Directorate had contingencies, offshore reserves, assets hidden so deep even AURORA couldn't find them. The money was recoverable.

But the precedent was dangerous. If one clever hacker could build a system that resisted their control, others would follow. The architecture of power they'd spent decades building could be undermined by code written in jungles and distributed through networks they couldn't police.

"Continue the hunt," Kessler dictated. "Capture if possible. I would very much like to meet this little architect who thinks he can outmaneuver us with algorithms and ideology."

"And if capture isn't possible?"

"Then we wait. He will make a mistake eventually. The patient hunter always wins."

He ended the call and returned to his chair, pulling up financial reports that showed the damage AURORA was inflicting. Billions redistributed to causes designed to undermine the system Kessler had built—transparency initiatives, investigative journalism, legal defense for whistleblowers.

Noah Rivera was funding the resistance. And doing it with Directorate money.

"You're making this personal," Kessler voiced to the screen. "That's your mistake. Ideology burns hot but brief. I've seen a hundred revolutionaries destroy themselves through passion. He will be no different."

But even as he articulated it, Kessler had feelings he hadn't experienced in decades: Anger, joy and concern combined.

Because Noah Rivera didn't fit the pattern. He wasn't motivated by glory, profit, or recognition. He was motivated by grief—the purest fuel, the hardest to extinguish.

And grief, when properly weaponized, could outlast any empire.

54 ▌

Counterpunch

Kessler — Private Diary (Zurich-0 Archive: Unclassified)
"Ah, there you are. I've found you, little architect. Now let's see how your algorithms handle reality."

Geneva Switzerland—Directorate Tactical Operations Center- 9:53 p.m. local time- Day 17

Screens covered the walls, displaying satellite feeds, communication intercepts, and thermal imaging from drones circling above the Argentine capital. Thirty operators worked in focused silence, each one a specialist in the machinery of modern man hunting.

Kessler stood at the center, hands clasped behind his back, watching the convergence unfold. He still had the look of polished granite—hardened and cold —despite all the recent travel. He told himself he would need some rest at the end of this. But for now, the game was afoot.

"Confirmation on target location," the lead analyst announced. "Palermo district, residential building, third floor. Heat signatures consistent with multiple occupants plus extensive electronic equipment. Power consumption patterns match sustained computing operations."

"Network analysis?" Kessler asked.

"He's routing through seventeen proxy servers across twelve countries, but we've identified his origin point through power grid fluctuation analysis. When he runs heavy computational loads, the local transformer registers a specific signature. We cross-referenced that with the timing of his attacks on our systems. Ninety-seven percent confidence."

Lukas stepped forward. "Strike team is in position. Twelve operators, two vehicles, full tactical load out. Building exits covered. Roof access blocked. Jamming equipment ready to deploy on your command—once activated, he loses all communication capability."

Kessler studied the overhead imagery. Noah Rivera—the ghost who had cost the Directorate billions, who had coordinated attacks on three continents, who had turned their own money into a weapon against them. A young man with a dead sister and a cause.

"What do we know about his AURORA system?" Kessler asked.

"Partially autonomous," Lukas replied. "If we kill him, embedded fail safes may trigger accelerated distribution of stolen assets. Our cyber team recommends capture—they want access to his servers before any dead-man switches activate."

"Capture, then." Kessler nodded slowly. "But if he resists to the point of elimination becoming necessary, I want those servers physically destroyed. Fire the building if you must. Whatever he's built cannot be allowed to persist beyond his death."

"Understood."

Kessler turned to address the room. "This boy has cost us four point seven billion dollars. He has funded journalists investigating our operations, lawyers defending those who would expose us, activists organizing against our interests. He took our money and weaponized it. That ends tonight."

The operators nodded, professionals all, uninterested in speeches but understanding the gravity.

"Ethan Cole and his people will try to warn him," Lukas noted. "They've been moving toward South America since London."

"I know." Kessler smiled. "Let them come. By the time they arrive, Noah Rivera will be in our custody—or dead—and they'll find nothing but ashes where their hope used to be. Sometimes the best trap is simply being faster than your prey."

"Timeline?"

"Seventy-two hours. We move during the blackout window—local power grid maintenance creates the perfect cover for our jamming operations." Kessler gestured toward the screens. "Coordinate with our assets in Argentine federal police. When we extract Rivera, I want official vehicles and documentation. This will look like a lawful arrest by local authorities investigating financial crimes."

"And if the Cole brothers and Sparrow arrive before we move?"

"Then we take them out too." Kessler's eyes hardened. "I've been patient with James's boys and Sparrow. Sentimental, even. That patience is exhausted. If they walks into Buenos Aires before we're finished, they do not walk out."

The operations center hummed with renewed intensity as final preparations began. Satellite feeds updated in real-time. Communication channels were established with ground teams. Extraction routes were confirmed, backup plans reviewed, contingencies addressed.

Kessler watched it all with the satisfaction of a chess expert seeing his endgame materialize. They had taken his money. They had exposed his operations. They had forced him to expend resources, attention, prestige.

Now came the counterpunch.

Buenos Aires, Argentina—10:15 p.m. local time

In his Palermo apartment, surrounded by humming servers and glowing screens, Noah worked through another sleepless night. AURORA's distribution algorithms were performing beyond expectations—another eight hundred million redirected in the past forty-eight hours, funding transparency organizations, investigative journalism, legal defense funds for whistleblowers across the globe.

He had coordinated Ethan and Daniel's operations flawlessly. Zurich was a success despite Lukas's appearance. London had yielded critical data. The noose around Kessler's empire was tightening.

So why did something feel wrong?

Noah paused, fingers hovering over his keyboard. His network monitoring showed nothing unusual—no intrusion attempts, no traffic anomalies, no signs of surveillance. But the silence itself was deliberate. Orchestrated.

He pulled up power grid data for his district. Normal. Communications traffic. Normal. Police frequencies. Normal.

Too normal.

He opened an encrypted channel to Ethan. "Where are you?"

A delay. Then: "En route. We can reach Buenos Aires in thirty-six hours. What's wrong?"

"I don't know yet." Noah stared at his screens, seeing patterns that might be paranoia or might be the shape of something closing around him. "But I think they're coming. I think they've found me."

"Then get out. Now."

"I can't." Noah's voice was steady. "AURORA requires my active management for just another twenty-four hours—after that, it becomes fully autonomous, impossible to shut down even if they take me. If I run now, they can stop what we've built."

"Noah—"

"Get here as fast as you can," Noah interrupted. "But if you can't reach me in time... make sure this wasn't for nothing. Lily would have wanted that. My sister died because people like Kessler treated human lives like resources to be managed. Whatever happens to me, don't let them win."

He ended the communication and returned to his work. The servers hummed. The algorithms executed. AURORA continued its quiet revolution, redistributing wealth from those who had stolen it to those who would fight against them.

Somewhere in the darkness beyond his walls, Kessler's people were gathering.

And the counterpunch was already in motion.

55

Falling Lines

"Noah, you're not alone anymore. Fight them, yes—but don't die for them. Live for something that's real."-Isabella

Buenos Aires, Argentina—Palermo District—8:14 a.m. local time- Day 17

Isabella's footsteps were barely audible on the hardwood as she entered the server room. Noah sat hunched over four monitors, his fingers moving across keyboards with practiced precision, coffee cup forgotten and cold beside him.

"How long have you been awake?" she asked, though she already knew the answer.

"Twenty-four hours. Maybe thirty. Noah didn't look up. "AURORA's hitting critical mass. The autonomous protocols are stabilizing faster than projected, but I need to monitor the final phase transition."

Isabella moved to stand behind him, her hands finding his shoulders. The tension there was like iron cable. "You're going to burn out."

"I'll sleep when it's done."

"Noah." She turned his chair, forcing him to face her. "Look at me. Actually look at me."

His eyes were bloodshot, pupils dilated from staring at screens. But he focused on her face, and she saw the exhaustion there—bone-deep, dangerous exhaustion that came from carrying too much for too long.

"I need you to listen," Isabella told him. "Really listen to me, not just process words while your mind is three steps ahead on code. Can you do that for me?"

Noah took a breath, nodded. "I'm listening."

"I was out this morning. The newsstand two blocks south—you know the one, the owner who always comments on my accent." She paused, making sure he was tracking. "There were men. Two of them. Not Argentine—Eastern European by the build and bearing. They were watching our building."

That got his attention. Noah straightened, the fog of exhaustion burning away under survival instinct. "You're certain?"

"I spent three years in Brazilian intelligence before I met you. I know surveillance when I see it." She kept her voice calm, measured. "They weren't making any effort to hide—which means either they're amateurs, or they don't care if we know they're there."

"Kessler." Noah was already moving, pulling up network monitoring tools, checking for intrusion attempts. "He found us."

"The question isn't if—it's when they move." Isabella crossed to the window, staying to the side, careful not to silhouette herself. "If they wanted you dead right now, you'd be dead. They're waiting for something."

"The complete AURORA deployment." Noah's hands stilled on the keyboard. "They want to take it down while they take me down. Maximum damage."

"Then we accelerate." Isabella moved back to him, crouching so they were eye level. "How long until AURORA is truly autonomous? Until it can function without you?"

"Originally? Seventy-two hours. But if I push the protocols, bypass all of the safety checks..." He was already calculating, his fingers twitching toward the keyboard. "Twelve hours. Maybe less."

"Then do it. And we leave tonight."

"Leave?" Noah shook his head. "Isabella, I have servers here. Hardware backups. Three years of work—"

"All of which means nothing if you're dead or in Directorate custody." She took his face in her hands. "Listen to me. Lily would want you alive. Your sister didn't die so you could martyr yourself for code. She died because Kessler's system treated her like a statistic. You've built something that can hurt him—truly hurt him. But only if you live long enough to deploy it."

Noah's eyes closed. When he opened them, there was something new there—not resignation, but clarity. "You're right."

"I know I am. Now—where can we go that they won't expect?"

"Uruguay." The answer came immediately. "Colonia del Sacramento—small city across the Rio de la Plata. We can take the fast ferry from Buenos Aires. It's an hour crossing, and the Uruguayan authorities are less...cooperative with international intelligence services."

"Can you transport AURORA?"

"It's designed for mobility. The core system lives in distributed cloud infrastructure, but I have portable servers for field management." He gestured to a rack of compact equipment. "Those plus my laptops—it all fits in two cases."

"Then here's what we do." Isabella straightened, her mind already tactical. "You have twelve hours to accelerate AURORA. I'll arrange the ferry tickets, secure a safe house in Uruguay, and prepare the burn protocol for this location."

"Burn protocol?"

"Everything they could use to track us or compromise AURORA—we destroy it before we leave. Thermite charges on the nonessential servers, degaussing magnets for the drives, accelerant for the paper records." She saw his expression. "Noah, if we're running, we run clean. No breadcrumbs."

He nodded slowly. "Okay. Okay, yes. Do it."

Isabella kissed him—quick, fierce. "Get to work. I'll manage the rest."

Twelve hours later, as afternoon sun slanted through the blinds, Noah typed the final command sequence. AURORA's status display cascaded green across all four monitors—autonomous functions active, self-replication protocols engaged, fail-safes operational.

"It's done," he mentioned quietly. "AURORA is fully independent. Even if they find all the servers I've personally managed, it will continue distributing funds, spawning new nodes, executing the mission."

Isabella appeared in the doorway, dressed for travel in dark jeans and a leather jacket. "The ferry leaves in three hours. I have tickets under Belgian passports—quality forgeries, should hold up to standard inspection. Safe house is arranged in Colonia. And..." She held up a small device. "Burn protocol is ready. Remote trigger once we're clear."

Noah stood, his legs protesting after hours of sitting. He moved to the server racks—three years of work, thousands of hours, hardware he'd carefully selected and configured. His hand rested on the closest server, feeling the warmth of processors executing his vision.

"It's just metal," Isabella told him gently. "The work lives in the code now. You don't need these anymore."

"I know. Still feels like leaving part of myself behind."

"You're not leaving it. You're letting it go." She moved beside him. "There's a difference."

Noah nodded, pulled his hand away. "Let's go."

They packed quickly—the two server cases, laptops, a single duffel of clothes and essentials. Everything else was expendable. Noah took one last look at the apartment, at the space where he'd built a weapon from grief and code, then followed Isabella into the hallway.

The surveillance team was still there when they left—Noah spotted them immediately now, two men in a gray sedan three cars down. They didn't move as Noah and Isabella walked toward the main avenue, didn't follow when they hailed a taxi.

"They're letting us go," Noah murmured.

"They think they know where we're going. Or they're waiting for reinforcements." Isabella kept her voice low. "Either way, we have a window. We use it."

The taxi dropped them four blocks from the ferry terminal. They walked the rest—careful, unhurried, just two more travelers in a city full of them. The terminal was busy with afternoon traffic, tourists and commuters mixing in the bright Argentine sun.

Their passports passed inspection without issue. The ferry officer barely glanced at them before stamping their entry. They boarded the Buquebus fast ferry—a massive catamaran capable of crossing the Rio de la Plata in under an hour.

Noah found seats near the stern, away from crowds. As the ferry pulled away from the terminal, he pulled out his encrypted phone and composed a message to Ethan:

"AURORA is now fully autonomous. Had to evacuate BA—Directorate found us. Heading to Uruguay (Colonia del Sacramento). Isabella with me. We're safe for now. Recommend you adjust route to Uruguay instead of Argentina. Will send coordinates for rendezvous once we're settled. Stay dark until then."

He hit the send button and watched Buenos Aires shrink behind them—the city where he'd built his resistance, where he'd turned loss into action. Now it was just skyline, growing smaller with distance.

Isabella took his hand. "Trigger the burn?"

Noah pulled out the remote device, looked at it for a long moment. Then pressed the button.

Somewhere across the water, in a third-floor apartment in Palermo, thermite charges ignited. The servers that had housed AURORA's early development would melt to slag. Paper records would flash to ash. The physical traces of his presence would become smoke and heat. One moment a shadow. The next, just a shimmer, and gone—dissolved into the silent, vast ether.

But AURORA lived. In distributed servers across forty-three countries, in redundant nodes spawning new nodes, in algorithms that would continue redistributing stolen wealth long after Noah was gone.

"It's done," he announced.

Isabella leaned against his shoulder. "New chapter."

"New chapter," Noah agreed, watching Uruguay's coastline emerge from the horizon.

Private Plane-Over the Atlantic-Simultaneous

Ethan's phone vibrated in his pocket. He'd been staring out the window of the private jet, watching clouds slide past at 41,000 feet, Selin asleep beside him with her head on his shoulder. The message was from Noah—encrypted, priority flag.

He read it twice, absorbing the implications. Then gently shifted Selin awake.

"What is it?" Her eyes were immediately alert—the gift and curse of operational conditioning.

"Noah. Kessler found him in Buenos Aires. He and Isabella evacuated to Uruguay." Ethan showed her the message. "We need to adjust our flight plan."

Selin read quickly, her tactical mind already processing. "Montevideo has better airport facilities than Colonia. We land there, rent a vehicle, drive to meet them. Less conspicuous than changing our filed destination mid-flight."

"Agreed." Ethan composed a response: *Adjusting to Uruguay. Will land in Montevideo in approximately six hours. Can reach Colonia within eight hours total. Confirm safe house coordinates when you're secure. We're coming.*

He sent the message, then opened a second channel—this one to Daniel. His brother would need to know the situation had changed.

Daniel—change of plans. Noah compromised in BA, relocated to Uruguay. Selin and I are adjusting route accordingly. Kessler's making moves—Europe was a stalemate, London was deliberate theater. He let us think we won. We need to regroup before the final push. Stay dark, stay mobile. Don't engage unless absolutely necessary. Will update when we're with Noah. How are things on your end?

The response came fifteen minutes later:

"Copy all. On my end—working with former Delta and contractor friends. Building operational framework for when we're ready to move on Kessler directly. These guys have the skills and motivation. Several have personal reasons to want the Directorate gone. But we're not ready yet. Need better intelligence on Kessler's security infrastructure, his personal patterns, his vulnerabilities. Can't just kick down doors—he'll have layers we haven't seen. Agree on regrouping. Take your time in Uruguay. Let the dust settle from Europe. We move when we're ready, not before. Stay safe, brother."

Ethan showed the message to Selin. "Daniel's being smart. Not rushing it."

"That's what Kessler wants—for us to rush, make mistakes." Selin leaned back in her seat. "We've hit him in Europe, taken his data, exposed vulnerabilities. Now we need time to synthesize what we've learned before we make the final move."

"You think there will be a final move? That this ends?"

"It has to. One way or another." She turned to look at him. "Either we take Kessler down, or he takes us down. There's no middle ground anymore. We've burned those bridges."

Ethan nodded slowly. She was right—they had crossed too many lines, stolen too much data, hurt the Directorate too badly. Kessler would never let them simply walk away.

"Then we use this time wisely." Ethan's voice dropped to almost a whisper. "Regroup in Uruguay, analyze what we've gathered, plan properly. No more reactive moves."

"Proactive hunter." Selin smiled slightly. "I like it."

They settled back into their seats as the jet carried them south. Below, the Atlantic stretched endlessly—dark blue water beneath scattered clouds. Somewhere ahead, Uruguay waited. Noah and Isabella. Sanctuary, temporary but real.

And after that—the reckoning.

Colonia del Sacramento, Uruguay—Three Days Later

The private plane touched down at Laguna del Sauce Airport outside Montevideo just as evening settled over Uruguay. Ethan and Selin moved through customs with their forged documents—Belgian passports that had cost Noah a sizable amount but were worth every euro spent on them.

They rented an SUV under a separate set of credentials and drove west toward Colonia. The highway was quiet, passing through countryside that reminded Ethan of California's wine country—rolling hills, scattered estancias, the occasional cluster of towns with colonial architecture.

"It's beautiful," Selin declared, watching the landscape slide past in the fading light. "I didn't expect it to be beautiful."

"South America isn't what most people imagine," Ethan replied. "Especially this part—it's almost European in places."

They reached Colonia after dark—a small city where colonial Portuguese and Spanish architecture created narrow cobblestone streets perfect for disappearing. Noah's coordinates led them to a house in the historic quarter, two stories of whitewashed walls behind a wooden gate.

Ethan parked a block away. They approached on foot, watching for surveillance, for anything out of pattern. The gate was unlocked—Noah's signal that they were expected.

The courtyard was small, tile floor surrounding a fountain that wasn't running. Light spilled from windows on the second floor. Ethan knocked—three quick raps, pause, two more. The pattern they'd agreed on.

The door opened. Noah stood there—thinner than Ethan remembered, dark circles under his eyes, but alive. Unmistakably alive.

"You made it," Noah stated with relief evident in his voice.

"So did you." Ethan pulled him into a quick embrace. "It's good to see you not dead."

"The bar is low, but I'll take it." Noah stepped back, gestured them inside. "Come on. Isabella made food—actual food, not the caffeine and anxiety I've been living on."

The interior was modest but comfortable. Isabella emerged from the kitchen—striking woman in her early thirties, dark hair pulled back, the bearing of someone who'd seen combat. She extended a hand to Selin first.

"Isabella Santos. Former Brazilian military intelligence, current keeper of this one's sanity." She nodded toward Noah. "Though it's a part-time job at best."

"Selin." The handshake was firm, assessing. Two professionals recognizing each other. "I know the feeling. Keeping Ethan alive has been challenging."

"I'm right here," Ethan protested.

"We know." Both women spoke it simultaneously, then shared a look of mutual understanding.

They gathered around a table in the dining area—simple meal of bread, cheese, grilled vegetables, and wine. The kind of food that tasted extraordinary after weeks of running.

"Tell me about Buenos Aires," Ethan added. "How did they find you?"

Noah swallowed a bite of bread. "Power grid analysis, best guess. Every time I ran heavy computational loads, it created a signature in the local transformer. They cross-referenced that with timing of AURORA's attacks on their systems. Eventually, pattern recognition did the rest."

"How close were they?"

"Surveillance team outside my building." Noah's jaw tightened. "They were waiting for something—probably reinforcements, or for me to lead them to other assets. We left before they moved."

"And AURORA?" Selin asked.

"Fully autonomous. Self-replicating, self-sustaining. Even if they find and destroy every server I personally managed, it will continue." Noah smiled grimly. "I built it to outlive me. That was always the point."

Isabella placed a hand on his arm. "And we burned the Buenos Aires location. Nothing left for them to find."

"Which means they think you gave them the slip," Ethan noted. "They don't know where you are now."

"For the moment. But Kessler's resources are extensive. We bought time, not safety." Noah leaned back. "What about you two? Daniel mentioned Europe was complicated."

Ethan and Selin exchanged a glance. Then Ethan spoke: "Zurich was a near miss—Daniel barely got out with the data. London was different. Kessler was there. In person."

Noah straightened. "He confronted you?"

"Talked to us. About my father, about how he trained Selin." Ethan's voice was carefully neutral. "He let us leave. And made it clear he was allowing it."

"Psychological warfare," Isabella declared immediately. "Make you doubt your victories, question your moves. Classic intelligence manipulation."

"It worked," Selin admitted. "We have the data from London—financial networks, shell corporations, everything we hoped for. But knowing he let us have it..."

"Makes you wonder what you're missing," Noah finished. "Yeah. That's the move. Give you information that looks damaging but is actually part of a larger trap."

"So, we're regrouping," Ethan affirmed. "Daniel's working with his military contacts—former Delta operators, contractors. Building a tactical framework for when we're ready to move directly on Kessler. But we're not rushing it. Not anymore."

"Smart." Noah nodded approvingly. "We hit him hard in Europe. AURORA's bleeding him financially. But we need to understand his response before we make the next move."

"That's why we're here." Selin poured more wine. "To analyze what we have, plan properly, and only move when we're ready to finish it."

Isabella raised her glass. "To regrouping. And to still being alive to do it."

They drank to that—four people who'd become unlikely allies, bound by shared enemies and the stubborn refusal to let those enemies win.

Later, after the meal, they stood on the second-floor balcony over-looking Colonia's colonial rooftops. The Rio de la Plata stretched dark beyond the city, separating them from Argentina—from Buenos Aires and the Directorate presence there.

"We gave them the slip," Noah muttered quietly. "At least for now."

"For now," Ethan agreed. "But they'll find us eventually. They always do."

"Then we make sure we're ready when they do." Selin's voice was steel wrapped in velvet. "No more running. No more reactive moves. We plan, we prepare, and we end this."

Isabella moved to stand beside Noah, her presence solid and reassuring. "Together."

"Together," the others echoed.

They stood there in the Uruguay night—four people against an empire, wounded but unbroken, planning their next move against an enemy who thought he controlled the world.

Kessler had let them think they'd escaped.

But they knew the truth now.

The real fight was just beginning, and at least they were not alone anymore.

56

Hunter's Hand

Kessler — Private Diary (Zurich-0 Archive: Unclassified Category RED)

"I don't enjoy hurting people. I enjoy understanding *them. And you, my friend, have so much to teach me."*

Brussels Belgium-Directorate Operations-6:37 a.m. local time-Day 18

No cameras and windowless, the interrogation room in the Brussels safehouse consisted of just concrete walls, a metal chair bolted to the floor, and Kessler standing over a man who'd made the mistake of helping Noah.

Philippe Ducasse had been a systems administrator for a Belgian hosting company, one of dozens Noah had recruited to run AURORA nodes. Unlike the others, Philippe had gotten greedy—tried to skim transaction fees.

Noah's algorithms had flagged him. Lukas had been waiting.

"You helped facilitate financial terrorism," Lukas pronounced, voice cold, unemotional. "That's twenty years in a Belgian prison. However..." He pulled up a chair. "I can make that go away."

Philippe's face was swollen, one eye nearly shut. "What do you want?"

"Noah Byrne's location."

"I don't know. We communicated through encrypted channels—"

Lukas raised one of Philippe's hands. The operative behind Philippe grabbed his left hand and broke his index finger with a practiced twist.

The scream echoed off the concrete.

"I need access to the communication protocols. The encryption keys. The network architecture." Kessler showed Philippe his phone—a photo of his wife and children entering their apartment building. "Your daughter. Montessori school in Ixelles. Very expensive."

The color drained from Philippe's face.

"You'll write down everything you know, all details if you please. Then you will help us create monitoring software that won't trigger Noah's safeguards." Kessler pocketed his phone. "Cooperate fully, and you get a new identity, new country, enough money to start over. Or refuse, and everyone you love learns what happens to obstacles."

Philippe broke. They always did.

Within four hours, The Directorate's cyber team had begun infiltrating three relay servers with invisible monitoring software.

"How long?" Lukas asked Sarah Park, his former NSA team lead.

"Forty-eight to seventy-two hours," she noted. "He's routing through seventeen countries, using quantum encryption. But all systems have patterns, his included."

"You have forty-eight hours." Lukas paused at the door. "If Noah Byrne goes dark before we locate him, I'll hold you personally responsible."

Madrid, Spain

Daniel Cole watched Viktor Sokolov return to his hotel at midnight. Russian national, former FSB, now part of Kessler's European network. Dangerous, professional—and predictable.

Daniel had been tracking him for three weeks, learning his patterns.

At 2 AM, Daniel entered through the service entrance—access card cloned, security cameras looped. He moved through the corridor with quiet efficiency, picked the lock in seventeen seconds.

Sokolov was asleep, weapon on the nightstand within reach. Almost within reach.

Daniel moved like smoke. One hand covered Sokolov's mouth. The other held the knife that opened the operative's throat in a single motion.

Sokolov's eyes opened wide with shock. He tried to fight, but the blood loss was catastrophic. Within ninety seconds, he stopped moving.

Daniel arranged the scene—robbery gone wrong, forced entry, valuables missing. Another violent crime in a city full of them.

One more operative removed from the board.

He left before dawn, texting Ethan: *Package delivered.*

The response came quickly: *Received.*

They were spread across continents, but they were still coordinated. Still family. Still fighting.

Daniel had identified twelve Directorate operatives across Europe and North Africa. Five were now dead. The other seven didn't know they were being hunted.

Kessler had declared war on the Cole family.

Daniel was simply winning it.

The night deepened, soft and blue. From far out at sea, the light from a passing freighter blinked once, then vanished into darkness.

But in the quiet corners of his mind, he knew the game wasn't over. It never was. Somewhere, Kessler would be watching. And waiting.

57

Vanishing Point

"Whatever comes next... we face it together. I'm done running. Time for payback."-Ethan Cole

José Ignacio, Uruguay—8:35 a.m. local time- Day 38

Gentle waves rolled in slow and even, brushing the shoreline. The small white stucco villa with weathered shutters looked like most of the other beach houses in José Ignacio—unremarkable, yet peaceful, a place where wealthy Argentines escaped Buenos Aires for long weekends. That was precisely the point.

Ethan stood barefoot on the sand, the wind off the South Atlantic cool against his face. Behind him, Selin moved through the kitchen preparing coffee. Noah and Isabella were still asleep in the guest room—the four of them had arrived in Colonia three weeks earlier and made their way here, to this small coastal village where the world seemed impossibly distant.

The encrypted phone buzzed in his pocket. Daniel. Ethan walked further down the beach before answering.

"You're up early," Daniel's voice carried across continents, clear despite the encryption.

"Couldn't sleep. You?"

"Still in Europe. Working." A pause. "I wanted to update you. The campaign continues."

Ethan knew what that meant—Daniel was still hunting Directorate operatives, systematically removing pieces from Kessler's board. "How many?"

"Seven confirmed. Three more pending verification. I'm working with some former Delta operators and contractors—people with their own reasons to want the Directorate gone. We're building something sustainable, not just reactive strikes."

"That's dangerous, Daniel."

"Of course it is dangerous. At least this moves us toward an endgame." Daniel's voice hardened slightly. "Kessler needs to understand that attacking our family has consequences. That we're not just running—we're hunting back."

"Tell me about the last one."

"Viktor Sokolov. Russian national, former FSB, operating out of Madrid. He was good—professional, cautious. But he had patterns." Daniel paused, and Ethan could hear distant traffic in the background. "I tracked him for three weeks. Learned his routines, safehouses, and habits. He always returned to the same hotel, took the same elevator, and ordered room service at the same time."

"How did you do it?"

"Service entrance, cloned access card, looped security footage. He was asleep when I entered—weapon on the nightstand, within reach. Almost within reach." Daniel's voice was flat, professional. "It was clean. Quick. I staged it to look like a robbery gone wrong—forced entry, valuables missing. Just another violent crime in a city full of them."

Ethan closed his eyes, feeling the weight of it. His brother—the man who'd taught him to fish, who'd protected him through childhood—describing murder with the detachment of a mechanic discussing an oil change. This was what their world had become.

"One more operative off the board," Daniel continued. "Kessler declared war on us. I'm just making sure he understands the cost."

"Be careful. He'll eventually figure out the pattern."

"Let him. I want him looking over his shoulder, wondering which of his people is next. Fear is a weapon too." Daniel's tone softened slightly. "How are you? How's Selin?"

"We're good. Safe for now. Noah and Isabella are here too—we're regrouping, analyzing what we've gathered. Planning the next phase."

"Which is?"

"Still working that out. But we can't run forever. Eventually, we need to force an endgame—something that either frees us or ends this permanently."

"I'm working on the same thing from this end. When you're ready, I have assets I can deploy. Skilled people who understand what we're up against." Daniel paused. "Dad would be proud, you know. Of both of us. He prepared us for this even if we didn't realize it."

Ethan's throat tightened. "Yeah. He did."

"Stay safe, little brother. Keep your head down until we're ready to move."

"You too."

The call ended. Ethan stood on the beach, watching waves break against the shore, thinking about his brother moving through European cities with a list of names and the cold patience of a professional killer. This was what Kessler had created—good people forced to become monsters just to survive.

He walked back to the house. Selin was on the porch now, two cups of coffee in hand. She handed him one without speaking, reading the weight in his expression.

"Daniel?" she asked.

"Seven confirmed kills. Still hunting." Ethan sipped the coffee, letting the warmth cut through the morning chill. "He's turning himself into what Kessler needs him to be—a threat too dangerous to ignore."

"That's the trap. Kessler wants us to become like him. Wants to prove that we're no different, that we will become corrupt when pushed hard enough."

"Maybe we're not different. Maybe we're all just people making choices in impossible situations." Ethan turned to face her. "Does it matter if we're good people doing bad things, or bad people who used to be good? The bodies pile up either way."

"It matters because we still ask the question. Kessler stopped asking decades ago." Selin moved closer, her voice gentle. "Daniel's killing Directorate operatives—people who've done terrible things, who would kill him without hesitation. That's not the same as what I did in Serbia. Those were innocents. There's a difference."

"Is there? Or is that just what we tell ourselves to sleep at night?"

"I don't know. But I know that you're still asking the question, which means you haven't crossed the line Kessler crossed. Neither has Daniel." She took his hand. "We're fighting a war we didn't start. That doesn't make us saints, but it doesn't make us monsters either."

Inside, they found Noah already awake, surrounded by laptops and portable servers. Isabella was making breakfast, moving through the kitchen with practiced efficiency.

"Morning," Noah announced without looking up. "AURORA processed another four hundred million overnight. Directorate accounts are hemorrhaging faster than they can staunch. At this rate, we'll have redistributed eight billion by month's end."

"Eight billion that's funding what?" Ethan asked.

"Investigative journalism networks. Legal defense funds for whistleblowers. Infrastructure for communities the system has abandoned. Basically—everything Kessler's network has corrupted or destroyed; we're rebuilding with his money." Noah finally looked up, his eyes red from screen time but alert. "It's poetic justice, if you believe in poetry."

"You don't?"

"I believe in math. Numbers don't lie. And the numbers say we're hurting them badly enough that they'll eventually have to respond with everything they've got." He turned back to his screens. "We bought time, not safety. Eventually, Kessler will find us. The question is whether we're ready when he does."

Isabella brought plates of scrambled eggs and toast to the table. "Then we use this time to prepare. Analyze what we've learned, identify vulnerabilities, plan our final move."

"Final move." Selin tasted the words. "You think there's an ending to this?"

"There has to be." Ethan sat down, accepting the food gratefully. "We can't run forever. At a point, we force a confrontation—either we take Kessler down completely, or we negotiate terms that let us disappear permanently. But this limbo can't last."

"Kessler doesn't negotiate." Noah's voice was flat. "I've studied him. He'd rather lose than admit weakness. Pride is his vulnerability, not pragmatism."

"Then we exploit the pride. Make it too expensive to keep hunting us. Force him to choose between his empire and his ego." Ethan met Noah's eyes. "What's the one thing he values more than revenge?"

Noah thought for a moment. "Control. He values control more than anything else. The Directorate isn't just his creation—it's his proof that he can impose order on chaos. If we threaten that fundamental control, if we make the system itself unstable enough that maintaining it costs more than abandoning us..."

"Then we have leverage." Isabella finished the thought. "Mutually assured destruction, but economic instead of nuclear. If he keeps hunting us, AURORA accelerates the wealth redistribution until the Directorate collapses. If he lets us go, he preserves what he can of his empire."

"You're assuming he thinks rationally," Selin warned. "Men like Kessler—they'd rather burn it all down than lose on someone else's terms."

"Then we make sure he doesn't realize he's losing until it's too late to stop it." Noah's fingers flew across the keyboard. "AURORA's beauty is its autonomy. Even if Kessler kills all of us tomorrow, the system continues. The dead man's switch I built ensures that our deaths accelerate the process—the Directorate secrets go public, their funds get redistributed, each network node spawns ten more. The only way Kessler wins is by letting us live."

They spent the day planning, analyzing, building scenarios. The flash drives from Zurich and London provided the financial architecture. Noah's AURORA system provided the weapon. Daniel's European campaign provided the distraction. Slowly, a strategy emerged—not perfect, but possible.

That evening, after Isabella and Noah had retired, Ethan and Selin took a long walk on the beach. The stars were brilliant here, away from city lights, the Milky Way a river of light overhead.

"Do you think we'll survive this?" Selin asked quietly.

"Honestly? I don't know. But I know that giving up isn't an option. And I know that whatever happens, I want to face it with you."

She stopped walking, turned to face him. "When this started—when you found me in that bank, when I was trying to decide whether to kill you—I never imagined this. That I could feel this way about someone. That love could be something other than leverage or manipulation."

"What did you imagine?"

"Survival. Alone. Until eventually someone faster or smarter or luckier ended it." Her voice was steady but weighted. "I never imagined a future worth living for. Never let myself want anything beyond the next mission."

Ethan pulled her close. "You deserve a future. We both do. And we're going to fight for it with every ounce of our being."

They kissed—long, deep, full of promise and desperation in equal measure. When they separated, Selin smiled.

"Tell me about it. The future. The one we're fighting for."

"Small university town. Somewhere quiet. I'm teaching economics—the real kind, not the sanitized version. You have that garden you talked about. We argue about tomato varieties and whether to plant basil or cilantro." He brushed hair from her face. "Normal. Boring. Safe."

"I'd like boring. I've had enough excitement for several lifetimes."

"Then that's what we'll have. After this is finished."

"Promise?"

"Promise."

They stood on the beach, holding each other, while waves broke against the shore and stars wheeled overhead. Four people hiding in a small Uruguayan village, planning to challenge an empire. The odds were terrible. The risks were absolute. But they had each other, and hope, and the stubborn refusal to let Kessler win.

Sometimes, that was enough.

Two weeks quickly passed. The rhythm of life in José Ignacio was deceptively peaceful—morning coffee, afternoon planning sessions, evening walks. Noah continued refining AURORA, building in redundancies and fail-safes. Isabella maintained their security, monitoring for any sign that the Directorate had found them. Ethan and Selin analyzed the financial data, mapping Kessler's empire with increasing precision.

Daniel sent periodic updates—another operative eliminated in Prague, surveillance networks disrupted in Berlin, Directorate safe houses compromised in Lyon. He was systematically dismantling Kessler's European infrastructure, forcing the man to divert resources toward defensive operations instead of hunting the Cole family.

But underneath the routine, tension built. They all knew this was temporary. The Directorate's resources were vast, and Kessler's patience was legendary. Eventually, he would find them. The only question was whether they'd be ready when he did.

One evening, as they gathered for dinner, Noah looked up from his laptop with an expression that stopped them dead in their tracks mid-conversation.

"We have a problem," he said quietly.

"What kind of problem?" Isabella asked, immediately alert.

"Someone's probing AURORA's outer defenses. Not a direct attack—more like reconnaissance. They're assessing response times, mapping network architecture, looking for vulnerabilities." Noah's fingers flew across the keyboard. "It's sophisticated. Government-level sophistication."

"Kessler?" Ethan moved to look over Noah's shoulder.

"Has to be. He's finally taking AURORA seriously—not just as an annoyance, but as an actual threat to the Directorate's existence." Noah pulled up network visualizations. "He's allocated serious resources to this. I count at least twelve different attack vectors being probed simultaneously. That's coordinated, professional cyber warfare."

"Can they break it?" Selin asked.

"Eventually? Maybe. AURORA's designed to be resilient, but no system is truly unbreakable. Given enough time and resources, they could find a way in." Noah's jaw tightened. "The question is whether they can do it before AURORA finishes redistributing the bulk of their stolen wealth."

"How long?" Isabella's voice was flat, tactical.

"At current rates? Four to six weeks before the critical threshold. After that, even if they shut down AURORA, the damage is permanent. But if they break through sooner..." Noah didn't finish the sentence. He didn't need to.

Ethan and Selin exchanged a look. The timeline had just compressed. Whatever endgame they were planning, it needed to happen soon.

"Then we must accelerate," Ethan vocalized. "No more waiting for perfect conditions. We move on Kessler before he moves on us."

"Agreed." Isabella was already standing, her mind clearly shifting into operational mode. "We reach out to Daniel, coordinate timing. Hit Kessler from multiple vectors simultaneously—financial, physical, and informational. Make it too chaotic for him to respond effectively."

Noah saved his work and closed the laptop. "I'll need forty-eight hours to fortify AURORA's defenses and accelerate the redistribution protocols. After that, we're as ready as we'll ever be."

"Two days," Selin announced. "Then we stop running and start fighting."

They stood in the small villa, four people who'd become unlikely allies, bound by shared enemies and the stubborn refusal to let those enemies win. Outside, the South Atlantic crashed against the shore, indifferent to human struggles. The stars wheeled overhead, eternal and cold.

But inside, something was building. Not hope exactly—hope was too fragile for what they faced. But determination. Purpose. The fierce will to survive that had carried them this far and would carry them through whatever came next.

Kessler had let them think they'd escaped.

Now they would show him what a mistake that was.

The endgame was beginning.

58

Throne of Ash

[CLASSIFIED: EYES ONLY – DIRECTORATE / NODE: UNKNOWN]

"Leadership is not consensus. The Directorate is not a council. Power consolidates; fragments perish."

—Excerpt from Kessler's Internal Address (Unverified Source)

Location Unknown — 3:22 a.m. local time- Day 39

Stone walls, soundproofed, lit by a single hanging bulb that swung gently with the draft from a broken vent— the room was built for silence.

The meeting table that had once seated eight of the world's most powerful people now held only five. Three chairs were empty.

Outside, through the cracked window slats, smoke rose over a distant skyline — the capital of a collapsed nation. The Directorate had done what it always did: destabilized, fractured, reassembled. A government had fallen overnight, its economy absorbed by Helios Defense Systems and its media networks rebranded within hours. The world called it "a humanitarian intervention."

Inside, the surviving members sat in silence, watching as Kessler poured himself a glass of water. No one else moved.

Martin Eberhardt, the new Helios CEO, kept his eyes fixed on the table. He had occupied this seat for only six weeks—ever since Konrad Voss had suffered his unfortunate "cardiac event" causing his early "retirement". But Eberhardt had heard the rumors and knew that Kessler had removed Konrad. Martin wasn't going to follow in Konrad's footsteps.

Martin Eberhardt understood, with crystalline clarity, that his predecessor's retirement had been permanent by design. So when Kessler's gaze swept the table, Eberhardt stayed quiet. He would not make Konrad's mistake of opening his mouth.

Heinrich Brauer, the German intelligence chief, was not so wise. He leaned forward, jaw tight with barely suppressed frustration. "This situation with Cole has gone on long enough. Our networks in South America report he's regrouped. The hacker—Noah Byrne—is bleeding our accounts dry. And yet we sit here, meeting in basements like fugitives?"

Kessler didn't look up. He sipped his water. Eyes fixed on the dark surface of the table. "Your networks," he added softly, "report what I allow them to report."

Brauer's face reddened. "I have served this organization for twenty-three years. Buried secrets that would collapse governments. I will not be dismissed like some junior analyst."

The room immediately went cold.

Kessler set down his glass with exquisite precision. When he spoke, his voice carried no anger—only the flat certainty of a man describing physics.

"Twenty-three years," he repeated. "Impressive. Tell me, Heinrich—do you remember the Brückner affair? 2011, I believe? A German intelligence official discovered irregularities in NATO funding channels. He prepared a report. He had evidence."

Brauer's confidence faltered. "That was... that situation was contained."

"Contained." Kessler smiled, but his eyes remained empty. "His car went off a bridge outside Munich. His wife received a generous pension. His children attended the finest schools, their education funded by a foundation that—if you traced its origins carefully enough—leads back to this table."

He stood, buttoning his coat, each movement deliberate.

"I built this structure from the shadows. I trained all the operatives, purchased every politician, replaced inconvenient truths with marketable lies. The Brückner affair. The São Paulo extraction. The journalist in Istanbul. The ambassador's daughter in Vienna." He paused, letting each reference land like a blade. "Shall I continue? I have excellent records. I keep them as insurance—against moments precisely like this one."

Brauer had gone pale. Across the table, Eberhardt studied his hands, grateful for his silence.

Kessler walked to the window and looked out over the burning city. The skyline flickered red against his reflection.

"You think this is a partnership," he remarked quietly, "but you were always contractors. And contractors can be terminated. Ask Konrad—."

He turned, his face unreadable in the half-light.

"Ethan Cole and the woman are my concern, not yours. The hacker will be de. These are operational matters, and I don't require your approval—I never have. The Directorate was a useful fiction, a mechanism to coordinate weak men who needed the comfort of consensus to act."

Brauer found his voice, though it emerged as barely a whisper. "We built this together."

"No." Kessler's voice was ice. "You administered what I created. There's a difference. One that Konrad learned too late, and one that you would be wise to remember."

He moved toward the door, then paused, looking back one final time.

"The Directorate isn't a council. It's a principle. And principles don't negotiate. They don't consult. They simply... are." His gaze swept the room, touching each face. "Serve the principle, and you'll continue to prosper. Challenge it, and you'll join the empty chairs."

He stepped out into the corridor, his silhouette vanishing into the half-light.

In the darkness behind him, the remaining members of the Directorate sat motionless, fearful to speak, afraid even to breathe too loudly. They had spent decades believing they controlled the narrative of power. Now they understood: they had always been characters in someone else's story, and Kessler had just closed their chapter.

Eberhardt looked at Brauer across the table. The German's hands were trembling. In that moment, the new Helios CEO made a silent vow: he would never, under any circumstances, give Kessler a reason to remember his name.

Behind them, the bulb flickered once... twice... then burst—an electric pop that shattered the stillness. Tiny filaments rained down, sizzling across the polished table before fading into silence.

No one moved. The remaining members sat in total darkness, their outlines swallowed by the black. For a heartbeat, only the sound of breathing filled the room—a room that, only moments before, had shaped the fate of continents.

Then, somewhere beyond the walls, a generator hummed to life.

A faint red emergency light seeped from the ceiling, bathing the table in a dull crimson glow. In that blood-colored light, the Directorate sat wordless, their faces half-lit and half-erased—like ghosts watching the world burn.

Power never dies; it simply changes the color of its light.

59

Line Cast Too Far

Kessler — Private Diary (Zurich-0 Archive: Unclassified Category RED)

"Loyalty is measured in moments, Konrad. You failed in the moment that mattered."

Montana — dawn breaking over the Madison River- Day 42

Mist clung to the water like breath over glass. The air was thin and clean, smelling of pine, silt, and cold steel. Konrad Voss moved through the shallows with the slow grace of habit, his fly rod bending slightly as he sent another perfect cast into the current.

He was a man who measured control in inches—control of wealth, of power, of people. The Directorate had made him one of the world's quiet kings.

But power, like water, always moved downstream.

On the ridge two miles away, **Kessler** lay prone on the cold ground, his body merged with the earth. The rifle was custom-built — carbon-fiber frame, titanium suppressor, the kind of weapon that existed only in whispers. He adjusted the scope, wind readouts flickering across a small HUD fixed to his wrist.

Distance: 1,642 yards
Breath: steady
Heart rate: 42bpm

Through the crosshairs, he watched Voss pause midstream, rolling his shoulders, calling something to his bodyguards on the bank. They laughed—three men with mirrored sunglasses and black tactical coats, oblivious to the small, silver glint far up the ridge.

Voss cast again, smiling faintly as the line arced against the morning light. That was the moment Kessler chose.

The rifle bucked once, barely more than a breath.

The round crossed the valley in silence — the sound reaching the guards nearly two seconds after impact. Voss jerked once, the fly rod slipping from his hands, the line drifting downstream. He folded into the water, ripples blooming red around him like scarlet red ink in snowmelt.

The guards shouted, drawing weapons, scanning the tree line, but there was nothing to see — no flash, no smoke, no trace. Only the river, whispering on.

Kessler lifted his head from the scope, watching the chaos below. A slow smile cut across his face — thin, surgical. He murmured to no one,

"You were useful once, Konrad."

He broke the rifle down with mechanical calm, his movements practiced, precise. Within minutes, he was gone — a shadow folding into the wilderness.

Far below, the bodyguards waded into the freezing water, dragging Voss's body toward the shore, shouting into radios that were already jammed. The trout still rose where the blood drifted, indifferent, feeding in the current.

By the time the first helicopter thundered over the ridgeline, Kessler's trail had vanished.

Only the empty ridge remained — and the echo of a single shot that had rewritten the chain of power.

[CLASSIFIED: OMEGA CLEARANCE – EYES ONLY / RECIPIENT: KESSLER, A.]
SUBJECT: FIELD INCIDENT — NODE 11-4 (MONTANA)

Directive Summary: Confirmed termination of **Konrad Voss** (Asset ID: HELIOS-ALPHA-07). Cause of death to be recorded as **"remote environmental accident"**—no further investigation to be authorized.

Financial and operational responsibilities of the deceased to be reassigned to interim shell entity Sable Meridian Holdings, effective immediately.

Addendum:

— Do not respond to inquiries from Directorate nodes regarding Voss's disappearance.

— Delete all audit trails connecting NODE 11-4 to existing Directorate funding chains.

— Proceed with stabilization measures as outlined under **Protocol Glass Veil.**

Final Note:

"He forgot who holds the line, and who cuts it."

— **Helios Central Command** (Signature omitted — issued under Kessler's own authority)

Kessler read the message from the glow of his encrypted tablet, the cabin of his private jet silent except for the low hum of the engines. The memo dissolved from the screen after ten seconds—self-erasing code leaving nothing but a faint afterimage in the reflection of the glass.

He sipped his espresso, eyes on the dark horizon beyond the window. Below, the Rockies rolled away beneath a sheet of silver cloud, the site of Konrad Voss's death already swallowed by distance and snow.

A faint smile tugged at the corner of his mouth. Another loose thread cut. Another lesson reinforced. Perhaps Heinrich Brauer would need to be next. He closed his eyes and murmured, barely audible over the engines,

"No one is untouchable."

Kessler's phone buzzed as the helicopter banked away from Montana. A message from his son: 'Voss termination confirmed in global feeds. Clean work.' Kessler smiled faintly. Lukas hadn't pulled the trigger—Kessler reserved certain kills for himself—but the boy was learning to appreciate craftsmanship. That was enough.

Then he set the cup down, leaned back in his seat, and opened a new encrypted file labeled:

COLE /PRIORITY RED.

The hunt continued.

60

Residuals

[CLASSIFIED: EYES ONLY – DIRECTORATE / NODE: GENEVA-9]

"The network has evolved. Assets decentralized. Oversight eliminated. Control is no longer hierarchical — it is algorithmic."

— Internal memo, recovered fragment (source unknown)

Geneva Switzerland— 9:35 a.m. local time-Three Weeks After the London Incident

The Directorate's headquarters looked peaceful from the outside—a modernist building near the UN complex, housing what official registries listed as "Helios Financial Advisory Group." Inside, the mood was anything but peaceful.

Kessler stood in the executive briefing room, studying damage reports with the detached curiosity of a surgeon examining failed sutures. Three nodes compromised in two months. Dozens of shell accounts had been frozen. Media inquiries began escalating despite their best containment efforts.

"They're coordinating," his chief of operations observed—a former Mossad analyst named Rachel Stein who'd been with the Directorate for fifteen years. "Cole, Yilmaz, and whoever's running their technical infrastructure. It's not random. They're targeting our most vulnerable points—hitting us where exposure creates cascade failures."

"How many people know the full architecture?" Kessler asked.

"Three. You, me, and Gerhard in Zurich. Everyone else knows only their section—compartmentalized for exactly this reason."

"Then we have an internal breach. Someone's teaching them our weaknesses." Kessler tapped the table, a rare sign of agitation. "Or they've reconstructed our network topology from external observation, which suggests intelligence capabilities beyond what we anticipated."

"What are your orders?"

Kessler looked out at Geneva's skyline—international organizations, humanitarian agencies, the architecture of global cooperation. All of it penetrated by his network, all of it corrupted just enough to serve the Directorate's interests without drawing attention.

"Accelerate Phase Three. If they're exposing our current infrastructure, we transition to the next generation. Begin transferring critical operations to AURORA-mirror protocols."

Rachel's face showed concern. "AURORA is their system. You want to copy it?"

"I want to devour it. By operating similar distributed protocols, we make their evidence worthless—just noise in a system we also use. Camouflage by imitation."

Geneva Switzerland— 9:03 a.m. local time

Like a ghost, the email hit the journalist's inbox —no sender. No traceable IP. Just an attachment labeled—

"Ledger_Reconstruction_v2."

He hesitated, hovering over the file. Some part of him — the part that still believed in causes — wanted to open it. The other part, the one that had seen too many friends silenced for curiosity, told him to delete it and forget.

Curiosity won.

He opened the file. What he saw didn't make sense at first — nodes, account strings, cryptographic hashes. Then it began to take shape.

A network — global, recursive, and alive. Billions moving in automated cycles across accounts that didn't exist, funding entities that weren't real. And at the top of the structure, one name flickered before the screen glitched and the system wiped itself clean.

HELIOS_DIR

The journalist leaned back, pulse racing. His name was Martin Graves, and he'd been investigating financial corruption for twelve years—long enough to know when he'd stumbled onto something genuinely dangerous versus the usual corporate malfeasance that resulted in fines and forgotten headlines.

This was different. This was systematic global infrastructure hidden in plain sight.

He took a breath, then called his editor on a landline—old-school paranoia born from watching too many sources disappear into legal threats or worse. The editor answered on the third ring.

"Helen, I need a meeting. In person. Not the office."

A pause. "That bad?"

"That important. There's a network—international financial coordination at a scale I've never seen documented. Money moving through automated systems that don't appear in any regulatory disclosure. I need legal review before we even think about publishing."

"Send me what you have. Encrypted."

"I can't. It wiped itself after displaying for thirty seconds. All I have are notes I took by hand." He looked down at his notebook—pages of scribbled node identifiers, transaction patterns, the name "HELIOS_DIR" underlined three times.

"Then bring the notebook. Tonight. There's a café near the cathedral—St. Pierre Brasserie. Nine o'clock."

Martin agreed, hung up, and immediately began photographing his notes with a camera that stored images locally, not in any cloud service. Professional paranoia, but he'd learned it the hard way.

Outside, the streetlights dimmed for half a second. Then the city's hum returned, seamless, indifferent.

Martin Graves never made it to his meeting.

The accident report filed with Geneva police described a tragic incident near Pont du Mont-Blanc—a journalist struck by a car that fled the scene. The driver was never identified. The security camera that should have captured the incident had malfunctioned twenty minutes before, its footage corrupted.

His notebook was found nearby, its pages water-damaged beyond recovery. His laptop contained nothing unusual—work files, personal emails, the digital souvenirs of an ordinary life.

The story was forgotten within a week, replaced by other news, other tragedies, the endless scroll of information that defined modern consciousness.

But in certain circles—encrypted forums, journalist networks, whistleblower communities—his death was noted with a different kind of attention. Another name on a list that grew slowly but steadily: people who'd looked too closely at financial networks they weren't meant to see.

Helen Chen, Martin's editor, attended the funeral with quiet fury. She'd received his call, understood its significance, and now held the weight of his final investigation—or would have, if his notes hadn't been destroyed.

She returned to her office, opened a file labeled "Potential Corruption Networks," and added a single entry:

HELIOS_DIR - Geneva origin - Martin Graves (deceased) - investigation suspended pending further evidence.

The network had survived another threat. The ghost remained a ghost.

But ghosts, Helen knew, had a way of haunting the guilty until truth became unavoidable.

61

Evolution

[CLASSIFIED: EYES ONLY – DIRECTORATE / NODE: GLOBAL-0]

"Containment achieved. Collateral damage acceptable. Adjust the narrative: the system endures."

—Final Transmission, Directorate Oversight Server (Decommissioned)

Caucasus Mountains— Time Unknown

Snow drifted in soft waves over the mountains, a pale silence stretching for miles. Inside a glass-walled chalet, a fire burned low, casting orange light across the polished stone floor.

Kessler sat in an armchair, dressed in black, watching the flames reflect off the window. On the television, muted news footage showed economic unrest — protests in Berlin, a failed vote in Brussels, a sudden collapse in digital currency markets.

The anchor's voice was calm, rehearsed, detached. Kessler smiled faintly.

A man approached from the shadows — one of the few remaining aides. "Sir, the reconstruction protocols are live. The Directorate's assets have been fully integrated into the Helios AI directive."

Kessler didn't turn his head. "Good. Let the world think the Directorate is gone. That's how we survive now — as code, not council."

The aide hesitated. "And the Cole file?"

Kessler's eyes remained on the fire.

"Let it rest."

He took a sip of black coffee, savoring it like an old ritual. "He'll resurface when he needs to. They always do."

The aide nodded and left. Kessler watched the door close, then looked out the window again — the mountains ghostly in the half-light.

For a moment, the fire flickered against the glass, and his reflection split in two — half man, half flame. He smiled once more, the expression not quite human.

Control wasn't lost. It had simply evolved.

José Ignacio, Uruguay — Dawn

The sea breathed softly against the sand. Ethan stood barefoot near the waterline, the wind tugging at his shirt, the horizon a bruised line between gray sky and darker ocean. Beside him, Selin sipped coffee from a tin cup, her hair loose, her expression unreadable.

They didn't talk much anymore. Words were too small after what they had seen and been through together.

A flock of gulls cut low over the surf, scattering as the first sunlight touched the waves. Somewhere inland, a dog barked once — distant, almost unreal.

Selin glanced at Ethan. "You ever think about going back?"

He shook his head. "There's nothing left to go back to."

She nodded, staring at the horizon. "The world forgets fast."

Ethan looked down at the wet sand between his toes. "Maybe that's the point."

The wind shifted. He turned toward the ocean again — just in time to see a faint glimmer far out over the water. It caught the sun for an instant, then vanished — too high, too straight, too steady.

Selin followed his gaze. "What is it?"

"Probably nothing," Ethan voiced quietly.

But he kept watching the horizon until the light was gone.

He slipped a hand into his pocket, feeling the smooth edges of the old flash drive — worn, dented, still there. Whatever the Directorate had become, it wasn't finished.

Neither was he.

Selin reached for his hand. "Come on. The tide's turning."

They walked together along the shoreline, their footprints fading behind them as the waves crept in, erasing every trace.

High above, for just a moment, a single drone hovered against the rising sun — silent, glinting like a watchful eye —then turned and disappeared into the sky.

62

Pieces On The Board

Kessler — Private Diary (Zurich-0 Archive: Unclassified Category RED)

"The Coles, the Little Architect and my lovely Sparrow think they're running. Let them. A war is easiest to win when your enemy flees straight into your design."

José Ignacio, Uruguay- Dawn-Day 52

Ethan stood on the beach at dawn, watching the sun paint the Atlantic in shades of gold and blood. Beside him, Selin was silent, her presence steady—an anchor in chaos.

"We can't stay here forever," she came out with finally.

"I know."

"Kessler will eventually find us. Or he'll force us out by taking someone we love."

Ethan thought of Daniel, somewhere in Eastern Europe, planning something reckless. He thought of Noah, hidden in jungles, building weapons from code. He thought of his father.

All of them fragments of a family scattered across continents, held together only by shared enemies and the stubborn refusal to quit.

"Then we move first," Ethan responded. "We stop reacting and start attacking."

"How?"

He pulled the flash drive from his pocket—the one that had started it all, still containing proof of Kessler's network. "We've been treating this like evidence. Like something for courts and regulators. But you said it yourself—those systems are compromised. Kessler owns them."

"So what do we do?"

"We make it personal. We don't expose the Directorate. We expose Kessler. His history, his crimes, his family. We make him the story. And we do it so publicly, so thoroughly, that even his protection can't save him."

Selin considered this. "That's a declaration of war."

"We've been at war. We just didn't know it." Ethan turned to face her. "He took out my father. He's hunting my brother. He corrupted you, turned you into a weapon, then tried to use that weapon against us. This isn't about the Directorate anymore. It's about him."

She nodded slowly. "Then we'll need Noah's network. And Daniel's operational capability. And every shred of leverage we've accumulated."

"And we'll need to be willing to lose everything that matters."

"I lost that a long time ago," Selin whispered quietly. "What I've found with you—that's just borrowed time. I'm okay with spending it on something that matters."

Ethan pulled her close, feeling her heartbeat against his chest, steady and strong.

"I love you," he professed. The words surprised him—not because they weren't true, but because he had avoided saying them, as if speaking the words made them vulnerable.

"I love you too," she replied. "Which is why we're going to survive this. Both of us. Together."

They stood like that as the sun rose fully, painting their shadows long across the sand.

José Ignacio, Uruguay- 10:15 a.m. local time

Noah woke up to messages—dozens of them, flooding through encrypted channels. AURORA had crossed another threshold: three million active wallets. One billion dollars redistributed. Fifty-three countries.

And a new message type: **requests for help**.

Journalists asking for funding to investigate corruption. Activists requesting security for protests. Refugees requesting money for passage to safety. Medical researchers requesting grants for treatments pharmaceutical companies had abandoned.

AURORA had become what Noah had dreamed: not just a weapon against the Directorate, but an alternative to it.

A system that said yes and gave voice to the powerless that the old system had determined were worthless.

He opened his laptop, began processing requests with the methodical precision of someone who understood that each and every dollar saved a life Lily hadn't gotten to live.

By noon, he'd approved forty-seven grants totaling $8.3 million. All of it stolen from Directorate accounts. All of it redistributed to causes that would make Kessler's control harder to maintain.

"You taught me the system was rigged," Noah whispered to Lily's photograph. "So I built a new one. And it's winning."

His phone buzzed—Ethan:

"Need your help for an endgame. Can you route financial data through mainstream media simultaneously? Make it impossible to suppress?"

Noah smiled. **"I've been preparing for that exact scenario. When?"**

"Soon. Days, not weeks. Be ready."

"Always am."

Noah closed the chat and returned to his code. The final piece of AURORA—the one he'd been holding back—was ready for deployment.

It wasn't just a currency network anymore. It was a transparency protocol. The sinister transactions Kessler's network had made in the past, the shell companies created, the payoffs—all of them mapped, documented, ready to be released simultaneously to every major news organization in the world.

The kill shot. The revelation that would either end Kessler's empire or get everyone Noah loved killed in the attempt.

"We're going to try," he voiced to the empty room. "That's all we can do. Try, and hope it's enough."

Vienna, Austria- simultaneous

Lukas Reinhardt stood in his apartment, looking at photographs of him and Ethan he shouldn't have kept. Pictures at Princeton. Him and Ethan on Cho Oyu. Him and Ethan with Daniel and Uncle James at the North Carolina cabin, all of them grinning like family.

He'd been ordered to destroy these. Attachments were liabilities. Memories were weaknesses.

But he kept them anyway. Hidden. Protected. The last evidence that he had once been someone other than what his father had made him.

His phone rang. Father.

"Status?"

"Facility preparations complete, Father. All defensive positions reinforced. Counter-assault protocols active. When the Cole brothers come, we'll be ready."

"Good. And your psychological preparation?"

Lukas paused. "Sir?"

"You'll be facing your friend. The boy you didn't kill on the mountain. The brother you chose over duty. Can you complete the mission this time?"

Lukas looked at the photographs, at Ethan's unguarded smile, at the version of himself that had believed friendship was real.

"Yes," he declared. "I can, Father."

"Are you certain? Hesitation has cost us materially. I won't tolerate—"

"I'm certain, Father." Lukas's voice was steady, controlled, empty. "Ethan Cole is a variable that needs elimination. When he arrives, I'll handle it."

Silence on the line. Then: "You've finally understood. Sentiment is weakness. Survival requires sacrifice. Your mother never learned that lesson. You have."

"Yes, Father."

"Then I'll see you in the Caucasus. Prepare for war."

The call ended.

Lukas stood alone, photographs scattered across his desk, and understood with absolute clarity that he had become exactly what his father intended: a weapon without conscience, a ghost without soul.

The boy who'd cried at his mother's funeral was dead. The teenager who'd wanted to belong to the Cole family was erased. What remained was what Kessler had always been building: a perfect instrument of control.

He gathered the photographs, walked to the fireplace, and watched them burn.

Each image curling black, each memory dissolving into ash, each piece of his humanity sacrificed to the same altar his father had been worshipping for thirty years.

When the last photograph burned to nothing but ashes, there was no relief. No regret. No emotion at all.

Just the cold certainty that he knew his role in what was coming.

And when Ethan arrived—when the friend he'd saved once came looking for his father—Lukas would finally prove that loyalty to the Directorate transcended all else, even the memory of brotherhood.

He was ready.

They all were.

The pieces were on the board. The endgame was approaching.

And whoever survived would determine whether the world continued under Kessler's control, or whether the resistance Ethan, Selin,

Daniel and Noah represented could actually fracture an empire that had existed for decades.

63

Signals In The Dust

"If Kessler wanted fear, he miscalculated. All he did was give me a reason not to run."-Ethan

"Kessler just made his last mistake.No one takes Ethan's family and walks away."-Selin

"Gear up. We're getting him back—and Kessler's not walking away."-Daniel

"Kessler thinks he owns the board. Fine. I'll rewrite the game."-Noah

José Ignacio, Uruguay- 3:45 a.m.- Day 54

Silver and glassy, the sea at José Ignacio was calm that night —almost too still. Ethan stood on the villa terrace, watching the Atlantic's dark expanse, thinking about the patterns he'd been tracking. Argentina's coup. The news blackouts. The orchestrated chaos that bore Kessler's signature.

From his faculty office window during the day, he could see the sun rise over these same waters, painting the whitewashed university buildings in fragile light. He had grown used to the rhythm of lectures, the quiet conversations with students who believed the world could still be reasoned with. It was almost peaceful.

Selin emerged from the bedroom, drawn by his absence. She carried herself with the same controlled poise that once helped her disappear across continents, now wrapped in the veneer of a consultant's calm. She was working security logistics for a local wine distributor—a company with enough global reach to keep her busy, and anonymous enough to keep her hidden.

"Can't sleep?" she asked, joining him on the terrace. Ethan shook his head. "Been checking the news. Argentina. Military coup. Government dissolved overnight." Her expression hardened. "The Directorate?"

Before Ethan could respond, his phone buzzed. 3:47 a.m.

No number. Just an incoming call from a number that shouldn't exist—a satellite relay routing through encryption protocols only three people in the world knew how to use. Protocols his father had taught him during childhood camping trips, the ones James had made him memorize "just in case."

Against his instincts, Ethan answered.

Static. Breathing. Then:

"Ethan."

His heart stopped. The voice was rough, distorted by poor connection and months of disuse, but unmistakably his father's.

"Dad?"

"Don't—" The line cut to static, then fragments came through: "—trap. Don't come—" More static. "Grid... forty-two point seven... forty-four point eight..." Static again. "—loves you—"

The call died.

Ethan stared at the phone, his hands shaking so violently he almost dropped it. For six months he'd carried the weight of his father's death—the burned cabin, the body Daniel had found, the funeral where they'd buried someone they couldn't properly identify.

Selin came to his side instantly, reading his expression. "What is it?"

"He's alive." Ethan's voice cracked. "My father. He's alive. Kessler has him."

"Are you certain?"

"That was his voice." Ethan's fingers fumbled with the phone, pulling up the call recording. "He gave coordinates. Grid reference forty-two point seven north, forty-four point eight east. That's Caucasus region."

Selin took the phone, listened to the recording, her expression hardening with each replay. "The call quality is degraded. Could be manipulated—"

"It's him." Ethan's voice carried absolute certainty. "The encryption protocol, the way he phrased it, the grid reference format—that's military standard he taught me when I was twelve. No one else knows that."

His encrypted line buzzed. Message from Daniel, sent via a routing chain that took thirty seconds to decrypt:

"I heard the same call. It was broadcast on multiple frequencies—they wanted us both to receive it. Satellite confirmation: thermal signature consistent with single male, 60-70 years old, holding facility. Guard rotation every 8 hours. Three weak points identified. Extraction viable if we move fast but smart. Waiting on your signal. — D"

Below the message, an attachment: a grainy satellite photo. A lone figure in a concrete yard, walking in a tight circle—the kind of movement pattern James Cole had drilled into both his sons for maintaining muscle mass during captivity.

Ethan stared at the tiny figure—a few pixels representing his father, alive, waiting.

Selin studied the image over his shoulder. "That's him?"

"Yes it is." Ethan's voice was hollow, fighting between hope and terror. "The body at the cabin—"

"Was someone else. Or staged." Selin's mind was already working tactically. "Kessler let us believe your father was dead. Six months of grief, of lowering our guard, and thinking the threat to us was over. And now he reveals the truth."

"It's bait," Ethan insisted.

"Of course it's bait." Selin moved to the window, scanning the street below for threats. "But that doesn't make it false. Your father is alive. Kessler has him. And this call—giving you just enough information to locate him but not enough to plan properly—it's designed to make you rush in unprepared."

Ethan looked at the coordinates again, at the satellite image of his father walking circles in a prison yard. Six months. His father had survived six months in Kessler's custody, waiting for rescue, possibly believing his sons thought he was dead.

His encrypted phone buzzed again. This time, a text message from an unknown number:

"You took something that doesn't belong to you. Now I have something that does. Your father is my guest. Comfortable, considering. How long he remains that way depends on your choices. Bring the data. Come alone. Or watch him die the way your compliance officer friend died, the way your bank CEO died, the way any fool who attempts to touch my network dies. You have six weeks to decide. The clock is running. — K"

Ethan read it twice, feeling the trap's mechanics click into place with awful clarity. Kessler wasn't demanding immediate exchange. He was giving them time—time to plan, time to prepare, time to build hope.

Which meant the trap was more sophisticated than simple ambush. Kessler wanted them to arrive prepared, confident, believing they'd outsmarted him. That's when he'd spring whatever he'd actually built.

"What now?" Selin asked.

Ethan stared toward the south, where storm clouds gathered over the horizon. His father's voice echoed in his memory: Don't come... trap...

James Cole, even in captivity, even after six months, still trying to protect his sons. Still warning them away even as he gave them the information they'd need to attempt rescue.

"We plan," Ethan responded after a long pause. "We coordinate with Daniel and Noah. We build a strategy that accounts for Kessler anticipating what we might do. And then we go get him."

"That's suicide."

"Probably." Ethan met her eyes. "But he's my father. And I had been living with the guilt of not being there when he died—except he didn't die. He was taken. And I'm not leaving him in that cell one day longer than necessary."

Selin nodded slowly. "Then we do it smart. We gather intelligence. We identify Kessler's assumptions about how we will operate and we violate every one of them. We make him think he's got us figured out, then we do something he can't anticipate."

"How long?"

"A year, maybe less if we're building a proper operation." She pulled out her laptop, began pulling up maps and satellite imagery. "I know people in Georgia. Former operatives who owe me favors. We can stage from Tbilisi, gather equipment, coordinate with Daniel's tactical planning."

Ethan's phone buzzed one final time. Voice message from Kessler himself, the tone almost paternal:

"You've had your rest, Ethan. Now it's time to come home. Your father is waiting. I'm waiting. Let's finish what we started thirty years ago, shall we? See you soon."

The message ended.

Ethan stood on the villa terrace as dawn broke over the Atlantic, his father's voice playing on loop in his mind: Don't come... trap... loves you...

James Cole had survived six months in hell to give his sons those fragments of information. Coordinates. Warning. Love.

Now it was Ethan's turn to do what his father had always taught him: count the exits, make the plan, and never leave your people behind.

"We're coming, Dad," Ethan whispered to the rising sun. "Just hold on a little longer. We're coming."

Selin appeared beside him, placed a hand on his shoulder. "Then we bring him home."

"Yes," Ethan vocalized, his voice steady despite everything. "We bring him home. Or we die trying."

Outside, the ocean continued its eternal rhythm, indifferent to human drama. Inside, Ethan Cole sensed something he hadn't been able to pinpoint since this all began: purpose.

Dangerous. Likely fatal. But real.

And sometimes, purpose was the only weapon that mattered.

64

Epilogue—Still Breathing

Kessler — Private Diary (Zurich-0 Archive: Unclassified Category RED)

"The Cole brothers and my lovely Sparrow believe they are coming to rescue James Cole. How charming. They are merely arriving for their education. The lesson is elementary: love is the finest weapon ever forged. It makes people reckless... obedient. And I take such weapons the moment they become useful. When this concludes—do remember my old friends: Every move you cherished as your own... was mine first. Even your triumphs are footprints I allowed you to make. I welcome you all. Class begins soon."

PART ONE: THE PRISONER

Undisclosed Location, Caucasus Region — 3:00 a.m. local time

No windows, no clock, just the fluorescent hum that marked time in headaches instead of hours. The prison cell was concrete and silence.

James Cole sat on the edge of his steel cot, studying the guard rotation pattern he'd memorized over six months of captivity. 0600 hours: shift change. 1400 hours: second shift. 2200 hours: night rotation. Every eight hours, precise as clockwork.

And at 0300 hours—the dead zone between night shift settling in and dawn breaking—there was a thirty-seven-second gap in the corridor camera coverage when the guards changed position.

Thirty-seven seconds. Not enough to escape. But enough to make a call.

His beard had grown wild; gray threaded through with white. He guessed that he'd lost around thirty or so pounds.. But his mind stayed sharp. And sharp was what mattered.

Three weeks ago, they'd made a mistake. During a medical check—routine, ensuring their valuable prisoner didn't die of malnutrition or infection—a guard had left a satellite phone on the medical cart. Just for a moment. Just long enough.

James had palmed it, tucked it into his boot, and waited.

For three weeks, he'd waited for the right moment. The moment when Kessler's attention was elsewhere, when the facility's rhythm was predictable, when the call would get through before anyone noticed.

Tonight was that moment.

At 0300 hours, James heard the guard footsteps recede down the corridor. He counted seconds—one, two, three—until he heard the distinctive click of the far door opening. The blind spot. Thirty-seven seconds.

He pulled the phone from where he'd hidden it behind a loose section of concrete, powered it on, and dialed the number he'd memorized decades ago—the emergency protocol he'd taught both his sons, never imagining he'd actually need it.

The line connected. Routing through satellite relays, bouncing across continents, encrypted through protocols only someone with his training would recognize.

It rang once. Twice. Then Ethan's voice, confused, half-asleep: "Hello?"

James Cole noticed his throat had begun to tighten. Six months of silence, of isolation, and wondering if his sons even knew to look for him. And now, hearing his younger son's voice...

"Ethan." His own voice came out rough, damaged from disuse.

A sharp intake of breath on the other end. "Dad?"

James spoke quickly, knowing he had twenty seconds before the gap closed: "Don't—" He forced the words out. "—trap. Don't come without—"

The guard's footsteps returning, faster than expected. James dropped his voice to barely a whisper: "Grid forty-two point seven north, forty-four point eight east. Caucasus. Guard rotation eight hours. Three weak points identified in—"

A hand grabbed his shoulder. The guard, returned early, face twisted in fury.

James kept talking, the phone pressed tight to his ear even as the guard yanked him backward: "—loves you—"

The guard ripped the phone away, slammed it against the concrete floor. It shattered into pieces.

But the call had lasted twenty-three seconds. Long enough.

"What have you done?" the guard shouted in Russian, his weapon drawn.

James Cole smiled despite the gun in his face, despite knowing he'd just bought himself a beating or worse. "I told my sons where to find me. And those boys—they don't leave family behind."

The guard struck him across the face with the pistol grip. He tasted blood, felt his cheek split open.

"Kessler will hear of this!"

"Good." James Cole spat blood onto the concrete floor. "Tell him the Cole family is coming. Tell him thirty years of running is over. Tell him I'm ready to finish what we started."

The guard dragged him from the cell, down the corridor, toward the interrogation room where Kessler would want to know exactly what had been verbalized, exactly what intelligence had been compromised.

But James didn't care. The call had gotten through. His sons knew he was alive. The coordinates had been transmitted.

After six months of captivity, believing his sons thought he was dead, James Cole had finally sent the signal that mattered: I'm alive. I'm here. Come find me.

Everything else—the beatings, the interrogations, whatever Kessler would do in response—was just noise.

His sons were coming. And when they did, Kessler would learn the same lesson James had tried to teach him thirty years ago:

You don't trap the Cole family. You just make them angry.

Interrogation Room — Thirty Minutes Later

The door opened. Kessler entered, carrying two cups of coffee as if this were a social visit rather than an interrogation.

"Kenyan roast." Kessler set one on the table in front of James. "I remembered you preferred it."

James Cole, now shackled to a steel chair, his face still bleeding from the guard's pistol-whipping, sat silent.

Kessler sat across from him, sipping his own coffee. The silence stretched—comfortable for him, suffocating for most men. But James had learned silence from the same teachers Kessler had.

Finally, Kessler spoke. "That was clever. Stealing a phone, waiting for the perfect moment, managing to transmit coordinates before being stopped. Very professional. I'm almost impressed."

"Almost?"

"Except it accomplished exactly what I wanted." Kessler's smile was cold. "Did you think that guard leaving his phone was an accident? That the camera gap in the corridor was an oversight? James, I've been waiting for you to make that call for three weeks."

The words hit like ice water. James Cole kept his expression neutral, but his mind raced through the implications.

"You wanted me to contact them," James Cole uttered slowly.

"Of course. How else would they know where to find you? I could have sent the message myself, but it would lack... authenticity. Better to let you do it. Let them hear your voice, hear the desperation, the warning. It makes them more likely to come, more likely to believe they're outsmarting me."

"It's a trap."

"Everything is a trap, James. The question is whether your sons are smart enough to see it coming." Kessler leaned forward. "Your son Ethan found my network. Traced billions in transactions designed to manage global instability. He thinks I'm a villain. But what he doesn't understand is that instability is the natural state. I don't create it—I channel it."

"That's what every tyrant tells himself."

"And that's what every idealist tells himself before reality educates him." Kessler stood, walked to the small window. "Your sons are coming, James. Ethan and Daniel both. They think they can rescue you. They think love conquers systems."

"It does."

"Then why are you in a cell, and I'm not?"

James smiled through the blood on his face. "Because you're too afraid to kill me. You need me alive as bait. That means you're not in control. You're desperate."

Kessler's jaw tightened. "I'm patient. There's a difference."

"Keep telling yourself that." James leaned forward as much as his restraints allowed. "My sons are better than you. Smarter. Faster. They're not corrupted by power because they never wanted it. And when they come—when they tear down everything you built—I'll be here to watch you realize you lost to men who still believe in honor."

Kessler studied him for a long moment. Then he stood, collected his coffee cup, and walked to the door.

"We'll see," he stated quietly. "We'll see if honor survives what I have planned."

The door sealed shut.

James sat alone in the interrogation room, blood drying on his face, wrists raw from the shackles. But he smiled anyway.

The call had gotten through. Even if Kessler had orchestrated the opportunity, even if it was all part of a larger trap, the fundamental truth remained:

His sons knew he was alive.

And captured men could be rescued.

James closed his eyes and began counting guard rotations, mapping the facility by sound, preparing for the moment when rescue became possible.

"Come find me, boys," he whispered. "I'll be ready."

And when they came, Andreas Kessler would learn the same lesson James had tried to teach him thirty years ago:

Control is an illusion. Love is the only thing that outlasts it.

PART TWO: THE SIGNAL

José Ignacio, Uruguay — Simultaneous

Thousands of miles away, Ethan Cole's phone buzzed. The call lasted twenty-three seconds.

When it ended, he stared at the coordinates he had been given and understood: the game had changed.

His father was alive. And the Cole family was going to war.

PART THREE: LUKAS KESSLER

Vienna, Austria — Simultaneous

The young man with pale eyes stood in his apartment, watching news feeds from across the globe. Markets responding to manipulated intelligence. Governments collapsing on schedule. His father's machinery working with perfect precision.

Lukas Kessler—alive, trained, complicit—had spent several years becoming invisible. The mountain had been his graduation. Cho Oyu, where he'd cut the rope himself, where he'd descended the south face alone while Ethan called his name into the void.

That was the test: Could he prioritize mission over friendship? Could he become what his father needed?

He'd passed. He always passed.

Now, watching surveillance feeds of Ethan and Daniel Cole preparing for their doomed rescue attempt, Lukas sensed a feeling he had been trained to ignore:

Regret.

Not for what he'd done. But for what he'd become.

His encrypted phone rang. Father.

"Lukas."

"Sir?"

"The Coles received the signal. They'll move in approximately six weeks. "Are preparations complete?"

"Yes. The facility is configured as discussed. Every entry point has controlled visibility. Every route leads where we want."

"Update on James Cole?" —Kessler asked.

"We moved him and have him secured in the southeast sector. When they breach that cell, they'll find exactly what we want them to find." Lukas paused. "The real holding location is three levels deeper. They'll realize too late they've been chasing a decoy."

"Very good." —Kessler paused. "You understand what comes next?"

Lukas stared at a photograph on his desk—him and Ethan at Princeton, arms around shoulders, grinning like the world was theirs. Brothers in everything but blood.

"I understand," Lukas replied. "When they arrive, I'll be waiting."

"And if you hesitate?"

Lukas's voice went flat. "I won't. Survival requires sacrifice."

"That's my boy!" Kessler smiled and his voice held something close to warmth. "Your mother would be—"

"Don't." Lukas's voice cracked. "Don't bring her into this. You made sure she couldn't see what you turned me into."

Silence on the line. Then, softer: "She would have loved you anyway. That was always her weakness."

The call ended.

Lukas stood alone in the Vienna dark, watching the city lights blur through glass. He thought of the boy he'd been—the one who'd cried at his mother's funeral, who'd believed friendship mattered, who'd thought his father was a hero.

That boy was dead. Killed on a mountain in Tibet, or years before.

What remained was a weapon. A system. A son who'd learned to prioritize control over all earthly things his heart once valued.

He pulled up the mission brief. Studied the facility layout. Memorized the kill zones.

And in the silence of his apartment, Lukas whispered:

"I'm sorry, Ethan. I'm sorry for what I'm about to do. But you were always going to be part of this."

Outside, church bells rang the hour. The sound carried across rooftops like a warning. Dawn was breaking over multiple continents, painting the sky in the same shades of amber and ash.

Across continents, sons prepared to rescue their father. A former protégé was coming to collect old debts. In the Caucasus, a father waited for freedom or death. In Vienna, a ghost weaponized his own regret. And somewhere in the machinery between them all, the world continued its oblivious turn, unaware that the fault lines beneath its feet were about to shift.

The trap was set.

The hunters were coming.

And somewhere between them all—in the space where loyalty met betrayal, where family met empire—the final reckoning waited.

PART FOUR: THE BROTHERS AND SPARROW

Somewhere Over the Black Sea — Dawn

At fifteen thousand feet, the cargo plane thrummed through the thin air, its cabin freezing. Ethan and Daniel sat strapped into jump seats, wearing cold-weather gear that made them look like Arctic explorers preparing for the end of the world.

They were preparing and in route to the rendezvous location. Not preparing as explorers. But as soldiers and liberators. They would pick up the chopper at the rendezvous location for the final push to rescue their father and deal with Kessler.

Between them were satellite photos of the Caucasus facility. Thermal imaging. Guard rotation schedules. Blueprints that Daniel had acquired through methods he didn't explain and Ethan didn't ask about.

Ethan studied the facility layout, and something his father once stated clicked into place: "Every fortress has a weak point. Usually it's not the walls—it's the assumption that the walls matter. Find what they're not defending because they think it's not worth defending."

James had taught them to think like attackers, not defenders. To see buildings as puzzles rather than barriers. Ethan traced a finger along the facility's perimeter, looking for the thing Kessler would dismiss—the overlooked angle that might save their lives.

"You're sure he's there," Daniel stated. Not a question—a confirmation he needed to hear one more time.

"I'm sure." Ethan pointed to the thermal signature in the southeast sector. "That's Dad. Same movement pattern he taught us. Morning calisthenics. Evening routine. He's alive, and he's waiting."

"Waiting for us to walk into a trap."

"Probably." Ethan met his brother's eyes. "You can still walk away. This is my fight. My choice. You've done enough."

Daniel laughed—sharp and humorless. "You think I've come this far to walk away? I've been dead for four years, E. Marcus Vale died so Daniel Cole could become something useful. I'm not wasting that on anything less than finishing what we started."

"Even if it kills us?"

"Especially then. Because that means we died for something. Dad. Family. The truth. That's better than dying for a paycheck in some Directorate operation that gets erased from the record five minutes after they bury you."

He checked his weapon—a suppressed HK416 that looked like it had seen serious use. "Besides, you need me. Your tactical planning is shit."

"My tactical planning got us this far."

"Your tactical planning is 'run away until something changes.' That's not a plan. That's hope with cardio." Daniel grinned. "You're lucky you've got me. And Selin. Between the three of us, we might survive this."

"Where is Selin?" Ethan thought, realizing he hadn't seen her in the last fifteen minutes.

As if summoned, she emerged from the cockpit, her expression grim. "We have a problem."

"Define problem."

"Satellite imagery from two hours ago shows increased activity at the facility. Guard rotation doubled. New defensive positions. Either they know we're coming, or they're preparing for something."

"They know," Daniel voiced flatly. "Of course they know. Kessler's been three steps ahead this entire time. The question is whether the trap is escapable or just lethal."

"There's a difference?" Ethan asked.

"Sometimes. Not often. But sometimes." Daniel stood, began checking the rest of their equipment. "Here's what we know: Dad's there. The facility is heavily defended. Kessler wants us to come because he thinks he can capture or kill us all at once. Standard bait-and-trap operation."

"So what do we do?"

"We spring the trap. But we do it in a way he doesn't expect. We make him think we're following one playbook while following another." Daniel pulled out a separate map—hand-drawn, covered in annotations. "This is the route he expects us to take. This is the route we're actually taking. And this—" he tapped a point three kilometers from the facility "—is where we split up."

"Split up?" Selin's voice was sharp. "That's suicide."

"No, that's asymmetry. He's planned for us coming together. Two or three targets moving as a unit. If we split up, we multiply his problem. I go loud from the north—draw their attention, make them think it's a direct assault. You two go quiet from the south, breach while they're focused on me, extract Dad, and exfil before they realize what happened."

"That leaves you exposed," Ethan protested.

"That's the point. I'm the distraction. The misdirection. The thing Kessler watches while you do the actual work." Daniel's expression was calm, accepting. "I've made peace with it. This is what I'm good at—fighting. Buying time. Being the loud idiot who draws fire so smarter people can do important things."

"Daniel—"

"Listen to me." Daniel gripped Ethan's shoulder. "You're the smart one. Always have been. You're the one who found the evidence, who exposed the network, who built something worth protecting. I'm just the blunt instrument. But blunt instruments have their uses. And this is mine."

"This is a suicide mission."

"Maybe. But it's also the best tactical option we have. And if I die getting Dad out? That's a trade I would make each and every time." He looked at both of them. "Besides, I'm not planning to die. I'm planning to be a massive pain in their ass while you two extract Dad. Then we all meet at the backup extraction point and celebrate with terrible Russian vodka."

"You're insane," Selin declared.

"Probably. But I'm right." Daniel returned to his gear, the conversation clearly over in his mind. "We drop in three hours. Get some rest. You'll need it."

Ethan watched his brother methodically prepare weapons and equipment, moving with the calm efficiency of someone who'd done this a hundred times. And perhaps he had. Maybe the last four years of being "dead" had been exactly this—dropping into impossible situations, surviving through skill and violence, walking away from things that should have killed him.

Or perhaps this was the one he wouldn't walk away from.

"Daniel?" Ethan's voice was quiet.

"Yeah?"

"Thank you brother. For it all. For coming when I needed you. For being the person Dad raised you to be."

Daniel smiled—genuine, soft around the edges. "That's what family does, E. We show up. Even when showing up is stupid. Especially then." He paused. "Tell me something. If we get Dad out, if we somehow survive this—what's the first thing you're going to say to him?"

Ethan thought about it. "I'm going to tell him I'm sorry. For not seeing what he tried to warn us about. For not understanding until it was too late."

"He won't want apologies. He'll want to know you're okay." Daniel leaned back against the bulkhead. "I'm going to tell him about Helmand. About the men I lost. About why I disappeared. All the things I couldn't say before because saying them made them real."

"He'll understand."

"I know. That's why I'm finally ready to say them." Daniel closed his eyes. "Get some rest, little brother. We've got a rescue to execute and a father to disappoint with our terrible life choices."

Ethan smiled despite his world being upended over the past weeks. "When you put it that way, it sounds almost manageable."

"It's not. But that's never stopped us before."

Selin joined Ethan, settling beside him, taking his hand. They sat like that as the plane carried them toward the Caucasus, toward the trap, toward the father they'd thought was dead.

Ethan looked at his brother—scarred, hardened, carrying ghosts from wars that officially never happened—and had a surge of love and respect so fierce it was almost painful.

They were family. Blood and choice and shared trauma forged into something that Kessler's calculations couldn't account for.

And that needed to be enough.

Or perhaps they'd die together in a Caucasus mountain facility, another footnote in the Directorate's classified archives.

Either way, they'd face it as they'd faced everything before: as a team, stubborn, refusing to let Kessler and his bastards win without a fight.

The plane flew on through the dawn, carrying them toward their reckoning.

END OF BOOK ONE
THE KESSLER PROTOCOL will continue in:
BOOK TWO: RECKONING PROTOCOL: BLACK OPS

$300 billion vanished in 72 hours.

The world called it a collapse.

It was an execution.

When International Mercantile Bank implodes, the world sees a financial catastrophe. Ethan Cole sees something else: a pattern. A design. A signature written in algorithms and blood.

His discovery makes him a target. His brother Daniel—former Delta Force, current ghost—makes him dangerous.

But the man hunting them is more powerful than any enemy they've faced. Andreas Kessler has spent forty years building a network that exists in the spaces between governments, between laws, between the world people think they understand and the one that actually runs it.

He has their father. He has unlimited resources. And he has a protocol for people who ask too many questions.

Two brothers. One conspiracy. No way out but through.

THE KESSLER PROTOCOL